Her Quiet Revolution

Her Quiet Revolution

A Novel of

MARTHA HUGHES CANNON

Frontier Doctor and First Female State Senator

MARIANNE MONSON

SHADOW
MOUNTAIN

Page ix: image of Martha Hughes Cannon used by permission, Utah Historical Society.

Visit us at shadowmountain.com

Library of Congress Cataloging-in-Publication Data
Names: Monson, Marianne, 1975– author.
Title: Her quiet revolution : a novel of Martha Hughes Cannon : frontier doctor and first
    female state senator / Marianne Monson.
Description: "This historical novel recounts the life of Martha Hughes Cannon, her early
    life in Utah, her studies in medical school, and her election as America's first female
    state senator."—Provided by publisher.
Identifiers: LCCN 2019049248 | ISBN 9781629726090 (hardcover)
Subjects: LCSH: Cannon, Martha Hughes—Fiction. | Women politicians—Utah—
    Fiction. | Women physicians—Utah—Fiction. | Suffragists—Utah—Fiction. |
    Mormon women—Utah—Fiction. | Mormon pioneers—Fiction. | BISAC: FICTION
    / Historical / General | FICTION / Biographical | LCGFT: Historical fiction. |
    Biographical fiction.
Classification: LCC PS3613.O539 H47 2020 | DDC 813/.6—dc23
LC record available at https://lccn.loc.gov/2019049248

Printed in the United States of America
Lake Book Manufacturing, Inc., Melrose Park, IL

10 9 8 7 6 5 4 3 2 1

For Andrew—my one and only

"THIS IS THE WOMAN'S AGE.
The universal voice of society proclaims the fact.
Woman must therefore lay the cornerstone of the
new civilization. Her arm will be most potent in
rearing the glorious structures of the future. Man
cannot prevent it, for in it is a divine intending."

—EDWARD W. TULLIDGE,
Women of Mormondom, 1877

MARTHA HUGHES CANNON
with her daughter, Gwendolyn, 1899

Part One

It is the chlorofil cell that gives the green color.
When it is not exposed to light it throws of[f] carbonic
acid gas; it is dependent on darkness and night.
—MARTHA HUGHES CANNON

Chapter One

SEPTEMBER 3, 1861
Mormon Pioneer Company, Utah Territory,
near modern-day Wyoming

The long and mournful cry of a hoot owl sounded through camp, causing horses to shift restlessly and campers to turn over muttering in their sleep, pulling thin woolen shrouds tight about their shoulders.

Elizabeth hung over the precious form of her baby, her littlest one.

Listening. Waiting.

An eternity's pause.

And then.

Annie's frail rib cage lifted, breath rattling through bones as flimsy as the wagons that had carried them these many miles—creaking over ruts, groaning beneath the weight, straining their way West.

The owl cry came again, haunting and solemn.

Elizabeth sought to push the old country's stories from her mind, to keep them safe behind walls of prayer and Bible verses taught by missionaries, but tonight the Welsh tales refused to be banished. In the darkness, legends seeped in at the edges, straining the gap of every seam. *Gwyliwr nos, gwarcheidwad duw. Night watcher, guardian of blackness.* Lady Blodeuwedd, formed from boughs of broom and meadowsweet, cursed to live out eternity in the form of an owl, harbinger of death.

Wishing for some magic to aid her, Elizabeth focused on the child before her, angling the dear feverish forehead upward to ease the entrance of breath. She added her frayed wrap to the baby's threadbare coverings, straining helplessly against her longing for a village healer, her own mother, or perhaps for medicine and understanding.

Others in camp had helped bless the child before sunset, but now the company slept, exhausted from the work of day and worn from caring for others afflicted with the dreaded mountain fever. So near the end of their journey, there were few able hands to help the suffering.

Elizabeth's older daughters slept on, unaware, and at last the baby, too, relaxed into slumber. Kneeling on the floor of the tent, the mother allowed the long hours of care to descend upon her shoulders, becoming one more burden to be hefted over eight hundred miles. Her daughters turned toward each other in sleep, leaving her alone with the dark edges of her mind.

Whooooo whooooo. The accursed bird sounded again, beckoning from some scrubby, gnarled pine sheltered in a crevice of wilderness. In the distance, a dog whined. The only animal that could see the approach of *Cŵn Annwn*, hounds of hell.

Unable to bear the sharp angles of such thoughts any further, Elizabeth pushed the tent flap aside, allowing the frosted September air to swallow her wholly. Culled clouds scuttled over the face of a vapid moon, throwing a swift succession of shadows across the cliffs rising near the edge of camp.

Flickering moonlight illuminated rocky formations plunging down the sides of the mountains. Witches Rocks, they were called, conjuring the Witches of Llanddona of her youth. *Please*, she tried to pray, struggling for the peace and faith she had felt at conversion, had felt many times on this journey since.

But she had so recently adopted a new truth, and her mother and her mother's mother had repeated tales from Glamorganshire far longer still. Winds howling through the canyon summoned stories of *Cyhyraeth*, the disembodied moan of death, and Elizabeth wished for a sprig of rowan to tuck in her pocket. Alone in this endless night, she could no more ward off superstition than she could breathe wellness into the body of her littlest one, anymore than she could heal the man she loved lying prostrate in a wagon.

But if Annie . . .

No. She could not think such a thought.

Skittering clouds sent terrible shapes over the face of the mountain, and the words her mother had said at their departure came unbidden to her mind. She could not help but whisper them, her breath rising in hoarfrost: *"Cadarn, cariad. Os ydych yn parhau yn y gwallgofrwydd crefyddol hwn, ni fyddwch yn dod i ben yn dda.* Sure, love, if you persist in this religious madness, you will come to no good end."

The ground glittered with crushed gems, hard and frozen, and Elizabeth's foot struck against a rock, sharper than the rest. Wincing, she tightened the stained and filthy rags bound round her feet to replace shoes that had shriven to pieces somewhere in Wyoming, becoming two more useless objects littering the edges of the trail.

"Please," she tried again to pray. "Please help us." Her words were snatched by passing shadows, torn and tangled by frantic winds.

During their ocean crossing, Elizabeth had watched a mother push a child-sized bundle into the sea, had seen that mother's body sail onward while her heart remained behind. Here on this trail of suffering, where shoes and bones collected on both sides of the roadway, why should her own child be spared?

She turned away from the night, returning to her sleeping dear ones. At the opening of the tent, two hazel eyes watched solemnly from beneath folds of fabric. Two arms waited patiently, trusting the night to return her mother. An oddly perceptive child, this one. Elizabeth hastened her steps.

"*Plentyn tawel.*" Hush child, though the girl had not uttered a syllable. "*Yn ôl i'r gwely,* Mattie. Back to bed with you."

But the four-year-old was still young enough to trust her heart more than her mother's placating words. "Mam," she called, knowing the tent to be far too quiet.

Brisk footsteps. A sharp cry of mourning against a baby's nightdress.

Mattie reached for her sister's unmoving hand, listened to her mother's choking sobs, and wished for the power to calm cries and breathe life back into stillness.

But the world outside Mattie's tent was big, and oh so dark. What could she do, such a small and girlish thing? Still even too young to walk with the children at the front of the wagons—*what could she do?*

They buried the baby at daybreak.

Elizabeth dug her daughter's grave with her own hands as her husband cursed his own helplessness from the nearby wagon. Though others in the company had sorrows plenty of their own, they brought butter, prayers, and condolences.

In Wales, Elizabeth would have stayed at home with the other women during the graveside service, but here they lacked both a house to hold vigil in and a gravedigger to open the earth. So she clawed away at the barren, rocky soil, scarcely feeling stones scraping across her palms. She carved rock and grime into an earthen cradle to shelter Annie through winter snows, through spring rains, to hold her safe from seasons passing in and out. Four-year-old Mattie and six-year-old Mary did their best to help, their stubby fingers swiping at the dirt.

Elizabeth longed for draped white linen to wrap around her precious child, for scented herbs, black gloves, funeral cake, and the ringing of a corpse bell to sound her pain. Instead, she sought to ignore her aching breasts longing for a baby who no longer needed feeding. She knelt beside a pile of rocks, next to her living daughters, as she spoke prayers both in English and the old tongue. "*Rhowch gylch i mi, arglwydd.* Circle me, Lord. Keep safety within, danger without," she prayed. "Circle me, Lord. Keep light within, and darkness without."

Elizabeth placed a single stone atop the shawl turned shroud, her face contracting as if she had set it upon her own heart and not her daughter's. "Those poor little bones," Mattie heard her mother whisper.

A tuft of mountain grass took the place of rosemary. A single candle glowed an eerie red in the rays of sunlight, leading Elizabeth's worried eyes back to the wagon where her husband lay, his cough grown worse. *What if?* She could not allow the thought.

Witches Rocks brooded down upon the grim assembly. In place of a hymn, Elizabeth sang a cradle song, the words finding new meaning as they echoed off the mountainside. "*Huna, blentyn, ar fy mynwes, Clyd a chynnes ydyw hon. . . .* Sleep my dear one, 'tis a mother's arms around you, make yourself a snug, warm nest; I will hold you, close enfold you, lay my blessing on your rest."

Elizabeth's voice broke as she struggled to finish. Mary's voice merged with her mother's and Mattie's, too, half wondering if this were not just another game and Annie would push aside the stones above her. But no. The rocks felt sharp, heavy, and oh so final.

"*Huna'n dawel, annwyl blentyn. . . .* Lovely darling, I will guard you. I will hold you, close enfold you, sleep upon your mother's breast."

Mattie marked her mother's worried glance as fear collapsed in a dense knot at the base of her stomach. If Annie could fall into this still and awful silence, then who else might follow? The girl tipped her head to watch her mother who, it seemed, could do anything, had done everything on this journey.

Her hands now hung shaking and helpless by her side.

Elizabeth murmured a final prayer, as Mattie trembled at this twisted discovery, for her mother had always been solid and immovable—a pillar of stone upon a hillside, there to remain through all millennia of time.

The rigidity of crystalline substances shut out the external impression.

—MARTHA HUGHES CANNON

Chapter Two

NOVEMBER 1873
Salt Lake City, Utah Territory

t a e r G

Mattie's hands flowed over and across the case of ten-point metal type—selecting a steel rectangle from among its companions, turning the notch upward, aligning it snug and square beside others in the metal composing stick. Bottom up, top down, notch to the right of the lead. Then a spacer.

y r c t u o

Sister Emmeline's distinctive scrawl was not the easiest to read, but the wit and humor made her work instantly recognizable, even if Mattie hadn't already memorized the way Sister Emmeline shaped each letter.

Great outcry. It was an interesting enough opening to pause over, and, for just a moment, Mattie stopped her movement between cases and let herself read forward instead of backward.

"Great outcry is raised against the much marrying of the

Latter-day Saints," the column began. The outcry over polygamy had captured the attention of the nation, and as a polygamous wife herself, Emmeline often used the platform of the *Woman's Exponent* to publicly defend the practice Eastern papers termed "barbaric."

"The tendency of the age is to disregard marriage altogether," Emmeline continued, "but there seems no indication of a desire to have the race die out." Mattie stifled an undignified snort and reached for another spacer. Of course Sister Emmeline would turn the debate over polygamy into a criticism of society's morality instead. The idea of sharing a husband seemed odd enough to Mattie, but plenty of women defended the system, even organizing indignation meetings to fight accusations of repression from one of two territories in the union outlandish enough to allow women to vote. "The season of scattering intellectual filth has set in over the country," the editorial continued. "It occurs quadrennially in the United States, commencing a few months before the Presidential election."

Mattie laughed aloud, then stiffened as a voice called out her name. Though she'd read only a line or two at most, she clenched her thumb over the last sort in the composing stick to keep it in place.

"Sister Emmeline wants to see you," said a girl with brown, braided hair and an apron identical to Mattie's.

"Very well." Mattie sighed, holding out the composing stick. "Finish this last line for me, won't you, Ruby?"

"I've work to do of my own before closing," the girl replied, glancing around for Brother Parry, before taking the mostly finished composition.

"You're a dear." Mattie smoothed her apron, though she could do nothing about the smudges. Well, it was a dirty job and nothing for it.

With her impeccably trimmed gowns, pinched nose, and severely drawn hair, Sister Emmeline reminded Mattie of a glossy black bird flitting around her formidable office—checking this, ordering that, and scrawling scathing words across slips of paper. Invariably, reading her tart replies in the paper proved far more enjoyable than speaking with her face-to-face.

Mattie paused in front of the heavy oak door. "Come in!" came the sharp invitation. Surrounded by stacks of paper nearly as tall as herself, Sister Emmeline sat behind her mighty desk, pin-tucked in gray silk, scribbling out sarcastic pronouncements on the nation. "Yes?" she asked briskly.

Mattie pushed the door open the rest of the way. "You wanted to see me, ma'am?" She shifted, feeling far too frumpy for such an office.

Legendary, this woman was, as an accomplished poet, author, and newspaper editor. She had been abandoned by her first husband, buried a second, and married a third with six other families to take care of. Yet a delicate lace collar circled her throat and a dainty amethyst ring rested on one finger, belying the whip-smart wit embodied in the woman they adorned. Emmeline glanced down at her papers. "Miss Paul?"

"Mattie, if you please."

"How old are you?" she asked curtly, as if they were already out of time.

"Sixteen."

"Apprenticed to learn typesetting from Hyrum Parry?"

"Yes, ma'am."

"I am told you can set Scandinavian type. You speak one of the tongues?"

"No, ma'am."

"But you can set the type?"

Mattie considered how to explain. "Languages are made up of patterns, ma'am. Though I don't know the meaning of the words, I can follow the patterns."

Emmeline set down her pen and took a hard look at the girl in front of her—apron smeared, messy curls parted down the middle, as disheveled as if she'd grown up on the hard side of a broom. "Not everyone can 'follow the patterns.' They tell me you're good at the work."

"Thank you."

"And you enjoy it?"

"Well enough, ma'am," Mattie replied, loathe to confess the work was a puzzle, interesting only until she had solved it. She held her tongue.

Emmeline nodded, unconvinced. "As you may know, Brigham Young opened this apprenticeship specifically for women. You could have a job here for quite some time should you want it."

"Thank you, ma'am."

Emmeline lowered her spectacles. "Is that what you'd like?"

"I suppose," Mattie said as those shadowed bird eyes seemed to bore into her soul.

Sister Emmeline studied Mattie like a cipher she could not quite solve. "You may go," she said, returning her attention to the paper before her.

Safely on the other side of the door, Mattie breathed a sigh of relief at having arrived at the end of another work day, still perplexed as to why she had been summoned. She tugged on her apron strings and drew the thing over her head, calling across the shop, "Good day, Ruby. Mr. Parry."

"Good day," they called back.

Snow, wind-driven from the western mountains, fell thick over the muddy streets of Salt Lake. Her boots would be soaked through by the time she reached the University of Deseret, but her heart beat faster at thoughts of the night ahead, of discussions and diagrams, of questions and wonderings.

How could she explain to Emmeline Wells that her work as a

typesetter was nothing but a repetitious game played to cover the costs of evening courses? How impudent would she sound admitting she spent most of the long hours of her days wishing for dusk to fall?

Clutching her schoolbooks strapped together with her work completed in neat and tiny letters, Mattie walked beneath the swiftly falling flakes, reciting the structures of crystalline molecules in a loving chant. How she admired the elegance of column crystals beside plane crystals, dendritic beside rimed. Precise and ordered by God Himself, hexagonal prisms were as organized as a row of type lined up, ready for inking and a launching into the world, destined to land where they may.

Arriving on campus, Mattie bid hello to John and Peter, Freddy and Nathan, classmates also enrolled in a course of chemistry. Did they also have to come up with their own fees every semester, she wondered, navigating such a thin and fragile line? She made her way to her desk, where she opened her notebook and a bottle of ink, nodding greetings to Phillip, Jonas, and Tom.

Professor Hooke rapped the lectern for attention. "Tonight, as you know, class, we shall discuss the molecular structure of quinine, which you should have reviewed in chapter eight." Mattie bent over her notebook, his words falling thick about her like a spell.

Where does heat—light come from?
—MARTHA HUGHES CANNON

Chapter Three

Even rows of adobe bricks welcomed Mattie home at the end of a long night of classes; a sturdy chimney puffed smoke into the frozen air, warding off snow gathered at the sills and lacing the walks. Her wet boots crunched their way across the rime of drifting white, and she wondered if they would be dry before it was time to put them on again.

Glowing windows hinted at a dear, familiar chaos waiting inside, and Mattie paused at the door to drink in one last, bracing breath before pushing it open. A whiff of potatoes mixed with the scent of smoke from the fire escaped from inside.

"Mattie's home!" her little brother Joseph shrieked, sprinting across the room to pull her inside.

"Scrape your boots!" Elizabeth called, though Mattie already struggled to separate mud from leather as she unlaced them.

"Just a minute, Joseph," she laughed, shaking the snow and damp from her cloak, tucking back her long, unruly curls.

Sliding stocking-footed into the kitchen, she found Papa in the rocking chair, bouncing three-year-old Lottie on his lap. Always she thought of him as Papa, though her real Papa had joined Annie in death three days after their arrival in the valley. Mattie had only the vaguest memory of Peter Hughes, too sick and weak to leave their wretched wagon before being laid to rest in a solemn coffin of pine.

It had seemed to Mattie that dark death had followed them into the valley, until James Paul, with four children of his own, taught her mother to laugh again a year later; more babies had followed swiftly ever since. With his Scottish accent bumping gently up against her mother's Welsh, James taught Mattie to work sums and sound out letters. He had noticed her quick mind and praised her efforts. Always he smelled of wood shavings mingled with a touch of metal from tools in his shop. "Our girl has a mind for numbers," he would say. *Our girl.*

Mattie placed her lunch bucket and school books on the table. "Your hair's a sight," her mother observed, pausing her brisk sweeping of the floor. Mattie tried to separate the sodden strands with her fingers. "There's a plate for you near the fire."

"Thank you, Mama." Mattie carried the simple meal of root vegetables and stewed greens to the table, where eighteen-year-old Mary held the newest member of the family, born just weeks before.

Lottie came running, open-armed, to climb onto Mattie's lap, a gesture impossible to deny to those sweet, silken curls, though her wriggling made it more difficult to reach fork to mouth. "It's snowing," Lottie announced. "I ate some."

Mattie settled the youngster on her knee. "And what did it taste like?"

"Like sparkles." Lottie ducked her head at the laughter that followed from her older brother.

"Those are snow crystals melting on your tongue," Mattie explained, throwing Joseph a look.

"And what are you learning at that school of yours?" Papa asked, joining them at the table.

"Miasmas," Mattie said, reaching for a slice of bread spread with sorghum syrup. "Poisonous vapors that cause diseases along with foul air and contaminated water—the black plagues and deaths in Europe."

Mama shuddered. "I don't know why you wish to spend your nights talking about such wretched stuff." Beyond the words, Mattie heard bewilderment, perhaps even reproach.

"Because if we don't understand how plagues happen, we won't be able to stop them, Mama."

"Quite right, Mattie," said Papa. "Important ideas you're studying."

"I don't know why it has to be you who studies it," Mama said softly. "There's enough work to be done here at home and never enough hands to do it. Plenty of others in the valley can worry about vapors and miasmas." *Plenty of others. Plenty of boys.* Mattie heard the words, unspoken though they might be. "You have a good, steady job setting type. In a few years, you'll be married and have more than enough to occupy your mind."

Would she? Would cleaning, cooking, and birthing children fill up her mind the way miasmas and crystalline structures and scientific lectures did? Mattie knew no way of saying she didn't think so without also intimating that her mother's life did not seem like enough. She held her tongue.

"Wipe your plate and put it back where it belongs," Mama said when Mattie had finished eating. *Where it belongs. There with the others.* Lined up in a neat stack, each one the same, the same, the same.

"Yes, Mama," Mattie said.

As they joined hands for prayer, Mama asked God to watch over and protect them, to guide them and reveal truth to their minds.

"Amen," said Mattie, wondering how she might explain to her mother that, to her, God seemed to work through the language of science, and when she understood those laws, she felt herself looking upon the glory of the universe.

Later, wedged in bed between Lottie on one side and Joseph on the other, Mattie listened to Mary's steady breathing across the room and considered the empty space between them. Had Annie lived, she would have been sandwiched somewhere in this tumbled pile of siblings. Had her hair been fair like Mama's and Lottie's? Or dark like her own?

Mattie could no longer remember.

Shadows morphed and changed across the floor as clouds scudded over the face of the moon, twisting miasmas and vapors into fantastical shapes both flickering and menacing. The shadows seemed to be waiting for someone to vanquish them—for someone who could peer into the face of all that darkness and understand.

Matter is something that offers resistance to
other matter—the resistance is a force.
—MARTHA HUGHES CANNON

Chapter Four

Mattie pulled the book closer, studying the diagram—puzzling it out in her mind, mentally rotating the image to view it from different angles—the structure of molecules bonding and forming, orbiting through space. How did they form? How did they function? What was the process and why? "The chemical compound of mercury has puzzled scientists from the days of the early alchemists," Dr. Albert Hooke explained. "See figure three."

She studied the diagram. If that were the case, then what reason could be found for the way mercury had reacted with phosphorous in the lab?

And if mercury could be compounded, then—

"—Mattie, did you gather the eggs yet?"

Pulled from a distance, her mind tumbled back to the cramped corner of a chaotic kitchen cleared to make space for slate, a notebook, and a bit of chemistry.

Flour dusted Mama's nose as her arms worked through stiff bread dough. Lottie played with wooden animals at her feet, and the baby wriggled in a basket near the hearth.

"I have a test . . ." Mattie began.

Elizabeth used a forearm to push aside stray hair escaping the bun at the nape of her neck. "Tests aren't going to keep your brothers and sisters full." Her voice was not one to argue with. "Take Lottie with you."

Mattie sighed and closed the book, still puzzling over the chemical compound for mercury as she crouched down to the three-year-old's level. "Do you want to help me gather eggs, Lottie?"

The little girl scrunched up her nose, unconvinced.

"Did you know that eggs are the largest single cells?" Mattie asked her sister.

"What's a cell?" She looked suspicious.

"I'll show you."

"Mattie?" She looked up to find Elizabeth considering her with as much puzzlement as she herself felt for the chemical structures of molecules. She could trace each line of her mother's face—each crease, each plane and angle as familiar as bread.

"Yes?"

"James and I talked about it. We think you should take next year off from schooling to do other things."

Darkness, madness raged at the edge of Mattie's consciousness. She forced her emotions down, as Elizabeth hefted the turned dough into a pan, pushing it into shape, forcing it to yield.

"Like what?" Mattie asked, tucking in the corners of her mouth in a gesture her mother had known since Mattie was a toddler. She did not have a will lightly broken, this girl. But how to help her accept her place in this imperfect, fragile world?

"Like what other things?" Mattie repeated.

"Like your siblings. You've already had far more schooling than James and I both together. You can help them with their schoolwork—heaven knows you've learned far more than you'll ever need to be a wife and mother. We need your hands here, Mattie."

Mattie tried to breathe through mounting emotions. Yes, they needed her hands, but what of her mind? What of that? It could not be swaddled and stuck in a basket beside the fire. Or could it? And if it were, would there be any point to go on living?

"Mama," she began, searching for her words like eggs nestled among straw. "Do you know women in Utah territory are training to be teachers and bookkeepers? Right here in Salt Lake, women are practicing law. Sophie Reusch is studying physic. Think of the good she will do with all she has learned."

"Yes, and she has a husband and children to come home to each evening. There may be time for that later. When you know what your husband and family need from you, you will better understand where to focus your efforts. For now, we need you here." With a movement she had done thousands of times, Elizabeth divided the dough, pressed it into a pan, and scored it across the top.

Mattie watched those hands, calloused and lined, strong beyond thinking. Those hands had guided them over a trail, had driven a wagon with a sick husband inside, and safely carried her little ones over mountains—what couldn't those hands do? Those hands had done everything for her since she could remember. And what did that mean she owed those hands? Gratitude, love, yes. Her labor, yes. But did loving your mother mean you had to relive her life? Was it possible to know you were different without disrespecting the body that had held and fed you before you could hold and feed yourself? Or was part of love giving up those corners and edges that didn't fit, chopping them off or pushing them into rough corners to stay in place, just so?

Fighting the panic that rose in her chest, Mattie took Lottie's hand and lifted the egg basket from a corner as Elizabeth swept her textbook from the table as though it were an object both dangerous and strange.

Outside in the yard, autumn morning light washed fantastical colors over the snow, pooling in frozen crevices of ground. Across the muddy valley floor, smoke puffed from chimneys of frame structures that would be rebuilt as the Paul homestead had been, evolving from a dugout built from the base of a wagon, to a framed two-room, to a snug adobe house. Mattie knew Elizabeth had fashioned the bricks of their house with her own hands, turning mud in forms until they dried in the sun. James had planed each wooden groove to fit each joint. Beyond the yard, a privy stood beside a sprawling garden where gooseberry, raspberry, and current vines twined together, now frosted over and decaying back into the organic matter from whence they'd come. All fall, the family had squirreled away pumpkins and squash, nestling them into the root cellar, to fill hungry mouths during the long winter.

At Mattie's approach, hens snug in their roosting boxes stretched and murmured their interest. Lottie's chubby fingers grasped handfuls of grain, giggling as the chickens rushed toward her in a flurry of feathers. Mattie collected warm spheres adorned with an occasional downy feather or earth from the feet of their mothers. When they were finished, Mattie cracked one egg, carefully pointing out the nucleus and membrane to Lottie, explaining the system that worked together like a family worked, each in their separate rooms.

They carried the eggs to the barn, where Lottie ran to snuggle into Mary's side, watching milk squirt from udder to bucket in a long, creamy stream. Mattie followed the smell of fresh shavings to the other side of the barn, where James bent over a wagon harness, puzzling out leather rivets and metal fastenings. Chisel and screwdriver sat beside a growing pile of shavings that smelled as safe as home and bread.

"Whit like?" Papa asked, nodding as she entered, using one of the few Scottish phrases he was still apt to use after so many years, a phrase she had heard the first time she met him. *"Whit like?"*—more than "How are you doing?"—seemed far more intimate somehow.

His phrase broke through her defenses and, though she'd had

no intention of saying it, Mattie blurted: "Mama wants me to be finished with school." Her throat constricted with the strength of emotion she'd fought to hold in check.

"Ay," said James, lining up the wooden beam and surveying the length of it. "Ay, she does." He set a metal planing tool atop the board. "Do this for me, my girl?" She took the tool and he guided her hands along the length of the board, shavings curling into the metal box as they moved, the wood growing smoother at each pass. "Ay, that's the way of it. You've always been a natural."

She knew she was not, but her body relaxed under the work, real and solid beneath her hands. He let her continue, moving down the length of the board, focused on the grain of the wood, on the curls twisting into strands like Lottie's flaxen curls.

Someone who did not know James might have thought he had forgotten, but Mattie knew he had not. Even as he moved about the shop, returning tools to their spots, running his hands along a span of wood to check the heft and length of it, he held her problem in his mind, considering it, turning it as he turned the task before him. "And what say ye?" he asked at last.

She raised haunted eyes to meet his. "I don't know how to explain it, Papa—learning, science—it's something I must do. I don't know why, but my mind is meant to learn those things." She paused and drew a shaky breath. "I mean no disrespect to Mama."

He nodded. "I know it." His worn hands guided hers across the length of the beam, allowing her to feel the surface she had created, and she marveled at his ability to have so many children and still manage to make her feel like the only one. "It's not her life you're living, my girl." He set a level against the plane of the board. "You can love her and not be her. We've always known your mind was a precious gift, Mattie. Best use it as you feel ye must. I'll speak to your mother."

She folded into him, his arm tucked around her shoulders, held safe against his chest—safe within those capable hands that could build and shelter, bend and shape the world to protect the ones he loved.

Nothing more was said of Mattie's quitting school. For now.

Chemical action may give rise to other kinds of heat.
—MARTHA HUGHES CANNON

Chapter Five

DECEMBER 1873
Salt Lake City, Utah Territory

The clerk at Edward Snelgrove's boot shop looked quite put out with the girl. "These are all the styles we carry for young women, miss. I think you will find they are quite the latest fashion." His expression indicated that it would not hurt her to consider his offerings a bit more.

After weeks of walking six miles each day through snow and rain and all that lay between, Mattie forced her voice to stay calm. "I have no doubt you are correct, sir, but it is not fashion I am after just now. You see, none of these oiled boots are sturdy enough to take me from home to work to school and home again without leaving my feet as wet and cold as a walkway in February."

The salesman lifted a dainty little contraption made of leather as soft as a baby's backside. "Surely this option is as practical as any lady should need?"

Mattie sighed. "Perhaps you could show me the men's work

boots? Certainly you don't expect everyone to work in footwear as delicate as a ballroom glove."

Looking about as if he hoped someone would interrupt this insolent customer, the clerk led her toward the men's boots on the far side of the counter. "I can't imagine you would wish to travel about town in any of these?"

Mattie flexed a sturdy heel, carved to hold its own against ice and sleet. A hardy leather hide with reinforced seams might take a person some place they wanted to go—through wilds and tempests, far beyond the length of a sitting room. "Yes, this is precisely what I wish," she breathed. "No laces. No buttons. Just below my knee. Do you have them in size five?"

"No," the clerk blustered. "They aren't manufactured that small."

"A special order then?" Mattie clutched the purse that held the savings she had scrimped for a month to hold onto—making worn dresses do, gathering scraps of firewood to sell to neighbors for coins to add to her typesetting earnings.

The clerk coughed and went to ask Snelgrove himself, who threw an equally bewildered glance in her direction. This strange girl now wanted, now insisted, on having men's boots. Snelgrove nodded, and the clerk returned reluctantly with an order form.

They would make them, he said, for an additional fee to cover the challenge of cornering so much strength into such a small contraption. *A fee for being practical,* Mattie thought as she filled out the form. Shoes, much like people, were not supposed to be merely decorative, she wanted to inform the clerk who couldn't be much older than herself. They were supposed to perform a function—to be useful and good for something beyond sitting prettily on a display shelf at Z.C.M.I.

She left clutching the receipt like a battle flag.

A few weeks later, Mattie picked up the newly finished boots and tugged them on for the journey home, luxuriating in every step. Even from down the street, the adobe house looked different and the windows shone brighter, as if they could not contain the light on the other side of their panes. School books clutched against her chest, Mattie hurried down the street, pausing by the walkway, charmed by the voices seeping around the edges of the door. She scraped her boots, so eager to be inside she could scarcely get them off.

"Mattie's home!" Lottie announced, and the family descended on her in a flurry of hugs and boisterous laughter.

Adam and Logan, her older stepbrothers, filled the house more than their tall, lank frames could account for. "What have you done to your hair?" Adam exclaimed as he turned her this way and that to examine the close cropping she'd had applied to her tresses. Mary and Elizabeth, too, shrieked over the transformation.

"I'm too busy for such nonsense," Mattie said as they turned her around.

"So I see," Logan said, lifting the books from her hands.

"And your boots? You actually wear those in public?" Adam laughed.

"I change into others." Mattie lifted a satchel holding proper boots for a lady. "It's not healthy to stand in wet shoes all day."

"A bold move," Adam pronounced, looking pleased. "And just as handsome as ever." Mary, perhaps, did not agree with her older brother's assessment. Papa sat in the corner, one arm around Elizabeth's shoulder, exuding happiness in the presence of his sons.

Logan unbound the leather strap that held Mattie's textbooks together and opened to the first title page. "Fascinating reading material, Matts. Ahem." He cleared his throat dramatically, and his cheeks dimpled with the hint of a smile. "*A Comprehensive Treatise on Inorganic and Theoretical Chemistry* in thirteen volumes by the honorable Sir Edward Thorpe. Inclusive of 274 diagrams. Shall we have a reading?"

"Let's have a taste of it then," Adam goaded. "If Mattie enjoys it, it must be pithy stuff."

"Oh, don't encourage him." Mattie elbowed Adam, but it was too late.

Logan chose a page at random, scanned it, and commandeered a glass of water from the table. "And now, dear students," he intoned, imitating a professor long practiced in the art of lecture.

"It's only his dimples and brown curls that make it impossible not to indulge him," Mattie whispered loudly.

Logan continued as if he had not heard: "You see, students, '*If* an aqueous solution of a substance is contained in a vessel the walls of which are permeable by water molecules but not by the molecules of the dissolved substance, and *if* the vessel is immersed in water, water will enter the vessel and the pressure on the walls will increase until equilibrium results, after which . . .'" Logan paused for dramatic effect, "'no more water will enter.'"

Joseph and Lottie, sitting at his feet, giggled and pushed each other.

Raising his arm above his head, Logan nearly shouted: "And yet! One must also ever bear in mind that '*If* the vessel were furnished with a movable piston . . .'"—Mattie rolled her eyes, but Lottie and Joseph leaned forward—"'. . . the *same* condition of equilibrium *might* be attained by merely compressing the solution.'"

The speech was nonsense, of course, but Mattie couldn't help noticing his presentation—the control of his gestures, his voice, and his awareness of space.

"That is correct, my friends," he continued, "you need only to furnish your vessels with movable pistons to achieve this enviable state of equilibrium—*or*—alternatively," here he picked up the glass of water, "you could simply *drink* your water and by this clever maneuver, accomplish quite the same thing." He bolted the water and bowed low.

"Bravo," shouted Joseph and Lottie, clapping.

"It's a wonder you get paid for such antics," Mattie said.

"Oh, come on, is your chemistry professor that engaging, Matts?"

"No," she admitted, "not nearly."

Still clapping, Mary crossed the kitchen and drew a kettle from the fire. Dipping a brush into the pot, she began applying the liquid to her hair.

"What's that? Witch's brew?" Logan asked.

"Steeped wild sage," she tossed back. "A hair tonic."

"Primping for the dance tonight?"

"Maybe, maybe not." She stuck her tongue out at him. Though she was eighteen years old, Mary felt her place as oldest waver in the presence of her older stepbrothers.

"At least Mattie won't steal your tonic," Logan teased. "Not enough hair to warrant it."

Mattie threw a pillow in Logan's direction. "What dance?" she asked.

"The one at the Bowery at Lindsey Gardens. You're coming," Adam announced.

"Am I, then?"

"Uh-huh. Remember when Mother used to tell us those old Welsh superstitions?" Launching into a falsetto, he intoned, "'Leave a knife in the leek patch on Halloween, girls, and you'll see the man you are to marry.'" Adam pulled her from the bench and twirled her briefly. He was older than Logan, with lighter, sandy hair and hazel eyes similar to Mattie's own. While his brother traveled with a theater group, Adam worked as a detective in Salt Lake, bringing home tales of intrigue and murder when he visited.

"Stop," she said, laughing and trying to catch her breath. "You've got a story to tell yourself, from what I've read in the paper. Weren't you involved in that sharpshooter scandal?"

"Yes!" Joseph begged. "Tell about the sharpshooter!"

"You're just trying to distract from the dance," Adam said. "Won't work though. You're going."

Mattie pretended exasperation.

"Fine, I'll tell you what happened," Adam said. "As you may or may not know, Salt Lake loves its sharpshooting competitions. They aren't that interesting though because the same marksman, name of Lafayette, wins every time. The only person who can beat him is this other fellow named Furey. Apparently, this got a bit boring, so a few of our local criminals decided to spice things up."

"What'd they do?" Joseph asked, glancing anxiously at his parents to make sure they had no intention of sending him out of the room.

"Well," Adam said, kneeling down, "first they told everyone that Furey would be out of town, so people would bet on Lafayette to win."

"And then?" asked Joseph.

Adam laughed. "Then Furey did come, only he wore a disguise, and the men used bogus checks to raise the stakes even higher. Using his fake name, Furey won, and the five men split up the money. Then they tried to skip town."

"How did you catch 'em?" Joseph asked, nearly jumping out of his seat.

"We'd been keeping track of Furey. When the stakes went so high, we knew something had to be up."

"But how did you get them?" Joseph plied again.

"Let him tell," Mattie said, laughing at Joseph's enthusiasm.

Adam lowered his voice. "We finally caught them at the railroad, wearing women's dresses. The skirts were lined with $2,600 in cash, $3,000 in checks, and one diamond stud pin."

Joseph and Lottie giggled. "Where are they now?" Joseph asked.

"Sitting on the other side of gridiron."

"Still wearing dresses?" Joseph wanted to know.

"I don't think so," Adam replied, as laughter filled up the room. These tales of Adam's hardly seemed like the Salt Lake Mattie knew, though the town had doubtless become more interesting since the completion of the railroad. Being around her stepbrothers always left her feeling dizzy and more alive somehow, as if she'd gulped down mouthfuls from a cold mountain stream, drinking water gushing straight from the veins of life. They lived life at full tilt, in a manner she found inspiring and enviable. No one tried to stop them. *They're men though,* her mind chided.

A button grease lamp Mama called a "witch's light" sputtered illumination around the bedroom for Mary and Mattie to dress by. Lottie sat cross-legged on the floor, watching her older sisters curl and brush.

"I don't feel well," Mary confessed in a low voice. "But nothing would keep me home tonight."

"I don't understand that kind of dedication to a party," Mattie told her. "But if you keel over dancing, I'll have my smelling salts ready."

Papa called everyone for prayer before they left. Through downcast lashes, Mattie watched candlelight flickering across the faces circled, asking for God's protection and grace.

After the last amen, Logan and Adam hurried Mary and Mattie to the waiting carriage, as Lottie and Joseph hung from the porch, peering enviously upon a world they could not yet enter.

Partygoers at Lindsey Gardens milled about the base of the whirligig and giant stride, some of the more adventurous jumping up to give the contraptions a go. Candles lit up every corner of the dance hall, and paper lanterns hung from the rafters like clusters of glowing fireflies. The windows offered a spacious view of the mountains across the valley and the Great Salt Lake glimmering in the West. The band struck opening strains as couples lined up for the grand march.

Mary's honey-colored tresses shone under the lights at the bowery, and she greeted friends effortlessly, tossing shy nods to the young men she found attractive. *How does she do that?* Mattie wondered, watching her sister move through the opening figures of the polonaise as if she belonged upon a dance floor. Mary's card filled up swiftly, and, hovering near the edges of the room, Mattie wondered, not for the first time, how they could possibly be sisters.

Just as gregarious, in his own way, Logan moved in a circle of admirers who pressed to hear stories of his thespian adventures, while Adam graciously pretended he wanted nothing more than to fill up the gaps on Mattie's dance card, claiming they were chances to spend more time with a sister he did not see enough. Mattie silently blessed him, hoping it was not obvious that, while drawn to the party with a curious fascination, she far preferred classrooms where people stayed safely put behind desks and didn't make sudden erratic movements like this young man was doing—what *was* he doing?

Oh heavens. Not attempting to talk with her. Yet, he was. Thrill and terror both rolled into one excruciating moment.

Blushingly, he asked, "Would you do me the honor of being my partner for the quadrille?" Not the confident sort, like those who buzzed around Mary, but a thoughtful chap who probably appreciated the molecular structure of crystals all on his own.

The color on Mattie's cheeks as she agreed to the dance matched his own. Dash it all. Surely there must be a less awkward way to go about this? But she made her way through the quadrille, answering his shy, gawky movements with every turn. "Jim Anderson," he stammered. "New to the valley . . . from Denmark," though it wasn't hard to guess the last part.

"May I fetch you a drink?" Jim asked after their turn on the floor. He managed to nearly spill cider down her gown, but missed and baptized the floor instead, coloring more, which she hadn't believed possible.

Arches of evergreen boughs bedecked with ribbons were carried into the center of the floor to use in the cotillion figures, the men holding the arches and the women passing beneath them. A young man near her coughed into a handkerchief, swirling miasmas and unbalanced humors through the air.

Together Jim and Mattie hurried away from the broad exposure of the dance floor, Adam cheered on her departure with a gesture Mattie ignored. Under cover of night, on the open pavilion, they both breathed more freely, knowing only stars above would mark their blushes. The celestial firmament had witnessed too many boys and girls stumbling their terrestrial way toward each other to mock the awkward process. "What are you studying?" Jim asked shyly.

"Chemistry," she replied.

"I find science fascinating," he confessed, as though it were a secret. "I might study zoology, you know. Which has been your favorite course so far?"

He listened to her responses and haltingly asked if he might see her again.

She nodded her head yes.

So this, then, was what it felt like. This courtship she had imagined, had watched from a distance, had puzzled over. Awkward and fumbling, but also sweet.

On the carriage ride home, Logan and Adam plagued Mattie about her conquest. Never mind that half a dozen young men tracked Mary's every movement, tonight the brothers' teasing was only for Mattie. "Come on, Matts," Logan said. "Tell us. What do you think of Jim Anderson? We all want to know."

"He was a sweet boy," she confessed, straining to remember the color of his eyes.

Try as she might, all she could land upon with any certainty was how her mother would be so pleased.

The origin of the disease is not as stated.
—MARTHA HUGHES CANNON

Chapter Six

The midwife studied Mary's flushed face, pressing one hand to the fevered brow and another to the wrist, her forehead puckered with concern. Not long after their return from the dance, Mary admitted she felt worse rather than better, and by the next day, she could scarcely get out of bed. Three days later, Mattie followed each movement of Patty's capable hands between Mary and the midwife's handbag, filled with instruments and medical wonders. Patty Sessions must be nearing eighty, and she had attended thousands of patients in her long career. Torn between concern for her sister and fascination for the process, Mattie tried to remind herself that her sister was no textbook.

Elizabeth rushed back to the room, carrying a bunch of dried leeks fetched from the root cellar. With shaking hands, she bundled them with twine and hung them above her daughter's bed. "An old practice from Wales," she explained a bit breathless. "My grandmother did it for me when I was ill." Elizabeth guarded every gesture.

"Leeks never caused any harm, for sure and certain." Patty shrugged, exchanging a glance with Mattie.

"What do you think is wrong?" Mattie asked.

Patty Sessions counted pulses through Mary's wrist, trying to calculate. "With a fever such as this, her humors must be out of balance."

"Humors?" Elizabeth asked, poised between Mattie and Patty as if she might pounce.

"Blood, phlegm, yellow and black bile," Mattie explained in a soothing voice. "I'm studying chemistry," she told Patty.

"I've seen it up and down the valley this winter," Patty said. "One woman after another has been stricken with fevers and the unbalanced humors."

"Like Hannah Thacker," Elizabeth said, her voice tight and constricted. "Left behind a husband and three small children."

"Eliza England last week," Patty added.

"I hadn't heard," Mattie said, fighting her own sense of mounting terror. *Mary stretched out in a long pine coffin. Mary pinned under a pile of sharp stones.*

"But you needn't worry," Patty reassured them, turning shadowed eyes toward Elizabeth. "Mary is young and strong and we've every reason to believe she will recover." Mary turned, flushed and feverish, pressing her face against the bedclothes. "I'll administer by prayer first, and medicine afterward. I imagine she's had a blessing already?" Elizabeth nodded yes.

Patty pulled out a small glass vial of consecrated oil from her medical bag, and dabbed a drop of it across Mary's forehead. Mattie and Elizabeth rested their hands on Mary's head, and Patty added her own, like autumn leaves drifting into a pile. Leaning in close, Patty closed her eyes and blessed her patient with healing by faith.

After they finished, Patty moved to the dresser, using the swift fall of pestle against the curved mortar to turn willow bark and dried hollyhocks into paste. With one smooth motion, Patty delivered the herbs into steeped water as curls of steam ascended heavenward.

The chemical structure of the hollyhocks combined with the healing properties of the willow bark in Mattie's mind, and her breathing began to relax.

"See that she takes this daily," Patty said. "And don't let the poison doctor with his nasty scarificator near her veins. I don't believe it does a bit of good." Mattie knew the instrument of which Patty spoke—the harsh brass box with its parallel hidden blades, ready to spring toward flesh at a touch of the knob and return the humors to their proper balance. Supposedly.

"I'll sprinkle salt around her bed. And a pinprick to her finger might ease her boiling blood, help her heal faster," Elizabeth said.

Mattie wondered if her mother saw yet another daughter falling into final stillness.

"Let's make some tea to calm your nerves," Patty said, leading Elizabeth downstairs.

"I'll stay with Mary." Mattie clutched the pestle Patty had left behind, watching her sister twist against the knotted sheets as soaked as a shroud. Here on the frontier, years away from the medical inquiry of Europe, debates raged on between midwives wielding herbed poultices and medical doctors with their lancing knives. Folk magic and rumors only added to the cacophony. And in between the debate, fallen on the field of battle, lay women's bodies alongside infant corpses—so many fragile bones.

Mattie wondered which position to take up, which weapon to wield in a battle that had already claimed her father and younger sister on a field that left survivors, but none free from scars.

After Patty departed, Mattie cocooned the little ones in bed, and set to cleaning up from supper. As she scraped river trout carcasses toward the pig bin, she glanced about the momentarily quiet kitchen and pulled the trout skeleton toward the fire's light.

Here—she traced the line with her finger—spine separated toward dorsal fin in delicate, evenly spaced bones as fine as cathedral spires, branching outward, perfectly suited to their purpose. God was a scientist like no other then, and the greatest of artists too, providing fish with cantilevered bones to aid the rise and fall of gills with no need of a diaphragm.

She separated flecks of skin from fins, marveling at the iridescence, wondering at the gills' ability to contract and expand, not unlike a bellows, aiding a creature capable of flashing through a creek bed or pooling in the shallows of a river.

The dorsal spine narrowed down the tail with an arc so—

"—*Mattie?* Whatever are you doing?" Elizabeth's eyes grew wondrous and baffled, as if she could not trust the scene before them. "Are the dishes washed?"

With her mother's words, Mattie tumbled back to a world of dishes and dirty floors and babies waiting to be fed. "Very nearly," she said, trying to toss off her mother's reprimand. But Elizabeth had pulled her far from the curved corners in her mind, far from a space where she could puzzle out answers.

Scraping the carcasses into the bin, Mattie chided herself under her breath. After all, who was she to believe she might find elusive explanations? She was nothing but a girl from a poor family living on the remotest frontier. What could she know, with her games of crystal structures, egg cells, and fish bones? So many times she felt like nothing more than a little thing stranded on a trail beneath a canopy of distant stars.

The brain is the medium through which the soul acts and enjoys. To reason and to will are its supreme functions.

—MARTHA HUGHES CANNON

Chapter Seven

Toward the end of the week, Patty Sessions returned to find Mary's fever broken. "She can sit up in bed now," Mattie told the midwife, who stewed herbs in a steaming cup of boiled water with gnarled but steady hands. Elizabeth's frenzy had tapered off with each sign of improvement.

"Disgusting," Joseph had pronounced the sickbed scene, and hurried out of the way. Though Elizabeth stood by her daughter's side, she had no interest in the methodology, while Mattie found herself as drawn to the scene as if Patty had arrived bearing sweets instead of medical instruments.

Patty measured tincture from tin, stirred, spooned, and mixed, explaining each step for Mattie's benefit. Mary watched the process through half-opened eyes.

"And who else is sickly in the valley right now?" Mattie asked.

"My daughter fancies herself a scientist," Elizabeth apologized.

"As well she may be someday. I'm afraid I can't do this forever." Patty chuckled and ducked close to check the consistency of her mixture. "Romania Pratt's baby is ill. And there's talk of her going back East to study medicine."

"Truly?" Mattie asked, filled with admiration.

"What will become of her children?" Elizabeth asked.

"Her husband and mother will watch after them."

Elizabeth's face indicated this was far from an adequate arrangement.

"How much easier it would be to go before one has a family," Mattie said, thinking aloud.

"And far easier not to go at all," Elizabeth added.

"Where did you train?" Mattie asked Patty, wishing she'd never brought up the subject in front of her mother.

"Not in a school, though I would have liked to," Patty said. "My mother-in-law was a healer and her mother before her, in Massachusetts and Mersea Island before that." She helped Mary sit up, smoothing hair away from her forehead and holding a cup to her lips. Mary murmured her thanks.

"That's the best way of it," Elizabeth agreed. "Mother to daughter. Learning at home and not in a classroom."

"Yet someone must have been the first to learn," Mattie said.

"The healers in my mother-in-law's family had to practice in secret, at risk for their lives," Patty said.

"In truth?" Mattie pictured healers gathering herbal remedies under cover of darkness on the slopes of a rainy, windswept English isle.

"Thankfully, the world has evolved past such madness," Elizabeth said. Her tone gave every indication the discussion was finished.

"We'll let Mary rest," Patty apologized. The patient sank back against the bed as the wan winter light fought its way through the rain-spattered window, coming to rest upon the midwife's black bag. Elizabeth held Mary's hand as Patty bottled up her tinctures and wiped down the mortar and pestle, wrapping them in rags threadbare from years of use, fastening them up and snapping them inside the dark container.

Downstairs, Lottie and Joseph played with the quietness of children who know someone is ill. Soup bubbled at the stove. Patty stopped to touch Lottie's curls and pat Joseph's shoulder as Mattie trailed after her.

"Mary will be fine," Patty said, turning at the door. "She should be up again in a day or two. Just see she doesn't overdo."

"Thank you," Mattie said, stalling. Looking down the street, she asked, "May I walk with you a bit?"

"If you wish. I'm heading to Romania Pratt's."

"Mother!" Mattie called into the house. "I'll be back presently." She wrapped a cloak about her shoulders, pinned on a simple hat, and then tugged on her practical boots. Seeing Patty's surprise, she explained, "I don't think it's healthy to walk about in wet and muddy shoes."

"It's a good idea," Patty acknowledged.

The women stepped into the swirling slush turning the roads to muddy rivers, holding their skirts high.

"Thank you for your help with Mary," Mattie said. "Illness is hard for my mother."

"She's not the first to feel helpless before it," Patty replied.

A storm raged its way over the mountains, obscuring peaks, throwing others into sharp relief. Across the valley, half-finished buildings stood halted and silent, waiting out the winter. "I'm intrigued at how Romania will manage medical school with all her other responsibilities," Mattie said.

"Thinking of joining her?"

"I'd never presume to think myself the intellectual equal to Sister Pratt," Mattie said, ducking her head. "Didn't she study at a Quaker school? And tutor Brigham Young's children?"

"She did."

"And she still has gold money to pay for the schooling, I'd imagine." Mattie didn't know her personally, but the story was well known in the valley, for Romania's father had found success in the gold fields of California, though he'd never returned from the expedition. His brother followed clues he'd left behind and retrieved the gold for his widow, which Romania's mother used to purchase a lovely home in the valley and the elegant pianoforte that adorned her daughter's front room.

"I don't know the details," Patty said, "but I've heard Romania is selling her pianoforte to cover the expense."

"She is?" Romania's determination to have this schooling, in spite of all that it would mean, dazzled Mattie. "And her husband?"

"Traveling East with her, chaperoning her to New York." Patty stopped near the entrance to Parley and Romania Pratt's elegant home. "Come in with me if you wish it. I can tell her you've come to assist me."

Mattie fought her mounting excitement at the labyrinth unfolding before her, but she hesitated, not wanting to intrude.

Romania greeted them at the door, her frazzled hair escaping the severe bun she wore at the nape of her neck, her wide-set eyes strained from exhaustion. "Thank you for coming," she said. "Irwin had the croup last week, and now Roy has come down with it, poor thing. He's miserable in spite of my best efforts. It's clear I'm no doctor yet."

"Miss Mattie Paul has come to assist me," Patty explained as they shed their layers in the foyer. Romania's expression held a twinge of annoyance, but she waved them back to the kitchen where three children played near a cobbled hearth. A baby writhed miserably on his grandmother's lap, drawing air in shallow, gasping breaths that reminded Mattie of a sound she'd heard before but could not quite place.

Patty fetched a pan from a shelf and filled it with water from the pump. "Once it starts to steam, let him breathe the water vapors," she said as she lifted the baby, demonstrating how to hold him above the pan. "Night air will also help." As Patty held the poor thing with his head below his heart, he cried, then coughed, and breathed a touch more easily. "How is his nappie?"

"Sore, to be sure," Romania said.

Patty handed the child to Mattie, who snuggled him against her at the angle Patty had instructed. "I believe I have some salve." Patty rummaged in her bag and produced a small tin. "Use this until the area clears."

"What is in it?" Mattie asked.

"Bark of indigo weed boiled down, mixed with beeswax, mutton tallow, and a little rosin," Patty explained. "When will you be leaving, Romania?"

Anguished by the suffering on her little one's face, Romania glanced up. "Next month if all goes well. It will be heart-wrenching to leave them, yet it must be done. Our community cannot continue this way. I cannot bear the thought of losing another child."

Mattie remembered hearing Romania had lost two of her babies. Two more pine coffins lowered into the earth. "Where will you go?"

"The Women's Medical College in Philadelphia," Romania replied. "As soon as I can get the children settled enough with mother and Parley to break away. It is a sacrifice, but the Lord knows we need more healers in this valley. People will keep coming, and Patty can't possibly treat them all. We need the medical knowledge of the East here with us in the West."

"Philadelphia," Mattie breathed in wonder, as if the word itself had magical properties.

"And the Church is encouraging you?" Patty asked.

"Brigham Young and Eliza Snow have advised us to leave as soon as possible." Mattie marveled at this new discovery, though it made sense given Brigham Young's desire to create a self-sustaining society.

"It's a brave thing you're doing," Patty said.

"Yes," Mattie agreed. "A brave and selfless thing."

They left Romania holding the baby, who rested more soundly now above the steaming water. As they headed for her front door, Mattie couldn't shake the feeling that Romania disliked her, but her coldness could not distract from the wonder she felt.

With the world shifting and morphing before her eyes, Mattie followed Patty up sidewalks slick with possibility. Contemplating Romania's sacrifices to attend medical school, she thought again how much easier it would be to go before one formed attachments. Though Jim Anderson might disagree. Mattie pushed the thought of him away, pulling her shawl tight against the wind. "Healing is a beautiful practice. Why did the women in your family keep their work secret?"

The aged woman inclined her head as she answered, bracing herself against a frigid gust. "My mother-in-law told me it was because priests felt local healing women threatened their power. They wanted the poor to come to them, though they did little beyond reminding them it was God's will they suffer. The Church of England viewed logic and reasoning at odds with faith and miracles, and taught we must suspend all thinking in order for prayer to work."

"People still repeat similar arguments," Mattie said. "But why would God give us minds if we aren't meant to use them?"

"Such logical thinking again," Patty said, smiling. "On Mersea Island, women met together to study the earth and its movements, to share their knowledge of herbal lore, and to help women through their cycles, through life begetting life. But many priests claimed women's healing power arose from carnal lust and consorting with devils."

"So they forbade them the practice of medicine?"

"If they didn't burn them at the stake. Meanwhile, doctors and priests treated their patients with prayers, alchemy, and poisons that often did more harm than good. My mother told me of a doctor from her youth who claimed a toothache could be healed by writing a verse of scripture along the edge of the jaw. They called midwives' techniques 'old wives' tales,' though they didn't mind pilfering their secrets. Anything doctors could not cure was blamed on witchcraft and the powers of the devil."

"That seems more than convenient."

"Indeed."

Mattie followed the bowed woman before her, turning into the heavy, pelting sleet as smoke rose sleepily from chimneys. What incredible strength lay beyond her frail exterior. On the other side of fences and beyond windows, Mattie caught glimpses of flames lit to draw people close and stave back the tempest. Shadows of flames rose and fell against panes of glass like hunters dancing round a burning pyre.

*The result of this force, the muscles are thrown into
action, and a contraction and the transmission
of this force is called reflex action.*

—MARTHA HUGHES CANNON

Chapter Eight

MARCH 1878
Salt Lake City, Utah Territory

Near the end of her typesetting shift a few weeks later, Mattie dragged herself before that imposing door, all black angles and edges. Inside the office, the editor darted, flurried, and momentarily perched.

You're not a young girl anymore, Mattie told herself sternly.

Gathering every scrap of courage about her, she knocked, waiting breathless at the void.

"Yes, Miss Paul?" Emmeline Wells asked, clearly baffled at the interruption from an innocuous typesetter.

"Sister Emmeline, I wished to . . . that is to say, might I seek your advice . . ." Mattie's eyes landed on the stacks of paper arrayed on Emmeline's desk, a multitude of tasks at hand surely far more important than any—

"Yes?" Emmeline's pen paused midstroke, hovering above the copy, reminding her guest that publishing a newspaper was no girlish whim. Her pen inched, barely perceptible, back toward the line, her eyes glancing down to her work. "Yes, Miss Paul?" Her voice forced toward patience, taking in the anxious state of the girl before her. "How might I help you?"

"I wish, that is to say, I have considered—" *Oh, out with it. Best toss it upon Emmeline's desk, a dull, flat thing to brush away with other vain imaginings.* ". . . I wondered if you would advise me to consider the study of physic? That is to say, ma'am," she cleared her throat, "I think I might wish to attend medical school."

Emmeline blinked.

Mattie moved one booted foot toward the door, ready to depart at the first hint that Sister Emmeline would dismiss her stammered confession.

But watch how she does it, lifting the pen to rest against her chin. "I see," Emmeline said at last. "I believe you have been studying chemistry at Deseret University these last few years, is that right?"

Mattie nodded, her throat too constricted to do more.

Emmeline placed her pen down on the desk. "Did you know the University of Michigan has recently begun accepting women into their medical program?"

Mattie shook her head, wondering if she were capable of further speech.

Emmeline raised her eyes to seek the upper corner of the room. Mattie thought of cutting off bread corners that never quite fit in a pan, only to realize they fit perfectly in a larger, different space where they would have worked all along, only you hadn't thought of such a thing. Emmeline's jaw tightened. "This valley is in dire need of smart, hardworking doctors such as you would make, Miss Paul. If you wish, I shall write to Eliza Snow and Brigham Young and tell them of your intention. And if you tell me of your financial arrangements and your application deadlines, I will know how best to assist you."

Mattie thought of lifting a kaleidoscope to her eye as a child.

Held still, the colored fractals rested in repose, paused in a moment of intricate stillness that seemed unending. And then. A flick of the wrist, the briefest turning and everything shifted: yellows slid into crimson, blues shifted into greens. How mesmerizing that movement, that turning, that melding of refracted light, meant in the end to turn, meant all along to change.

Some weeks later, Mary's eyes shone in the candlelight, her honey hair coifed and wrapped in elegant waves. Shyly, she leaned into the young man at her side, pressing the new band circling her finger.

"We are so very happy for you," Mama said, glowing as much as her daughter. She placed a rhubarb cobbler on the table.

Engaged. The look of belonging was unmistakable, and at age twenty-two, Mary was the ideal age for matrimony. Jim Anderson, who had long since become a regular fixture at the Paul household, glanced sidelong at Mattie.

"Have ye considered a date, then?" James asked his oldest step-daughter.

"A summer wedding," Mary said, smiling into Parley Neeley's face, then veering off into ramblings of colors, flowers and shades of her trousseau before circling back. "Yes, summer. And Mattie will be done with school then. She can help Mama around the house, unless . . ." She broke off with a glance at Jim.

Mattie started to hear her own name invoked. Not wanting to detract from her sister's moment, she gazed around at the expectant faces, all hopeful for something she could not give. "Actually, I won't be done with school. I am planning to try for medical school." An awkward silence ensued, with Mary and Mama exchanging alarmed glances over the head of a distraught-looking Jim. Mattie rushed to fill the void. "It's far from settled, of course, but that's my hope."

"Medical school?" Elizabeth asked, aghast. "Unaccompanied?"

"Well, possibly not, Mother." Mattie squirmed, wishing she could hide herself in the pantry like a child.

Jim's expression relaxed at her acknowledgment, and James came to the rescue. "That's a big decision, Mattie. Congratulations to you as well."

"Thank you," she said, silently blessing him. "But, Mary, what flowers did you say you wanted to carry in your bouquet?"

With her question, the focus of the room shifted back to the engaged couple and their weighty deliberations, though Mama's expression indicated she didn't plan to let the matter drop as easily as that. Jim's hand sought hers beneath the table in an encouraging squeeze.

On the front porch later, preparing to depart, Jim whispered his devotion, his willingness to go with her to medical school so she need not go alone.

"Thank you, but I don't want to overshadow Mary's engagement right now, Jim."

"I understand," he said, although he didn't, for she hardly understood it herself.

Closing the door behind him, she wondered why she felt no thrill at the thought of going to medical school with him by her side, why the prospect left her a little deflated, with no trace of the shine that hovered over Mary's face. As she watched him walk away with an air of eagerness, she tried to name the emotion in her surging heart and landed on only guilt.

Some days later, James entered the sitting room carrying a bulky object wrapped in a quilt, which he placed at Mattie's feet as she sat darning a hole in Lottie's dress. "What's this?" she asked, setting aside the sewing. "Mary's the one receiving gifts at the moment."

"Ay," said James. "But this one's for ye."

Mattie moved aside the quilt, lifting it up and over one side. Wooden planks, hewn and fitted tongue to groove, sanded smooth and stained, a lid decorated with red leather tacked in place. Sturdy leather handles bolted to each side. "What is this?" she asked, moved by the artistry, each inch of it bearing the mark of her stepfather's hands.

"You'll be needing a trunk to take to medical school, won't you?" James said. "Now ye have one."

Mattie lifted the lid, and the scent of James's shop, of labor and fresh-cut pine, escaped. "But I've not even been accepted!" Tears sprung to her eyes at his gesture, knowing the hours he must have spent, never saying a word as he labored to give her a piece of home to carry her onward into this wide, broad world.

She rose and threw her arms around him, hugging him tightly. He laughed, taken aback by her fierceness, and the sound rumbled through his chest as he rested awkward hands upon her shoulders. "Thank you, Papa," she said again and again.

Mattie carried the trunk upstairs, and nestled an umbrella box full of coins at the bottom of it, coins she had already begun to squirrel away for medical school, just as her mother hoarded acorn squash and root potatoes against the long cold winter.

Some months later, Mattie carried a letter inside, with shaking hands. Soap making had taken over the house; filled molds cooled on every flat surface, and the remaining liquid boiled over a fire built in the backyard. Mama wiped the sweat from her face as Joseph struggled to hold the molds steady.

"What's happened?" Mary laughed at her sister's expression. "You look like you've seen a vision."

Mattie laughed. "Perhaps I have. University of Michigan has accepted me. Without an interview."

Eight-year-old Lottie bumped against her mother, and melted soap spilled to the floor. "Oh bosh!" Elizabeth said, as two-year-old Maude began to cry. "Can you please help your sisters, Mattie? We haven't time for anything more right now."

"Sorry, Mama," Mattie said, scooping up Maude, as Lottie directed Bonnie toward a pile of blocks on the back porch.

"Congratulations," Mama said, as she steadied Joseph's hands and began pouring the melted soap mixture. "If that's what you're wanting to hear."

"A B C," Bonnie spelled with her blocks, and the baby fussed against Mattie's shoulder.

"I can't say I think it's a reasonable idea," Elizabeth continued, as she swiped her wrist across her damp forehead. "Galavanting across the country alone, away from your family, away from your beau. I hope you plan to marry him before you go, lest you find him scooped up by another."

"Yes, A B C," Mattie spelled for her sister, keeping silent, like a wick that had been lit only to be blown back out.

Contraction in the animal is excited by external stimulus.
—MARTHA HUGHES CANNON

Chapter Nine

Conference-goers milled about in family groups: greeting friends, straightening bonnets, brushing miles of road dust off dresses, and gawking at the footprint of the temple, beginning to rise from the desert floor. Momentarily silent, pulleys and angled cranes brooded over the structure, where each stone had been hand chiseled on site. Train tracks now pulled the massive stones to the construction area, relieving oxen that had hefted previous blocks cartload by excruciating cartload.

As a child, Mattie had attended conference gatherings in an outdoor bowery, but the new Tabernacle timbers had been crafted by pioneer hands, then topped with a domed roof that reminded Mattie of an egg. After hours of waiting to be seated inside, she shifted on the pine bench painted stroke by stroke to look like oak.

"If all who attend conference will leave their coughing at home and sit still while here and omit shuffling their feet, they may have an opportunity of hearing pretty much everything that may be said," Elder George Albert Smith said, speaking from the pulpit hundreds of yards away.

Asking thousands of people to be quiet seemed like a pointless task, but the crowd quieted and, thanks to the egg-shaped roof, most of the speakers' voices carried the length of the hall. Mattie peered around a velveted, feathered hat in front of her, considering what made some of the speakers far more engaging than others, crafting their pauses and forming words to heighten suspense, while others hurtled words into the vastness.

Growing bored, Mattie stifled a yawn and leaned into Mary, weary from the long walk compounded by heat rising from hundreds of bodies. The benches managed to be hard, despite layers of petticoats.

With Mama's watchful eye chiding her inattention, Mattie sat up straighter, focusing on the pipe organ's lines to distract from the stale air circling closely packed bodies. Elder Smith sat down to a flurry of "amens" and Brigham Young, resplendent in vest and top hat, approached the pulpit. Mattie leaned forward in her seat, for Brother Brigham's voice carried easily through the cavernous building, and his talks were never dull.

"Death must come upon us," he began. *Hmm . . . an auspicious opening.* "I don't know how far it is where the dead dwell, but it is not very far." Mattie thought of Papa and Annie, wishing she could sense them. "I pray the Lord will give us wisdom to know how to sustain and preserve ourselves." *Isn't that what medicine does?*

Brother Brigham lowered his voice and plunged into his chosen subject with a fervor well known to his followers. "Our religion incorporates and includes all the duties devolving upon us every day of our lives, and enables us, if we live according to the spirit of it, to discharge those several duties more honorably and efficiently. I do not think there is as good a financier on the earth as my Father in Heaven is; and I believe the same with regard to any other branch of human knowledge, or of anything which affects the peace, happiness, comfort, wealth, health, and strength of the body, and in fact the entire welfare, whether political, social, or physical, of the children of men. Consequently I would like to have Him dictate my affairs."

Mattie's mind wandered down paths of fish bones and the properties of mercury, all of them fathomed and designed by the God she believed in.

Brigham continued, "Our religion incorporates every act and word of man. No man should go to merchandising unless he does it in God; no man should go to farming or any other business unless he does it in the Lord. No lawyer—no, hold on—I will leave the lawyers out, we have no use for them." Laughter burst forth freely.

Brigham waited for it to quiet and continued with a dry smile. "Our work, our everyday labor, our whole lives are within the scope of our religion. This is what we believe and what we try to practice." Mattie, her heart thrilling with his words, glanced over at her mother's face, unreadable, unmoving. Of course, Mama would say he wasn't talking of women.

Brother Brigham shifted, smoothing his beard with one hand. As if he'd read her worry, he said, "Now, I wish to say some words to the sisters," and Mattie hoped he might offer assistance to her cause. "Do not dress after the fashions of Babylon, but after the fashions of the Saints." She sighed, disappointed, unsure as to why so much attention was directed toward the clothing of women, a sermon topic she found endlessly dull.

"Suppose a female angel were to come into your house, how would she be dressed?" Well, his question was at least mildly intriguing. "Do you think she would have a great big peck measure of flax done up like hair on the back of the head?"

Mattie snickered. "Would she have a dress dragging two or three yards behind? Would she have on a great, big—what is it you call it? A Grecian or Dutch—Well, no matter, you know what I mean."

She laughed outright now—she couldn't help it. Listening to this imposing man trip over descriptions of fashion styles was too delightful. She was not the only one laughing, though Mama flashed a warning again.

Brother Brigham continued unabashed: "Not at all. Instead

of going to parties to dance and indulging in this nonsense, go to school and study; take rocks and analyze them—tell the properties and what they are. Instead of going 'right and left, balance all, promenade,' go to work and teach yourselves something."

Mattie sat up straighter at the abrupt joining of topics. Joseph tugged at her hand and tried to distract her with a whirligig he had smuggled in his pocket. At another time she would have been happy for the distraction, but now she shrugged him off, leaning left of the feathered hat, waiting for the next words.

Brother Brigham did not disappoint. "As I have often told my sisters in the female Relief Societies, we have sisters here who, if they had the privilege of studying, would make just as good mathematicians or accountants as any man; and we think they ought to have the privilege to study these branches of knowledge that they may develop the powers with which they are endowed, to study law or physic, or become good bookkeepers and be able to do the business in any counting house, to enlarge their sphere of usefulness for the benefit of society at large. The time has come for women to come forth as doctors in these valleys of the mountains."

An electric shock passed through Mattie.

This, then, perhaps, was what the full power of the Holy Ghost felt like. She dared not raise her eyes to meet her mother's gaze, but continued tracing the lines of those exquisite pipes rising from the floor of the Tabernacle building toward the roof, pointing straight at heaven.

As if sensing skeptical reactions from his listeners, Brigham countered, "Someone, perhaps, will use some little argument against women doing anything of this kind. Shame on the boys, and shame on the great big, fat lazy men! Let these women go to work; learn some good, solid sense." There were a few nervous titters in the crowd and Mattie knew many in the audience would dismiss Brigham's words as another one of his tirades, dabbling in realms better left to the female Relief Society leaders. He would soon enough move onto another pet obsession, Mama would say. But to Mattie, no one had ever been more prophetic. She wanted to stand up and say to everyone: *Are you listening? Are you hearing this?*

Brigham's voice turned thoughtful as he finished his remarks. "I hope we may live so that God will bless and enable us Latter-day Saints to live our religion; if you do, there will be no necessity to fear all the powers of earth and hell, for God will sustain you."

The electrified feeling remained, and Mattie wondered if her hair would rise on end with the waves of it. She kept her eyes fastened on those pipes, not wanting to move or turn away, hoping someone had written down his words so she could read them again and again.

Surely Mama could say nothing against her schooling now, with both Brother Brigham and Emmeline Wells on her side. Mattie scanned the rows of people—dusty men, women, and children arranged in sedate and ordered lines. "The time has come for women to come forth as doctors in these valleys of the mountains." Women. Doctors. How many plumed hats rested on the heads of women who would go for training? Romania. Mattie. And who else? In spite of Mama's gaze, in spite of all obstacles that lay ahead, when the choir rose to sing their number, Mattie felt like rising up and singing "Hallelujah" alongside them.

Were it not for the extreme mobility,
there could not be that interchange.
—MARTHA HUGHES CANNON

Chapter Ten

d   e   e   c   c   u   S

Mattie's hand moved swiftly between the cases, top to bottom, right to left. Flick, switch, place, next—setting the letters, each of Sister Emmeline's words, speaking in praise of a new candidate for medical school departing from the valley.

Flick, switch, place. Pleasure tugged at the corners of her mouth as she set the type for Emmeline's newest editorial announcing that Martha Hughes Paul would be departing for medical school.

> Miss Paul has been qualifying herself for some time past in the study of medicine and surgery, preparatory to going East with the intention of perfecting herself in these attainments. She has educated herself by her own energy, industry, and economy, and earned money to defray her college expenses, and her example of diligence and perseverance is worthy of imitation. Miss Paul is a young lady of exceptional ability and deserves to succeed.

Other announcements continued, Sister Emmeline's cheeky voice speaking through every line—praising those she felt deserving, slamming a rival local paper for "abusing 'Mormonism' and 'woman's rights'" in recent editions. "We merely allude to the fact, as an evidence of how poorly informed some of these editorial persons are," Emmeline ranted, telling the editor off in the most well-bred manner.

Mattie supressed a smile. That small and pointed bird lady held powers which belied her tiny frame. Even while she enjoyed Emmeline's approval, the thought of ever crossing to the wrong side of her opinions filled Mattie with a simmering terror.

She double-checked the kerning and leading to avoid distracting rivers in the lines of text, then bound the completed square in her composing stick with string. She carried the precarious bundle to the proofreader's stone to await inking and proofing before the words would be smeared across papers, dried and folded, sent out into the world, announcing the event in black and white words, right there for the touching.

Some weeks later, Mattie's delicate boots hurried down the Salt Lake street as the imposing bronze eagle peered down curiously at the young woman with close-cropped hair. Her boots had danced with excitement often as of late: When her ward, the Salt Lake Tenth, held a benefit evening to help raise funds for her schooling. When Eliza Snow had presented her with a homemade silk purse sheltering two gold pieces inside. When she counted her savings and found she had enough for the first year's tuition if she made beds and cleaned rooms at a boardinghouse near the University of Michigan.

Her boots lay still, though, the evening she told Jim Anderson she had decided to journey to Michigan alone. That night, after speaking the words, "I cannot marry you," Mattie scuffed her way home, devastated by causing Jim so much pain, wishing she understood why she couldn't be his wife. And why the thought of going alone, a prospect that horrified her mother, thrilled her to the fiber of her being.

But that sadness was several weeks behind her, and today her boots tripped lightly to a brick building sandwiched between the Lion and Beehive houses.

In the Church Office Building waited a circle of women, including Dr. Romania Pratt, just back from medical school, where she had studied the art of cataract surgery. She was as plain and severe as ever but held herself with a confidence and poise Mattie admired and envied. *Did they teach you that in medical school?* She felt a chilly distance in Romania's greeting, and Mattie wondered if Romania shared her mother's view that Eastern universities were no place for unmarried young ladies.

The Shipp sisters greeted her too, more warmly it seemed. Dr. Ellis Shipp, curls piled fashionably at the crown of her head, had just returned from Michigan to establish the first midwifery school in the valley. Her sister wife, Maggie, elegant in starched taffeta stripes, who had cared for Ellis's children, would soon depart for Women's Medical College of Philadelphia, trading the responsibilities of home for the duties of the medical student's lab.

So much knowledge, so much experience centered in these women, all of them with families of their own. There they stood on the other side of this great divide while she—scarcely twenty-one years old, the only one unmarried—had only just begun. Mattie felt herself a child among her elders, though Maggie and Ellis reached to reassure her that she would be one of them soon enough.

The door to the Church office opened, and the women were beckoned in by John Taylor, iconic leader who would inevitably be set apart as president of the Church in the aftermath of Brother Brigham's death, a man with deeply shadowed eyes who had faced down a mob in Carthage Jail at the side of Joseph Smith, and whom she had only seen across the expanse of the Tabernacle. Behind him came George Q. Cannon, first counselor to Brigham Young, a Liverpool accent marking the edges of his speech, as he greeted the women, one by one. She had heard him give sermons in fluent Hawaiian, a tongue he had learned on his mission to the Sandwich Isles. The man had represented the Church before the U.S. Congress, and now he had invited her—*her, her, her*— to receive a blessing before her departure, setting her apart for medical school just as missionaries were set apart for their service. Though she'd had weeks to consider the invitation, it was no less baffling, no less thrilling.

President Cannon's balding head reminded Mattie of a billiard ball, all curves and bulgings, framed by a white scruff of fringe. But his kindly eyes helped her continue to breathe. "Welcome, Sister Paul," he said, shaking her hand most cordially. "We look forward to hearing great things of you from Michigan."

She murmured something like a response as the group assembled in the office and shut the door. The men laid their hands upon Dr. Pratt first, and John Taylor blessed her with power and health as she established her practice in the valley. Then George Q. Cannon blessed Dr. Ellis Shipp with the ability to balance home and family as she trained new midwives in Zion. John Taylor, in turn, administered to Maggie Shipp, granting her a quick-thinking mind to aid her learning, trusting her children would be cared for in her absence.

After each blessing, Mattie watched the women with new strength in their eyes, supported by their faith and its leaders.

"And now, Sister Paul," George Cannon said kindly.

She rose, trembling, and seated herself in the chair, feeling the eyes of her sisters resting upon her. The men stood behind her and placed their hands upon her head, and Brother Cannon's accent cast each word as British poetry:

"Sister Martha Hughes Paul, inasmuch as you are going forth to learn the duties of your chosen profession to store up in your mind, we feel to bless you, in the name of the Lord Jesus Christ."

Mattie felt warmth start near the crown of her head and flow through her until it reached every muscle and molecule.

"We say, be thou filled in your heart and made strong by the Spirit of God. We endow you with strength and health and ask that you will be preserved from disease and affliction. We pray that the Lord will be with you day and night, upon the land and waters and preserve you in His keeping."

As the words continued on, Mattie felt empowered and protected, enveloped with a love and acceptance she had glimpsed rarely before.

"Sister Paul, we bless thee that health and peace shall drop from the ends of thy fingers, and consolation and comfort from thy lips. We ordain thee and set thee apart to administer peace and comfort to the afflicted."

The loveliness of the promises took her breath away, and she felt for the first time that perhaps her mind was not an accident she needed to hide or atone for, that this choice was God's will as well as her own. Never mind that her mother still couldn't look her in the eyes when she spoke of her departure. Never mind Jim's disappointment. She knew she was following the path of her heart and eventually all would be right.

"The sick shall rise up at thy touch, and sickness and death shall flee from thy presence. We bless thee to this end in the name of Jesus Christ, amen."

"Amen," repeated Mattie, echoed by the women seated in front of her. She raised her eyes. And though she still had much to do to pack, prepare, and put in order, Mattie felt herself ready, at last, to depart.

Part Two

The stark, cold corpse of man, the cadaver, awakens
in the reflective mind admiration and reverence. The
surgeon dissects with an ever-increasing interest.

—MARTHA HUGHES CANNON

Chapter Eleven

SPRING 1880
Ann Arbor, Michigan

Spring in Ann Arbor swept over the city in one fell swoop, tossing aside the last remnants of winter, bursting through each bud on campus. Birds flitted as if this were the first spring to ever enrapture the earth. Few students crossed campus at this hour, though a handful of the more determined professors yawned as they endeavored to recall today's upcoming lectures or where they had left their students' exams.

The early dawn light struggled to enter a pale basement where motionless forms stretched upon exam tables, a lone figure in skirts moving among them. Scalpel in hand, she used her instruments to peel back the fragile wrappings and probe beneath the surface, marveling at muscle, sinew, and connective tissue, tracing the length of intersecting fibers. Pausing to annotate a measurement, she confirmed the diagnosis of ovarian hemorrhage that had taken the life of a woman in her mid-thirties. The overworked reproductive organs

had birthed before, which meant she had died leaving children behind, most likely. She wore years of care upon her face.

"Thank you," Mattie said softly to the woman's body as she
worked. "You must know how much I appreciate you allowing me
to learn this way. No textbook or lecture or diagram could ever be
as helpful."

Did newly departed spirits hover near their bodies? Her habit
might be dismissed as paranoia or prayer, yet Mattie felt dissections
went better when she spoke to the cadavers, when she explained
what she was doing and why. For this reason and others, she arrived
first to the dissection room.

Mattie nudged the woman's uterus aside to better examine the
pelvic cavity, which had recently been discussed in lecture. Adding
a sketch to her notes, she continued to probe and cut, probe and
cut, averting her nose from the pungent smell emanating from the
decomposing body. "Thanks to you I can help other women, keep
them from your suffering," she explained to the draped figure before
her. Footsteps sounded in the hall, and Mattie lowered her voice. "I
am sorry we couldn't have done more."

"Miss Paul?" Dr. Silas Douglas appeared at the doorway, closer
than she had realized. He looked round the room in bafflement. "To
whom are you speaking?"

Mattie blushed, feeling like a sixteen-year-old caught playing
with a fish carcass. "Excuse me, Dr. Douglas. I did not hear you enter." A chin-curtain beard defined the stern angles of Dr. Douglas's
face with grizzled fuzz, and Mattie miserably considered that there
was no other professor she would have been less excited to see at the
door.

His question hung in the air, awaiting an answer.

"I was speaking with my patient," she admitted at last.

"With your patient?" Dr. Douglas asked, raising his substan-
tial eyebrows. Professor Douglas had taught at the University of

Michigan for over twenty years and made no secret of his position that women lacked the intellectual and psychological strength to practice obstetrics. He had objected to their entrance to the program and had not yet forgotten the discomfort of being overruled. "Your patient, miss, is dead."

"Yes, sir."

"As you know, if you've gained anything from your two years here, once brain activity has ceased, the ears no longer resonate from sound, nor is language processed in the brain's receptors. Based on this information, speaking to a dead patient as you exhume her stomach and measure her uterus would be entirely nonsensical. Would you not agree?"

Mattie stammered. "There may be no scientific reason to support this practice, sir, but I find that when I do, dissection goes better. . . ." Her voice trailed off. "And certainly there can be no harm in it?"

Dr. Douglas adjusted his spectacles. "Except, of course, until the living overhear you. Would you like to explain your intriguing theory to our anatomy class this afternoon?"

Mattie's cheeks flamed. "No, thank you, sir."

"Then I suggest you finish your exam preparation and refrain from further discussion with the school cadavers, Miss Paul."

"Yes, sir." Mattie turned back to the corpse. With shaking hands, she took final measurements and resolved the diagram in her notebook, then drew a sheet over the woman's face, returning her body to anonymity and unbroken silence.

Some physiologists believe that intellectual forces are generated upon the brain surface in a manner analogous to that in which electric currents are developed.

—MARTHA HUGHES CANNON

Chapter Twelve

Medics-in-training jostled into the lecture hall hours later, fighting their way up the steep stairs of the wood-paneled amphitheater, swapping exam scores and the best moments of the rugby game from the evening before. An air of anticipation whispered of graduation only weeks away and summer internships after that.

Into this scene ventured five women attired in modest skirts, dark hems sweeping the ground, hair brushed back in tidy knots and buns. Viewed from the floor below, the men arranged up the steep, circular room seemed to hang suspended like dangling marionettes.

As the women entered, the lecture room erupted with laughter and scoffing, and an electric current seemed to pass down the rows. "Hen medics!" several voices jeered. Ignoring them, Mattie swept across the worn plank floor following Lavinia Carter and Mildred Butternup, fellow second-year medical students.

The women stepped over a red line separating one row in the hall from the others, settling themselves into chairs. "Honestly," Mattie breathed. "You'd think they would tire of these antics after two years together."

"It's the coming summer holidays that inspire them," Lavinia whispered back. "They are trying to make up for the months when they cannot pester and assail us."

"However shall they occupy their time?"

Granted, there were a few friendly faces among the lot. Mattie found Leolin Bennet a row behind them, smiling down apologetically, as he tried in vain to hush the most obnoxious provokers.

"Gentlemen." The voice of Dr. Silas Douglas, Professor of Practice, sounded from the threshold of the door. His decisive steps across the floor silenced the jeers, though he seemed to find the outbursts amusing.

At that moment, another woman rushed through the door with an apologetic smile. "Sorry I'm late, sir," she said. "Barbara Replogle, if you please."

A hundred faces turned toward the newcomer in amazement, and Dr. Douglas turned in the unknown student's direction, appalled. "Barbara Replogle, new student observation?"

The woman's unbuttoned jacket billowed open, revealing a white shirtwaist tucked hastily into a simple gray skirt, and her wide, round face showed no hint of timidity or awareness of what she had done. "Yes, sir." Ignoring his expression of disdain, she made her way toward the women's row, stepping over the red line as "Bwaack" sounded from the back row.

"Miss Replogle," Dr. Douglas blustered, "the first thing you will learn at Michigan, should you decide to pursue your studies, is that the suitability of women for the medical classroom is still in its earliest experimental stages." Barbara's face remained impassive as Dr. Douglas placed his medical bag upon the table in the center of the lecture hall. "Considering the scientific fact that every woman monthly becomes a quasi-invalid unable to think clearly, there is considerable concern over the presence of women in these so-called 'mixed classes' of instruction. We will excuse your breach of protocol this morning, but I hope I can assume that you will not discredit your sex again in this way."

"Understood, sir," Barbara said, dismissing the public degradation without the slightest sign of mortification. Mattie felt she'd spent the last two years navigating this minefield, doing all she could to avoid a confrontation like the one Miss Replogle had plunged herself into on day one. Douglas's gaze rested upon this new pupil, eyes slightly narrowed.

Turning on one foot, Douglas strode back to the podium, laying a dummy torso on the table, fixing its fabricated, unseeing eyes into the crowded auditorium. *Poor creature,* Mattie thought. *Which hypothetical ailment will befall it today?* If Miss Replogle felt kinship with the figure exposed to so many hostile gazes, she did not show it as she drew out a bottle of ink and notebook. Mattie opened her own notes to the most recent page of ciphers, so small they were nearly illegible.

"As you know from your syllabus," Dr. Douglas announced, "today's lecture is on insanity and its prevention." He squinted down at his notes and ran a hand through his fine, thin hair. "My discourse this afternoon is based on Dr. Daniel Tuke's recent research in London wherein he documents a higher rate of insanity among civilized people than among savages, though accurate numbers among savage populations are unreliable at best." Mattie considered what to write down and contented herself with drawing a scroll about the title.

Dr. Douglas joined his hands behind his back, getting into the stride of his lecture, clearly enjoying the sound of his voice carrying through the hall. "It appears that an increased liability to insanity may be the penalty which superior organisms have to pay for their greater sensitivity. Then again, in more primitive cultures, the medically insane may be quickly disposed of without charitable institutions to keep him from becoming a burden on his fellows, and this may account for the variation."

Higher rates of insanity among the civilized, Mattie wrote, wondering when the fact might be useful in medical practice.

"And now we turn to a discussion of female hysteria," Dr. Douglas said. "You will recall it was Hippocrates who advanced the view that women's wombs wander at will throughout the female body, 'blocking passages, obstructing breathing, causing disease,' an example of which we had a brief reminder earlier today." Here, he looked pointedly to Barbara, and titters came from the back rows. Barbara kept her head bent over her notebook, and Douglas continued. "Aretaeus of Cappadocia termed the organ an 'animal within an animal' and noted that the womb responds favorably to smells, hence the usefulness of smelling salts, or the most efficacious solution—happy marriage and regular coitus and pregnancy to keep it from becoming bored."

Mattie and Mildred exchanged a slightly mortified glance.

"Symptoms of classic female hysteria, of course, include emotional outbursts, anxiety, fainting, insomnia, irritability, and marked sexual desires. At times it is exhibited by engaging in nonsensical behaviors. A person speaking to a cadaver might be a useful example."

Mattie's face burned red, and beside her, Barbara's hand rose into the air.

Incredulous, Douglas turned toward her. "Miss Replogle, though I understand you may be confused, now is not the time for questions. Take thorough notes, and you may direct your question to your discussion group. You may meet with me in office hours if you need further clarification."

"Very well," Barbara replied crisply.

Mattie and Lavinia exchanged a baffled glance. What on earth had this naïve newcomer planned to say? *Hippocrates and the wandering womb,* Mattie wrote. *Cause of classic female hysteria.*

Dr. Douglas cleared his voice and continued, "Today I would like to share with you a new research from France on the use of metalloscopy and metallotherapy to treat hysteria and hystero-epilepsy. In this procedure, iron, copper, zinc, gold, silver, tin, arsenic, or antimony may be applied to the skin." He unlatched his bag and removed a circle of metal discs, each the size of a large coin, and applied it to the dummy's arm like a bracelet. "Some experimentation may be needed to determine the best metal for patient response, but in many cases, when the discs are removed the anaesthesia disappears completely. Can anyone explain why?"

Barbara raised her hand again. Along with an eager boy on the first row.

Sparks emanated from Douglas as he called, "Thadeus?"

"Is it because the contact of metal with dry skin gives rise to an electric current?"

"Someone has been reading ahead," Dr. Douglas complimented. "Yes, and the strength of the current could be determined by the deviation of the needle of a galvanometer. Of course with a disease as complicated as hysteria, no approach can guarantee success. Please note that metals may also be ground to micro-fine powders for ingestion, which may prove more effective for some patients." Dr. Douglas lined up several vials on the lecture podium.

Ingest ground metal, Mattie wrote, wishing she could examine the methodology of these experiments herself instead of hearing about them secondhand.

"The experienced medical man will no doubt wonder how we can trust reports from patients who are hysterical after all," Douglas continued. Mattie hadn't been wondering that, but then, she wasn't an experienced medical man either.

"No doubt patients lie," Douglas continued, "but their deception can be detected when an impartial, careful observer is at work." He concluded, "We will break now for discussion groups in which you will summarize the findings, and respond with your analysis, due next week. Dismissed."

The initial step is friction.
—MARTHA HUGHES CANNON

Chapter Thirteen

Throughout the auditorium, students hurried to gather their belongings and join study partners. A few scoffed in the direction of Barbara, no doubt discussing the interruption. Always a gentleman, Leolin stopped on his way out to introduce himself. "Welcome to Michigan," he told Barbara sympathetically.

"I imagine you'll be joining us?" Mattie asked her, feeling drawn to this student who had managed to remain unperturbed by Douglas's public scorn.

"Thank you, yes," Barbara said, greeting Lavinia and Mildred as well. Inclining her head conspiratorily, she whispered, "You must tell me. Are all the professors here so impossibly archaic in their estimation of the fairer sex?"

Lavinia stiffened and cast an eye toward the crowded lecture platform. "Now is not, perhaps, the most suitable place for a discussion, Miss Replogle."

Barbara nodded. "Understood. Another time. In the meantime, I look forward to hearing your views on the promise of metalloscopy as a way to manage the most hysterical amongst us."

Mattie stifled a laugh and found herself falling toward the side of liking the unabashed Miss Replogle.

They jostled their way into the hallway, where students and professors swooped past, medical coats billowing as they discussed the day's lectures and procedures. Classical pillars held up the dark edges of the building in carved, heavy marble. From above, portraits of past college presidents looked down upon the scene with an air of slight dismay.

On the other side of an arched doorway, study groups assembled and debated across the flat surface of tables. Mattie brushed her long skirts beneath the heavy breadth and propped her notebook open.

"I, for one, found the French experiments compelling," Lavinia Carter began, lines of books behind her like sentinels of centuries of tradition. "Their results were consistent, their methodology sound." Lavinia launched into a mini-lecture of her own, summarizing the science behind the procedure with an astuteness calculated to impress all listeners, leading Mattie to once again admire Lavinia's insights, though she remained less confident about the future Dr. Carter's sickbed manner. She focused her attention back in time to hear, "though the metallic application may have removed the *existing* anaesthesia, in all probability, it only *transferred* the hemianaesthesia."

Mattie had lost the train of logic, but Mildred nodded. "That would be consistent with Dr. Douglas's observations." Mildred dipped her pen in ink and scrawled something in her notebook.

"And with Regnard's galvanometer measurements as well," Lavinia added, decisively. "Any other ideas we should consider?"

"Only to question the basic concept of female hysteria at all," Barbara said. Five pairs of eyes focused on the newcomer.

"Hysteria is quite well documented as an ailment," Lavinia said, in a voice meant to silence all opinions to the contrary. A few students from nearby discussion groups glanced over at the elevated volume.

Barbara countered nonchalantly. "Oh, certainly there are instances where symptoms are extreme enough to warrant a diagnosis and intervention, but much of what is termed 'female hysteria' by the medical community seems to be simply a woman's biological system functioning as it is intended to, that is, differently from a man's."

Mattie stifled a laugh, fascinated to hear Miss Replogle say aloud something she had often wondered in private.

Lavinia seemed far less intrigued by the cheeky outsider. "And what would you suggest? Tell the women suffering from female hysteria to cease complaining?"

"The diagnosis is complicated," Barbara acknowledged, "but the remedy probably lies around this table—women need more opportunities to develop their intellectual faculties."

"That theory is scarcely supported by the evidence that academic overwork only contributes to women's emotional ailments," Lavinia shot back.

"Have any of you felt such indications?" Barbara asked. Mattie shook her head. "I think we need more female physicians doing research on female diseases. Theories like wandering wombs would never have been entertained if someone who actually owned a womb did that analysis."

Mattie laughed—she couldn't help it. It was such a simple, yet brilliant observation that left all measurements with a galvanometer ridiculously superfluous. A thin, wan light streaming through the arched window landed on Barbara's brown tresses, setting her aglow, and she seemed like an angel who had swooped in from the ether above proclaiming simple truths to confound the learned.

Lavinia, for one, however, did not enjoy the unexpected visitation. "And what, pray tell, would you suggest we write down for our group response to Dr. Douglas's lecture then, Miss Replogle? I doubt he would be interested in hearing he is unqualified to research the subject due to his lack of having a uterus."

"He doesn't mind finding us unqualified due to our having one," Barbara responded. Silence hung in the air, and the observational student seemed to remember they were not friends engaged in a discussion over tea. "I am sorry," she apologized. "I'm new, and I am afraid I don't understand this group process very well, obviously. Perhaps I should have just listened today." She tucked a loose strand of hair behind her ear. "Personally I'm much more impressed with Jean-Martin Charcot's observations that hysteria occurs in men as often as in women, though, and that it might come from the brain rather than the uterus."

Mattie leaned forward, excited. "Perhaps Dr. Douglas's information is outdated then? He is ancient as dirt and far too enamored of the ancient Greeks. I have always thought so."

"Medical women throughout the ages could have corrected such preposterous theories," Barbara said, perking back up at Mattie's enthusiasm. "Unfortunately, Professor Douglas is clearly not interested in hearing their accounts."

Lavinia blotted her notebook and capped her ink well to indicate the discussion was drawing to a close. "Do you have anything published by this Charcot? We can mention it in our response, which is due next week, but only if we have a documented source."

A laugh burst forth from a study group nearby, and Mattie wondered whom they were mocking. She longed to ask Barbara more about these medical women, though now was not the place or the time. *Shouldn't medical school be exactly the right place and time?* she wondered, wishing this Miss Replogle had arrived sooner in her medical education—she was highly entertaining. Definitely on the liking side, she decided.

"I can find something," Barbara promised.

"Fine," said Lavinia. She stood up, blocking the light from the window. "I'll summarize the lecture and send it around for input from the rest of you." She picked up her satchel and bid the group good day. Mildred followed close behind her.

Barbara sought Mattie's eyes apologetically, "I hope I didn't offend . . ."

"Not at all," Mattie said, rising with a smile. "Your comments were most enlightening, Miss Replogle. Don't mind Lavinia. Or Dr. Douglas. Neither of them is used to being challenged." She wiped off her pen and closed her notebook. "I would suggest if you want to survive your next few years here, you might save some of your enthusiasm for conversations held off-campus."

Barbara smiled with relief. "Is there somewhere you'd suggest?"

"I like to take a canoe out on the Huron River sometimes," Mattie offered. "I have to prepare for an exam, but if you meet me outside in a few hours, I could show you."

"Thank you," Barbara replied. "I have much to learn here, and I do hope to make more friends than enemies."

"You have one," Mattie assured.

But how much is there imperfectly known, how
much undiscovered in the mysterious little world even
after the incessant exploration of thousands of years.

—MARTHA HUGHES CANNON

Chapter Fourteen

The drifting canoe cut through ripples on the surface of the Huron River, sending them outward in concentric waves growing larger at each interval from the epicenter. Light shafts plunged below, where fish flashed among the shallows and organic matter accumulated cell by precious cell.

There was nothing untouched by science, Mattie thought, marveling at the way medical school had made it impossible for her to see light weaving its way through a canopy of trees and not consider protoplasm's response to the presence of chlorophyll. Impossible to drift across the surface of a river without wondering at the properties of water that made life possible on earth at all.

What a scientist was God, what a master of scientific inquiry in ecology's design. This river cut its way downward, winding through caverns and crevasses until it met with the same ocean that rose and fell against the crags of Wales where she had taken her first steps.

Across from her in the canoe, Miss Replogle reclined in pinned skirts and practical galoshes, just as pleased as Mattie to drift in silence. Hollyhocks and early thistleweed raised unfurling stems along the bank's edge where ducks paddled. Swallows darted after insects in maneuvers through the softness of sound.

"Do you recall the first time you looked at a drop of river water through a microscope?" Mattie asked, remembering the day two years ago when she first peered through a "magic glass" and discovered a fairy world of tiny creatures moving erratically through a striated jungle. The microscope revealed a world not so different from our own, for all its minuscule nature. And if slime from a rock pool held the wonder of protozoa and nematodes—writhing little animalcules endowed with independent life—then what else remained upon this broad earth yet to be discovered?

Barbara leaned over the other side of the boat, careful not to tip, watching light descend to depths teeming with unseen creatures. "Each time I'm near water that initial wonder returns. It's nice to remember why we entered this work in the first place. Wonder and mystery are likely a rarity in Dr. Douglas's lecture hall."

Mattie laughed. "For sure and certain. I can promise you Dr. Douglas is the worst among them though. He views women as monstrosities and told us in our first year he was opposed to our presence at the school because women are incapacitated by childbirth for at least a year, and the forced interruption might lead female doctors to end their pregnancies or kill their own infants."

Barb shook her head in disgust. "How can someone intelligent be so ignorant?"

"Dr. Palmer is far more tolerant, though he makes no secret of his opinion that women may make good students but will never amount to good practitioners. Dr. Ford is the only truly welcoming professor here. He taught Elizabeth Blackwell at Geneva. I would suggest you introduce yourself at once, particularly after today."

"Thank you, I will," Barbara said, laying her straw bonnet on the seat beside her, allowing the broad sunshine to turn her hair to amber fire. "I'm afraid I've never been very good at staying silent."

"I was much intrigued with your comment about medical women in earlier ages." Mattie trailed a finger through water that curled and spread about her finger, wet with light. "From all I have gathered, Miss Elizabeth Blackwell was the first woman courageous enough to consider medical school and her graduation set off a bevy of women brave enough to follow her lead. According to professors at the University of Michigan, female physicians are an entirely new phenomenon."

Barbara laughed. "Women have been healing for centuries of time. They trained female doctors at the ancient Egyptian Temple of Sal."

"They did?"

"Many worked secretly at the risk of their lives, but in ancient Greece, Agnodice disguised herself as a man and practiced obstetrics until she was brought to trial. Trotula wrote Italian gynecology textbooks used for hundreds of years. The University of Paris accused Jacoba Felicie of illegal practice, and six witnesses testified she had cured them. They banned, fined, and threatened her with excommunication should she ever practice again."

"Agnodice. Trotula. Jacoba Felicie." Mattie repeated the strange names in wonder. "But why would female physicians be seen as such a threat?" She probed the story, reminiscent of Patty's, for a possible explanation behind each mock and jeer she had encountered in the classroom no matter how hard she tried, no matter how high her scores.

Barbara trailed a paddle through the water of the wide river bend. "For years women practiced healing arts in secret, developing natural remedies using intuition, trial and error, and empirical thinking." Patty and the skilled hands of her ancestors had practiced their art under cover of night.

Barbara continued, her voice gaining momentum as she plunged along. "The church taught that scientific inquiry contradicted faith.

Priests said childbirth was God's curse for Eve's sin in Eden, so when midwives used ergot to ease the pain, they mocked the will of God. Anything a doctor could not cure was blamed on a witch who could be sought out and destroyed. Variations of these same fears continue to this day, seeping down through centuries like wine spilled into water."

Sitting straighter, Mattie grasped the paddle with clenched knuckles turning white at the thought of the veiled animosity she had confronted at so many turns. "How did you learn this? Not in a medical preparatory course."

"No," Barbara laughed again. "My mother is a midwife. She raised me on this history, and encouraged my desire to obtain certification, though it might be challenging to obtain it."

"I think Dr. Douglas has a long two years ahead of him," Mattie said appreciatively, and Barbara smiled.

"Healing used to mean curing *and* caring, but now those roles have been split in two. The mystery that used to repose in religion has transferred to science, wielded by male doctors. Female nurses and family members are allowed to do the mundane work of caring, but the credit of curing goes to the doctor alone. Mattie, every time you and I step into the medical classroom, we threaten these ideas, these established orders. No wonder they taunt us."

Mattie felt Barbara had handed her glasses to see the past two years through. Determination surged through her, and she appreciated Barbara's earlier defiance more than she had before. Knowledge and power might have allowed her mother to help her father along that pioneer trail. Knowledge might have saved Annie. "Knowledge and power need to be returned to the hands of the lowly. We cannot let them intimidate us."

Barbara leaned back, soaking up the diffused light slanting between branches. "You're ahead of me on this journey, Mattie, and it doesn't seem they've succeeded with you."

"Not in driving me from practice, no," Mattie said, "but I admit that the weight of criticism has given me many moments over the last two years where I have doubted myself, my instincts, my aptitude. . . ." Her voice trailed off thinking of the many times she had allowed herself to be talked over, dismissed, dissuaded, had almost come to believe the criticism would stop if she were only more competent.

"It's nearly impossible not to allow it to affect you," Barbara responded. "But you will see it now. Know that it is not *you* they rail against, but something larger altogether." She dipped her paddle into the water, pierced shaftways with light. "And what brought you to this place? I imagine you must have a forward-thinking family."

Mattie considered how much to trust. Barbara seemed accepting and warm, but would that acceptance extend to a strange frontier religion? During medical school she had learned that the less she said about Utah the better unless she wanted to answer awkward questions about multiple wives. "In my church, women are believed to have a special propensity toward healing," Mattie admitted, glancing up to see how this would be received. "Usually as midwives or spiritual healers, but I was blessed by church leaders to seek my training with the hope that I would return to establish a practice."

Barbara looked impressed. "What religion do you practice?"

"I was raised in the Mormon church, in Utah territory."

Surprise passed over Barbara's features, but she recomposed her features quickly. If she had preconceived notions, she fanned them away. "There is no question you are lucky to have the support of your community in a work so many find threatening."

"Of course, not everyone is supportive," Mattie admitted, the gentle face of her mother shimmered back at her from the creased surface of the pond.

Barbara grimaced. "That would be too much to ask. But, Mattie, you have a strong mind and a good heart—you will make an excellent doctor. You must resist the temptation to doubt it."

Mattie did not respond, but plunged her paddle deep into the surface of the river with a fresh fierceness, shifting silted layers of boggy sediment that had been allowed too long to accumulate, resting beneath the surface, blurred and undisturbed.

Chapter Fifteen

"Agnodice." Mattie straightened her gown.

"Trotula." She perched the square-paneled cap on top of her cropped curls and secured it with pins.

"Jacoba Felicie." She pinched each cheek for a touch of color and bowed into the mirror. "Hello, Dr. Paul," she addressed to the reflection. *Not quite yet.*

On her desk lay a newspaper clipping, mailed to her by James, who had torn a page from the *Woman's Exponent* and circled the announcement:

> We tender our sincere congratulations to Miss Mattie Hughes Paul who has recently passed her examination and will graduate in the medical class of '80 at the 30th Annual Commencement of the Department of Medicine and Surgery of the University of Michigan. . . . Miss Mattie was a favorite of ours and earned her first money towards defraying the expense of her medical education by setting type for the *Woman's Exponent*. She is an interesting, intelligent, and brave young woman.

Brave young woman. The words echoed in her mind as she

pulled on the woolen cloak her parents had sent her as a graduation gift, which rested like a hug around her shoulders. She made her way from her boardinghouse on Maynard Street to the diagonal walk of campus beneath wide elm trees unfurling fresh leaves toward the light. Barbara met her there, squealing with pleasure. "Dr. Mattie, your graduation gown is perfection! Happiest of birthdays!" she exclaimed. Mattie hugged her warmly, thinking over the past few weeks during which she'd introduced her to Dr. Ford and helped her settle into the same boardinghouse.

"Happy birthday!" Mildred and Lavinia called, joining them in caps and gowns of their own. All around them, students in black robes streamed across campus and rushed to line up with classmates.

"Congratulations!" Leolin called, and gestured the women over to meet his family members.

"Hello," Mattie said, greeting his mother and father who were clearly a bit awed by these female doctresses, but every bit as gracious as their son.

Holding tight to Barb's arm, Mattie navigated around the groups of visiting friends and family, none of which belonged to her. How she would have loved to have Papa and Lottie, Mary and Mama here for this moment.

Travel-weary visitors yawned and arranged themselves in the gilded main chapel as graduates filed in and assembled themselves at the front. In solemn tones, the dean invoked the accomplishments of the new scholars yearning to be set free upon a world where they had earned the right to intone the phrase, "When I was in medical school."

In grandiose platitudes, the dean called down venerable blessings of the university to watch over the esteemed graduates, imbuing them with power as they set forth to cure through the mysteries of science, inducted by their professors into the secrets thereof. He droned on, enjoying the echo of his own voice across cavernous arches as he complimented his own profession's efforts in a slowly sickening world.

On the stand between Lavinia and Mildred, Mattie stood surrounded by row after row of fellow students who had taunted, encouraged, hindered, and helped her on this journey. The dean's words became a blur in her mind. Never mind that the graduation speakers spoke only of male doctors and never once acknowledged the handful of women among them. Through her mind ran the refrain *Day of Days*.

Never mind the snubs over the past two years, the challenges, the difficulties. Never mind. Today was her Day of Days. Her twenty-third birthday. The culmination of years of work and longing. Her mother had not stopped this. Professor Douglas had not kept her from this podium. She was here. The light streaming through the stained glass windows, bathing the floor in rose and golden hues, was real. It was all gloriously, unforgettably real.

Mattie sought out Barb's eyes and exchanged a glance of triumph and knowing. Her friend understood, more than anyone, what this moment meant. In two short years, they would reverse places and Barb would mount the brink of this broad precipice.

When Professor Palmer called "Dr. Martha Hughes Paul," time paused for one moment in its journey, stilled and hushed by her lone footsteps across the hall, a hall that had been built anticipating men's footfalls alone. But here was a light, firm step, here a young woman with close-cropped curls and a determined smile, the edges of her mouth tucked firmly in place.

As Mattie's leather boots clicked across the dais, she carried other names with her. With each step she silently said a name. *Agnodice*. Head held high, colored light staining her curls like a benediction. *Trotula*. Feeling the weight of those eyes resting upon her. *Jacoba Felicie*.

Reaching to accept the rolled-up diploma, Mattie shook hands with the president, the dean, with professors Palmer, Douglas, and Ford. She shook hands with them all, carrying the names of those women healers upon her lips, as they had carried her own upon theirs, though they had not known they worked not only for their patients alone, but for women coming after them, for mothers and grandmothers aiding the mystery of life itself.

Now there would be one more name to add to this list of women healers: Dr. Martha Maria Hughes Paul. And once again the unspoken words echoed through her mind across the cavernous hall, *Day of Days.*

The heart's muscular coat consists of seven layers,
each made up of an incredible number of fibers twisted inward
and woven together in the most compact and intricate way.
—MARTHA HUGHES CANNON

Chapter Sixteen

One month later, Dr. Martha Hughes Paul set a scalpel aside and bent over her work, drawing a needle through flesh and pulling it taut, reinforcing the stitch with unnoticeable sutures, as she'd done many times before. Mattie arranged the tiny hand just so, encouraging it to wave overhead like a flag unfurling. Such perfection, she thought, marveling at each miniscule bone and sinew, familiar and yet different from her own.

A sharp rap sounded at the door, and Dr. Paul jumped, pulling the needle too sharply so the skin nearly tore through. "Drat," she said to the project before her.

"Mattie . . ." Barb's voice sang around the corner of the door. "A tall and handsome stranger is waiting for you in the parlor."

Mattie laughed. "I don't believe you, Barb. You're just trying to distract me from my pressing project."

Barb made a face, as Mattie bent over the remains of the field squirrel she had been sewing onto an armature. Other taxidermy projects watched the proceeding in furry, solemn silence. "Shall I tell Dr. Bennet you're too engaged with your 'fascinating pastime' to speak with him?"

"Oh, so it isn't a stranger," Mattie baited.

"No, but wouldn't it be exciting if it were?" With a flourish, Barb turned down the hallway and Mattie grinned as she set down her tools.

Leolin raised his eyebrows when Mattie entered the parlor. "So I caught you playing at your morbid pastime again, Dr. Paul?"

Mattie made an indignant noise. "Indeed I am. The light is best at this hour, and my newest piece was coming along quite nicely before you interrupted it."

"Pray tell, what does your landlady think about your choice of pastimes?" Leolin asked, teasing.

"I'm afraid like most lay people, Mrs. Crosby finds the ancient art of taxidermy to be rather disgusting, not appreciating its finer points as the medically trained among us are more wont to do. So long as I clean up thoroughly afterward, she endures it."

"I'm afraid you dramatically overestimate your fellow practitioners, Dr. Paul. We may tolerate your eccentricities for the sake of your brilliant mind and sharp wit, but none I know share your enjoyment of sewing poor dead creatures back together."

Mattie sighed, sinking into an armchair facing Leolin. "I only find it surprising more people don't pursue the hobby. But I can take solace in the knowledge that to be great is to be misunderstood. I find myself in good company looking back through the ages."

Leolin laughed and lit a cigar, drawing on it luxuriously as he watched Mattie with a veiled, appreciative gaze. Remembering where he was, he coughed and stopped short. "I'm sorry, you do not mind?"

She shook her head. "But you better not let Mrs. Crosby see you."

"Understood." He opened a window, wafting the smoke outside.

Mattie smiled at his feeble attempt to cover the nervous blunder. "And to what do I owe the pleasure of this visit? Certainly you did not call to offer your suggestions on my latest squirrel?"

"No." Leolin took a long slow draw upon his cigar. He had been a favorite in medical school, beloved by the professors who found him attentive and adept at his work. To Mattie, he had always been encouraging and kind, quick to compliment her insights and gently correcting when she made a miscalculation. He had become like a brother to her these past years, and she realized looking upon his slicked black hair and the easy languor with which he reclined in the parlor chair, how much she would miss him when they parted ways.

Leolin considered the cigar in his hand, turning it as if seeing it for the first time, enjoying the slow and lazy path of the smoke curling upward, seeming in no hurry to come to the point. "I came," he said at last, "to invite you home to Boston with me."

"Why, Leolin," Mattie said in surprise. "How thoughtful of you. I should very much like to see Boston, if I were in a position to travel."

"Would you indeed consider it?"

"I found your family to be most amiable when I met them at graduation." Mattie distractedly picked up a fan that lay upon the side table and began applying it with haste. The afternoon was warm but began to feel much warmer. "You must know my budget does not allow leisure travel. I'm afraid I must finish my preparations and return to Utah territory to set up practice." Never mind that she had prolonged purchasing the return tickets. Never mind that each time she set out to do it, a cold dread lay upon her stomach like sifted charcoal.

"It would be my pleasure to pay your way, if you would allow me," Leolin said, his voice carefully steady.

"But I couldn't possibly . . ."

"It would be anything but an imposition." He let the silence stretch out in the haze, as his words hung unanswered on the air. "It would be my honor if you might consider returning . . ." Here he cleared his throat. ". . . As my intended wife."

Mattie opened her mouth to reply, but found herself unable to formulate a syllable. She shut it once more.

"This may be unexpected," Leolin said, kindly reaching to cover her shock. "But surely you've noticed my regard for you, how well we get on, both professionally and personally."

"But, Leolin," Mattie breathed, "I never dreamed . . ."

"I am sorry to have startled you, perhaps I should have spoken sooner. I didn't want to distract from your studies. But now . . ." He studied his cigar once more as if her answer might lie tucked between paper and tobacco. "It would be my honor to join my life with yours, to practice together. Think of the good we could do."

Mattie considered it. Leolin was a kind man—an honest man. By his side, they *could* do much good in the world. She pictured a joint practice with her husband, the two discussing patients at night around a fire, pictured her hand in his, his lips upon her cheek, and found—she could not.

All she could think of was her mother's laughter ringing through the rafters of their adobe home on the mountain frontier, James Paul whispering a taunting refrain in her ear, the two of them kneeling together in prayer. She wanted that type of love. Someday . . .

Why not now? Why not with Leolin? And why then had she delayed buying her ticket home? With Leolin waiting before her, Mattie forced herself to take a sterner look at her motives. Certainly Barb's newfound friendship was part of it, but it was more than this. In spite of a two-year medical degree, she still felt so unprepared to practice in the real world. Just as Logan spoke with polish before a public audience, she longed for that ability. She wanted to better understand the newest theories of contagion coming out of Europe that seemed to contradict everything she'd been taught. She'd had so little practice with actual patients—she glanced back up at Leolin, waiting.

And for some reason she could hardly explain, she still wanted to do these things—alone.

Leolin watched her struggle, saw the emotions moving across her face like ripples set to spinning over the languid surface of a pond. He marked her wrestle and saw something triumph at last, as he held his breath, wondering . . .

"I'm sorry," Mattie said, breaking the silence. "You are such a dear friend to me, and I hate to disappoint you." She crossed her legs at the ankles and tucked them beneath her settee. "I can't explain it, but I feel there is more I still must do, must learn. I am not ready to marry anyone yet."

"Yet," he repeated.

Mattie raised her eyes to meet his and found naked emotion behind them. She sucked in her breath, surprised by the intensity. "I do not want to keep you in hope, Leolin. You have much to offer any woman."

"Just not you?" He spoke the words quietly and without anger.

"I am so sorry, my friend," she said, tucking in the corners of her mouth. Had he recognized the gesture, he would have known the matter had been settled forevermore.

The brain remains in many respects,
a puzzle to the scientific investigation.
—MARTHA HUGHES CANNON

Chapter Seventeen

1882

Philadelphia, Pennsylvania

University of Pennsylvania signs wreathed with Ivy League laurels and architectural turrets stood far from the smog produced by Philadelphia's textile mills and iron foundries, far from the Liberty Bell and gracious pillared halls of early U.S. history. The medical school was one of the first in America to accept the latest findings from across the ocean, and Dr. Paul had come to study pharmacology and bacteriology in the first clinical hospital in the country. As Mattie was the only woman in a class of seventy-five, professors and students had initially questioned, some not so subtly, about whether she had the ability to perform. After exam scores began posting, they stopped speculating.

As she strode across campus and entered the hospital, Mattie fastened her white lab coat over her simple gray muslin dress and picked up a sheaf of patient chart notes detailing various complaints. Fairly routine issues were presented for her review: dysentery, a fractured tibia, a case of pneumonia. A few patients might offer a possibility to gather laboratory samples.

Flipping over the pages, she stopped at a new chart: *27 years old, female hysteria, wife of a riverboat captain. Patient's husband complains of nervousness, insomnia, irritability, and fainting spells.* Mattie's pulse quickened. The patient was scheduled to be seen by an attending physician and a university intern.

Approaching a nurse filing paperwork, she forced her voice to sound casual. "Clara, do you know which doctors have been assigned to this case?"

The nurse glanced at the file. "Bertha Stomlar?" She scanned down her register with agonizing slowness. "She's scheduled to be seen shortly, ma'am, in the third examination room. Doctors Moore and Slocum have been assigned to her case."

"Now there's a third," Mattie said. "Please add my name to the patient's file."

"Yes, ma'am."

Bertha Stomlar sat on a table wearing a worn hospital gown, and Doctors Moore and Slocum glanced up sharply when Dr. Paul entered. "I'm also working on this case," Mattie explained, introducing herself to Bertha and her husband, ignoring his obvious surprise at the arrival of a lady doctor.

Doctors Moore and Slocum hovered around the patient, measuring vital signs while her husband slouched in the corner, considering the scientific instruments with clear discomfort.

Bertha looked even more alarmed as the men held an ear trumpet up to her heart and measured her pulse with their fingers. "Nervousness, insomnia, and irritability," Dr. Moore said. "Can you tell us more?"

"Bertha hasn't been herself for some time," her husband, George, explained, straightening the cap on his head. "Nervous fits, awake all night, hates me to leave her alone when I go to work. I don't know what to do with her."

"Does that seem right?" Mattie asked Bertha, noticing the faint scent of stale urine. Bertha sheepishly nodded.

"The other day when I came home," George continued, "she had fainted dead away. What would have come of her if I hadn't come in then, I don't like to think."

"She certainly has a strong case of hypertension," said Dr. Moore, concluding his count of her pulse. "I have some suggestions for potential remedies."

"If you will give us a moment to consult," Mattie said, addressing the patient and her husband, "we will need to discuss the case." They nodded and the doctors filed into the hall, consulting their notes.

"It seems clear that her condition is deteriorating," said Dr. Moore. "I have seen metallurgy do wonders with patients such as this one."

"Agreed," said Dr. Slocum. "But if she does not respond, we should consider recommending a hysterectomy. Her system is clearly out of balance and drastic measures may prove necessary to restore her body to normalcy." Mattie tried to contain her mounting rage.

"Surely, we do not have enough information to make such a determination yet," Mattie insisted. "I believe we need more information from the patient."

"But her husband said . . ."

"From the patient," Mattie repeated. "It may be she has some insights on her own symptoms that her husband does not."

"In such a condition, should her opinion be trusted?" Dr. Slocum countered.

"I see no reason to doubt it," Mattie replied.

"If we agree to start with metallurgy, I need to verify what metal compounds we have on hand," said Dr. Moore, his gaze moving between the two physicians.

"I can check the surgery calendar," suggested Dr. Slocum.

"Very well," Mattie said. "While you check, I will speak again with the patient, then we can assess next steps." She knocked on the door and edged it back open. "Mrs. Stomlar, may I have a few words with you?" The woman's hair was dirty and tangled, but she nodded.

"Is there any more information you can tell me that might give me insight into your condition? When your husband leaves for work, how long is he gone?"

"A week or two at a time," George interjected, "depending on the route I travel."

"Have you ever had any children?" Mattie asked. At the question, Bertha's face crumpled like a crust of bread thrown into a pond, and she shook her head furiously.

"Have you ever been pregnant?"

Tears flowed fast down Bertha's cheeks, and she swiped them away. She nodded, and her husband stood up from his chair in the corner, placing a protective hand about her shoulder. "I lost a baby eight months ago," she said at last, and Mattie breathed a sigh of relief that the woman could actually speak.

"I am so sorry to hear that," Mattie said, searching out Bertha's haunted gray eyes. "Do you feel yourself fully recovered from your delivery?"

Bertha shook her head a second time.

"Do you live by other family?"

Bertha stiffened at the question, turning her face to her husband's coat. "Her mother lived with us, but she passed six months ago," he explained.

Mattie rested a gentle hand upon Bertha's arm, allowing her sobs to come louder and stronger. "I am so sorry for your loss. I will give you both a moment. Then I'd like to perform an examination with your permission, ma'am."

Mattie stepped into the hall, waiting for the other doctors to return. Dr. Moore hastened down the hallway carrying a set of vials and metal bracelets. "We have arsenic, tin, and copper on hand," he reported.

"Excellent," said Mattie.

Dr. Slocum returned from verifying the surgery calendar. "We could have her in to receive a hysterectomy within a month."

"I have some new information that may inform our diagnosis," Martha explained. In quick, even tones, she updated the other doctors on what she had found out. They could hear Bertha's sobbing from the other side of the door. "It seems like normal grief," Mattie argued, "compounded with possible complications from childbirth. I'd like to examine her further, but at this point I believe she needs rest and support, not medical interventions."

"As you are the senior physician, we must defer to you," said Dr. Slocum. "But they wouldn't be here if they didn't need medical intervention. We should at least give them options."

"Very well," Mattie reluctantly agreed.

When they opened the door to the exam room, Bertha held her husband's handkerchief, and his arms circled her thin shoulders.

"Bertha, you have suffered a great loss," Mattie explained.

"But it was quite some time ago—" George shrugged helplessly, looking to the male doctors.

"No matter. It is a great loss, and she needs to be properly cared for. She should not be left alone. She must have help. Can you bring someone in to assist her?"

"Our niece lives up river . . ."

"When you travel for work, particularly, she must have company. Bertha, your heart and mind have been through a tremendous difficulty, and they need time and care to fully recover, do you understand?" Bertha nodded and drew closer to her husband. Mattie turned to George. "There are things we can try—medicines, procedures—but none of them will begin to help her as much as you yourself can, sir."

"We'd like to try some medicines if you have them," George said. "We're at our wit's end, in truth."

Dr. Moore held up his vial of arsenic, but Mattie continued, "The physician Trotula found great benefit for patients in grief by prescribing herbal sedatives like musk oil and mint teas, but before we get ahead of ourselves, I'd like to make a further examination. Gentlemen, shall we allow the patient to undress?"

Once alone with Bertha, Mattie asked her, "Can you tell me again about any pain you're experiencing?"

Bertha listed the same symptoms as before, then hesitated and confessed that she'd struggled to control her bladder since giving birth. Mattie recorded her words, reaching into her mental storehouse of medical knowledge, then completed the examination.

Sitting before her patient once more, Mattie weighed the likelihood of a vesicovaginal fistula. "There is a fairly rare condition that seems to fit the complaints you're having, Mrs. Stomlar. A surgical procedure is often quite successful at correcting it, if you don't see improvement."

Bertha's face visibly relaxed at the possibility of finding relief.

Mattie opened the door and the physicians returned, accompanied by George. "Gentlemen," Mattie said, "I believe we may have discovered the source of Bertha's complaint. After further examination, I believe she may be suffering from a vesicovaginal fistula, which can be solved with a fairly minor operation. I am suggesting Bertha try herbal supplements for two weeks, along with plenty of rest, and adequate care and support. If she finds herself still troubled, she will return and we will proceed further." Mattie turned to Bertha and George and gently said, "I think you'll find your health greatly improved if you both do your part."

George's fingers trembled as he drew back his wife's hair, and Mattie felt instinctively they would be all right. There was real love between them. By far the most disturbing cases were when there was not.

In the face of abuse and neglect, there was only so much a physician could do—for as much as you might wish, you could not fix parts and pieces of a person like a mechanical spring or a hinge.

"Are we in agreement, doctors?" Dr. Paul asked Slocum and Moore.

"For now," Dr. Slocum said.

Dr. Moore added, "If things do not improve, I highly suggest you look further into metallurgy."

George nodded.

Seeds germinate in the dark and are exceedingly nitrogenous.
—MARTHA HUGHES CANNON

Chapter Eighteen

A few evenings later, in the city of smoke and bridges, a lamp-lighter smudged with coal lit a gas streetlamp as evening faded into night. Patrons of the arts streamed past him into a nearby building, few noting his lonely work on their behalf nor considering the darkness he kept at bay.

In nearby hills, thousands of men, like inked mice, tunneled daily into the earth to remove bituminous coal from the earth, lump by precious lump. Black gold they called it, Pennsylvania's coal every bit as valuable as California's oranges, though it might leech sludge into rivers and turn noonday to a smudged resemblance of itself. These men labored to light up the streets, or at least to add a ha-loed semblance of light smothered by smoke and haze. Smelting steel to span the chasms of the earth, the Irish, German, and Polish immigrants labored, joined by constant new arrivals. Smokestacks brooded over the city, belching smoke into the air in exchange for neat and even numbers to enter onto columns of a ledger.

Patrons streamed into the concert hall pressing cloths against their faces to filter the street air, sighing in relief when they passed inside. In the National School of Elocution and Oratory, William

Pittenger held courses in Theory, Practice, Dramatic Recitation, and Rhetoric. As the gaslights dimmed to a more manageable flicker, Master Pittenger announced a series of one acts and monologues for the audience's pleasure.

Backstage, Mattie waited in a long white gown, rocking on her feet, as she watched a fellow acting student sweat beneath the stage lights. Jonas recited his chosen soliloquy from *Hamlet* well enough, and she ignored the tremor in her own hands, hoping it would suit her character well. To stop her voice from trembling, she whispered vocal exercises into the draped curtains and bristled ropes hung from the rafters of the theater.

Inhaling slowly and deliberately, Mattie expanded her chest to its fullest capacity as her instructors had taught her these many months, then released as she formed the phrase:

'Tis now the very witching time of night; when churchyards yawn, and hell itself breathes out Contagion to this world.

The words felt fitting among the dusty, lurking shadows.

On stage, Jonas swayed more dramatically now. Her cue to be ready.

Wishing her stepbrother Logan could be there to see her foray into the acting world, Mattie inhaled using the school's patented "Dorsal Breath" method of which Mr. Pittenger had taught: "Inhale as if endeavoring to thrust out the muscles of the back by the force of air." She appreciated the creativity, and thought it better not to question the anatomical soundness of his analogy.

Another section of Pittenger's textbook entitled "Unfortunates Who Never Can Extemporize" advised, "Persons are met every day who are fully persuaded that the possibility of ever becoming effective speakers has been placed by nature forever beyond their own reach. In some cases this persuasion is well founded. How shall such persons be made acquainted with their condition, and thus save themselves years of painful and fruitless toil?"

Tonight, filled with dread and anticipation, she could not stop his questions running through her mind: "Do the subjects with which you are most familiarly acquainted still seem shadowy and confused in your own mind?" *Did they? Certainly, there were scientific concepts she did not know exhaustively, details that at times still escaped her.*

A second question: "When you try to tell a friend about any passing event, do you use words so bunglingly as to give him no clear conception of the matter?" She had puzzled over that one. When she tried to explain concepts in lectures, certainly she was not always successful. *Perhaps.*

"Hardly a speaker lives who does not at some time fall into unsightly or ridiculous habits." Yes, of course she was guilty at times of ridiculous habits. *Speaking aloud to empty laboratories and dead cadavers, for one.*

Mattie repeated Hamlet's words a touch louder, since no one would hear her over Jonas feigning death in writhing turmoil. *You've practiced this many times,* she told herself sternly, hoping to quell the rising panic mounting in her throat. *But this time is different,* she countered. *This time is in front of a live audience and you're no longer on a frontier town in the desert—perhaps you are not ready. Perhaps you will fail here, and also in medicine, perhaps you will fail.*

She needed a more hopeful recitation beyond Hamlet's contagion, and cast her mind about, reaching for Brigham Young's practical God who could lend insight on acting methodology as well as medical procedures. "I would have Him dictate my affairs," she said, forming each word. "The Lord is my shepherd; I shall not want. He leadeth me beside the still waters. He restoreth my soul."

Jonas collapsed, and the theater fell into blackness. As the audience clapped their appreciation, the vise around Mattie's throat tightened. Under cover of darkness, Jonas made a miraculous re-covery and passed her backstage, striding toward the wings of the theater. "Well done," she whispered.

The lights sprang up once more, and Mattie swallowed, finding only dryness in her throat, as she willed herself onto the stage, be-neath stage lights that pounded in waves.

They sprang to illuminate her white gown, trailing behind her, to a rosary dangling from her girdle, to a coronet of precious stones wound through her hair. With each step she took across the stage, she became less a doctor and more a young queen forced to abdi-cate her throne to her one-year-old son, sentenced to death by her cousin.

With quiet majesty, Mary, Queen of Scots, cast her gaze around the theater, confronting the walls of a castle prison on every side. She addressed her assembled subjects as they recoiled in anguish.

> *Why these complaints? Why weep ye?*
> *Ye should rather rejoice with me, that now at length the end of*
>   *my long woe approaches;*
> *My shackles fall off, my prison opens, and my soul*
> *delighted mounts on seraph's wings . . .*

The young queen clasped her hands in an expression of soul-felt pleading.

> *As an earnest friend, beneficent and healing death approaches.*

Mattie felt the audience rising with her, moved by her words and the eloquence of her pleading. Entering into the thrill of the scene, she mourned the betrayal by Elizabeth who placed the strangeness of her religion and the threat to her own power above the ties of blood.

> *All the indignities which I have suffered*
> *On earth are covered by his sable wings.*

Queen Mary turned to face the sharpened guillotine. She prepared to kneel down and place her head into the cradle where she would await the descent of a sharp blade to sever life from consciousness.

Having thus confessed, Mary knew herself ready to reunite with all that lay beyond this fragile world. She handed her crown to an attendant, as her loyal subjects averted their gaze, tears streaming down their cheeks.

Just before the blade descended, the Queen turned once more and spoke with an otherworldly radiance.

I feel again the crown upon my brows.

All went silent.

The audience erupted, and Queen Mary strode into the shadows, becoming Mattie once more, heaving with the relief of having the ordeal behind her and hoping the audience's applause to be sincere.

When the show concluded, one audience member pushed her way backstage, insisting she had been given permission. Mattie took one glance at this intruder and swiftly closed the distance between them.

"Barbara!" Mattie said, throwing her arms around her friend. "My dear, dear Barb, how very good of you to stop on your way overseas."

"Mattie, what a vision you were! You captured us entirely. We hung upon your every word!"

"Oh hush," Mattie insisted, as Jonas passed by. "Perhaps *you* did. Jonas, you died a most heroic death."

But Barb refused to hush. "'*I feel again the crown upon my brows.*' You delivered that line to perfection. Truly, my friend, is there nothing you cannot do? Advanced medical training is not enough? You needed to earn an oratory degree as well?"

Mattie colored under the compliments, dismissing them with one hand. "As you well know, I needed the training to better explain scientific concepts to an audience and not embarrass myself completely."

Barb leaned her head close to Mattie's conspiratorially. "Let's escape into the night. I want to hear all that is happening to you in Philadelphia."

Mattie guided her friend toward the dressing room. "If you are planning to ask about romantic entanglements, I will tell you straight off, I've found the fastest way to lose a suitor is to show the slightest bit of interest. But I've many other fascinating things to tell you, all the same." Removing the white linen from her shoulders, Mattie rubbed at the makeup that remained in the concavities of her cheeks like deep bruises. She took Barb's arm. "Let's make our getaway."

Walking together beneath the streetlamps, their two shadows blended eerily into one as they disappeared into the smoky lanes and corners of Philadelphia. The hazy glow of a streetlamp lit a flyer advertising an anti-polygamy lecture in nearby Wesley Hall. Mattie cast the sheet a wondering glance, then pulled her friend on into the night.

The body is a vast laboratory.
—MARTHA HUGHES CANNON

Chapter Nineteen

Two weeks later, Mattie welcomed George and Bertha Stomlar back into her office. Bertha's hair was combed and washed, and she looked far more rested than she had before. "I feel much better, Doctor, but I'm still troubled by many of the symptoms we discussed last time."

"I'm sorry to hear that," Mattie said, "but I think we can get you feeling better very soon. Let's get you scheduled for the procedure, and I will need to consult with the other physicians on your case."

"You plan to perform this operation, Dr. Paul, and you wish *me* to be your second?" Dr. Slocum could not hide his disbelief.

"I am the senior physician on this case. Would you prefer not to assist me for a particular reason?" Mattie asked.

"I believe the patient clearly needs a hysterectomy, firstly." Dr. Slocum said, rising and reviewing Mattie's chart notes.

"And secondly?"

He blustered after an answer, finally blurting out, "I will not consider it."

Mattie straightened. "No matter. I'll check with Dr. Moore. Perhaps he will be available."

Dr. Slocum raised his eyebrows. "Good day to you, ma'am."

As Mattie and Dr. Moore entered the operating room where Bertha waited, already etherized, they passed George Stomlar in the hallway, twisting his hat in his hands. "Don't worry, Mr. Stomlar, Mattie said, "We will take good care of your wife."

"I do thank you," he replied.

Probing beneath the surface of Bertha's skin, Mattie found a fissure that had formed, probably during childbirth, allowing a discharge of urine into the vaginal vault. "Aha," said Dr. Moore, working at her side. "It is as you suspected, Dr. Paul. We can proceed with confidence."

"I appreciate your trust in me," Mattie countered, concentrating on the difficult maneuver to repair the rupture. "And your willingness to stand second in surgery to a female physician. Not all would be so broad-minded."

He chuckled into his surgical mask. "It is a privilege to work beside you, Doctor," he said, watching her deft sutures.

As the sun slanted low in the sky and other researchers began to think of dinner, Mattie entered UP's medical laboratory. Dr. Spencer, washing out a beaker, looked up in surprise, "Are you just arriving, Dr. Paul?"

"Yes, I have some experiments to take care of, and I don't mind the quiet," Mattie said. With an air of admiration mixed with astonishment, Dr. Spencer set the clean beaker beside the sink and headed for the door. "Good evening, Doctor."

"Good evening."

Alone, Mattie eagerly opened a book by Ignaz Semmelweis, *Etiology, Concept and Prophylaxis of Childbed Fever,* with her own notes, small and measured, in the margins. Firmly tucked between the pages, lay a letter from Barb bearing a German postmark.

> *By now you may have heard of Koch's recent publication proposing agar-agar for growing specimens in the lab. It's quite groundbreaking, as it remains in solid form at optimal temperatures and keeps the culture pure.*
>
> *During my time here, I met one of his laboratory assistants, a Lina Hesse, who prepares cultures and produces illustrations for his lab. She told me that she made his previous beef stock preparations in her own kitchen, then suggested Koch explore agar-agar, as she used it for jellies and puddings after receiving some from a friend native to Java, where it is quite common. You will, however, notice Koch gives Lina no credit for her contributions in his publication.*
>
> *I haven't yet tried it myself, but if you do, write at once and let me know how you find it.*

The recipe was scrawled below.

There were those at the university who still argued in support of the humors theory, defending them as vehemently as they would Galileo's orbits. But new intriguing ideas proposed by lone voices in academia had begun scoffing at three centuries of scientific practice, positing that illness was caused not by vapors, but by microscopic, wriggling creatures too small to be seen with a human eye. Was an ill person inhabited with swirling miasmas or infinitesimal, acrobatic worms? One hypothesis seemed nearly as fantastical as the other. Mattie hoped to test Lina Hesse's recipe while at the same time confirm Semmelweis's findings.

She pulled out a cotton apron her mother had sent, smocked with Elizabeth's tiny stitches, probably made by candlelight after the children were asleep. Tying it over her dress, Mattie knew Elizabeth had intended her to wear the gift for housework, though she wished her mother could understand that laboratories had much in common with well-ordered kitchens. *Now,* Mattie thought, *let us see for ourselves who is right and who is wrong about this miasma microcreature dilemma.*

Following Barb's directions, she added ingredients and stirred the gelatinous mess over the Bunsen burner, adjusting the gas heat. With one hand, she reached over to Barbara's letter, scanning the section: "Add three more grams of meatbone liquid and peptone."

Turning down the gas, Mattie poured the mixture into three glass dishes, which she set aside to cool beside a collection of glass beakers, flasks, and funnels.

While they cooled, Mattie placed a sample labeled "puerperal fever" beneath the lens, bending over the brass compound microscope and sighted in on the round margin of space where animalcules reigned. Adjusting the dials, she turned the brass knobs toward better focus, and the enemy came into view. Seemingly innocuous, grapelike clusters trailed across the slide like trails of pebbles dropped by a child's hand.

"My doctrines exist to rid maternity hospitals of their horror," Semmelweis had written in his book, and Mattie understood what he meant. Though the creatures under her glass looked benign, she had seen what the pebble trails could do to a new mother still weak from giving birth, had watched headache and cold fits give way to heat, perspiration, and thirst. Had held women as they clutched their abdomens in pain worse than labor, had seen their tongues turn from white to furred black. Far too many women descended into delirium and mania before the disease had its lethal way, leaving behind a helpless infant rooting about in vain for its mother.

Mattie's fear of puerperal fever was compounded by the knowledge that her sister Mary was now pregnant with her second child, a twisting reminder that time ticked onward as Mattie continued her schooling. Jim Anderson had also married; she pushed the thought away.

Semmelweis hadn't lived to see his controversial stance vindicated and had been widely mocked by the international medical community, who called him naïve for claiming something as simple as hygiene could really stand as the difference between life and death, and for being ignorant enough to believe that fevers were not caused by dissecting-room miasmas, unclean bowels, or shrinking uteri. Semmelweis had died in depression and insanity, lured into an asylum where he turned every conversation to a babbling incoherent mumbling about childbed fever. Severely beaten by guards and straitjacketed, he had died alone after fourteen days in the sanitorium. Sometimes it seemed to Mattie that the scientific world could be just as brutal in their own way as the gladiators of ancient Rome.

"And now, Semmelweis and Frau Hesse, let us see if you were right," she said to her assembled supplies. The community now began to acknowledge the validity of Semmelweis's work, but far too late for him to enjoy his triumph.

Mattie laid in front of her a sample she had gathered from puerperal fever patients and used a piece of cotton wool to inoculate the first dish. She washed the wool with simple soap and swabbed the second, then rinsed it with a solution of chlorinated lime, Semmelweis's recommended recipe, before inoculating the third.

After washing her hands, she covered each dish with a glass bell dome, then set them beside a window where the morning's sun would warm the bacteria colonies, spurring them to new and burgeoning life.

Three days later, Mattie's light step sounded down the hall, hurrying as if it were Christmas morning, though the presents this morning would arrive wrapped in bells of glass.

She uncovered the lids, marveling at the transparent agar-agar, still solid on this unseasonably warm spring morning, the untreated sample now growing a lovely colony of clustering pus. The inoculated dish, washed first with soap, contained fewer bacteria colonies than the original, but the final one, oh the final one, washed with Semmelweis's concoction, was pure and clean as her mother's kitchen table.

"Ignaz," Mattie said aloud, speaking to potentially nonexistent ether, "I wish you could see this moment and understand what you accomplished. Somehow, I hope you know you were right. The Galileo of microbiology, you were, my friend, sacrificed for your vision, decades ahead of your time."

"And you, Frau Hesse," she tilted the agar-agar to shimmer in the morning sunrays though it remained beautifully solid, "your work demonstrates once more the impossibly fine line between a 'woman's work' and the quests of humanity."

Critics had once told Dr. Semmelweis that cadaverous particles were too "unreasonably small" to cause harm. Lounging together in their superiority, the medical community had been certain nothing so tiny could possibly be responsible for diseases so grandiose and devastating. Many had been offended at the implication that, as gentlemen of medicine, their hands might be anything other than clean.

Looking around the room for somewhere to direct her scorn, she found it in a row of scientific textbooks lined up on a dusty shelf. "You have quite the habit of underestimating small things you do not understand," Mattie informed them.

Hands trembling with emotion, she turned back to her samples. If something as seemingly insignificant as sanitizing hands and instruments meant the difference between thousands of women returning home with their babies, and thousands more who would be moved from maternity ward to graveyard, what wouldn't this knowledge mean for her mother and so many other women struggling to survive in the West? Mothers needed to know how to protect their children—not just from runaway horses and desert snakes, but from strings of microscopic clusters unwittingly passed by loving hands. Here, she thought, here was work worth giving one's life to—that people might know their own power.

Development is the body undergoing certain changes,
a paramount necessity in the living body.
—MARTHA HUGHES CANNON

Chapter Twenty

Through the smoke of the stage set, which could have been the mining hills surrounding Philadelphia as easily as medieval Inverness, a grim and battered Scottish warrior, smeared with blood and grime, held his sword loosely, madness building in his eyes. "How now, you secret, black, and midnight hags!" spake Macbeth. "What is't you do?"

"A deed without a name," the crones replied.

Hours passed as ancient poetry lived and breathed upon the stage, and a woman with an odd tuck to her mouth was particularly vivid as Hecate, leader of the witches. Decked in coal-colored fabrics, she commanded the stage, imploring the darkest corners of the room:

> *Great business must be wrought ere noon:*
> *Upon the corner of the moon*
> *There hangs a vaporous drop profound;*
> *I'll catch it ere it come to ground:*

Hecate pronounced each word with relish, adoring and cherishing the edges of the language she spoke into the night:

And you all know, security
Is mortals' chiefest enemy.

Hecate's loathsome companion, adorned in hideous rags, bent over a scratched and marred cauldron, cackling:

By the pricking of my thumbs,
Something wicked this way comes.

Like apparitions, the witches danced eerily into the night, as the soldier looked round in confusion.

Where are they? Gone?

Macbeth's hand tightened on the hilt of his blade, as if the solid object might protect him from supernatural visitations.

Sometime later, the weary warrior found lunacy tracing circles round his wife's eyes, her hands stained with blood she alone could see. Though Macbeth sent for a physician, the doctor diagnosed:

More needs she the divine than the physician.
God, God forgive us all!

A heavy curtain descended and the audience applauded, finding their way back from Inverness to Philadelphia. The house lights blazed, and Mattie returned to the stage for a bow beside her fellow classmates.

Professor Pittenger, who had instructed her class for the past two years, approached Mattie, and her hands involuntarily tightened. A ruthless critic, she imagined he must be coming to offer parting correction in the short time remaining before graduation. "It is not usually wise to tell our hearers, or to ask their opinions," he often repeated to his students.

"Miss Paul," Professor Pittenger said, removing his silk top hat and inclining his head. "May I congratulate you on a lovely performance."

"I thank you, sir," she replied with surprise.

"Truly, you shone upon the stage tonight. Your audience could not tear their eyes away."

"Thank you, sir," she said again, knowing he was not one for flattery.

"Are you still determined to return to the desert to practice medicine?" he asked. "I believe you could stay in Philadelphia should you wish to pursue a career as a tragedienne."

Oh, how Mattie wished Logan could stand by her side, hearing these words at this moment. But far away among the mountains of the West, Annie's bones decayed beneath stones. She straightened. "Sir, I thank you, but I must devote whatever talent I possess to saving lives among my people."

His eyes rested upon her youthful face, perhaps seeing something she did not. "As you wish," he said, inclining his head with admiration.

Filled with her professor's encouragement, Mattie exhaled through imaginary dorsal fins upon her back. *Perhaps then. Perhaps after four long years, I am ready.*

Life is a continuous adjustment of internal matter.
—MARTHA HUGHES CANNON

Chapter Twenty-One

Mattie boarded the train, stowing her luggage above the compartment and settling into her seat, a space that would serve as home for the next few days. Other passengers organized themselves around her—an elderly man in a top hat who nodded good morning, a family with young twin girls bidding a teary farewell to their grandmother, and a businessman securing his satchel. Each passenger held a story, each culled from a separate trajectory, drawn together for the span of this brief journey.

The whistle blew a warning for passengers to take their seats, and the great steam engine churned smoke into oblivion. The iron wheels turned, carrying Mattie away from Philadelphia, away from East Coast refinement, turning her, finally, in the direction of home. She had travelled this direction once before, though she no longer remembered it—jolting forward mile after mile in a rude wagon pulled by oxen, part of a wagon train stretched over the land. And now, the word *train* had morphed into a new experience, propelling her at unimaginable speeds over blurred ground.

"Hold onto the handles," the mother instructed her daughters as the locomotive picked up steam. Below greetings and casual conversations, a tension simmered through the passenger car as they gained speed— if the train derailed . . . well, they had all seen photographed images of twisted metal bent like broken, distorted appendages. No passenger walked away from such a collision. Mattie grasped the side of her seat.

Four years. Had it really been four years? She hardly felt like the same young woman who, at age twenty-one, had cautiously set foot into the broader world. For four long years she had seen her family only through lines of ink. The most recent letter from Elizabeth and James divulged that women physicians in the valley had opened a new hospital; it also reminded her how eager they were to welcome her home.

Mattie ate and dozed and found herself on the outskirts of Chicago. Rail travel was still a new enough sensation that she couldn't help marveling at the slowness of horses outside the windows, at the coach lines that had grown inefficient in an instant.

Chicago came into sight, with new buildings launching upward—skyscrapers they called them, pinnacles of glass and steel thrust into space. The iron horse carried her forward, but also backward, away from progress and development, toward remote frontiers, open vistas, and a length of rocky mountains folding into each other. Home.

Though her delineation of home now also included laboratories and hospitals. Stuffed squirrel and bird collections. Scientific instruments. Barbara. Home was no longer solely Utah territory anymore, as the places and people she loved had expanded and broadened manyfold.

Looking about, she no longer saw her fellow passengers only as people. "I am going to California to see my daughter," the elderly man explained to her, and she knew from his jaundiced skin and distended belly that he likely suffered from liver-grown, and it was good he was going to see his daughter now.

When the train conductor bent to mark her ticket, she couldn't help but note his clubbed fingernails and fought the urge to ask him about his ragged breathing. Observing the children playing quietly, she wondered, given the shape of one girl's skull, if she might have a connective tissue disorder.

"Mama, my tummy hurts," said one of the twins an hour into the journey. Mattie listened, not wanting to pry.

"Drink your milk," her mother instructed. But a little while later, when the girl still held one hand to her abdomen, Mattie leaned over.

"Excuse me, ma'am, I don't mean to meddle, but I am a doctor, and milk might make her stomach worse. I have a ginger lozenge that should help, if you would like."

"Thank you!" the woman said gratefully, taking the lozenge. The girl, perhaps seven, with red braids and freckles sprinkled across her nose, sucked on the offering, eyes resting upon Mattie like she'd said, "I am a magician," rather than a doctor.

At some point over the last four years, the milieu of humanity had become not only people, but also patients—beings housed in fragile bodies, whose neurological, respiratory, musculoskeletal, and dermatological states could be both read and deciphered like living puzzles careless about their clues. Mattie knew her fellow humans to be incalculably precious, capable of harnessing power from steam and coal, of pulling iron from great depths below and shaping it into lengths which they could bend the very surface of the earth to accommodate. Yet, she had seen these same creatures reduced to corpses by small strings of pebbles smeared upon the surface of jelly. Had watched these brilliant breathing machines reduced to rotting filth within a matter of days. They were one-part animal and one-part goddess, these little girls at play. Remembering the illnesses of her youth, Mattie knew this ability she had honed for four years of seeing each person as a cipher to be decoded—it was this she needed above all else to bring home.

The westbound train left Chicago behind as it sped for the open flatlands of Iowa and Nebraska; swaths of sod and grain fields turned to green and golden blurs beyond the windows.

In Mattie's bag rested letters from Barbara and Leolin. Both had offered to accompany her West. Though she longed to see them, she had written, "Come in a fortnight after I get things settled." But what she truly meant was, *I have to go alone to this space and decide what is still mine—to see the place I came from with new eyes, for I now know not only what it is, but also what it is not.*

Utah Territory was not Philadelphia with its charming, graceful ways. It was not Ann Arbor in its flatness. Her simple family, their quiet frontier ways seemed dearer than ever but also quaint, edging so very close to backward. She had seen the way East Coast papers portrayed women in polygamy, like slaves and hostages held against their will. The thought of anyone trying to hold Emmeline Wells against her will made Mattie smile, but it was a wistful smile, for many people believed the papers.

As the train retraced the route Mattie had taken four years before, she felt old longings return to her: a desire to make something of herself, to prove she could accomplish something important. Even with graduation behind her, she feared her inability to establish a practice. In the years since leaving Ann Arbor, she'd heard from Lavinia, Mildred, and Barb about the challenges of pioneering medical practices given the prejudice against women doctors. She had the schooling, but would her skills hold up in the real world before her?

Miles churned by, turning flowers to brilliant streaks, changing broad distances to dust, and hurtling her toward the future whether she were ready to go or not.

Part Three

Matter is constantly changing its form.

—MARTHA HUGHES CANNON

Chapter Twenty-Two

The locomotive slowed as it approached the station, gears grinding against forward momentum. *Salt Lake City.* Mattie grasped the edge of the window, eagerly devouring the wide dirt streets with new eyes. Horse-drawn trams traced routes down the center of the streets.

New gaslight posts stood ready to come to life at dusk, oddly incongruous with the wooden walkways they illuminated. The walls of the temple now scaled two stories, still climbing upward, and an Assembly Hall had been raised beside it—a gothic-inspired edifice whose towers and white spires would have been more at home in Philadelphia. In this struggling frontier city, she could now recognize allusions to the refinement of the East, strengthened over her absence, like a younger sibling playing dress-ups in an older sister's clothes. Salt Lake had been as busy growing up as she had been.

Passengers surged forward and the twin girls, whose family had transferred trains at Promontory Point in Ogden, as she had, squealed at the sight of their destination after long days of travel. On the train platform, throngs pressed together hauling the trappings of travel as they shepherded parcels, hat boxes, and hand baggage through the station. Still seated, Mattie scanned the crowd, marveling at the mélange of clothing styles and tongues spoken in this city of immigrants drawn from every corner of the earth—Polynesian, Asian, and Scandinavian. Moving across the assembly, her eyes landed, at last, upon faces with angles as familiar as her own.

James's hair had thinned and grayed in the intervening years, but his eyes were as kind as ever. Spidered creases traced the corners of Elizabeth's eyes. Her hair was parted severely down the middle as it always had been, and Mattie drew back from the window, confronted with the realization that her parents were growing old. From the doorway, she could see Mary had transformed into a young mother, one hand tugging the baby's bonnet to settle it squarely on the child's round head, her stomach rounded once more beneath her skirts. And Lottie, *could that possibly be Lottie?* At fourteen, all that remained of the child Mattie remembered were her flaxen curls, now coifed and shimmering. The girl looked as awkward and misplaced in her growing body as Mattie still sometimes felt beneath the postures she'd learned to adopt in oratory school.

As Mattie struggled to descend with jostling bags, her family pushed forward to hug her, but Mama reached her first. "Heavens, look at you," Elizabeth said softly, overwhelmed at the sight of her daughter who had covered in mere days the same route she had once walked over many months.

"Hello, Parley," Mattie said, kneeling down to shake hands with her nephew for the first time. She hugged her sister, who had moved far beyond her on the path of adulthood, a fact that left Mattie feeling both oddly envious and simultaneously relieved. "He looks like you, Mary, with a slight touch of his father about the nose. And Lottie!"

The young woman hugged her older sister as if she'd never let her go. "Lotta," she corrected.

"Yes, of course. All grown up."

Baggage staff handed down her wooden trunk, each angle still holding strong and true. "Well now," James said, and Mattie leaned into him, years falling away, breathing in the smell of wood shavings and the wool of his vest. "Whit like, Mattie?" he asked, and she was home.

The buggy rattled its way down the street as their voices tumbled over each other in their eagerness to say everything at once. "There's the new blacksmith shop," pointed Mary.

"And that?"

"Eliza Snow's silk mill," Lotta explained. "We've planted mulberry plants for the silk worms to eat!" The city hummed with productivity and growth. Large granaries had sprung up.

"That's Emmeline Wells's project," Mary told her sister. "She's like Joseph in Egypt storing for a famine I hope never comes."

The city couldn't compare with Philadelphia's elegance, but Mattie loved the brash scrappiness of this settlement scrambling to become a city, scratched from valley dirt so recently it still brushed residue away from the hem of its skirts.

Every corner held a new surprise—a new residence gone up, a new business opened. "That's the Deseret Hospital," Mary said, gesturing to a white frame building. "Run by women doctors trained in medical schools back East."

"I'll have to call," Mattie said, knowing the Shipp sisters must be behind the project, as well as Romania Pratt. "I imagine home will be the only place unchanged since I've left."

Her parents exchanged a glance. "You'll find it different enough," Elizabeth said, with a slight trace of resignation.

At Mattie's confusion, Mary added, "Papa has a surprise for you."

"Oh, yes!" Lotta bounced on her seat as though she were once again four.

"Hmm. I bet Lottie will be a dear and tell me the secret." Mattie tossed her sister an entreating glance.

"Don't you dare!" Mary chided.

"Lotta!" the girl corrected again, and clapped her hand across her mouth.

Mattie laughed. "Well! You've all become a great deal more mysterious while I've been gone, that's a fact. Papa?"

James leaned back in the carriage with an expression of contentment beneath his bushy brows, a smile tugging one corner of his mouth. They turned the corner onto Ninth East, and Mattie traced the familiar adobe structure with its dear little roof, sturdy chimney, James's shop and the garden behind. But the silhouette of the back of the house rose where she had expected to see it descend—*What on earth?*

The buggy pulled up, following a new approach between the kitchen and James's shop, with an entrance and mounting stoop that had not been there four years ago when she departed. Mattie's eyes filled with awe. "What is this?" she murmured, a catch in her throat, as she began to grasp what she was seeing.

"He started building it right after you left," Lotta explained, clapping her hands. "And he made us keep it secret *for four years!*"

Mattie tumbled from the carriage. Four new walls had been raised, covered by a tight roof to keep it warm, space big enough for a small office and examination room, with a separate entrance for patients. A hand-lettered sign, done in James's steady script, hung beside the door of the addition and declared the space belonged to *Martha Hughes Paul, M.D.*

Mattie could not keep tears from falling fast and thick as she turned to hug James. How could she possibly ever repay him? Four year ago, even as she struggled in Ann Arbor, as Professor Douglas goaded her for speaking to cadavers, as students hazed and teased her, here, here, *here* was what Papa had been doing in the West. Without a word, he had been carving out space for her profession, creating a way for her to be a doctor and overcoming any potential awkwardness as a single woman setting up office in an unchaperoned space. No one could be scandalized by this new venture, for here she was, fully supported by her parents. Both parents, she realized, for though Elizabeth might have resisted the sacrifice, she had also relented. For here it stood.

"Jim Downey down the street is selling a buggy about the right size for house calls," James said. "I told him you might want to see about buying it."

"Papa." Mattie looked at his lined face through eyes fogged with tears. "Mama." She reached for her hand too. "Thank you."

Heat, light, electricity, and nerve force is generated in all animals.
—MARTHA HUGHES CANNON

Chapter Twenty-Three

Early dawn suffused the valley, wrapping around mammoth cliffs, filling crevices with the first blush of day. Through the brambles and briars of the foothills, a lone figure wended her way, pausing to pinch off a cluster of red raspberry leaf, stopping to snip a stalk of yarrow. A simple hat and scarf covered her short curls, warding off dew, and she carried a flat-bottomed basket.

Mattie inhaled a bracing breath of morning mountain air—truly no other air tasted quite like this, full of scented streams as they tumbled down the side of rocky cliffs, of pine-clad copses and towering heights fanned by birds in winged ascent. She began her days searching streambeds for dense clusters of stinging nettle and graceful stalks of scarlet lobelia, replenishing her store of remedies. For a frontier doctor needed to know the herbs and their seasons for gathering and drying, must be able to cure with the medicines of a patient's pantry in addition to writing prescriptions compounded by a druggist. Watching the day break over the tops of the mountains, Mattie felt as if she stood upon a rocky precipice of her own, with the glory of a future nearly ripe for the plucking.

When the first true rays penetrated past canyons and into the valley, it was time to turn her steps in the direction of her office. In early weeks, patients tread cautiously, marveling at a lady doctress newly returned from the East, wondering among themselves if she had learned anything beyond fancy book learning in her time away. She spent hours gathering office equipment and setting rates for nonexistent customers: 5 dollars to deliver a baby, 2 dollars to set a bone, 50 cents for a consultation, 75 cents for a house call plus 25 cents per mile outside of town.

Her first customer had been Billy Andrews next door with tears dripping down his chubby cheeks, holding up a puppy who had managed to get a fishing hook lodged in his lip. "Please, Miss Doctor, help my pup?" Billy fearfully regarded the brass scales, test tubes, and measuring cylinders, the hunched microscope and rack of medicine bottles and needles, as Dr. Paul lifted the whining puppy onto her newly sanitized examination table.

"I'm not a veterinarian, Billy, but if you hold Chocolate's face against your shoulder, I'll see what I can do." Billy swiped at his tears and held the wriggling creature while Mattie clipped the barbed end of the fishing hook and threaded it back through the punctured skin.

Mattie cleaned the wound, thinking with a wry smile that she hadn't needed four years of medical school for this. But when she set the squirming puppy back in his young master's arms, his grin was also exactly why she had gone for training.

"I'm awful sorry, Doctor, but I don't have any money," Billy said, as sick realization broke over his face. "I can ask my parents though."

"Never mind the charge," Mattie said, knowing the boy's family didn't have a nickel to spare. "I'm happy to help. But no more casting your fishing rod beside Chocolate."

Billy went home and told his mother about the lady doctor's steady hand and kind smile, and the next day, when Mattie returned from gathering herbs, she found a clutch of vegetables and a nosegay of wildflowers on her step. Though they wouldn't cover the cost of office equipment, they seemed payment enough.

Her second customer was Walter Allen, a neighbor who had always been a friend of James. Walter stood ill at ease on her stoop, eyeing the sign. "How may I help you, Mr. Allen?" Mattie asked.

"Um . . . er . . . actually, Doctor, my horse is in labor and it's coming poorly. I know horses are not your particular specialty, but . . ."

Mattie sighed, wanting to proclaim again that she was not a veterinarian, but also sensing she needed to gain people's trust in her skills, even if that meant starting with their animals. And knowing, too, that among a community of small farmers, animals often meant the difference between survival and starvation in a way city people would never understand. "I can do my best," she told Walter, putting on her hat and following him to his barn, where his chestnut horse writhed through a difficult birth.

"She's my best mare," he explained, straightening his hat. "I'd be most obliged if you can help her."

Mattie ran her hand over the horse's flanks and distended belly, feeling after the position of the foal, finding it not so different from a breech presentation in a human. "Her foal isn't presenting correctly," Mattie explained. "I've little experience with doctoring horses, but I will do what I can to help the foal turn." Just as she'd done with many women in labor, Mattie soothed the mare and placed her hands upon the belly to ease the youngster's passage.

When the slippery new life descended into her hands, and the mare, spent and exhausted, bent over her foal, Mattie felt a familiar thrill of joy.

"Well now," Mr. Allen said, "I reckon you did as well as any horse doctor." He paid her three dollars for her efforts and spread word that Miss Paul had a steady hand and clear head and must have learned something worthwhile in the school she'd traveled so far to attend.

Patients began arriving after that, bringing broken bones for setting in plaster-of-Paris bandages, complaints of bladder stones and swollen joints, of heartburn and toothache. They paid when they could or returned with a basket of eggs or a plucked chicken when they couldn't. Mattie handed the food over to Elizabeth who watched the process, awed to find that the frivolous pursuits of Mattie's youth now conjured something as practical as food to set upon the dinner table.

Feeling at last that she could welcome guests, Mattie wrote Leolin and Barbara saying they could come if they wished. Barb replied: "Oh Mattie, I'd love to, but I must confess I'm smitten with a new beau and busy trying to maintain a practice beside such distraction. There might be wedding bells in the future, and how I wish you were close enough to be my maid-of-honor. Loving you from afar."

But Leolin wrote to say: "I suppose I'd better come see this rocky mountain settlement that holds so much allure for you. Thank you for the invitation."

And so one morning, while Mattie watered the sage, rosemary, and spearmint planted beside her office door, Joseph brought the buggy around to escort his sister to the train station.

As the train pulled up to the platform, Mattie strained to catch a glimpse through the windows of a familiar black mustache. Holding her arm, Joseph said, "Now we finally get to meet this chap who's come chasing you across the country."

"Oh hush." Mattie elbowed him lightly. "He isn't chasing me. Besides, everyone in the valley dismissed me as an old maid long ago."

"Nonsense, you're just a choosy woman with a good head on your shoulders. Not the type to swoon over the first man who tries to sweep you off your feet."

"Can you please explain the difference to Mother?"

The train completed its stop, and a whistle sounded. A window in the first compartment opened, and Leolin's jaunty head appeared, mustache intact. Mattie waved.

At the light on her face, Joseph raised an eyebrow.

"We're *friends*," Mattie insisted.

Leolin descended, valise in hand, shaking Joseph's hand and by-passing Mattie's formal greeting for a swift hug. "Since I could not lure you to Boston, there was nothing to do but seek you in this desert instead."

His black eyes were as mischievous as ever, and she found herself reaching to touch his arm in spite of herself, happy to see a familiar face who had known her when her head spun from knowledge acquired in the relentless rush from lecture to lab to textbook.

Joseph settled Leolin's valise in the carriage and picked up the reins, drawing the party away from the station and into bustling Salt Lake City. Leolin's eyes swept up the wide, muddy streets skirting a hodgepodge of structures to the granite walls of the temple humming with construction. Brilliant, stainless blue spread above the mountains, craggy and constant. "A lovely city you're building here," Leolin said, nodding appreciatively. "Though I expected nothing less would draw the illustrious Dr. Paul from gracious old Philadelphia."

"As much of a flatterer as ever, I see," said Mattie.

"At your service, though I assure you my compliments are most sincere."

Mattie ducked her head remembering his words, spoken more than two years ago, *Surely you must have noticed my regard for you.* He would, of course, had to have put such sentiments behind him in the intervening years. He must have. And yet. He had not married. She kept her head averted so he would not see the color of her cheeks.

While Joseph unbridled the horses, Leolin paused to admire the sign and entrance to Mattie's office. Eager for his input on her practice, Mattie showed him her tinctures and ointments, and told him how she longed for belladonna and found stinging nettle a poor substitute.

"I don't think you can be charging enough for your services," he confessed when he saw her rates.

"Well, firstly," she explained, "I am in a valley of immigrants where many of us still struggle to survive. And secondly, I am a woman and therefore assumed, by some, to be less adept at my work."

"Assumptions have a way of being wrong," Leolin said, "for I remember your work in medical school as never short of glorious."

A touch too hastily, Mattie opened the door connecting her office to the main house, where James and Elizabeth pretended not to be waiting, eager to meet this man who had swooped in from the East in pursuit of their daughter. Mattie made the introductions and could not unsee the eagerness with which James grasped Leolin's hands, nor the easy camaraderie that sprung up between them.

The trouble lies in the blood.

—MARTHA HUGHES CANNON

Chapter Twenty-Four

Within the week, Leolin had settled himself at a boardinghouse a short distance away and busied himself with his own professional projects, though he never resisted the Paul residence for long. One morning, Mattie compounded a tincture for bruises on the reclaimed table that served as her laboratory. A sharp rap sounded at the door, and a panicked child's voice called, "Doctor Martha?"

Mattie found ten-year-old Mette Niels—out of breath, brown braids disheveled—standing on her stoop.

"What is it?" Mattie asked, concern mounting.

"My little brother, Jens, is wretched. Mama sent me to ask, can you please come?"

"Come inside while I pack my things," Mattie said, rifling through a list of potential ailments, knowing if Dorthe Niels was worried, there was solid reason. "What's wrong?" she asked as she placed bandages into her medical bag.

"His stomach," said Mette. "He's been retching and moaning. Mama's terrible worried."

Mattie's pulse quickened. Dorthe was a Danish immigrant, and an experienced mother who doctored her babies at home, and her husband, a bigamist, had been under investigation lately. How discreet must she be? She mentally ran through a list of illnesses that might fit the description. "Has he perhaps eaten something out of turn?"

"I don't know, ma'am," Mette said, braids dancing as she shook her head. "All I know is Mama said please come alone." Alone. There it was.

"Thank you, Mette. I'll come at once." Opening the door, she gestured across the yard. "Can you ask my father to fetch my horse and buggy? Tell him it's an emergency."

"Yes, ma'am." Mette set off across the yard.

Tossing lancet, scalpel, and syringe into her bag, Mattie glanced frantically around the office for anything else she might need. Needles for sutures. A thermometer, still rare in Utah. Plaster bandages, stethoscope, and a vial of Lister's antiseptic.

By the time she had gathered a handful of spearmint leaves from the container near the door, James was leading the hitched horse and buggy from the stable, Mette trotting by his side. "Thank you, Papa." Mattie tied on her bonnet and hoisted the medical bag to the floor of the buggy, gesturing for Mette to settle beside her. "Emergency at the Niels's. Not sure when I'll be back, Papa."

"The Lord keep ye, Doctor," James said, placing the reins into her gloved hands.

She smiled at his kindness even as she flicked the traces onto the horse's back. "Hold tight, Mette."

Mattie kept a sharp eye for passersby, knowing that if Mette's family was under investigation, any unfamiliar face was suspect, for federal marshals had been known to disguise themselves as peddlers in order to question local children for information about the cohabitators they sought.

Peder Niels eased open the door, looking for anyone who might have followed Mattie, eyeing her with a sniff of suspicion. Wary of outside contact, he had been in favor of calling a nearby midwife, but the boy was indeed in danger, twisting and writhing in a knot of bedclothes, a pan of vomit nearby. Dorthe Niels sat beside him in a blue-and-white checkered apron, her hands skittering from the boy's feverish head to his shoulders to keep him still.

"Thank you for coming," Dorthe said, when Mette led Mattie inside.

Mattie set down her bag, and removed her hat. "I came as quickly as I could." The young boy, perhaps four years of age, turned miserably on the bed, and Mattie's mind eliminated possibilities even as she came toward him. "Hello, Jens, I'm Doctor Martha." She knelt beside his bed. "I've come to help. Is that all right?" He nodded, and she lay a hand upon his forehead. *102, maybe 103. Not gastroenteritis.* "Has he eaten anything usual lately?"

Dorthe shook her head.

Food poisoning? "Where does it hurt?" Mattie asked, and the child motioned to his stomach, pushing away her touch. *Centered on the lower right side.*

"I imagine you've administered consecrated oil?" she asked the parents.

"Several times," Dorthe answered.

Mattie drew an instrument from her bag. "This is my stethoscope, and I need to listen to your stomach, would that be okay?" In response, Jens moaned and shook his head vigorously. "How about if I promise to be very gentle?"

Jens turned his head from Mattie to his mother. "Will it hurt?" Dorthe asked, for her son's benefit.

"Not at all," Mattie promised, and at last Jens pulled his hands away.

Holding the instrument to his belly, she imagined globules of bacteria swelling his intestines, though his small body struggled to ward them off. She straightened. "Brother and Sister Niels, may I talk to you?" Following them to the front room, she noticed parcels and trunks hastily thrown together near the door, prepared for a swift departure. "Your son has appendicitis," she explained. "He needs to have the infection removed by surgery, and it must be done quickly."

Father and mother exchanged tortured glances. "And what if we don't?" Peder asked.

"There is a risk it could burst," Mattie said. "Even a chance he may die."

"Should we call a midwife? Have you done this before? We can't have any trouble, not right now," Peder blustered.

"We're going underground," Dorthe explained.

Ah. The Mormon polygamist underground: shuffling between communities, eluding federal agents. Not much of a life for small children. Mattie's heart swelled for them. "I performed several of these surgeries in Philadelphia," she said, shaking aside a longing to have Leolin by her side, knowing the parents' concerns would likely lessen if he were here.

Belief and distrust struggled visibly on Peder's face, mingled with a touch of awe this woman before him could do something for his son that he could not. He clenched and unclenched his fists and finally said, "How can I help?"

Knowing it was too risky to transport the child to her office, Mattie considered the surgical setting; the cramped log cabin was a far cry from a hospital. "Can you boil water to sterilize the instruments?" He nodded, and her eyes fell on the even planks of the kitchen table. "The table will probably be the best spot for the procedure, but ether is flammable so we must remove it from the hearth."

Peder followed her directions and added wood to the fire, while Dorthe fetched clean linens. Three other children, stair-stepped in height, hovered in the corner of the room, watching the proceedings with solemn, round eyes. With everything sanitized, Mattie administered consecrated oil a second time and pronounced a blessing on Jens's head. Then she draped a hood about the child's face, applied the ether, and waited for his eyes to close and his breathing to soften.

Once she was sure he was asleep, Mattie hovered the knife over the child's belly, gauging the distance and the site, and then pressed the blade against the boy's skin, drawing an incision more than an inch long.

Peder and Dorthe huddled with their other children at the far side of the room as Mattie controlled the bleeding, inserted her index finger into the opening, and probed near the large intestine. After some prodding, she located the pus-filled inflamed appendix, flipped it out upon his stomach, tied it off, cut it, and sterilized the aperture with a deft movement.

After reinserting the youngster's innards, she drew a needle and thread from the tray and sewed up the opening as if she were sewing up a pillow. The parents watched this more familiar gesture with relief. Mattie applied a bandage, and it was over so quickly the children had not stirred from their corner.

The parents gathered near their son, still etherized upon the table. "You must keep the bandage clean and dry until the wound heals completely," Mattie instructed. "It's very important to allow only clean clothing and bedding near the site. He will sleep off the effect of the ether in an hour or so, and I can stay until he awakens, but I would not advise moving him from the house for two days at least."

The parents exchanged looks of anguish, and Mattie wished she could offer more comfort. "I'm so sorry," she said again, humbled by the family's struggle.

An hour later, Jens's eyes fluttered open, his eyes clear and lucid. Dorthe cried as she held him. "I will check back tomorrow to see that no infection has set in," Mattie promised the parents. As she cleaned her instruments and put them away, Peder pressed a silver dollar into her hand. "I couldn't possibly," Mattie said. "Not right now. When things are better for your family," she insisted, knowing she would find the bounty of the Niels's garden on her doorstep all autumn long if they had anything to spare.

Returning to her buggy, Mattie glanced toward the mountains, so close they appeared practically on top of her. Her eyes searched out a particular canyon, and though she said nothing aloud, she hoped Annie heard the prayer sent in her direction all the same.

From where comes all the energy we find in a nerve center?
—MARTHA HUGHES CANNON

Chapter Twenty-Five

Through the curved view of the microscope, Mattie studied the outer envelope of oval shapes circling through a backdrop, reminiscent of the new, mottled painting style she'd seen in Philadelphia— Impressionism, they called it. The swirls in front of her were far more deadly than paint, however. Strains of smallpox virus shifted across her slide.

Working by her side with a culture of his own, Leolin confirmed her conclusions. "Yes, it's as you suspected."

Mattie's shoulders sagged at the weight of the news she would have to bear to the Frane household, the measures that would need to be taken to prevent it from spreading. "We need to increase the rates of smallpox vaccination in rural areas before we have a massive outbreak to contend with."

Mattie enjoyed having Leolin work beside her and knew Papa and Mama would be happy if they announced their engagement. The whole family—indeed the whole community—expected it, and they would be correct that Mattie could do much worse than marry the tall and handsome doctor who had traveled the length of the country to work by her side. But she felt little joy at the prospect, only a dull longing to be more than a rural doctor married to another rural doctor, presumptuous though the thought might be. So she delayed questions about the future, pushing it off and away.

Buggy wheels turned in the driveway before Leolin could reply, pulling their attention from the brass microscopes to a trim and elegant buggy drawn by a fine chestnut mare. Mattie pulled the homespun curtain aside for a better look at who might be paying a call, clearly not a social one, as the buggy stopped in front of the office rather than the front door. A footman opened the enclosure and Mattie glimpsed yards of pressed and puckered blue silk, trimmed lace petticoats, and elegant black-and-white leather boots buttoned up the side.

"Dash it all!" Mattie exclaimed.

"Who is it?" Leolin asked, peering over her shoulder.

"Only one of the most important women in Salt Lake." Mattie hurried to remove her simple work apron and pull on a pair of gloves, as a coachman helped the aged but fashionable Eliza Snow down from the carriage. "She might have sent a note of warning!" Mattie removed the microscope to a distant table to keep deadly samples out of the way, and then swept the remaining jumble of instruments into a nearby drawer.

"Would you prefer to meet her alone?" Leolin asked, closing the books upon her desk.

"It would be simplest, I think, if you don't mind. Be a darling?"

"I would do much less to be a darling," he said with a light touch of her hand. Color rose to her cheeks, as he made his escape. *Soon. She would have to decide about him soon.*

Mattie scarcely had time to set the books in a straight pile before a tap came at the door.

Though Mattie had formally met President Eliza Snow before she left for medical school, she'd always found herself stiff and tongue-tied in front of this elegant woman, reminiscent of hand-painted airy china. And now, here she was, rapping at her office door. Mattie ran a quick hand over her hair and down the front of her dress, wishing she had worn something less practical than a smocked work dress for office hours.

"Good morning, President," Mattie said, holding the door as the silk-clad figure rustled her way into the office. "I apologize for not being better prepared to receive you." Eliza wore a starched white collar pinned with a delicate pink cameo at her throat; a dainty lace cap sat atop hair that remained stubbornly brown despite her age.

"No matter, my dear." Eliza dismissed Mattie's concern with a wave of her lace-gloved hand. "You are working, and that is, after all, why I've come to see you." Her brown eyes were kind and generous, at odds with the fussiness of her clothes, and Mattie relaxed a touch, trying to forget that this famous poetess had met Queen Victoria, Charles Dickens, and Abraham Lincoln himself.

Moving medical references from the only reasonably comfortable chair in the office, Mattie gestured, "Won't you please have a seat?"

Eliza settled herself, considering the instruments, the racks of medicines, the lines of herbs drying above the windows. "It's a neat little practice you have set up here," she said. "I'd heard as much. My dear, it seems only a moment ago we were holding a benefit in your honor to raise funds for your schooling, and now here you are, an accomplished doctress in your own right. How grows your practice?"

Mattie took confidence in the kindness of her brown eyes. "Slow at first," she confessed, "but better every month. People in the valley are still learning to trust doctors at all, much less women doctors."

Eliza nodded. "In my experience, the best medicine combines faith with herbs of the earth, mingled liberally with the best science can contribute."

"That is very much my own perspective," Mattie agreed, impressed at the energy and clarity of thought emanating from this woman nearing eighty. Perhaps if a person continued working at the same pace, one's body and mind might forget to slow down? "I hope to focus my work on public health and education, to help mothers in the valley heal their children when they can and seek assistance, both spiritual and scientific, when they need it."

Eliza inclined her head as if imparting a secret. "I believe I know of a path that may help you advance in this direction."

"Please tell."

"You have no doubt heard that in your absence the Relief Society has embarked on several ambitious projects. One of these, of course, is Deseret Hospital, a place for doctors to administer religious healing as well as medical care. Our resident physician will be taking a leave of absence, and I have come on behalf of the governing board to see if you might be interested in applying for the position."

Of course, Mattie knew the hospital and had meant to visit many times, though the endless work of setting up her own practice coupled with the awareness that Romania Pratt was also a visiting surgeon there had kept her away. She'd meant to go. *A hospital run by LDS women—really how had she not found the time?* She floundered for an adequate response.

"This comes as a surprise, no doubt," Eliza said, graciously coming to her rescue.

"And my private practice?"

"I would imagine you could continue it as time allows. The board is interested in starting a school to train nurses and midwives. We hope the new resident physician will be interested in helping with this endeavor."

Mattie's mind swirled with possibilities. To open a school training nurses, holding faith and science side by side as weapons against the shifting viruses infecting the valley. Her goal to study medicine had carried her far beyond the rim of the Rocky Mountains. Though she had accomplished much of what she'd planned, now she found her desire far from quenched, as if she'd set out for one point only to find, once arrived, she did not stand on the highest peak at all, for others stretched beyond it she'd not glimpsed before. "I imagine you'll have several applicants? I must consider my time, of course." *How could she possibly find enough hours in the day?*

President Snow seemed intimately familiar with the problem. "I have often thought that unless we had more to do than what seemed possible for us to accomplish, we should not perform all that we might."

Mattie nodded slowly. To be resident physician of a hospital run by women. The prospect left her dizzy and filled with a courage not merely her own. Something like this was exactly what she'd gone through medical school for. *But how could she do* all *these things?*

Ready or not, she stood upon a darkened theater in Philadelphia once more, pushed onto the stage beneath a glaring spotlight. Mattie reached through the shadows, grasping for her lines: "President Snow, I believe I would love to apply."

Some days later, Mattie pulled her buggy in front of the gray brick building and tried to steady her shaking hands. The two-story building that had once held the Catholic hospital was small compared to hospitals in Philadelphia and Michigan, but the clean white lattice windows set a cheerful tone. A receptionist bustled her toward an office labeled Resident Physician and Surgeon Dr. Ellen B. Ferguson, directly across from the office space for Hospital Matron and Visiting Surgeon Dr. Romania B. Pratt. Mattie couldn't help noticing that her own potential office was a good deal larger than Romania's. She shrugged the ungracious thought aside and greeted Eliza Snow who stood when Mattie entered the room.

"Thank you so much for coming," Eliza said. A stout woman in stiff silk bustled through the door behind Mattie. "And I imagine you have met Dr. Romania Pratt?"

"I have," Mattie said, feeling like a poor country girl in a twice-turned dress when Romania's heavy lidded eyes raked her up and down. Certainly no one had asked Romania for recommendations for the new physician.

But if Eliza sensed any tension, she ignored it. "I think we will begin with a tour of the facilities."

"If that's all that's needed, I'll see to my patients, President," Romania said.

"Thank you, Doctor."

Romania swept away with a cold glance over her shoulder.

Eliza led the way to the back of the building behind the offices. "It may seem odd to start with the storerooms, but we established this hospital through generous donations of funds, goods, and supplies, so I like to begin here."

Sacks of grain and folded blankets ranged in careful stacks on broad shelves. "You were away at medical school when we began this project," Eliza explained, "but it was a true community effort. Primary children collected pennies and blankets, families held benefit concerts and donated washbasins and coal they could ill afford to spare. We try to spend hospital resources with these sacrifices in mind."

"Very impressive," Mattie said, taking in the orderly rows. "Both the supplies and their organization."

Eliza led the way toward the wards themselves, where nurses and doctors moved between sickbeds, taking notes, stopping to administer medicine or change bandages. Mattie paused to savor the sight, unique in all her medical experience, for the only men in this hospital ward were patients.

Eliza stopped near the end of the ward. "As you might guess, our patients are Welsh, Danish, Chinese, Irish, Eastern European, and American, my dear. They work as housewives, loggers, miners, farmers, stone masons, and chambermaids and suffer with everything

143

from ovarian tumors to pneumonia and typhoid fever. It is essential our doctors understand the multitude of situations with which they may find themselves confronted within these walls."

"I understand," Mattie said. "The public hospital in Philadelphia was similar in scope." She paused before a collection of medical textbooks, microscopes, and anatomical references. An intact skeleton dangled, waiting to demonstrate a fracture or the shape of the pelvic cavity.

At the end of the hall, Eliza pointed out rooms designated for surgery and areas for quarantine, simple but functional. One private room held a woman with soft features who couldn't have been more than thirty years old. Mattie watched two men and a matronly woman with deep-set dimples lay their hands upon the patient's head, administering consecrated oil and speaking the words of a blessing.

Once out of earshot, President Snow explained, "Adeline Savage came to us bedridden. As I told you when we met at your office, we established this facility primarily to allow patients to be healed by *both* faith and medicine; healing ordinances are part of all medical procedures, so long as a patient desires it."

"You've succeeded most impressively," Mattie said.

"Thank you. Several of the rooms upstairs are empty," Eliza explained. "That is where we hope to create a school for training midwives and nurses to serve this valley and the settlements beyond."

A thrill ran through Mattie at the thought. If she'd had such encouragement as a girl, such opportunity so close at hand, how much easier would her own journey have been? What an incredible visionary this woman was, beneath her prim lace cap and papery skin.

"Shall we return to the office?" Eliza invited. Mattie trailed after her, determined more with every passing minute that she wanted to be a part of all this woman was creating. Even seeing Romania daily didn't seem enough of a threat to detract from the excitement she felt at the prospect.

Dropping into a chair behind the desk, Eliza gestured to the ward, the offices, the beds both empty and filled. "I know we are far from the most prestigious place you could choose to practice, Dr. Paul, but we are considering several applicants for this position. Can you tell me how you might see yourself fitting into our work?"

"President Snow." Mattie cleared her voice, ordering it not to tremble. "My earliest childhood memories are of burying my little sister on the westward trail. My father followed her in death days after our arrival. My mother was helpless to aid them, and this is why I went to medical school. I feel called to help our people heal and fight disease. To use *all* the tools God has given us to this end. Your work here aligns with my most sincere aspirations, and it would be my honor to work by your side."

Eliza demurred, thanked her for coming, and promised nothing at all, while Mattie knew tonight she would lie awake in her cot, unable to sleep with anticipation, her mind lit up by this shifting kaleidoscope that had slipped to the right, fallen into place as unexpectedly as if an angel dropped from above, though this particular angel had a pronounced preference for frilly petticoats and brown-watered silks.

We are considering the oxidation of tissue
which is the agent of life.
—MARTHA HUGHES CANNON

Chapter Twenty-Six

Mattie checked her patient charts again: A case of gallstones. Still critical. A man whose arm had been caught in a threshing machine. Improving steadily. She stopped by the bed of a diphtheria patient. "See that he gets morphine," she instructed the nurse. Autumn sunlight slanted through westward windows, angling across the room from bed to bed.

Lucy Young leaned against the doorframe of Adeline Savage's room. Lucy, the dimpled matron Mattie had noticed on her initial tour, had no training as a nurse, but worked as a healer in the temple and came often to the hospital to offer comfort. It had been a month since Mattie had first seen Adeline, and still she lay pale and waxy, despondent in the dying light. Other than the slow, labored rise and fall of her chest, one might easily mistake her for a dummy used in demonstrations, if not for a corpse from the autopsy lab.

Lucy stopped Romania Pratt approaching from the opposite direction. "Please, Dr. Pratt, what more can I do to help her?" Romania's gaze flicked to the patient who had shown no improvement in the months she had been here.

"She is bloodless and practically lifeless, sadly," Romania answered before moving on.

Advancing in Romania's wake, Mattie stopped beside Lucy, drawn by her grieving expression. "I think you feel their pain almost as much as they do, Sister Young."

"Is there really no hope for her?"

"None that we doctors have been able to deduce." Mattie studied the woman before her, her gray eyes the expression of calmness itself. Lucy was a legendary healer who had directed the healing work in the St. George and Logan temples for years. Incredible stories spiraled in her wake. "But then again, I believe the most hopeless cases are your particular specialty?"

Lucy looked away, flattered. "I have already administered to her with Patriarch Brimhall, but perhaps another blessing would bring her comfort."

"Yes . . ." Mattie allowed her voice to trail off. President Snow had hinted that Adeline should return home so the room could be readied for a new patient, yet administering to her again could cause no harm. Mattie stepped into the room and rested a hand upon Adeline's pale fingers. "Adeline, Sister Lucy Young is here. Do you remember her? She is a healer in the Logan and St. George temples. She will administer to you, if you wish."

Wan and lashless eyes flickered open momentarily, confused at their whereabouts, focusing with difficulty on Mattie's face. Adeline took in the figure of Lucy hesitating near the doorway and seemed to comprehend for a moment. She nodded almost imperceptibly.

"I'll fetch some water," Mattie said, as Lucy drew out a bottle of consecrated oil.

Standing to one side of the patient, Mattie struggled to hope despite the fact that Adeline had been sick for a year and a half before her arrival here. And here she had lain, two months in the hospital, the recipient of blessings and prayers from her husband

and numerous other loved ones. Lucy bowed her head, and Mattie mumbled a prayer, beseeching help she scarcely believed possible. Still, if nothing else, the blessing might grant the woman peace.

"Amen," Mattie said, raising her eyes to Lucy's face, surprised to find it lit with hope. Adeline's thin form lay upon the sheets, prostrate and unchanged. Whatever inspired Lucy, Mattie found no evidence of it.

With exquisite care, Lucy washed Adeline's legs with water, blessing them as she touched each limb. She held Adeline's head as she washed her face, folded with pain, anointing each spot with consecrated oil.

The two women closed their eyes once more, and Lucy lay her hands upon the feeble, thinning hair, calling down healing power with a quiet confidence that burned its way into Mattie's consciousness.

Mattie's hands rested upon the crown of Adeline's head; though her eyes remained closed, through her fingertips she sensed a quickening, a sudden surge of warmth.

Surely . . .

Mattie peeked from one eye, and sucked in her breath. Even as she watched, the waxy pallor faded from Adeline's skin and a faint blush stole across it, steady and unmistakable. Beneath her very fingers, Mattie felt the body relax as tension drained way, and the patient's breathing gained strength.

Pulse quickening, Mattie opened her eyes, taking in Lucy's tearful gaze, as beneath her trembling fingers, the patient struggled to sit up. "Heavens!"

"Slowly, Sister Savage," Lucy said, reaching to support Adeline's head. "Don't attempt to rise unless the doctor thinks it safe."

But Adeline's skin glowed with life and her frail hand reached for the edge of the bed as she edged herself forward. "I can get up now," she said, guiding her legs toward the floor like a foal preparing to stand for the first time.

Mattie rushed to catch her, but the sudden strength in Adeline's arms took her aback. Overwhelmed, Mattie choked out: "Slowly, Adeline. Just a moment ago we thought you were done for this life."

Adeline pushed off the cot, taking one shuffling step and then another, her eyes filling with tears. "It's a miracle." She looked from Mattie to Lucy. "The Lord healed me through your hands—I was bound, but you set me free."

"Not us," Lucy assured her, shaking her head, humble and triumphant.

"What in the world?" came Romania Pratt's exclamation from outside the room. Nurses and other patients crowded the doorway as Adeline turned this way and that, holding her arms out in wondrous display.

"Send a message to her husband at once!" Mattie directed, watching Adeline as if she might disappear into the air above. In all her training and experience, she had never seen anything that could compare with the event that had just transpired.

If Mattie had not felt the body animate beneath her own hands, had not watched the color wash over that face with her own eyes—and even though she *had*—still, she wished she could experience it all over again, for she could scarcely find strength to believe it.

What gives opacity to the white matter of the nerves?
—MARTHA HUGHES CANNON

Chapter Twenty-Seven

A week later, Mattie still could not forget it. Could not forget the energy returning to Adeline's ashen skin, the life breathing into itself. The scene played through her mind over and over like a play under rehearsal. The vacated room did not encourage acceptance, for Adeline's husband had rushed to whisk her away. Adeline had walked to the buggy of her own accord, leaning firmly on his arm, but walking, walking, walking, as if she had done it every day and had not spent the last year watching life unfold from the center of a bed.

The room she had occupied was now filled with an ornery miner with lead poisoning who complained loudly, leaving it easy to forget Adeline had ever come and gone, that Lazarus in petticoats.

"The sick shall rise up at thy touch," George Q. Cannon's blessing had promised Mattie years before, and she held the wonderment of the moment again this morning before brushing it away, knowing there were patients to attend to, and a troubling case of a mountain man who had lost his way on a high canyon pass, managing to freeze both his feet to the ankles before being rescued. She would need to amputate both legs below the knee, a procedure she had not done since Philadelphia, and she was weighing the benefits of a transtibial extended flap amputation as she followed the attendant nurses toward the operating room where the etherized patient awaited them.

At the end of the hallway, Mattie sanitized and properly scrubbed her instruments and then her hands, praying for the best way to approach so daunting a riddle.

Upon entering the room, she came to an abrupt halt.

For there, in her operating room, facing her patient and the nurses preparing for the procedure at hand, stood a man in a fastidious suit and silk cravat, hat in hand, conversing with Betty and Lina as casually as if they were chatting over tea.

"Dash it all!" Mattie said aloud, bewildered at the sight of him. *Did this man know nothing of surgical procedure?*

He turned toward her, and she found herself noticing the blue clarity of his eyes, the fine shape of his full lips beneath a tidy mustache; she shook her head, annoyed at herself for noticing these trivialities at such a moment. "I beg your pardon?" he asked in a charming English accent.

Taken aback, Mattie grasped for words as if her foot had landed on an uneven floor board. "This, sir, is an operating room, and we are about to begin a procedure. Visitors are most certainly *not* allowed. Kindly remove yourself at once." Betty drew back in shock, as Lina smothered a sound of surprise.

"Excuse me," the stranger said, humor dancing about his eyes. "I do most truly hope that you'll forgive me, Doctor . . . ?" He extended his hand in greeting.

Protests gathered around Mattie's lips, as Betty and Lina exchanged tortured glances. "Dr. Mattie Hughes Paul, sir, but I have just prepared my hands for surgery."

"Oh, of course, do forgive me," he returned the offending hand to his side and bowed slightly. "President Angus M. Cannon at your service, Doctor. I'm delighted to make your acquaintance."

What in heavens had she done? The nurses stifled smiles, trying to pretend that she, Mattie, had not just ordered stake president Angus M. Cannon—a member of the board of directors over the hospital and a nephew of the prophet himself—*ordered* him from her operating room.

Well done, she groaned internally, wishing she could throw herself out the window along with the wash water. He could have her removed from her post within the hour if he wanted to.

Dragging apologetic eyes back to his face, she expected to find him angry, or at least perturbed. Yet his mustache twitched suspiciously, and he appeared nearly amused. Sensing her discomfort, he placed his hat back on his head and bowed. "Please forgive my intrusion, Doctor. It was a pleasure to meet you. I wish you a most successful procedure." His even steps crossed the floor between them, and he pulled the door closed behind him.

The women let out a collective sigh of relief.

"Heavens." Mattie sighed. "It must be obvious I did not know who that gentleman was."

"Sorry, we could think of no way to tell you," said Lina, tying on her apron. "With all the congregations in Salt Lake to oversee, President Cannon is seldom at the hospital. He makes only brief appearances here."

"Are you saying in all likelihood I won't have to face him again? It's clear enough I made a mess of that." She struggled to focus back on the patient arrayed in front of them, who had far greater problems to worry about. *Would she never?* And *why* could she not shake the clear kindness of those light blue eyes? Mattie took a full breath and released it. "Shall we see if I can do better with this surgery than I did with that encounter?"

The heart's curious valves open and close with rhythmic precision.
—MARTHA HUGHES CANNON

Chapter Twenty-Eight

Days at the hospital passed swiftly, with patients to see and the planning of the new school. Yet in spite of Lina's promise, Mattie saw President Angus Cannon again only two weeks later, striding down the hall, wearing a different silk cravat, President Eliza Snow beside him. The stark hallway offered no route for escape. Mattie considered turning on a heel and retreating in the opposite direction, but he called out, "Doctor Paul, isn't it?"

Steeling herself for a deserved tongue-lashing, she chanced a swift glance at his face and stopped in surprise. Taking his proffered hand she began, "I must apologize—"

"Not a bit," he stopped her, British accent still intact, holding her hand as if she had trusted him with something quite precious. "I told President Snow how impressed I was with the care you showed your patient in the short time I had the privilege of being a guest in your operating room." His eyes shone with a slight hint of teasing.

Mattie stopped short, wondering what game he was playing, but his face held only graciousness, and she had no reason to assume he was being insincere. "Thank you, sir," she said, withdrawing her hand in complete confusion.

The following week, Mattie was surprised to find him present once more, this time in a meeting of administrators and physicians. He sought out a seat beside her, and leaned toward her conspiratorially. Whispering just low enough for her to hear, he said, "Here's another member of the board of directors, Dr. Paul. Perhaps we should not order this one from the room, just today?" She ducked her head to muffle her laugh, while he maintained a straight face.

Over the subsequent weeks, President Cannon sought her input about administrative matters, consulted over procedure, and then inquired after her views on the smallpox vaccination. Remembering Lina's remark that President Cannon was seldom at the hospital, Mattie wondered if his recent appearances had anything to do with the way his eyes seemed to linger on her face longer than strictly necessary.

She found his presence magnetic and intriguing, and as weeks passed into months, Mattie found herself waiting to catch his eyes across the room, to hear his voice speak her name.

She attempted to be subtle, for Romania's and others' eyes were quick to notice, and Mattie had no desire to elicit gossip. After all, Angus was several years her senior and already had three wives. She harbored no intentions to add to his already burgeoning household.

One morning, when Romania asked Mattie for her input on a procedural matter, Mattie thought of his measured counsel and responded, "Perhaps we should seek President Cannon's input."

Dr. Pratt's eyes narrowed triumphantly. "The President should not be bothered over such a trivial issue, Dr. Paul. As you seem to forget, his older brother is in the First Presidency, his uncle is the prophet. President Cannon has little time to spare, though you alone seem blind to that fact."

Mattie drew back as if she'd been stung, wondering if she'd made an embarrassment of herself and Romania was not the only one who thought so.

She managed to avoid him for several days, but when she arrived to look in on an irascible railman few could tolerate, Mattie found President Cannon seated beside him, talking as if he had no other place to be. "Oh, excuse me, President," Mattie said, turning to leave. "I didn't know you were here."

"Please," he insisted, reaching toward her. "Disregard my presence, Dr. Paul. Carry on with your work. I was just telling Mr. Xu about my arrival in Nauvoo as a child."

Determined to complete the examination quickly, she checked the old railman's vital signs, noting the first spark of vitality Mattie had seen on his face.

"We didn't stay long, you know," Angus continued, as the patient turned back to hear his story. "Mobs ran us out in mid-winter. I huddled near the banks of the Mississippi River with my brothers and sisters, half starving and frozen, until a flock of quail descended upon us. We roasted the birds on spits, and devoured them. Nothing I've ever eaten in my life tasted quite as good as those quail." The railman nodded as if he knew a thing or two about consuming a good meal under harsh conditions.

"Mr. Xu," Mattie said, "I'm going to change your bandages now. Please try and relax while I take care of this, sir." Gently she unwound the covering, checking for signs of infection or gangrene. Usually when she did this, he cursed and complained, but today he lay still as Angus spoke of his journey west under the most primitive conditions, only two years after Brigham Young. When Mattie finished, she deftly tucked the bandages back around the wound.

Glancing up, she sucked in her breath at finding Angus's eyes resting upon her with obvious admiration. "Mr. Xu," he said, "you are quite lucky to have a doctor as dedicated as Dr. Paul. You are in most admirable hands, sir. Many, under such circumstances, would be envious."

Mattie blushed, trying to shake off the compliment as if he meant nothing more than her work. *Didn't he?* She could not dismiss his look of adoration, and she tucked the memory away, where she might retrieve it again.

At home, James wondered why Mattie set off so eagerly for the hospital each morning, why her laugh came so freely, filled with little jokes and quips for Bonnie and Maude; why, in moments, a sly smile would tug at the corner of her mouth as if she were reliving a private secret—a look, a word, or the brush of a hand.

Leolin noticed too, and wondered at the changes, so subtle they could be explained away, but impossible to miss if you noted Mattie's every expression as he did. Busy with work of his own, gathering herbs to take East, consulting on difficult cases for the druggist, he watched Mattie smile at empty corners of the room and began considering his next step beyond the rocky confines of the valley.

Exhausted by demanding hours at the hospital, the anticipated nursing school, and her own private practice, Mattie's thoughts of Leolin consisted primarily of a nagging sense of guilt. He had not spoken of marriage again directly, and committing her future to him seemed more impossible than ever since Angus's arrival in her life.

Though she tried to drag her thoughts away from Angus, Mattie found that she could not. She'd never felt the slightest inclination to enter into plural marriage, especially given the controversy with the government, but since meeting Angus the thought had begun resting on her mind. She longed for the close companionship of her parent's marriage but had no wish to spend the rest of her life having baby after baby as her mother had, bless her. Eliza Snow and Emmeline Wells were two of the most accomplished women she knew, and their lives in polygamous marriages held a balance few women in monogamous relationships could claim. Maybe the system *was* a solution to many societal problems, as some Church leaders claimed.

From what Mattie could gather from conversations couched in hospital protocol, Angus's three wives—two sisters followed by a widow with children—had mainly been marriages of convenience. Surely he had never looked on them as she felt his gaze rest on her when he believed no one else was looking.

The lightness in her heart, the thrill of excitement, the peace, the soul-filling joy she felt with him—it was everything that had been missing with Leolin, with Jim Anderson, with every boy she had ever known. And "boy" was what they seemed next to Angus's experience.

Knowing that life with him would be anything but easy even if he were inclined to seek her hand, Mattie tried to stay focused on the work before her. Yet, seated at her desk, pouring over patient notes, she often found herself gazing into the distance, longing to consult Angus on medical matters, or perhaps to linger for some moments in the goodness of his clear blue eyes.

The following week when she went to the hospital storeroom to fetch supplies, she was startled to find Angus had followed her. He drew back at once, apologetic. "Excuse me, Dr. Paul. I saw you come this way and wondered if I could be of help to you?"

She blushed at finding herself alone with him for the first time. "Thank you, President. I am looking for a particular instrument I used in Philadelphia, though I'm not sure we have it."

"Such a lovely city," he said.

"You know it?"

"Very well. From my mission to the East. Did you enjoy the medical program there?"

"Very much." Encouraged by his inquiries, she went on to describe her work, the experiments she had performed, her oratory training. "You see," she told him, "someday I want to be able to stand upon a public stage. I cannot imagine a more important work than bringing a knowledge of patient care to every mother in this valley."

"It is a pleasure to see a woman fulfilling her life's work and mission," he said in response. "You inspire me greatly, Dr. Paul." Mattie dropped her eyes under his gaze, blushing at his words.

A shadow fell across the doorway. From her vantage point, Romania Pratt could see only Mattie in the room. "Have you collected the dirty bandages from your patients yet?" she asked.

Mattie stammered after a reply, but Angus stepped forward.

"It is my fault," he said. "Please forgive me, Dr. Pratt. I will assist Dr. Paul with that task since I have taken up her valuable time." And Angus set off to collect the dirty bandages before Mattie could even protest that he of all people surely should not.

Scared lest her feelings drag her under, Mattie did her best to avoid him, or at least keep him at a distance. From things he had said, to patients, in meetings, in passing, she couldn't help but wonder at their similarities. Both children of converts from the British Isles. Both had worked in printing offices. Both had explored life beyond the valley, for Angus had settled St. George, explored the Colorado River, and traveled by freight wagon to Montana. Though he'd planned on an education at West Point, he'd postponed it for missionary service which led him to Connecticut, Maryland, Pennsylvania, and New York instead. She wondered if she'd ever met another person who seemed to truly appreciate and understand the ambition of her soul, rather than feeling threatened by it.

One day as Mattie had to unavoidably check on the vital signs of a patient Angus was visiting, the patient asked after Angus's parents. He appeared inexplicably moved by the question, and silence stretched out as he worked to find a response. Hinting at a sorrow that still haunted him, he cleared his throat and said simply, "I regret to say I lost both my parents on that journey westward."

Jumbled fragments returned to her—a pile of stones raised upon a mountainside, and her father, so frail he could do no more than watch from the wagon. The feel of her father's cold cheek as she stood on tiptoe to kiss him goodbye.

Wondering if this, then, explained the connection between them, she waited until the patient fell asleep to lean across the bed. "I, too, lost my father, my baby sister," she whispered over the sleeping form. As she studied the long shadows resting on Angus's face, she felt, as she often did, he would understand what she meant.

That evening, Angus found Mattie struggling into her coat and hurried to help her with the offending sleeve. He offered, casually, to return her home in his buggy, as their eyes met with a swift glance of hope. "Thank you," she said, striving to sound far more nonchalant than she felt.

He brought his buggy around and lifted her into the seat with the strength of a much younger man. "Dr. Paul, meet Roscoe Conkling," he said, gesturing to the black stallion pulling the trap.

Mattie laughed. "Very pleased to meet you, Roscoe." The night was brisk, and she leaned close to Angus, thinking how much she would like to ride on like this for a good piece yet, far longer than home.

"Dr. Paul, I hope you don't think me too forward in seeking out your company," Angus said, glancing toward her sideways, as if she might have vanished.

"On the contrary," Mattie admitted, "I think it no small secret that I enjoy your company very much, sir."

"I'm afraid I've done a terrible job of hiding how much I enjoy yours." His tone made her blush in the darkness. She fastened her hand more firmly about his arm, and they rode on in silence for a block or two as drops of rain and snow slushed down upon the streets, turned into flickering fireflies by the light of streetlamps. All Mattie could think was how incredibly beautiful water turning to snow looked as it fell.

"I wonder . . ." Angus said, letting the phrase trail off into the night, swept up by the brisk wind. "I wonder . . ."

Mattie's heart began to race most erratically.

He pulled the buggy to the side of the road, reining in Roscoe, whose breath puffed out in billows of mist rising up to meet the almost-snow's descent.

Angus turned to face her, taking both her hands in his own, and she noticed for the first time how warm and safe they felt, like settling down upon your own hearth after a long walk through a winter storm.

"I wonder, Dr. Paul, if you might consider becoming my wife." Color washed over her cheeks in the shadowy buggy; emotion rushed in her ears so she could barely hear his words.

He dropped his gaze to her hand resting lightly on his own. "In these difficult times, perhaps you feel me brash and even reckless for daring to ask. I'm already under investigation by authorities for polygamy, and I wouldn't want you to think such a path would not be difficult."

She did know. Like everyone else in the valley, she had seen federal agents interviewing children, spying through windows, subpoenaing women to testify against their husbands. *Still* . . . though no one in her immediate family practiced polygamy, Eliza Snow did. Emmeline Wells did. These women were tremendous pillars of wisdom. And with Angus as her husband, she could take her place among them. With him by her side, what couldn't they do? Everything. All of it. It seemed they could undertake every great thing she could ever imagine. This. Something like this was what she had waited for.

"Though I have faith that eventually the laws will change in our favor, I don't know how long that will take," Angus said. "But, Dr. Paul—Mattie—if you will?" She nodded. "I *do* believe in time things will change, and we will be able to live as we choose." She felt his eyes upon her in the darkness, felt them hover near her mouth. "In truth, I feel as though we were made for each other," he confessed. "I have never felt such longing to simply be beside someone."

Though they were sitting in near-darkness, Mattie felt as if she had swallowed the sun and was surprised to find no evidence of its light emanating from her every pore. She reached up shyly, running her fingers along the line of his jaw. "Nor have I," she said, daring to turn her lips in the direction of his own.

Did she believe in polygamy? She wasn't sure. But she knew she believed in him. And in the joy fork-lighting through her soul, unmistakable and true.

The heart is strong and tough, and yet smooth, soft, and elastic.
—MARTHA HUGHES CANNON

Chapter Twenty-Nine

OCTOBER 6, 1884
Salt Lake City, Utah Territory

Secret. I must not say. Secret. I cannot tell.

The words punctuated each footfall; with each pass of the brush through her hair, they rang in her mind. The house rested in mid-morning stillness, everyone else away at their respective labors, while in her bedroom, Mattie brushed her hair with tonic until it shone with the sheen of silk. She buttoned up her best dress, a deep green taffeta trimmed near the wrist with pink silk and black crocheted lace.

Leaning toward the looking glass, Mattie pinched her cheeks to beckon a touch of color and fastened a carved cameo, a gift from her mother, near her throat. Her chest rose against her stays in sharp, shallow pants as she struggled to breathe through the voice tugging at her mind. *Secret. I must not tell.*

In a sense, it was incredulous everyone hadn't read the secret upon her face these past weeks. Unbelievable that Mama, Papa, and Lotta could have failed to notice her expression as she choked down a few bites of gruel this morning.

Elizabeth's eyes had rested upon Mattie, weighing if something might be amiss with her daughter, but she had dismissed the concern, distracted by the daily rush to feed the mouths circling her table. Meanwhile, Mattie watched those familiar strangers, wondering at their ability to go about their chores as if it were yet another day on the calendar, no different from those before, never sensing that *everything* had changed. Or was about to.

Tying on her best bonnet, Mattie glanced one final time at her reflection, regarding the flash of her eyes, the fluttering of her hands. She stopped and leaned against the door of the bedroom, listening for sounds of someone who might question her midmorning departure in her finest gown, as her heart kept time with the pounding words: *Secret. For what if they knew? Secret.*

It had to be this way, Angus had explained, to protect her family from the investigation against him, from prying federal agents. It was better for her family's safety if they knew nothing for now, until the situation improved.

Mattie lifted her reticule from the bed, packed with a nightgown and things to keep her for a few days. Stepping into the hall, she listened again for any movement beyond the sound of the empty house settling into itself. Nothing.

Venturing downstairs, she found the morning fire from breakfast turning to ash and placed a simple note upon the wooden planks of the table. Though she offered excuses and begged them not to worry, they would know something was amiss as soon as they read it.

Passing to her medical office, a space that had been neglected as of late, she made her way to her buggy tied up and waiting, where her horse stamped in the brisk October air. Only a few yards now. She hurried down the steps and placed her reticule on the bench, lifting a foot toward the mounting step.

"Mattie?" It was a voice she loved beyond all reason. Coming from his workshop, James crossed the yard, surprised to find his daughter departing for a midmorning ball. She hesitated, one foot upon the step, unable to add one more ounce to his burden. As he ambled toward her, she noticed how much more slowly he moved, how gray had encroached its way over his beloved head bit by bit.

"Yes, Papa?" she asked, as guilty as if she'd been found wasting time with chemistry books in the middle of chores.

His expression of surprise settled into confusion. "Whit like?" he asked, using the old childhood phrase. Mattie had spent the last few weeks reminding herself that she was an autonomous adult nearing thirty years of age, yet confronted with this greeting, she failed entirely.

Impulsively, she leaned into him, seeking the comfort of his arms around her. He smiled at the unexpected gesture, holding her against his chest as he had always done, and she soaked up the strength she had ever found there.

Drawing a deep breath, she pulled back to look at him. "I'm afraid I need you to trust me, Papa."

He took in her hat, her finest dress, and her face glowing fiercely and gathered up all his questions, settling them into the buggy beside her reticule. He handed her up to the driver's seat, placing the reins firmly in her waiting hands. "God bless you, my daughter."

Tears blurred her vision. "Thank you, Papa. I promise I'll return." He looked more concerned than before she had spoken but nodded slowly. Images from Mary's wedding day flashed through her mind then: the flowers, the party, the cake and celebration, her sister arrayed in white, holding Papa's arm. Mattie swallowed hard against those trappings of longing and started the horse forward, turning it onto the road.

Guiding the rig across a town dressed in the vibrancy of autumn, she made her way toward Temple Square and the two-story Endowment House. Entering alone, Mattie's heart beat erratically and her face flushed with rising panic at the thought of the commitment she was about to make.

But when she knelt down at the altar and saw Angus's face across from her, his clear blue eyes filled her with the hope of all that lay before them, the promise that somehow, someday, this action done in secret would be held up for the world to acknowledge. As she reached for his hand, peace flooded her heart, and she felt a reassurance that things would come out all right.

She scarcely heard Angus's older brother George as he pronounced miraculous blessings, scarcely heard anything before, "I now pronounce you man and wife . . ." and, "you may kiss each other over the altar." Mattie leaned over that altar, scarcely thinking that it was an altar of sacrifice, a place where anciently, people lay their most cherished possessions to be consumed in fire by God—felt only a thrill at his lips upon her own, felt only that this was exactly where his lips belonged. Along with the thrill of believing, though no one outside the walls stood witness, the angels in heaven—perhaps Annie and her father among them—knew she and Angus had promised to be one.

Mattie slipped from the Endowment House alone, returned to her buggy alone, made her way to a hotel across town alone, where she signed the register with a name that was not her own and waited for her bridegroom. There would be no flowers, no parties, no announcements in the paper. For it was—all of it—*secret*. Angus arrived sometime later, drawing her close as he never had before, his hand upon her head, her hair, her cheeks.

"So we are really married?" she asked.

"I believe we are," he said with a laugh, and she thrilled at his closeness, at the time that stretched before them, at the end of a courtship that had seemed but a series of brief and stolen interludes.

Quiz: What is farce?

—MARTHA HUGHES CANNON

Chapter Thirty

Mattie sidled in the door of the hospital, three days later, cheeks burning. She had never taken leave before, and she was never ill. "Where were you?" Romania asked bluntly.

"Caring for patients in my private practice," Mattie answered, hating the necessary lie, for she'd never counted dishonesty among her faults. To distract herself, she passed several satisfying moments imagining Romania's expression if she had spoken the truth and said she'd spent the last three days in a hotel room with Angus.

To keep their secret, Angus began avoiding the hospital, a simple enough solution, as he had spent far more time there of late than necessary. "Just for a short time, my love," he promised. "Until this investigation blows over." He did, after all, have three other wives to attend to, as well as church and business duties.

"And then I'll meet your other wives and children?"

"I promise."

Going home was worse than facing the hospital, for though Mattie had planned to maintain secrecy, when she opened the door, a strange and awkward silence confronted her.

The angle of her mother's body bespoke betrayal, and Mattie

could not look away from the pain and confusion etched into every line of James's face as he jerked forward and back in his rocker. Lotta and Joseph came forward to hug her, formally, as if a great sorrow had come upon the house.

"I was gone but a few days," Mattie said, wishing they could return to the rush of the busy morning before her departure.

But her voice echoed through the stillness of the house and Elizabeth finally said, "Oh, Mattie, what have you done? Your letter was more confusing than helpful."

"You must tell no one," Mattie confessed, realizing she couldn't continue the lie. Not to them. "But I got married. To Angus Cannon."

"The stake president who is under investigation for plural marriage?" Elizabeth asked. In response, Mattie burst into tears, for though the past few days had held joy, the pain in Papa's eyes was not worth any price. Getting married in secret had made sense at the time, but now it seemed cold and fabricated. For the first time she realized she no longer belonged in her parents' house, yet neither could she claim a home with her husband as long as he sought to elude prosecution.

"I'm sorry," she said again and again, wishing she could say anything to lift the worry from Papa's eyes or Mama's hunched shoulders.

"But *why*?" Mama asked, seeking through her daughter's words for the strands to connect, to weave together some sensible pattern out of the mess before her. "When the government pressure worsens daily?"

"Because I *love* him, Mama," Mattie said, letting her heart rest plain upon her face. "Because I love him, and he loves me."

Elizabeth's pain lessened then, a touch of hope returning to her eyes. Finally, they put their arms around her, allowed her to cry against their shoulders, as if a parent's hug could still set everything right.

"This is not an easy path you've chosen, daughter," James said, still holding her. "But if you truly love each other, it will come out all right in the end. I assume we'll meet your groom?" Mattie nodded, and over their daughter's bowed head, James exchanged an anguished glance with his wife.

Lotta chose the moment to casually announce, "Leolin was looking for you," and Mattie's heart dropped. *Dear Leolin. How had she forgotten?* She laughed bitterly through her tears, for she had long congratulated herself for being the sort of person who never allowed romance to carry reason away. Yet here she stood, with no right to chastise anyone again.

She sent Leolin a note of apology, of brief explanation with no details, and some weeks later he came to fetch his things from her office: the medical textbooks he had lent, the microscopes and other equipment, the medicines they had compounded together. As Mattie saw how difficult it was to extricate their combined belongings, she realized at last he had never planned to separate them.

How little she had understood—that much was plain, because the angles and corners of his face, hollow with suffering, struck her anew with the selfishness of what she had done—how she had allowed herself to enjoy their friendship, always teetering on romance, then betray their partnership with hardly a thought. He didn't know *who* she had married, but that scarcely mattered since it was not him. "Leolin, I am so sorry," she said, reaching for his arm. He drew back as if her touch would burn. "I—I—didn't mean to . . . I care—"

"Do you?" he asked, cutting her off, speaking as if from a great distance.

"Yes," she said, knowing it was true and also that it was not.

He gathered his ointments, instruments, and spare shreds of dignity, and bowed in a way that was more aloof than angry. "Good day, Martha." He turned to leave her office.

Tears coursed down her cheeks, and Mattie wondered if the emotions she felt might have anything to do with the strange sensations in her stomach, the churning every morning and sudden desire for crackers and tea. The thought intensified her sorrow, for if anything might make this situation more fraught and dangerous than it already was, it was *that*.

And, not for the first time, she realized the reactions of those she loved to the most important event of her life felt more like a funeral had taken place than a wedding.

Make as little as possible of superficial appearances and changes.
—MARTHA HUGHES CANNON

Chapter Thirty-One

MAY 1885

Barb's letter lay heavy in Mattie's swiftly diminishing lap, filled with gossip and the challenges of her career, the thrill of a wedding, and an invitation to visit. Writing by faintest candlelight, Mattie sought for words to answer her friend.

Dear Barb,

The City of the Saints is more like the City of Desolation now a-days as the persecution that is going on against the poly-gamists is almost unendurable. The U.S. is determined to put down polygamy . . . I am having no peace, because I am considered a leading Mormon Woman.

Mattie studied the corner of the desk. How would her friend react if she knew the truth? Truth. Truth couldn't be trusted to a letter that might be intercepted anyway.

Barb, you will hurt yourself laughing when I relate to you some of my experiences. They have had me married to one of the Mormon Leaders, and arraigned me before the Grand Jury to

*answer to the charge of being an associate in polygamy—of course
I was acquitted.*

Yet another lie, this one to her dearest friend. Why not confess the truth? That she had narrowly avoided appearing in court,
hiding her pregnant bulk beneath layers of petticoats, swearing she
had never married a man she *had* married. Why didn't she tell her
friend the truth? Partly because the risk was too great and partly
because she feared Barb would not accept this abrupt evolution. But
she needed to speak of it, even if only in half-truths and lies. How
she longed to sit down with that dear soul and confess everything,
longed to know her as she once had, in a lifetime so different from
the one before her.

She longed to tell Barb she'd been forced to resign her post at the
hospital after an agent served a warrant there. How she had slipped
out the back door, abandoning, in the turn of an hour, her patients,
the work she loved, and her plans for a nursing school. She wanted
to confess how much she missed the smell of the surgical wards, the
feel of a scalpel in her hands.

A knock at the front door below came harsh and sharp, seeking entry at all costs. Mattie dropped Barb's letter, dread spreading
through her hands as she blew out the candle.

They had a plan, she forced herself to remember. Creeping silently on stocking feet, she crossed the room and breathed her ever-
increasing belly inside the false door James had fashioned in the old
armoire, heard Elizabeth below moving slowly in the direction of the
knocking, which grew louder and more insistent.

"Open up!" demanded a voice outside.

Through the muffled angles of wood, Mattie could hear
Elizabeth's voice, calm and steady in spite of the terror that must be
mounting behind her façade. "No sir, there is no one named Martha
Hughes Paul at this home. Yes, she is our daughter. The family is at
dinner at the moment."

Heavy footsteps sounded across the floorboards of the kitchen—James's voice also now, denying his daughter's presence. A moment of hesitation stretched where Mattie guessed the federal marshal weighed the option of searching the house. In town, agents often disguised themselves as peddlers or census takers to gain information, but this officer was playing no games. "You will guarantee you do not know where your daughter is?" the voice demanded.

Soft murmurs of ascent, pacifying him, reassuring him they had no idea where their daughter may have run off to, while upstairs Mattie struggled to control her frantic breathing by pressing her mouth against the coarse fabric of a blanket. So many lies, tangled into each other, and now from her parents, whose words had never held anything but truth.

"I will leave this with you in case you happen to see her," the marshal said. Angry footsteps retreated the same way they had come.

Moments passed with only the sound of Mattie's jagged breathing against the woolen fabric. She placed one hand to her swollen stomach. *What kind of life awaited this child?*

Quiet steps into the darkened room. "Mattie?" Elizabeth whispered. She carried no light.

Mattie eased open the false door of the wardrobe. "Are they gone?" Her voice shook with the weight of long days of hiding, long hours of unreprieved darkness. She tumbled into her mother's arms that reached around her bulk.

"They're gone," Elizabeth said, circling her daughter, who seemed at age thirty to need her more than she had when she'd been little.

The words should have been reassuring, but Mattie knew there was more. "What is it?"

Elizabeth pulled her closer, as if she would use her shoulders to shelter her daughter from the world outside. "He left a warrant for your arrest—the court has summoned you to testify. And—" She hesitated. "They've captured Angus."

A cry burst from Mattie. She'd seen him a handful of times since their wedding. How she longed for him, her husband. And now, he was in custody. In all likelihood, bound for prison like other Church leaders, sent off with parties from their congregations, as if they were leaving for a mission, rather than for months at the state penitentiary. "If they have Angus, isn't that enough? Why are they seeking me, if they have three other wives to testify against him?"

Elizabeth ran her hand back and forth across her daughter's back. "You're far more valuable to them," she whispered. "Rumors fly he's married a rather famous doctress who would be able to testify about women she's delivered and the polygamous fathers that stood at their side."

Mattie struggled to hold back the choking sobs starting inside her chest. "What should I do?" She wished she were a girl asking for advice about her hair or dress, though in truth, she tried to remember if she'd ever sought her mother's advice with the urgency she felt at this moment.

Thin arms held her fiercely. "For now, eat some supper and get some sleep. We will find a place for you to have that baby." Mattie's heart swelled toward her mother, who was too kind in this moment to say what she must be thinking, *If only you'd asked me, I could have told you so.*

After supper, carrying no light, Lotta ran to the neighbor with a note, returning a short time later with an address scrawled on a scrap of paper. James readied the wagon and helped Mattie pack the wooden trunk he had built for her never dreaming it would be needed for its present purpose.

Wrapping Mattie in blankets, James and Elizabeth smuggled her to the wagon, where they tucked blankets around her, sheltering her from rough wooden planks. Heaping hay around and on top of her obscured figure, James jolted the wagon forward, leaving Lotta and Joseph behind.

This must be what a corpse feels like being taken to the cemetery, Mattie thought as they rumbled over the road, rattled by every bump and pothole. She wondered if they would pass the Deseret Hospital, where Romania Pratt had taken over her vacated position, a discomfort as galling as the boards grinding into her shoulders.

Elizabeth kept a lookout at each crossroad as James hurried the horses into the night. Each rider on the road could be a federal marshal looking for "cohabs," each horse might carry an unsympathetic neighbor to report their passage.

After hours of journeying, they reached the flat wilderness surrounding the Great Salt Lake, and Elizabeth pulled her daughter from the wagon bed so she could relieve her cramping muscles and remember what it meant to breathe freely.

By the light of a pale moon, Mattie watched foam skim across the surface of the lake, coming to rest against salt-crusted rocks, draped like a bridal veil, jagged and torn. Culled from the water and turned silver by the alchemy of a waxing moon, the glittering gravel evoked, for Elizabeth, another moonlit night scented with fear.

All too soon, Mattie settled back to that strait coffin for the final jolting hours to Grantsville. There, on a wind-tumbled ranch of sagebrush and cattle, James helped his daughter and wife settle into a bedroom at the back of the Woolley house—built on land remote enough to shelter one more refugee on the Mormon underground.

At long last, Mattie eased onto the mattress, so exhausted from the journey and the child growing within her, she could sleep anywhere. She held tight to her mother, craving Elizabeth's presence in a way she had never needed her before.

Living bodies differ from non-living bodies by producing life.
—MARTHA HUGHES CANNON

Chapter Thirty-Two

SEPTEMBER 1885
Grantsville, Utah Territory

Rachel Woolley, the envelope read, but Mattie recognized the handwriting as Elizabeth's. She sliced the seal, sliding out a piece of paper with one line written across the top:

Rachel, much love to you. Emma

Anyone who intercepted the note would find its contents puzzlingly brief, but Mattie carried it inside, hefting her bulk over the threshold.

She stoked the dying embers of the breakfast fire, reviving them with a gentle blow, and holding the letter close to the low flame until lines and dashes began to appear, called to life by the heat like the writing on the wall at Belshazzar's feast, while she, like Daniel, waited to interpret.

Lines that had been written in milk turned brown before the heat and began to arrange themselves into letters:

We've seen no agents near the house.

Mattie exhaled with relief.

We believe it is safe to come for the gathering. Unless we are followed, we will be there Thursday night.

Joy at this prospect.

Much love to you and our new little one.
　　　　—Mother

Thursday afternoon, Rachel Woolley, who had sheltered Mattie these months, shooed her children out the door with her husband and began stoking the fire to heat pots of water to fill the copper tub set in the middle of the kitchen.

Mattie helped with the preparations for the ceremony she had seen done many times, but never for herself. She recalled her first confinement ritual, shortly before Lotta's birth, and her own alarm at seeing her mother's body swollen and distended.

She had helped with the celebrations for expectant mothers at Deseret Hospital as well, and as Mattie watched the steam rising from the bathwater, she drew strength knowing that her baby would not be deprived of this. True, there would be fewer women than usual, but when the beloved women of her family arrived, nothing else mattered.

"There you are!" Mary embraced her, as Lotta squealed with joy at seeing her so large. Elizabeth just wrapped her arms around her, holding her for a moment in silence.

The tub stood ready, steam rising in curls from the surface, and Mattie stepped from the bedroom wrapped in a towel. With love and great care, the circle of women eased her gently into the fragrant water. Light from a dying fire left the room in shifting shapes of shadows, and the constant pull of pregnancy eased for a moment, as Mattie sighed at the comfort of floating in a dimly lit primordial sea, surrounded by faces she dearly loved.

They laid their hands upon her then, sponging her clean, washing grime and dust from her body. Together these women, her sisters, surrounded her, anointing her with consecrated oil, blessing each part they touched one by one: "We anoint your back, your spinal column that you might be strong and healthy," Elizabeth said, her voice full of love.

They continued onward across her body, touching and blessing as they went. Mary spoke next: "We bless your hips that your system might relax and give way for the birth of your child." Mattie could hear the faith in her sister's voice.

"Your breasts that your milk may come freely," said Elizabeth.

Having petitioned for her body, the women laid their hands upon Mattie's swollen belly, blessing her unborn child, supplicating God that the child might be "perfect in every joint and limb and muscle."

Lotta's voice chimed in and Mattie reminded herself that her sister was no longer a child, but a woman ready to take her place in this gathering. "We bless you that when its full time shall have come, that your child shall present right for birth."

Once more, the women circled her, placing their hands, full of power, upon her head. Elizabeth's voice sang through the darkened room, carrying the joy of blessing her own baby's baby: "As we unitedly lay our hands upon you to seal this washing and anointing for your safe delivery, we ask God to let His blessings rest upon you, that the good Spirit might guard and protect you and your child." Slowly she drew the ceremony to a close. "In the name of Jesus Christ, amen."

"Amen," Mattie said, as they helped her from the tub and plied her with towels. When she was dressed once more, they celebrated together, eating cakes and pies that Rachel had prepared for days. Mary bequeathed simple booties cut from linen, while Lotta urged Mattie to unwrap a tiny bonnet she had crocheted and a smocked cotton baby gown held together by her mother's perfect, even stitches.

Lying in bed that night, after her mother and sisters had departed for home, Mattie could still feel those circling hands resting upon her head, could still hear their voices pronouncing benediction upon herself and her unborn child. She sighed into sleep, knowing that although Angus might be miles away locked up in prison, with the women's words around them, her baby would not enter this world alone.

Contractions began two days later. Spasms of pain radiated through her uterus and around toward her back, as Mattie watched the process, feeling both oddly outside and within it. She had studied the process copiously, had attended hundreds of births, knew the procedure intellectually from start to finish, and could picture each contraction of the lateral wall as it shrunk in preparation to expel the child. Remembering uteri she had examined in dissecting rooms, she could imagine the very texture of the organ sheltering her child. As she felt her cervix soften, she understood that as the infant descended, the bones of its skull would compress to ease its way through the vaginal canal.

Rationally, she knew she must stay calm, must breathe through each contraction, squatting upon the bed to bring the child into proper position. She knew biting down upon a wet towel or pulling against a sheet tied to the bedpost might ease the pain, and she breathed and pulled as she rode out each wave that surged beneath her.

She knew all of these things, and yet found that watching the process from without was not the same as experiencing waves of pain radiating through the core of her being. Knowing anatomy was not the same as rising to meet this endurance race with every ounce of strength, or doubting—as the birth pains grew closer together and more intense—her own ability to surmount this mountain. The face of Rachel Woolley, who had brought four children into this world, hovered by her side, murmuring encouragement, moving from boiling water and back to the bedside, carrying strength and a reminder of a world outside this pain.

Tearing at the sheets, Mattie craved the reassurance of her mother and the calm, even voice of Angus—both miles away. While she sought to logically reassure herself, the lightning rod of pain splitting her insides apart cast her into a headlong spiral, banishing all rational thought. Spinning through a dark and rocky wilderness, she focused on the face of Rachel Woolley, clinging to her grasp, and screaming into that void, shocked and humbled that millions of women before her had also traveled, barefoot, this desolate and winding road.

The urge to bear down grew irresistible now. She grunted and pushed with all her might, felt a mighty stone within her body descend downward, centimeter by blessed centimeter. "The head is out!" Rachel reassured, as Mattie cried out in relief. "You are doing beautifully. Slowly now. Just a bit more."

Mattie summoned strength she did not know she had and bore down again, feeling a tremendous weight slip free, as a waxen wet thing, all flailing limbs, emerged from her body and into Rachel's waiting hands. A thin, fragile cry, insulted and floundering, broke the stillness of the house, and Rachel laid the child, still connected to her mother's body by a pulsing chord, upon Mattie's bare chest, covering them both in a soft quilt.

Joy coursed through her body, euphoria and exhilaration, as Mattie pushed the quilt aside and examined each perfect fingernail, each exquisite eyelash plastered with vernix. "It's a girl," she announced, sobbing with waves of emotion that crashed against the beach of her heart, swollen with a growth as dramatic as her belly had undergone these past many months. In awe, she examined each centimeter of this little being with whom she had first become acquainted from the other side of her own skin.

Rachel's eyes mirrored the awe of Mattie's face, the circle of motherhood closing to completeness, as Mattie choked with joy at the feel of her littlest one, flailing in her arms. Her exhausted, fumbling hands guided lips toward her breast, where they nuzzled into her, seeking sustenance with an instinct neither taught nor learned.

Sometime later, Mattie fell into spent slumber. Days and nights began to blur into one as she slept only when the baby did, awakened only at the alert of her cry. The sun on its orbital passage scarce mattered now—all that mattered was the soft rise and fall of a tiny chest beside her, life compressing to the rhythm of her daughter's sleep, and she rose only to relieve herself and eat more than she'd ever consumed before.

Floating in and out of consciousness, Mattie dreamed she felt Angus's hands upon her, believed for a moment she heard his voice in her ear. Struggling upward through layers of consciousness, she found his image floating before her, a mirage no doubt, one she wished she could hold onto. Reaching for it, she cried out when her fingers touched upon flesh, as his arms circled round her, solid and real. "Is it you?" she demanded of this phantom.

"My brave and precious girl, it is I."

"But—you're in prison," she said, sifting through dream and reality. "I thought your sentence was extended—"

"It was. It was. But they let me out," he said, holding her as if he would never let her go. "And of course I came right here to you, my love. To you and to our child."

Joy coursed through her at his presence, at the reality of his hands, the smell and sight of him. She had forgotten, so nearly forgotten what it felt like to be at his side, his smallest gestures familiar and dear. She leaned toward the cradle and scooped up their baby. "Meet our daughter," she said, placing the squirming bundle, indignant at being disturbed, into his hands.

Angus knew what to do with a baby, for he was not a first-time father after all. Settling the child into the crook of his arm, he examined the creature with a joy like Mattie's own. "Hello, then," he said to the baby. "I'm very sorry not to have made your acquaintance sooner." The infant swatted at his fingers with her tight little fist. "She has a firm handshake, just like her mother," Angus observed. "Do you know what you will call her, my dear?"

Mattie had spent hours considering this question, wondering what Angus would say if he were here, had planned to write to him, but this moment was ever so much better. "If you also agree, I'd thought to call her Elizabeth. Elizabeth Rachel, for two of the bravest women I know."

Angus's eyes shone. Addressing the baby again he said, "Well then, Elizabeth Rachel Cannon, it is mighty fine to meet you at last."

Molecules of gasses have great mobility.
—MARTHA HUGHES CANNON

Chapter Thirty-Three

Three days. Three precious days were all Angus could spare and then, once more, he was off. Needed for business demands, for pressing Church matters, for three other wives and a dozen other children. He bid Mattie goodbye with a lingering kiss, holding their babe as a precious treasure he was loath to part with. Mattie watched his carriage pass down the road in the direction of Salt Lake wondering if she would ever have a right to claim him as her husband openly before the world. He believed they would—believed laws would change, that the government would relent and allow them to practice their religion unmolested. For if not, why had the Saints been driven from their homes time and again to settle in this valley, miles away from the lands of their birth, directed, he believed, by a prophet of God to practice this celestial order of marriage—*why*, if not to know all would come out right in the end.

Mattie tried to also believe, to trust him and other leaders, to hope that God was in it and eventually she would be able to publicly claim the man she loved. She was proud of him—proud of their family—and grew heartily sick of hiding in corners and slinking in shadows, as if she had reason to be ashamed of all she held dear.

And if things didn't change? They had touched on other options. Options Mattie hoped would never become necessary.

A handful of weeks had passed since Angus's departure when Mattie bundled up little Lizzie, as she'd begun calling her, to take her outside to enjoy a rare moment of waning sunshine. She carried her daughter toward town, pausing as children scampered after each other, piling up leaves and jumping into them with abandon, shrieking as they ran in circles through the falling autumn flowers, crimson, yellow, rose.

Thinking of a day when Lizzie could run after them, she whispered, "I will keep you safe," to the precious bundle in her arms, and began singing a song she could not remember learning, though she could not manage the Welsh as her mother could: "Lovely darling, I will guard you. I will hold you, close enfold you, sleep upon your mother's breast."

Basking in the sunshine, Mattie continued down the simple dirt street, past mothers calling their children, past farmers in the fields, harvesting the last of the autumn crops. She turned onto the main street, wondering why it lay oddly quiet. A lonely sign swung on its rusted hinges in a whisper of a breeze.

Wondering where everyone might be, Mattie stopped, gaze fixed in fear, panic mounting. The final homestead before town center belonged to the Judd family, and a clothesline bordered the side of their yard. Persis Judd had strung up her morning wash, all whites, clipped neatly at the edges with wooden pins. Crisp linens and dish towels, sheets and cheesecloths flapped in the wind like ghostly specters darting this way and that.

In the middle of the line, between petticoats and pantalets, fluttered a red bandana, unmistakably out of place. It was no accident. It was a warning.

Instinctively, Mattie pulled Lizzie closer, sheltering the babe against her shoulder. Turning on her heel, she scanned the wide streets for anyone who might be watching from a shadowed corner. The only sound came from children still at play, and the snap and flap of laundry tumbled by the wind. But who could know who might be lurking in the edges of a doorway, marking her movements? She tugged her shawl to cover her hair and turned for home.

Rachel hovered on the other side of the doorway, frantically haunting the hallway. "A warning," Mattie said in a rushed whisper. "At the Judds." She closed the door tightly behind them.

"I tried to go after you," Rachel said, choking on relief. "But I didn't want to draw attention. I had a message just after you stepped out." Rachel pressed her littlest boy, Andrew, against the shelter of her skirts. "Federal marshals have been spotted in town asking questions. They've put a bounty on your head, Mattie. Two hundred dollars in exchange for information leading to your arrest."

Mattie sagged into a chair. "But why?" she beseeched the heavens. "Angus already served one prison sentence."

Rachel nodded. "For his third marriage, right? But if they can prove he married you, they can put him back in prison. I imagine they also want to know about the polygamous mothers you've delivered."

Mattie bowed herself low over Lizzie, longing to shelter her daughter from this hailstorm of worry. "Wherever else can we go?" she sobbed, feeling the weight of her husband's freedom descend upon her shoulders.

"I know a safe house in Centerville," Rachel said, "though it will be a long, cold journey by wagon to get there. Are you feeling up to it?"

Mattie nodded. "I think we have to be."

Passengers thronged the Centerville station as a locomotive slowed and approached the platform, gears grinding. Drawing a lace veil low across her face, Mattie threaded her way through the holiday crowd, trying to maneuver her skirts above the slick and sooty walkways, holding Elizabeth with one hand and managing a small reticule in the other. A porter hefted her trunk, wending his way between men in derby hats and women in bonnets, maneuvering packages and bundles, much like the day she had arrived home from medical school. And yet, so very different. She sought to shake the memory of a miserable journey to Centerville in the bed of a sheep wagon, covered in straw, the terror of lifting Lizzie near the end and finding her blue with cold and barely breathing.

Yet Centerville had not proven as safe as Rachel had believed. Unbelievably, agents had been spotted in town, still tracking her, drawing ever closer on her trail.

"Number 62 to Ogden will depart in ten minutes!" a conductor in uniform barked from the bottom step of the locomotive. Ten minutes. Silently, Mattie prayed she would not be recognized before she could manage to get onboard.

"You can place the trunk here," Mattie directed the porter, indicating the assembly line where he dropped her trunk and waited for a coin. As she rummaged through her reticule, Lizzie puckered her lips in frustration at the strange noises of the station. Making a calming noise for the child, Mattie tried to distract herself from the fear mounting behind her chest. *Eight minutes now. They needed to get out of Centerville.*

A shrill whistle rang from the other side of the platform, and a man in uniform, standing near the conductor, pointed in her direction. Terror gripped Mattie's throat as another man, clearly working with the first, started toward her. "Excuse me, ma'am!" he called across the sea of passengers.

She did not wait to see if they were confusing her for someone else. Heart racing, Mattie pressed her baby against her shoulder and ducked into the crowd, for once blessing her short stature, as she hid behind businessmen engrossed in conversation. *Her trunk.* There was nothing to do but leave it.

A whistle sheared the air. *"Stop!"* came the voice, harsh and insistent.

Lizzie cried out, complaining at her mother's sudden motion. "Shhh," Mattie soothed her fiercely, wishing she could likewise calm her own speeding heart.

Bless the crowd, larger for the holidays, and the low fog wreathing its way through the station. Darting from one group to another, she paused only long enough to spy the next patch of shelter. "Excuse me," she said, pushing her way past faces both sympathetic and suspicious. Given the uproar over polygamy, a fleeing woman with a baby offered no great mystery for the crowd to unravel.

Mattie's heart pounded at the unexpected exercise, and her lungs burned as she raced toward a cluster of conveyances for hire. Flying to the far side of an open carriage, she put its black bulk between herself and the pursuing officer.

"In a hurry, ma'am?" the driver said, awaking.

"Yes," she cried, barely able to speak the word as she thrust open the carriage door. "I need you to hide us." He comprehended at last, turning the latch behind her and moving away, pretending not to listen to her instructions at the cracked window.

Slinking to the floor of the carriage she hissed, "Take us to the next station north. Stop for no one. There's extra fare if you get us out safely."

He was a good actor. As she hushed Lizzie from the floor of the carriage, he returned to the driver's seat and lit up a cigarette, puffing intently. Her pursuer rushed past the carriage, never glancing inside, still scanning the road ahead for her fleeing form.

The driver lazily picked up the reins and turned his rig into the street, whistling a shanty as he moved out of the station. Mattie collapsed against the seat, gasping for breath, and did her best to hush an indignant baby.

Five minutes. Five minutes until the train departed from the Farmington station. Mattie kept her veil drawn close about her face and counted the agonizing minutes before the locomotive drew them away.

They changed trains in Ogden and chugged their way toward Evanston and the territory border. Miles churned beneath them, every passing minute putting space between herself and those who sought her. She unfastened her shirtwaist to feed a very hungry Lizzie, as images she had seen on her way home from medical school scrolled past the window like a magic lantern turned in reverse.

With Lizzie settled for a nap, Mattie pulled out paper and ink:

> *My love, we have made it out of Utah. We were nearly apprehended at the station and in the terrifying scramble, my trunk was lost. Can you see if my parents can reclaim it? I can replace the items inside easily enough in New York, but not the trunk Papa made with his own hands.*
>
> *Babe and I are fine after the fright, though both in need of sleep. Going abroad seems to be the best way to avoid arrest for us both. I could not live with myself if you were returned to prison on my account. Though I fear an ocean crossing with our little one, I wish to put as much of the wide world between us until the warrant for my arrest expires or until the laws become more favorable.*
>
> *As we discussed when you were with me, I may go in search of my family's land—England or Wales, perhaps—I know not where exactly, but will write to Mother for the information. I have had quite enough of hiding and scrounging. I would rather be an exile in a strange land than ashamed to show my face in public at home. You can send mail ahead to New York, where it should reach me before we sail. L— and I bring you in our hearts.*

She paused and considered how best to sign it. Surely not with her own given name. Her middle name was Maria, and Angus's was Munn. The combination together felt like two halves of themselves placed side by side, when they could not be, and she knew he would understand their meaning.

Yours forever, Maria Munn

Matter is something that offers resistance to
other matter, the space occupied by itself.
—MARTHA HUGHES CANNON

Chapter Thirty-Four

APRIL 1886
New York City

Shock and anger coursed through Mattie's body, leaving her scarcely able to stand, let alone read the words that swam before her. She sat down hard upon the nearest stone wall near the wharf, a broad retainer set against the perils of the sea. Ships creaked and sighed in their berths and soon, very soon, she and Lizzie would be upon them, their world shrunk to the size and space of a narrow wooden cabin and walkway. Lizzie, in her perambulator, sucked on the frilled edge of her blanket, oblivious to her mother's distress.

Mattie spread the letter from Angus on a rock, flattening it before her, trying to focus and read it again. *Surely she had misunderstood.* Letters swam before her eyes and she tried to make them behave, to line themselves up in sensible arrangements upon the page, but she was too upset. In a haze of anger, she looked back to the wharf, to the ship that waited to take them across the ocean, the scent of salt and brine sharp in her nose.

Forcing herself back to his words scrawled some weeks ago upon this bit of parchment, she assembled them one at a time, as she'd done long ago when laying type:

M a r r i e d

She swallowed past a strangling sensation in her throat.

> *Please forgive me, my love. I know this is sudden and I hope the surprise will not be too unpleasant. I have married again. A woman you may know. Maria Bennion. She is near your age. Her father asked me to marry her, and it seemed right to me to do so. Please know no one else could ever dampen my affection for you. I wish you and our little one safe passage across the sea, and remain your devoted husband always.*
> *Angus*

Thoughts rushed through her mind—none of them generous. She had met Maria, and Mattie tried to bring her into focus. An ox of a girl, as she remembered. Built to survive frontier life and bear a dozen children. *Married? Again?* So she wasn't to be the last. Or the youngest. She had hoped—oh, it had been a silly romantic notion. But she had hoped he would never want to marry again now that they had found each other—that together they would be enough— that *she* would be enough.

Of course, romance was not the only reason to marry, particularly for a man like Angus, there might be any number of reasons for him to take another wife. But he had just gotten out of prison and she had fled only to protect him—had brought her whole career to a halt—and now he'd married again, placing himself in jeopardy despite her exile. Even while she'd labored with Elizabeth, he had courted another, kissed another. She pushed the wrenching image from her mind.

A sea breeze whipped the water to a dancing froth, blowing sea scum laced with grime into putrid foam along the shore. She had been born beside the sea's mighty power, and beneath a rocky headland she had taken her first steps, though she had no memory of it. It was different from what she'd imagined. Seagulls combed over flotsam and jetsam, shattered bits of driftwood and bits of broken crates—things discarded, picked over and shattered—she felt kinship with them all. Lizzie began to fuss and Mattie hurried to comfort her, this darling creature who had met her father exactly once.

Knowing she would regret it, but unable to restrain herself, the next day Mattie dashed off a furious, ranting reply and sent it toward the Rocky Mountains.

How dare you? How could you? I thought we had agreed?

Bearing documents for Maria Munn (a name now turned loathsome in her mouth), she calmed Lizzie in a cramped berth aboard the ship that would serve as home for more than a month.

Breezes from the wide Atlantic caught up the sails, filling them to a crisp bulge as the vessel navigated its way through New York harbor, heading toward the gray, shifting surges of open ocean. Her stomach complained at the waves pulling all directions, and Lizzie seemed just as disoriented.

"Throw a penny over the ship's bow when you're going out of dock," Elizabeth had written, but Mattie ignored the Welsh superstition, feeling she needed more help than pennies could provide as she remembered legends of drowned souls racing white horses over the breakers.

Her mother had once made this crossing, with a sick husband and three small girls in tow. Now the clock turned in reverse, and she herself sailed past years and decades as the ship ploughed onward, cutting its way through the swath of ocean.

Passing below the Statue of Liberty, hampered by scaffolding, Mattie turned her face toward the shining copper sculpture. It would corrode over time, the metal oxidizing in the presence of salt air—the Roman goddess of freedom with her arm raised, holding a torch aloft, would turn from copper to black and someday, green. *Libertas.* Completed with help from Emma Lazarus's poem: "Give me your tired, your poor, your huddled masses yearning to breathe free . . . Send these, the homeless, tempest-tost to me."

Holding Lizzie close, Mattie recited the lines with a grim twist to her mouth. The last months beneath this banner, she'd felt anything but free. Now as she left Angus behind with a new wife to hold, left also the fragments of her career, she wondered if somewhere on the other side of this broad expanse, she too could hold up her head above the discarded links of shackles littering her feet.

Part Four

Sometimes in wounds, H_2O is the best remedy that can be given.
—MARTHA HUGHES CANNON

Chapter Thirty-Five

APRIL 1886
Birmingham, England

A great and mighty wind carried Mattie's ship across the heaving Atlantic, where it washed ashore in Liverpool, then turned her upstream to Birmingham. In that great city of industrialization, factories breathed in lumber from the forests and coughed out a gloomy cloud of sludge along with buttons, cutlery, nails, locks, and ornaments. To produce the world's first steam engine, cotton mill, and a flaccid substance known as plastic, Birmingham's blazing fires rained ash upon the streets while its clanging smithies evoked the clinking of hell.

Drawn by the promise of work in factories and forges, people sought refuge in shanties and row houses when each shift drew to a close. Upon rising, they tossed the contents of chamber pots into rivulets of sludge skirting the edges of the street. Clean water could be had in Birmingham for the wealthy alone, but clean air could not be had for any price.

Careening through the street, a madhouse of conveyances

transported coal and barrels of oil, past street urchins who haunted the back alleyways. Picking her way through the sodden mess, Lizzie in her arms, Mattie sought for a foothold free from refuse, her skirts already filthy. Lizzie had fallen ill on the ocean crossing, and her cough lingered on, needing relief from cramped spaces and endless rocking, though this filthy, clanging city seemed an unlikely reprieve. Imagining smallpox and typhoid breeding happily in the vile soup lacing the streets, Mattie lifted her poor, miserable Lizzie higher, wondering how this filthy, smoky hell could possibly be the England she had always dreamt of seeing. Her mother had urged her to visit distant relatives, writing introductions on behalf of her daughter, Maria Munn, a name Mattie hoped to discard as soon as possible.

She stopped before a cramped row house, no cleaner than the rest, propping up a tired and sagging roof. *Surely, this couldn't be what Mother intended.* Rapping on the door, she half hoped she'd copied the strange address incorrectly: 61½ Great Brook Street.

Fanny Evans parted her hatchway just a crack, partly because she never knew what kind of riffraff might wash down the street with the latest blowabout, and partly because she didn't want any of her brats to escape into the mess and her with nothing to do but run after them.

"Ee-yar! Elizabeth's bab and babby? Maria, innit? Ain't you got a face as long as Livery Street, en?" Mattie had grown up around English accents, but she watched Fanny's weathered mouth with fascination, trying to understand how the language spilling from this woman's lips could also be her own. "Come in! Come in!" Fanny beckoned, hurrying her inside, stopping to rap a child on the head. She prattled on, and Mattie tried her best to decipher, saying "yes" whenever Fanny paused for a response.

Lizzie clung to Mattie's sodden cloak, alarmed by the numerous urchins with tangled hair surrounding her, making it impossible for

Mattie to extract herself from either cloak or baby. Fanny's three-year-old, Charlie, ran close, mucus running down his face, and poked Lizzie until she cried. "Deff off your mithering," Fanny ordered the boy, but he paid her no mind.

Drenched, filthy, and exhausted, Mattie sat down, where at least a fire waited. Fanny set a "cob" before her, which turned out to be a round roll, not too dry, with tea served in a cracked cup hastily wiped with a dishrag.

The corners of the house gathered cobwebs and cozy piles of dust. Had Mattie been home, she would have felt only compassion for Fanny's attempt to keep house with soot coming in at every corner and so many mouths to feed. But as she wiped Lizzie's running nose and tried to comfort the coughing baby, she wondered how to comfort a sick child while surrounded by so much chaos.

"It's your first time in West Midlands, bab? A bit black over Bill's mother's, innit?" Fanny's voice rolled up and down, each line ending on a high note, like every sentence held a question.

Mattie nodded. "It most certainly is a bit black." It couldn't yet be five o'clock, but darkness had fallen fast and thick upon the sooty city, and Fanny placed a bowl of boiled bacon fat and cabbage in front of her. Mattie's stomach turned over at the smell. "Thank you," she managed, thinking gratefully of the bit of cheese and hard crackers stashed in her bag. "I'm not hungry."

Smelling food, Lizzie began to fuss, so Mattie did her best to cover herself with a blanket and feed her, though the baby continually batted the covering aside, distracted by the bedlam. Fanny's husband Thomas arrived home at that moment, and the children rushed to greet him. Hefting one urchin in each arm, he called, "Ow bin ya?" to Mattie.

"Hello," Mattie said, as he settled the children on the bench and lay into the bowl she had declined to touch.

"So yer travel wiffout yer husbind?" Thomas asked, curiously, paying no mind to Lizzie's commotion beneath the blanket. Fanny glanced over, just as interested as Thomas.

"Yes," Mattie said, trying to remember Maria's backstory. "Unfortunately, my husband is kept at home with business."

After an awkward pause, Thomas said, "Ar," a response that made sense to Fanny. Charlie pinched his sister who began to pout, and the parents turned their attention back to the table. "Put yer fizzog straight," Thomas ordered.

Mattie wrestled a miserable Lizzie and tried to keep her own eyelids from drooping. "Imagine you must be cream crackered, the bof of you," Fanny said, rising. Followed her gratefully up a tight staircase, Mattie realized this family had even less space than her parents did, and her arrival must have turned several of the children out of their beds for the night.

"Thank you so much," she said. "Goodnight."

"Ta-ra a bit," came Fanny's mystifying response.

Lizzie fussed and coughed before falling into an exhausted sleep, and Mattie, Maria—whoever she was—turned her face into her pillow and tried to recall if she had ever felt so utterly and completely alone.

Change in the living body is from a stable to a less stable matter.
—MARTHA HUGHES CANNON

Chapter Thirty-Six

Each day in Fanny's house felt like a month of bedlam. Of incessant soot prying round the windows, of rain descending down the chimney to hiss in the fire. Of over-boiled cabbage and kidney pie. Of a language less familiar than the food. Every time Charlie came within pinching distance of Lizzie, she began to scream. And Lizzie's cough turned worse rather than better, small surprise given the foul air and the strange noises that awakened her.

Fanny, for all her kindness, didn't mind swearing up and down at her children, or smacking them upside the head when she felt they had it coming. When Lizzie panicked at the sight of Charlie, Fanny patted her on the head, a tad too roughly. "All that ails the little wench is she needs a bit of hardening." Mattie swallowed and tried to ignore the comment, just as she ignored the sly sips at the liquor bottle Fanny took throughout the day, recognizing this woman's life doubtless required a stiff, bracing substance of one kind or another.

Days blurred together, and Mattie found herself living for letters addressed to Maria Munn carrying chatty news from Mary, declarations of love from Angus, and notes from her mother, though they were weeks old by the time they reached her hands. The familiarity of Elizabeth's letters, the thought of those warm hands setting down words in swirls of ink, folding the paper in even, well-creased lines, made Mattie's breath catch in her throat. There was no greater symbol of home than those two beloved hands. *You were very small when you left Llandudno, but it is a lovely spot of earth,* Elizabeth wrote. Though Mattie had planned to visit Wales, now that she was here, it seemed too difficult to take Lizzie down the street, much less make her way to another country.

While letters alleviated her loneliness, they also heightened Mattie's drifting purposelessness. Her family's lives were busy with responsibilities and projects, just as hers had always been. For the first time in her life, she lacked a goal requiring all her effort. Now she floated, frozen in time, caring for her daughter, yes, but beyond this, only waiting. Waiting for laws to change. Waiting for a warrant to expire. Waiting for a time when she could return to a community that did not watch her with suspicion. Waiting.

Some weeks after her arrival, Fanny handed over a letter written in Angus's hand with distinct crumples about the seal. Carrying the thin treasure upstairs, Mattie waited for Lizzie's breath to settle into the long, slow pattern of sleep before she lit a sputtering candle on the desk and spread the letter before her.

"My own dearest love," it began. *Oh, but was she?*

The humility of his next words took her aback, and she could hear his voice speaking through the words upon the page:

> *When I have done my best, if I feel anything, it is the thought that rises within me of my weakness and inability to do all that I feel I ought to do for you. I fear I have inadvertently hurt you with my recent marriage—please write and tell me how I can better be all you need from me.*
>
> *Then again, I only wonder, my dear girl, that you have held out as well as you have. You have done above and beyond what I could have expected anyone to do under the circumstances in which you have been placed. I am ready to go through anything*

to promote the life of our child and your happiness as well as all others that God has given me.

Breath caught in her throat at the sweet sincerity of his words. Almost he seemed to realize how difficult it would be to travel with a small babe in tow, hiding under another name. Her heart eased up a bit. *All others.* She did not like to think about those others, and yet, polygamy was, in fact, what she had signed up for. She wondered how his previous wives had felt at learning Angus had married *her*— it was not the pleasantest of thoughts.

I imagine your money must be growing short and I enclose a check and ask you to inform me of what you need. Do you see any opportunity to practice medicine while you are abroad?

Oh, how she would love to, though she had not the slightest idea of how she might go about it.

I have wondered what you might think if I joined you overseas and stayed a month with you? I have been tempted to ask permission—although there is no one in sight to take charge.

Mattie's heart beat faster at the thought of Angus all to herself, free to travel openly as husband and wife in the great broad daylight. No one to share him with. No demands of church and work—only her own husband. Her own.

If it is not proper that I join you, I am willing for you to do anything most agreeable to you. I trust, notwithstanding all looks dark and somber, that God will yet overrule all things for His glory and our joy on this earth and we will yet be able to live openly as husband and wife. If ever mortal man poured out his soul to God that he might be worthy of you, and make you happy, it is your humble lover.
I am as ever and forever yours.
          Munn

It was the last line that tossed her over the edge. Yes, he had married another. Yes, she had assumed she would be the final one. And hoped. In this area, he had certainly failed to understand her expectations, adept as he may be in other arenas.

Before she could change her mind, she took out a little wooden writing box which held paper, extra nibs, and bottles of ink.

My own loved one,

Have reached our destination at last. Can't say that I am particularly pleased. I am thankful to meet my relatives, but it distresses me to see them so very poor. Regarding my precious little charge, she stood the trip remarkably well, in spite of her illness. I thank God she is holding up. My relative's house is small and crowded, and I will have to make a change, though I scarce know where to go.

I've received your letter. If we ever live through this present strait I trust we will be better men and women, but I admit I grow heartily sick and disgusted with it, polygamy that is. I wish we could look at the divine part of these things only, it would avoid much psychological disturbance—and be better all around, but with so much earthiness in our nature (mine) this is not always easily accomplished. Of course I am only one of hundreds who are situated thus, and many of them worse. The knowledge that it is God's plan is the only thing that saves us from despair—almost madness, I fear. Prominent in it all is the love I bear you; and taking it all together—I attempt to swallow the dose of contending emotions.

I admit the thought of having you here beside me quite thrills me. But I know the many burdens you carry. I understand if it cannot be so.

Much love,

Your rebellious Maria (and not the other one)

Mattie blew out the candle and settled herself in bed, listening to Lizzie's breathing as Angus's question about practicing medicine tumbled through her mind.

Simple attraction overpowers polarization.
—MARTHA HUGHES CANNON

Chapter Thirty-Seven

The coach turned down a wide, muddy street called Bath Row, and stopped before a three-story building supported by columns. Balancing Lizzie against one hip, Mattie reached forward to pay the driver, and a doorman helped her descend. Mounted on a carved column a sign read: Queen's Hospital, Royal School of Medicine and Surgery. A familiar rush of smells welcomed her inside—the fragrant twinge of ether, a hint of quinine and sulfur.

"You all right?" a receptionist asked, her accent clearly from Birmingham, but far more understandable than Fanny's.

"Yes, I hope so," Mattie said, unsure of how to respond to this greeting. "My name is Alace Bennett. I am a doctor, visiting from America." The receptionist swallowed her surprise. "I sent an inquiry a few days ago. To a Dr. Martin, I believe?"

The woman's face puckered in apology. "Oh yes, ma'am. Inquiring about a hospital position and our nursing curriculum, wasn't it?" Mattie nodded. "Let me just see about the doctor."

While the woman was gone, Mattie peered down the long row of beds in the ward. Much like the hospital where she had worked in Philadelphia, this was a large teaching facility. The front doors opened, releasing a class of medical students, donning lab coats and jostling each other. *Nothing had changed.* There was not a single woman among them.

The receptionist returned with a middle-aged man walking briskly, his starched white coat flapping behind him. "Alace Bennett?" he asked. She nodded at her new alias. "Matilda tells me you are the doctor visiting from America who wrote to us?"

"Yes," Mattie said. "I would be very obliged to learn more about your hospital if you might be so kind." His tired eyes swept up and down, taking in the baby squirming in her arms. How she wished she'd left Lizzie behind.

"Come in," he said, leading the way to his office. "I don't know how much you know about our hospital, but we treated more than sixteen thousand patients last year. Ten years ago, we became a free hospital, where a one-shilling admission is charged, but even that can be waived for those in need."

"What a great work you are doing," Mattie said with sincere admiration.

"Thank you," he said. "Where did you do your training, Mrs. Bennett?"

"Universities of Michigan and Pennsylvania."

"Ah, two excellent schools, and I believe a tad more progressive, having graduated female medical doctors. Women are not currently admitted to our programs."

"Yes," Mattie said, rushing past his comment. "I will be here with relatives in Birmingham for a time, and I'm interested in continuing my practice, if possible."

"You are here with your husband?" Dr. Martin asked pointedly.

Mattie cleared her throat. "Unfortunately, he is kept at home on business."

"I see. And you have credentials? Letters of introduction?"

Again, Mattie stalled, "Not at the moment, but I can easily have them sent."

"Yes, well, it would be quite difficult. Given the circumstances," Dr. Martin explained. "We are very busy working with medical students from the school. However, if you wished perhaps to volunteer as a nurse, we might be able to accommodate your request."

Mattie floundered. "But, sir, I have no training as a nurse."

"Yes. Well. As I say, it's quite difficult given the circumstances." He stood to indicate the interview was finished. "I do wish you pleasant travels with your little one."

Mattie made her way to the door, face burning with frustration, ashamed of her naïvety to believe she could waltz through the doors and find her skills welcomed so far from home.

She gave no glance to the receptionist who noted her humiliated retreat. "Are you finished talking with Dr. Martin?" the woman asked.

"I am," said Mattie, sweeping on.

"You also wished to see our nursing curriculum, isn't that so?"

Mattie stopped and tried to calm her breathing. "Yes," she admitted, "I did."

"I could watch your wee one while you take a look, if you like? My name is Matilda."

Mattie assumed Lizzie would refuse, but to her surprise, she held her arms out to the woman. "Hello, little miss," Matilda said, and Lizzie ventured a smile.

"Thank you ever so much," Mattie said.

Matilda led her toward an office stacked with textbooks and journals. "And how do you find Birmingham, Dr. Bennett?"

"Quite smoky, I'm afraid," Mattie confessed.

"Yes, ma'am, though our mayor has a great many plans to clean the air, close up the sewers, and build clean water reservoirs."

"I don't see evidence he's making much progress," Mattie said wryly.

"We've a long way yet," Matilda acknowledged, "but you can see inklings if you travel around Corporation Street."

"Hmm," said Mattie, finding the idea of attempting to remediate a city like Birmingham a daunting one. "It must take a great creativity to see beyond the current reality."

Matilda nodded. "I'll leave you here to peruse our resources. If you find something useful, do let me know, and perhaps I can find you a copy."

Mattie dove into the curriculum files and textbooks with a zeal she'd not felt in a long time. After reviewing the curriculum organization and diagrams of several textbooks, she settled on one far better than anything she had seen at home. All too soon, Matilda opened the door, ushering in the sound of Lizzie's plaintive chatter. How deceptively angelic Lizzie appeared when happy and clean.

"Thank you ever so much," Mattie said, hefting that sweet weight back into her own arms. Lizzie's blue eyes, so much like her father's, lit up as she cooed to find her own mother returned to her once more. "I thank you most sincerely," Mattie said. "This has meant more than you could possibly understand."

"Have you found something then?"

"I have," she said, enthused by the nursing school she'd constructed in her mind with each passing moment. "I would love to take a copy of this textbook and its ordering information."

A short time later, the two women headed back to the entrance, book and pamphlets tucked firmly beneath Mattie's arm.

Out past the medicine stores, the infirmary, the lying-in beds, Mattie carried Lizzie, pausing at the door to breathe in one last whiff of the battleground of life and death before burying her nose in her daughter's baby hair, wondering how the exchange could manage to be both beautiful and loathsome.

*Cells may undergo atrophy, they may die, those
that manifest life are subject to death.*

—MARTHA HUGHES CANNON

Chapter Thirty-Eight

Mattie settled Lizzie on a blanket, where she batted her small limbs about with a fierce helplessness. Slicing across the opening of the latest missive from Mary, she turned out pages that had once breathed the air of home.

Bless her, Mary had enclosed several copies of the *Woman's Exponent*, and Mattie spread the papers before her, devouring the lines. Romania had managed to stall the opening of the nursing school and have a falling out with the hospital matron that necessitated the summoning of police. Anger mingled with jealousy at the thought of that woman barreling roughshod through the hospital groundwork she had so carefully laid.

Emmeline and Zina Young had traveled to DC to speak at the National Women's Suffrage Convention, another headline announced. The women had met with Susan B. Anthony, Elizabeth Cady Stanton, and the president of the United States after testifying before the House Judiciary Committee, requesting relief from federal agents. The news filled Mattie with envy she could scarcely contain. *Oh, to be engaged in such work, publicly claiming her own name once more.*

But the following edition turned her envy for Emmeline to pity, for it contained an obituary for Louie Wells. Clearly written by her mother, the article praised her goodness, grace, and talent, which anyone who had known the vibrant, theatrical Louie could confirm. Salt Lake's darling had died, the article said, of dropsy. *Poor Emmeline.* An image of Emmeline's youngest daughter, petted, artistic, and charming, flitted through Mattie's mind, and she glanced instinctively at her own dear daughter attempting to inch her way across the floor.

Mary's letter was chatty and conversational, filled with news of her children and the Relief Society's silk production. Mattie smiled at her sister's description of the mulberry boughs that had taken over the kitchen and the sounds of munching silkworms that kept her up at night.

> *I am unsure if Angus has written about Louie Wells's funeral? I hope the news will not be too much of a shock to you.*
> *As I'm sure you could guess, Louie's death came as quite a blow to her mother. I'm afraid since the funeral, there's been a dramatic falling out between Emmeline and Angus.*

Mattie sat upright. What could have possibly transpired? Emmeline's oldest daughter was married to Angus's own nephew, John C. Cannon; the two prominent families had always been close.

> *Emmeline never could be unbiased when it came to her own girls, particularly Louie, you will recall.*

A bit of an understatement, that.

> *But there are many people who feel Angus was far too harsh.*

What on earth had he done?

Perhaps he's already explained it, but I thought you might want a woman's perspective on the situation. We assembled for the funeral over which he presided, as solemn and mournful as you would expect. Then Angus chose that moment to reveal that Louie had not died of dropsy as had been announced, but from the complications of pregnancy.

Good heavens. He would never . . .

There had been rumors of an affair between Louie and John C. Cannon, but Angus announced that the rumors were true. And that the resulting pregnancy killed her.

Mattie could scarcely drag her eyes away from her sister's letter in time to prevent Lizzie from scooching under the bed. Could this possibly be true? What in heavens could he have been thinking?

You must imagine us, arranged in black, there to support Emmeline, beyond shocked by his announcement. No one contradicted him, but several people in the audience called: "For shame!" horrified he would dare dishonor the dead. Emmeline, poor soul, fainted on the spot. As did her daughter Annie.

Good gracious heavens. This letter sounded more like the plot of a cheap dime store novel, not happenings among people she knew and loved.

You can see from the paper, Emmeline recovered enough to write an obituary for her daughter, leaving out all the details and controversy. Emmeline's daughter Mel met Angus in the street a few days later and slapped him across the face. Some reports say he slapped the girl back, but I'm not sure I can believe that.

I do not know the whole of it, and perhaps he has written himself to better explain his actions. I hope the whole debacle

will not damage your friendship with Emmeline. You have
always been her protégé.

How could such a mess *not* hurt her friendship with Emmeline? Mattie buried the thought at the edge of her mind, hedging up the question with worry.

Lizzie fussed at Mattie's feet, chiding her mother to pay attention to her. She picked up the child, teased her with a toy giraffe, and turned to read the obituary for a second time, now more remarkable for what it left out—an affair with her brother-in-law, a sudden departure for California. A hushed-up birth. Also no mention of the ruckus at the funeral, where Angus had apparently taken it upon himself to reveal the particulars of the affair, an appalling decision Mattie could not account for.

She tried to imagine Emmeline, overcome with grief, facing the funeral of her youngest daughter, having to deal with the shame of Angus's revelation. What could *possibly* have been his motivation? Mattie wondered if she even knew the man she had married.

After settling Lizzie to sleep, Mattie started a letter to Angus, meandering around the edges:

> *It is an absolute fact that a woman can't travel here in*
> *Europe with a baby, unaccompanied by her husband, without*
> *having that child branded with illegitimacy and herself looked*
> *upon as one who has submitted herself to prostitution. I become*
> *discouraged at times and wonder if some of us will ever have any*
> *respectable married life, on this sphere anyway. Though your*
> *letters are doting, a part of me thinks your words are just a bit*
> *of taffy given to cheer me up while you are having a jolly time*
> *with others. I put these thoughts on paper to let you understand*
> *that my isolation has not quite made an angel of me yet, but*
> *your blessed neck is at stake if you ever tell I am jealous.*

Finally she could hold back no longer:

I have heard of the death of Louie Wells. How my heart aches for Emmeline. I am young in experience, but can realize something of a mother's feelings. May peace & comfort come into her heart. Oh Angus, how could you? Though I am trying to trust you followed what you believed to be the best course of action, I do not know how you could have added to Emmeline's burdens at this time.

Lizzie is sleeping and I ought to be.

Alace

The food appreciated and thoroughly masticated
shows that the nerve is not paralyzed.
—MARTHA HUGHES CANNON

Chapter Thirty-Nine

In the dark and smoky row house, Fanny Evans drummed day and night upon her children's heads. Mattie wondered if she dared untangle the children's knotted hair filled with lice nits. After a few weeks of listening to Fanny's West Midlands accent, Mattie found her words more understandable, but half wished she could return to incomprehension, particularly when Fanny reached into the liquor cabinet. Lizzie fussed and clung to her mother each morning when they returned to the unwelcome scene. Somehow Birmingham felt even more cold and damp behind those four walls than on the other side of them.

Fanny's "Ow' bin ya?" seemed decidedly chillier one morning a few weeks later, and Mattie wondered if she had imagined the change. As usual, Mattie gulped down the offered morning "cuppa," trying not to think about the cleanliness of the cup. Charlie crossed his eyes and stuck his tongue out at Lizzie when his mother's back was turned, and Lizzie clung to Mattie's neck.

"That little pale-faced madame 'as bin thoroughly spoiled," Fanny chided as she watched Lizzie, "and you will have more 'en enuf to put up with before you get through with her."

Mattie bit her tongue and pulled her "spoiled madame" closer.

When evening fell, Thomas returned, dusty and covered with the dirt of the day and also asked, "Ow bin ya?" though he watched her sidelong through suspicious eyes. Following his wife into the pantry, the two whispered in a heated exchange. Mattie could hear "wrong 'un" and "gi'it some 'ommer."

They made it through dinner—a soupy porridge boiled too long with peas long since turned to mush. When one child began to fuss, Thomas warned, "Stop your pithering, or I'll give ye a good cog-winder."

After supper, the children escaped from the table like a scruffy mess of puppies, and Thomas and Fanny exchanged glances. "Anuver letter came for ye," Thomas said, as Fanny drew a crumpled envelope from a drawer. "From yer husbind?"

Mattie took the thin letter, recognizing Angus's hand, and turned it over. The seal was broken and clumsily repaired just as his previous letter had been. "Yes, from my husband."

Fanny elbowed Thomas, and he cleared his throat. "Tell us true, babs, are ye in some kinda trouble? Because we donna want trouble, and canna have wrong 'uns around the childun."

Mattie looked in disbelief from husband to wife.

Thomas shook his head. "No trouble." When Mattie did not reply, he added, "We're not so green as we're cabbage-looking." Well, this was a new expression to add to her list.

"Not around the childun," Fanny added. "Donna need a copper firking about to give us a bell-oiling."

"There is no copper, uh, firking after us, I assure you," Mattie said, feeling the color rise to her cheeks. "But you needn't worry. I was planning to move on soon enough."

"We donna mean to be grizzling. Yer family, ain't ya?"

Mattie considered the filthy floor, the nit-infected children, and the offal that passed for supper on their table. "My mother says so." She rose, hoisting Lizzie to her hip. "We can leave tomorrow morning if you wish. I do thank you." She started for the stairs, and heard their lowered voices speaking furiously below.

"Must fink we're saft in the head."

"Don't want no argy bargy."

Above the roar of the tussling children and the clink of dishes came the pronounced response: "A wench traveling with a babby and no husbind ain't on no holiday."

The stairs felt far more steep and narrow than the last time Mattie had climbed them. *Where would she go?* The question settled like a weight upon her heart. Months into her exile, and already she was being passed on like unwanted goods. No family to claim, no friends to fall back on. She longed to go to Manchester where Emmeline Wells's husband led the LDS congregation and she could connect with other members of the Church, but she hesitated knowing the constant communication with Salt Lake would make it far too easy to report her whereabouts.

Rocking her daughter to sleep, Mattie sang the old lullaby, feeling she'd been turned adrift upon a surging sea, no land in sight. "I will hold you, close enfold you, lay my blessing on your rest."

An hour later, Mattie settled Lizzie into her cradle with still-wet lashes. The child hiccoughed in her sleep, fist still clinging to her mother's finger. Mattie bent forward to kiss the sweet thing and slyly slipped her finger away. How could one small child require so much time and attention? Even while she loved her Lizzie, she grew weary of the solitary relentlessness. The knotty problem of where to go descended upon her again, and she lit a candle and turned to Angus's letter.

The epistle was brief, dashed off in between meetings, barely worth the price of postage, but Mattie scrambled after the words:

> *Kiss my little babe for me and accept my warmest love. How I would like to carry her for you, were I there. I tell you in all solemnity that I never bow my knees to the Lord but what my*

thoughts go out after the one so remote from me, amongst strangers, first of all.

My sweet, I am sorry, but I cannot join you in England. I spoke with President about it, but he is too ill and with other leaders already overseas and in prison, I am needed here. How sorry I am to wait longer for your embrace.

She hadn't realized how much she had been hoping he might be able to come until she read the news that he couldn't, his words only increasing her utter loneliness. Resting her head upon the desk, she coughed back tears so she wouldn't wake the baby.

In the dim and sodden light—if you could call the city's incessant gloom "light"—Mattie rose. A soft and steady rain beat about the eaves like a lullaby, softening the sounds of morning to a gentle rolling cadence. Lizzie awoke with a stretch and a yawn, watching her mother's movements from her cradle with steady eyes, waiting her turn, for there were only so many things her mother's hands could hold at once.

Mattie packed their few belongings into a case that felt as stiff and awkward as her name. In the kitchen, the Evans children scampered forward to see if there would be a "bell-oiling."

"I thank you for your help," Mattie said to Fanny, for she had arrived in this country knowing no one, and having any relations were better than none. She said nothing of regrets, though, for she had been surrounded by lies as of late and preferred to speak truth.

Charlie peered from behind his mother's apron to cross his eyes at Lizzie one more time. "Ta-ra a bit, now, babs. I hope ye understand," Fanny said, with a touch of apology.

"I do. Goodbye."

A coachman stowed her case, and helped her up to the carriage, closing the door tight behind them. Steady drizzle accompanied them up the muddy streets, and Mattie pulled Lizzie closer, hoping the child wouldn't catch another illness from this damp cold that settled right to the bones.

In the railway station, Mattie covered Lizzie's head with a cloth, trying not to think about her pink lungs attempting to filter factory grime. The train's churning wheels carried them away from the haze and smog hovering over Birmingham like a circling cloud of industrialized wrath, bearing them past row houses and factories until green began to fill up the windows. The countryside unfolded in great swaths of lushness, a bolt of fabric unbound and rolled over the land, its seams trimmed in hedgerows.

They traveled east to Stratford-upon-Avon, the birthplace of Shakespeare, where Mattie hoped to breathe country air and determine where to go next. The train rounded hills crisscrossed by aisles of thick gorse and dotted with thatched roof cottages. Lambs scampered after their mothers beside gardens run wild with hollyhocks and climbing roses. Mattie's eyes ate up the verdant feast.

Lizzie awoke as they descended from the platform and blinked in the light, and Mattie laughed at the child's bewilderment at finding blackness changed to green, like a fairy's spell cast over the world while she slumbered.

When Alace Bennett signed herself into a boardinghouse near Stratford-upon-Avon, the woman of the establishment asked, "End yer husband?" in the same suspicious voice Thomas Evans had used.

"Kept in America with business," Alace replied, cheeks burning.

"I see." The woman believed her no more than the Evanses had, and Mattie's color rose faster, knowing the woman would find her actual marital arrangement just as scandalous and strange if she knew the truth of it.

She nearly broke down and sobbed when she saw the boardinghouse room, quiet and clean. Within a few days, Lizzie's cough began to ease and she woke in the morning with smiles and giggles Mattie had not seen for many weeks.

Chapter Forty

After a fortnight of settling into a routine of meals, naps, and reasonable bedtimes, Mattie found herself yearning to explore beyond the narrow rooms. Packing up supplies, she dared venture to Warwick Castle to distract herself from troubles at home she could do little to remedy. Lizzie rarely allowed any person besides her mother to hold her, no matter how friendly or kind, so there was nothing to do but carry her through the medieval fortress that had guarded the river Avon for the last eleven hundred years. Alace Bennett signed the guest registry balancing her baby against one hip.

A guide who introduced himself as Nigel, and appeared nearly as old as the castle, led them through the great halls and staterooms, summarizing a thousand years of rebellions, invasions, captures, and beheadings. "In the year 1153," Nigel intoned, "Henry of Anjou tricked Gundred de Warenne into surrendering the fortress by informing her that her husband was dead. In truth, her husband was, at the moment, engaged in battle for the estate, until he received the news his wife had relinquished the castle. At that point, he died, devastated by the loss of the fortress."

"A medieval Romeo and Juliet then?" Mattie asked. In her dark mood, she thought the story sounded just about right for marital communication. With its portcullis and stone turrets, the mighty fortress was truly the dream English country castle, with as many towers as one might wish for. But stone walls seven feet thick turned out to be far colder than one might imagine. Walking through the space, Mattie couldn't help noting that, as with other anticipations she might name, the reality of living in a castle wouldn't be nearly as charming as it sounded.

Nigel led them through the largest armory in Europe, then past towers and ramparts to view the celebrated "Warwick Vase" and on through the tapestry collection. Following his shuffling steps up a rampart ascending 150 feet above the river, Mattie wondered if his heart would last longer than her aching arms.

She turned to the western vista, where, beyond those rolling emerald hills and across an ocean, the man she loved might be imprisoned again or even dead for all she knew. How she longed to have him here beside her. Lizzie struggled to be put down, crying in frustration when her mother held her tight. "Not right now, baby," Mattie soothed.

Nigel led the way down a steep descent. "If you'll follow me, we will descend to the dungeon," he said. Down a narrow labyrinth of steps she trailed after him. Down and down and down, where the air grew stagnant and moist. "You'll notice prisoners' inscriptions etched into the walls if you look carefully," he remarked. Examining the hatch marks, Mattie again thought of Angus in prison, and wondered if he'd been bored enough to write on prison walls. Probably not, she decided. More likely, he had spent his time in more productive pursuits, like writing adoring letters to all four of his wives.

By the end of the tour, Mattie's arms ached and the sensation in her abdomen made her physician's diagnostic mind spin along the subject of prolapsed uterus—that old curse of the wandering womb back to haunt her once more.

She settled a cold, hungry, and unimpressed-with-castles Lizzie against her throbbing shoulder. Returning to their boardinghouse, Mattie paused on the bridge, savoring the irony that the most beautiful place to experience the castle was not inside of it at all, but across the river Avon, with the reflection shimmering over an expanse of wide, clear water—a very long distance away.

Struggling not to give way to despondency, Mattie set off again the next week, armed with clean nappies, playthings, wiping cloths, and a happy baby in tow, to see the town where Shakespeare had been born. Cobbled streets, picturesque cottages, and Tudor-timbered houses attracted a steady stream of Bard worshippers who came to walk the river Avon, reciting lines from *King Lear* and *The Tempest* in a cadence that matched Fanny's own.

Listening to the voices around her, Mattie realized that the original Shakespearean actors likely sounded a great deal like the Evans family, the iambic pentameter of the verses rolling along the rhythms of the British midlands.

Mattie schlepped her child through the cottage where Shakespeare had been born, the theater that had staged his great works, and Anne Hathaway's cottage, Lizzie growing heavier with every cobblestone she crossed. The child began fussing, sick of the adventure, and trying anything to appease her, Mattie began reciting words she had once spoken aloud in a gaslit theater in Philadelphia:

> *Great business must be wrought ere noon:*
> *Upon the corner of the moon*
> *There hangs a vaporous drop profound;*
> *I'll catch it ere it come to ground:*

Lizzie stopped fussing and looked solemnly at her mother, as if the world had ceased its order. Fragments came back to Mattie like an incantation:

How now, you secret, black, and midnight hags! What is't you do? A deed without a name.

Mattie's voice slowed, to the culminating lines:

And you all know, security is mortals' chiefest enemy.

The wisdom of those words struck her anew. The danger of security. How casually she'd rushed into marriage, holding it like a new and clever game. Remembering knowing glances between her parents told her they had seen what she could not understand. She consoled herself with the thought that as Shakespeare had penned his lines in the fifteenth century, she had not been the first to rush headlong into folly.

Mattie searched the narrow, crooked streets, half-expecting to see Macbeth's apparitions, but only the damp and misty streets of Stratford-upon-Avon lay before her, only Lizzie's insistent fussing turning now to a cry. Searching for a place to feed the hungry child, knowing she couldn't hurry over lumbering cobblestones without turning an ankle, Mattie sank upon a stone bench beneath a statue of the Bard arrayed in a dapper cloak and flawless cravat, lounging against a scrolling pedestal.

Mattie covered a red-faced Lizzie with a blanket and fumbled with the hooks upon her blouse, wondering if Shakespeare had ever had baby spit-up run down his shirtwaist. It seemed doubtful. The last time she'd recited those lines, she'd been in oratory school, with so many possibilities before her. What might Shakespeare have accomplished without a wife to bear his children and prepare his meals while he engaged his mental powers in the pursuit of his craft?

Lizzie settled into a hungry rhythm of sucking as Mattie's dark thoughts continued their spiral. If he had been born a Wilhelmia, would those same plays ever have been called into existence? Or would his rhymes have died somewhere between the hungry cries of a child and the endless churning of nappies? Perhaps greatness throughout all time had depended, in some way, on the silencing of a woman's dream, the hushing of her ambition.

Though Mattie adored everything about this child wriggling in her arms, she could not help longing for the sense of purpose, of skill and efficiency she felt in a hospital—the resolution at the end of a full day's work. Though she hadn't wanted her mother's life, she hadn't wanted this underground existence either, and Mattie's exhausted brain tried to retrace the swift transformation, as startling as a babe fallen asleep upon a moving train. How had she gone from that world of possibility to this blur of uncertainty while the child's father . . . Mattie bent her head over the Lizzie's blanket so her tears would mix with the mist settling upon Stratford. She did not want to think of Angus.

Mattie craned her neck for a closer look at the poet's fastidious mustache, his cavalier expression, his crooked arm and finger pointing to a pithy inscription carved into the solid weight of stone. She adjusted her sucking child so she could read the quotation: *"There is no darkness but ignorance,"* the stone proclaimed.

"Indeed," Mattie whispered.

Some weeks later, a letter arrived from Angus, professing his love and insisting his declarations were anything but taffy.

> *Please do not chastise me over the matter of Louie Wells's funeral, as I cannot bear hearing your disappointment. I was acting on directions from my older brother George, who instructed me to say the things I did, though in retrospect I think his judgment was clouded by his own son's involvement in the matter. I tell you in*

confidence that I regret the action, as I would not do anything that increased the pain of those suffering as Emmeline has. Even more, of course, I know the regard you have held for her and it brings me sorrow to think of any difficulty it may cause you.

Mattie sighed, imagining the awkwardness of trying to smooth over this breach with Emmeline and wishing Angus put half the effort into exercising good judgment as he did into offering pretty apologies and explanations.

I recalled you saying you might need information about your family in Wales, and collected the given names of your grandfather and grandmother in Wales from your mother. These I enclose with additional funds, in case you wish to go in search of them.

Wales. She felt a tugging at her heartspace to stand upon that ground once more. She had planned to go. Now, with nowhere to turn, lost and adrift, with so little sense of who she was remaining, she felt the pull of her first home. Though she could no longer remember standing upon that ground, it was her birthplace and her parents' home too. Certainly she had more connection to Wales than to distant cousins in Birmingham or sights of interest in the British countryside. If people journeyed to Stratford-upon-Avon seeking connection with Shakespeare through his birthplace, perhaps she should seek out her own.

Mattie opened the lid of her wooden letter box and pulled out a letter-in-progress she kept for Angus, penning a line or two as she was able, to send when all edges were filled.

I am sorry you cannot join me, but I do understand. I feel there is nowhere upon this earth my feet belong at the moment and little know where to go next. Thank you for the information on my Welsh family and the funds. I think to put them both to good use. I do not understand how the Louie situation could possibly have escalated as it did, but I hope you have apologized to the Wells family as nicely as you have to me. I imagine it will be better understood when you and I can converse again in person someday, if ever such a moment is to be ours. My own loved one, imagine yourself kissed, hugged, and a piece taken out of your ear. Lizzie has learned to turn over and thinks herself the epitome of clever.

I remain yours, Alace

Mattie tried to seal up her despair along with the letter, blowing against the candle flame until the room lapsed into darkness.

Grecian mythology declares that Prometheus compounded the first man of clay and particles taken from various animals. The Mohommedans say God made Adam of seven handfuls of earth, from different depths and colors, collected by the angel Azrail.

—MARTHA HUGHES CANNON

Chapter Forty-One

The train headed north, then west, west to Wales—not so distant really, yet distances were deceptive here, with cultures and languages long rooted to the earth beneath them, a matter of mere miles bringing vast shifts in cultures and languages. As the train crossed into Wales, the more sedate British midlands gave way to rockier ground breaking through the surface of the earth, its green skin pierced through with rough outcroppings of stone. Afternoon shadows stretched and shrank over grotesque formations, taking on the shape of mystical creatures from Mattie's youth, selkies, witches, and goblins.

The language shifted too, as Welsh began appearing on signs and the voices around her spoke in breathy, higher intonations. Gutteral sounds and tongue rolls ran over and around vowels like a mountain stream circling stones. "*Noswaith dda.*"

"*Sut mae?*"

If ever there was a language meant for spell casting, it was Welsh for sure and certain. It sounded the part of one of the oldest living languages in Europe, descended from Celtic and Brythonic tongues. A couple sat down behind her, and Mattie listened to their conversation, marveling at the words and sounds that had first filled her throat, sensing their familiarity from her mother's lips, though she could no more understand them than she could pronounce the signs beyond the windows: *Llansanffraid, Cefn-ddwysarn, Vale of Clwyd.*

The train pulled into Llandudno, the town of her birth, and Mattie hushed a rather miserable Lizzie, looking about for a place to change a wet nappy. Leaving the station, she traversed the seaside promenade running the length of a crescent of sand, where sandpipers fished in the shallows and gulls turned circles overhead. From shops crowded beneath pastel candy-colored row houses, vendors sold mint cakes, bonbons, and lollies to children on holiday. "I want a sweetie!" a child demanded of his parents.

Faced with bracing salt air and waves rolling in the Irish Sea, Lizzie quieted, wide-eyed and wondering. "Llandudno: Queen of the Welsh Watering Places," Mattie read from a sign. A paddle steamer from Liverpool docked at the pier, unloading families on holiday, come to walk across the strip of sand and tell their friends they had been to Wales.

Mattie carried Lizzie over cobblestoned streets, past beachgoers and gift shops selling trinkets, heading for the sheer limestone headland at the end. Somewhere, in a house named Tanygraig, near the Great Orme, she had been born. "Tanygraig," she said aloud for Lizzie. "Beneath the rock," it meant. In that house, adjoining copper mines and her father's joiner's shop, her parents had first listened to missionaries from across the ocean.

The Great Orme stretched before her like a sea serpent, and she climbed, child in arms, turning back to see Llandudno fall away, sheltered by the curve of the land. Tracing her way up a footpath carved into the limestone cliff, she paused to rest when the ascent became too much. The air was soft somehow, far different from

Utah's dry desert; it rested against her skin with a gentle exhale carrying the scents of wild succory and wood sage.

Wild Kashmiri goats frolicked alongside nesting puffins, and a peregrine falcon screeched against the sky, sending a cluster of cormorants into the water. Somewhere nearby, more than thirty years past, her mother had once held a small version of herself. For one moment, those years turned mistlike, and Mattie wasn't sure which side of the blanket she was on.

Though the seaside town was charming, she felt no strong desire to stay there. Families on holiday only served to remind her of her own loved ones far away. After a handful of days trying various tea shops and setting Lizzie's small toes against the sand, Mattie wondered where to go. Llandudno, lovely reprieve though it was, felt little more welcoming than Stratford-upon-Avon.

Her mother had written,

> Llanddoged, a small village near Llanrwst, is where you will find your father's parents, if they are still living, and their graves if they are not. I've had no contact with them since we left, and if they are alive, I've no idea how they will feel about meeting you after so many years, but your father's family lived in that area for generations.

Generations passed in Llanddoged and Llanrwst, bound through her blood in serpentine connections. Moving from boardinghouse to boardinghouse as she'd been, the allure of a place her family had stayed for generations drew Mattie southward.

The modern ingenious and beautiful theory of evolution,
recognizing the kinship of man with all that lies below him—is
it not symbolized and foreshadowed by the old philosophies?
—MARTHA HUGHES CANNON

Chapter Forty-Two

She hired a trap to carry them past Conwy castle, road tracing the river as it flowed seaward from the peaks of Snowdonia. Llanrwst was a small medieval town where St. Brigid had once turned rushes to fish to feed the poor. Tudor architecture twisted about a central square clock tower, a convergence for cobbled streets. Mattie paused to let Lizzie play along the river's edge, before the carriage ascended narrow roads bordered by hedgerows so dense and tall nothing could be seen on either side. They traveled through a tunnel of green, dotted with foxglove and fern, stopping at the top of a hill overlooking the valley, where wooded hills folded into each other, the vast mountains of Caernarfonshire rising in the distance.

The driver delivered them before a cluster of stone cottages with sagging slate roofs in Llanddoged, where he promised they would find room for the night.

"*Noswaith dda,*" Mattie said to the woman who opened the door, doing her best with her scant Welsh.

"*Noswaith dda,*" the woman replied. "*Sut allai eich helpu chi?*"

"*Diolch*, I'm sorry . . . do you speak any English?" Mattie asked, embarrassed to be at the end of her Welsh.

"*Ie.* A little," the woman said.

"I'd like a room, please. My name is Alace Bennett and this is my daughter."

"Bronwen Davies. Welcome."

As she filled in the ledger, Mattie explained, "I've come to Llanddoged because my grandparents live near this village, or they did at one time."

Bronwen cast a curious look at Mattie that seemed to ask why, if her grandparents had lived in the village, she couldn't speak Welsh, and instead paraded about with a horrible American accent. "They are still alive?" she asked.

"I don't know," Mattie admitted, realizing how impossible it might be to find some remnant of a family, maybe now long dead. "Their names are Mair and Thomas Hughes, but I'm not sure if they are still living."

Mattie bent over Lizzie, feeling foolish, but the innkeeper encouraged, "I do not know your grandparents, but if anyone did, it would be Gwendolyn in the Vale of Elwy. She is as old as the trees and knows everything. She may remember."

Mattie's heartbeat picked up at the name, as alluring as an enchantment. "Where might I find her?"

"She is caretaker of Tythyn Bodrhyll." Bronwen walked to the door, smoothing her apron as she went and gesturing across the road to a gap in a stone wall. A small footpath continued, nearly lost in tangles of green growth. Mattie could distantly trace the stone outline of a church beyond. "Follow that path yonder a ways, through the circular churchyard and onward. It will lead you right."

Lizzie nodded in Mattie's arms, her tiny mouth opening in a yawn.

"Put the child down for a kip, if you like. I can have a listen." Bless this woman. Lizzie settled down easily for once, and Mattie placed her in a cradle in the corner of her room.

Reveling at the lightness of walking by herself, Mattie crossed the street and followed the path to a stone church with diamond-shaped, leaded glass windows. Yew trees circled the churchyard, planted so the devil had no corner to hide in, Bronwen had told her. The path continued behind the church and through the grave-yard, chiseled slate stones tilting in every direction. Yew trees with branches gnarled and twisted as a Celtic knot guarded the edges of the cemetery, their roots emerging from the earth and returning in looping shadows impossible to untangle.

Mattie paused as a rustle overhead and a rush of air brought the largest owl she'd ever seen to settle on a yew branch above her, turn-ing its head from side to side, regarding her passage. Mattie exam-ined the mottled tawny crest, feathered grasping talons, and glowing pumpkin eyes in dismay. She glanced back toward the village, be-yond headstones fading into arched and ghostly specters. Somewhere in the back of her consciousness, she recalled her mother telling an old Welsh story of a woman who could assume the shape of an owl. Lady Bodeuwedd, perhaps.

The wind picked up, playing through the trees with a slight whistling, even as she eyed the owl and the copse ahead, lost in lac-ing, flickering shadows. *Her grandparents and their parents before them had lived near these woods.* Drawing her cloak close about her, Mattie bent her head and scurried forward beneath the owl's sharp gaze.

Underneath the boughs of yew, silence reigned save for the hushed whisperings of trees. Ivy clambered over the forest, lacing rivers of vines up tree trunks like the veining on a hand, flowing from this world to the next and back again. Pushing through tangles of undergrowth, Mattie gaped as green upon green sprouted from every inch of forest.

The footpath ended abruptly at the edge of a boggy swamp,

where large carved blocks of limestone continued across the expanse. They were . . . stepping-stones.

Oh surely, *this could not be the way to anyone's home?* The ancient stones must have been chiseled in place by Druid hands some centuries past. Having come so far, there was little to do but cross over, and Mattie raised her skirts, grateful she'd worn practical broadcloth lest a slick boot send her tumbling into the water. She sprang gingerly from one block to the next.

So intent on guiding her feet safely to the other side, when she raised her head, she gasped aloud. Directly ahead stood the crumbling ruins of an older sanctuary, decaying fragment by fragment back to the stone from which it had been hewn. Two archways—once windows—and a connecting passageway remained, where ivy and creeper vines ran riot through the stones, sprouting joyfully from the apex of a crumbling nave. Directly in front of the ruin rippled a bubbling spring. The well had been outlined in stones cut in the shape of a Celtic knot, cool water shimmering at its center.

Mattie found her throat dry as parchment. Tiptoeing to the edge of the well, she peered through the riffled surface to depths below, and bent before it, hoping it was clean, yet so thirsty she nearly didn't care. Her physician's mind reminded her that such a spot could carry typhus, but she bade her mind be quiet and sank to her knees, leaning forward before such an unexpected offering. The water tasted of cool shadows and river rushes, of bracken forest things, and she drank down mouthfuls.

Sitting back on her heels, she noticed bits of rags tied to a scraggy bush beside the well. Wonderingly, she touched the fabric. Homespun. Where to possibly go next, she had no idea, for this was certainly no habitation for the living. Making her way through the ruined churchyard, Mattie inhaled, the way growing more curious at every bend.

Across a small clearing, at some distance from the church, stood a cottage built of chiseled stone, the edges pieced together like a child's building blocks. A slate roof descended to chains waiting to shepherd rainwater from eaves to wooden barrels. Flowers and climbing plants wound over and through the walls of the cottage, and it might have been abandoned but for the plantings in barrels and hollowed tree stumps, and but for a thin wisp of smoke curling from the weathered chimney.

What century had she wandered into when she tripped across those stepping-stones? The edges of time grew as slippery as the bottom of a mossy well. Mattie approached with caution, as though if she traversed too far into this world, she would find herself unable to return. These thoughts were madness, but in the soft exhale of the forest, firmly within nature's grasp, reason held little sway.

Up the pathway she went, and then hesitated before the battered door held together with corroding fasteners. She knocked and waited.

"*Dewch i mewn*," came the response, from a voice as old as the forest.

Hoping the words spoke of invitation, Mattie pushed against the frame. It gave way beneath her hands, opening inward, revealing a sheltering space not unlike a stone cave. A colorful hand-knotted rug lay upon the stone floor. The remnant of a fire glowed in the hearth. On a wooden shelf stood an assortment of simple crockery. And from the eaves, bundled herbs filled the air with scents of rosemary, elderberry, and wood sage. Beside the fire, in a rocker, an ancient woman worked, steadily weaving from a basket of rushes at her feet. Her skin was as tortuous as the bark of yew trees, but her knobbed fingers deftly twisted each fiber. "*Prynhawn da.* Madam— Gwendolyn?" Mattie asked. "I apologize, I am afraid I do not know much Welsh. Nor your surname, neither."

The woman did not stop her rocking, or the smooth plying of the rushes. "*Croeso. Dim pryderon.* Gwendolyn is fair enough."

Mattie stepped further into the cottage, struck by the utter simplicity and cleanliness of each surface, the polished stone floor and the windowpanes so clean they bent the forest beyond into lovely, liquid angles. Such a difference from Fanny's home.

I'm Alace, she meant to say, but confounded by the cottage, the forest, the mystery of this woman, she forgot. "I'm Mattie," she said instead, gasping at the sound of the forbidden word spoken aloud. But who would this fairy woman tell, after all?

"There's a bit of raspberry leaf tea, should you like some, Mattie," Gwendolyn said, gesturing to a kettle hanging over the fire. The sound of her name felt as welcome as the scene before her, and she wanted to lap up the comfort of the cottage as she had lapped water from the spring. "And speckled bread." Two mugs stood waiting upon the table.

"Were you expecting someone?" Mattie asked, not wanting to intrude.

"No," Gwendolyn said with no further explanation. She poured steaming water over mugs filled with leaf shoots, then placed a saucer on top to steep. The dense speckled bread tasted of labor and forest fruit.

Gwendolyn resumed her weaving, gesturing for Mattie to have a seat. "*Nawr.* What has brought you to my door?"

Mattie brushed crumbs from her mouth. "An innkeeper told me you might know of my grandparents, who live nearby. Or did at one time."

"Their names?"

"Mair and Thomas Hughes."

"*Ie,*" said Gwendolyn, dropping her weaving and lifting the mug to her lips.

"Did you know them?"

"But of course, I knew Mair and Thomas," Gwendolyn said, her eyes resting upon Mattie with new interest. "And here you've come, looking for your grandmother, and you passed her, though you did not know it."

"I passed her?" Mattie stopped.

"*Ie*, that you did."

"But—" Mattie stumbled over the words, wondering if this ancient woman could be confused. "Is she still alive then?"

"I'm afraid not, though that matters little," Gwendolyn said. "Shall I take you to see her?" She set down her weaving, a piece resembling a four-pointed star, and then turned her head from side to side, as the owl had done. "You look a bit like her, you know. When she was younger." Gwendolyn lifted a shawl from a hook and wound it around her shoulders.

Though age bowed her shoulders, Gwendolyn moved down the path with surprising agility. Mattie followed her around the trees bent with ivy. "Your grandmother Mair died decades ago," Gwendolyn explained. "But she and I were *gwerin cyfrwys*. Cunning folk, I believe you call it."

"Cunning folk?"

"That's an English name for a folk healer. When a person wants to be complimentary, of course. They have other names, too, don't they, not quite so nice."

"Witches?" Mattie guessed, thinking of Barb and Patty.

"*Ie*. That's another."

They crossed the crumbling remains of the churchyard and skirted the calm surface of the well. Mattie peered down at the fissure in the earth, where water flowed upward, rippling like a womb in contraction.

Gwendolyn leapt over each stepping-stone, quite at home in the swampy divide. In the copse of yew trees, swelling, sinuous branches flexed like muscles against the curvature of the earth, and the owl waited in her tree, feathers ruffled by a passing wind.

"Have you seen her now?" Gwendolyn asked, not waiting for an answer. Mattie looked about her and wondered if she had. Ducking beneath branches of yew, they returned to the cemetery, where two names had been etched in slate with the broad edge of a chisel: Mair Lloyd & Thomas Hughes. A posy lay upon the stone's broad edge, a four-pointed star woven from rushes at its base.

"Thank you," Mattie said, overwhelmed to find the resting place of these people who had known her as a baby, had once held her father in their arms.

"She isn't here truly," said Gwendolyn. "You have passed her already."

Around Mair's grave, slate boxes holding the dead were pried open, inch by inch, by green and curling fingers pining for resurrection morn. David Lloyd and Catherine Davies lay next to Mair, and beside them, Margaret Huges and John Davies, then Hugh Owen, Margaret Jones, and Elizabeth Hughes. With a start, Mattie realized these were her aunts, uncles, grandparents, and cousins bearing dates spanning to the 1700s, and others, probably older, fading into stones filed down by time. "Why, my whole family is here," Mattie said fighting an urge to fall to her knees. Here at last was her own source, her own beginning, a spring she had never known.

"Gwendolyn, what other names did they have for cunning folk?"

"That depends on how many centuries back you are wanting to reach." A breeze tousled the old woman's hair, pulling softly at the edges of her simple cloak. "Witch, healer, poet. Those will be recent ones, you know. A fair bit farther back, they might have said druidess, goddess, or prophetess. I'm not sure there's any difference."

Mattie reached forward to touch the edge of Mair's stone, softened like a book worn from overreading. "Perhaps not."

*The early alchemists and astrologers in their vague but
grand speculations have much to say of the human
body as a microcosm or "little world," made up of
every element in the three kingdoms of nature.*
—MARTHA HUGHES CANNON

Chapter Forty-Three

Mattie returned to the graveyard the following morning to copy information from the stones to send to her mother. Though there was little to keep her here, she found herself wanting to linger in Llanddoged, feeling for the first time in her exile she had found a place to which she had some claim.

Mattie settled Lizzie on a blanket some days later, where the child immediately pushed up to all fours and began rocking back and forth, in a practice crawl. "Ba ba ba ba ba," Lizzie prattled.

"Yes, baby." Mattie ran a hand over her child's head, covered with whisps beginning to form silken curls. "Mother needs to write a letter to Grandmama, little one."

She opened her letter box and smoothed a sheet of parchment before her, as Lizzie scootched forward and back, reaching for her mother's skirts. Grasping the folds with tiny fists, she began pulling herself up as if she were scaling a mighty mountain, her latest mischief.

Mattie set down her pen with a sigh. "Here, little one." She offered a wooden ABC block, but the child batted it away. Why did the child play independently until the very moment her mother began a task? Looking about for something novel to distract her, Mattie removed paper and pen from her wooden writing box and set it before Lizzie. "See now? What clever toy is this?"

Lizzie set to pulling open the empty drawers, and Mattie dashed off a greeting, knowing the child would not stay distracted for long. Just as she dipped the pen and returned it to paper, a clatter and a terrible strangling echoed from below.

Mattie dropped her pen and took in the scene in one horrified glance. A glass bottle of ammonia, kept on hand for cleaning, had been forgotten in a drawer of the writing box. The empty bottle rolled across the floor, stopper beside it. Lizzie fell back senseless, gasping for breath.

Great heavens above. Surely the child had not drunk . . . Mattie flung herself over her baby's convulsing form, pulled the shaking child onto her lap. Lizzie's eyes rolled back in her head, as the small body stiffened in her helpless arms. *Oh, dear Lord.* Mattie could not stop herself from imagining the powerful base making its way down that precious esophogus toward the crescent of a stomach, chewing up delicate tissue along the way. The child was now senseless.

Reaching for a glass of water, Mattie doused Lizzie's face. Revived momentarily, the child sputtered and resumed breathing. *For now.* But the powerful chemical mixture had only just begun its descent into her system, and she'd taken enough to kill an adult, much less an infant. *God in heaven above.* Clasping Lizzie in her arms, Mattie scooted toward her medicine bag, searching for a weak acid to neutralize the base. Nothing. And here in this remote town in the Welsh countryside, where might she find such a substance?

Panic closed her throat, and Mattie felt the absence of Angus to the core of her being. She was blessedly and utterly alone with this. A vial of consecrated oil lay in her bag, on hand for blessings and healings, only a teaspoonful remaining. Cradling Lizzie in the crook of her arm, she pried off the lid and poured it down the child's throat, mumbling the most sincere prayer of her life.

Beautiful hands had surrounded Lizzie before birth, when she still floated safely in the womb, beyond the reach of contagion and mishaps. Oh, how Mattie longed for those hands—her mother's, her sister's, her husband's—to join with her now. Lucy Young had called upon the power of God to help Adeline Savage stand and walk across those floorboards. Mattie needed such power because she could not face, could not consider, losing this daughter sprung from her womb. And if she did lose her . . . she would prefer to seek shelter in the cold and solid ground beside her daughter rather than continue down this rocky trail.

"Don't leave me, Lizzie, dear," Mattie begged the child, who convulsed violently and began vomiting over her mother's skirts. Thinking enough like a doctor to turn her, Mattie pulled Lizzie to one side so she would not choke upon her vomit. Lizzie retched and coughed up a frothy soaplike substance, and Mattie noted mucous membrane mixed with lather bubbling from her daughter's rosebud mouth—fragments of her precious internal organs, she diagnosed, her heart contracting in time with Lizzie's stomach.

The child's face strained red in agony, her jaw clenched and shuddering. Mattie dragged her to the door, threw it open, and screamed into the expanse: "Help! Please help me!"

A clatter below sent Bronwen to the bottom of the stairs, where she took in Mattie's panic, and the shaking child upon her lap.

"I need an apothecary," Mattie demanded frantically. "Or a doctor."

Bronwen rushed up the stairs. "But there is nothing nearby," she apologized desperately.

Mad despair threatened to take hold, and Mattie fought against its ragged edges. "Where can I go?"

"*Gwerin cyfrwy.* A village healer?"

A village healer. Gwendolyn. *Of course.*

Clutching the writing child, Mattie used the railing to pull herself upright. "Will you fetch my shawl?"

Bronwen snatched it from the room, and Mattie wrapped it around the babe, feeling Lizzie turn chill in her arms. "Hold on, darling," she sobbed as she made her way downstairs and across the street to the churchyard. The familiar path grew far longer with a trembling Lizzie to manage. Shuddering at the sight of the grave-yard, she ducked beneath the trees and lurched toward the bog. The owl had disappeared.

At the sight of the stepping-stones, Mattie nearly cried aloud. "Please help me," she said aloud, to God, to the trees, and all that listened. She willed herself forward, to one stone and then the next, skirts dragging at her ankles. Leaping to firm ground at last, she nearly fell down upon the earth, but instead struggled forward, across the meadow and around the burbling well. Through the re-mains of the churchyard, and up the stone path, Mattie lurched to-ward the ivy cottage, calling Gwendolyn's name.

At the sound of panic, the old woman pushed open the door, reading the situation at once. She helped carry Lizzie to a cot, laying an ear upon the dear little chest, paying no mind to the mess.

"Ammonia," Mattie said, her voice breaking. "She drank a vial I keep on hand for cleaning. I need a weak acid, hydrochloric per-haps? To counteract the effects."

"Did she vomit?"

"Yes."

"How long ago did she drink it?"

"Twenty minutes perhaps?" Mattie calculated the rate of her pil-grimage. *Had it been only twenty minutes?* "Maybe thirty." Under-standing her own words, she cried, "Has it been too long now to be helpful? Oh, dear God in heaven."

Gwendolyn pulled mortar and pestle from a shelf and drew a

piece of charcoal from the fire. She raised and dropped the stone, crushing the carbon, while Mattie pushed back the hair from her daughter's face, contorted in agony. Yes, charcoal might aid absorption of the poison, she thought dimly.

Mattie pictured Lucy Young's hands upon Adeline's head. Adeline had been some woman's daughter, a woman who suffered as she suffered now. "Do you have any cooking oil?"

Gwendolyn pointed to a cruse of golden liquid on the counter.

"In my faith, we use oil for healing," Mattie said, and Gwendolyn did not seem surprised. "I gave her some before, but I don't have more. I need to bless it. I wish someone else were here to do it. My husband. Or Lucy Young. Or anyone else." She buried her face in her hands, knowing she sounded incoherent.

"You can find the way," Gwendolyn said simply.

Yes, she had helped bless oil before, and surely if God heard prayers, it would be a mother's prayer at a time like this. Comforted by Gwendolyn's calm, Mattie knelt, offering a petition to bless the oil for healing the sick.

Propping Lizzie's head back, she spooned a teaspoonful into the baby's mouth and placed her hands upon the child's head once more. If the child's throat and stomach had been destroyed, perhaps it would be better . . . Mattie couldn't finish the sentence. She didn't want Lizzie to suffer. She would rather . . . she stopped again, trying to push away fear and conjure Lucy Young's faith. The child's breath softened, and she moaned.

Gwendolyn spooned the charcoal mixture into a cup of water, swirling the particles like rising mist, and Mattie cradled Lizzie's head while Gwendolyn administered the liquid. Lizzie swallowed. Charcoal could absorb the chemical, ease its passage, and Mattie pictured it moving through the intricate twists and turns of her daughter's system, praying it was not too late.

Lizzie stopped thrashing and lay inert, but breathing still.

"Shall we tidy you up?" Gwendolyn gestured to the sick stains down the front of Mattie's dress.

"I don't want to leave her," Mattie said. "I'm sorry, but I had nowhere else to go."

"Here's the proper place for you, isn't it?" Gwendolyn helped her undress so she need not leave the baby's side, then wrapped a robe about her and carried her soiled things away for washing. Mattie sank to the floor, tracing Lizzie's skin flushed with fever. Better fever than white waxen stillness. *Anything. Anything but that.*

Hours later, Gwendolyn prepared supper, which Mattie choked down, Lizzie by her side. Watching the jagged and forced breathing, she knew the poison had been more than enough to kill a frail baby. Lizzie's only hope lay with the divine.

As the light outside gave way to darkness, Gwendolyn stoked the fire. Mattie held fast to her daughter's hand, as flames danced and flickered in the hearth.

Back and forth, Gwendolyn rocked, weaving rushes into another four-pointed star. "How came you to healing?" Mattie asked.

The old woman chuckled. "Ah, you're seeking for a story, then?"

"Time is one thing I've plenty of tonight."

The wise woman nodded, knowing stories could work as well as medicine to pass the long, aching hours of a vigil. "My family came from Myddfai, south from here. Part of an old healing family, we are," Gwendolyn explained. "The legends say that a woman, not completely human, of course, walked out of a lake, and my ancestor loved her immediately. He asked for her hand in marriage, and within a handful of years, they had three sons. But as sometimes happens, the husband grew careless, and this goddess, or whatever she was, returned to her lake, taking her husband's wealth with her.

"After she left, her sons haunted the shores, longing for their mother. She came to them, bringing a book filled with ancient medical lore. The Lady of the Lake taught them herbal traditions to make them great healers, and they became known as the renowned physicians of Myddfai.

"Passing their vocation from father to son, they did, but these healers also had daughters. It is from these daughters I am descended. They called us wise women rather than doctors, though many of us excelled at the art."

Mattie clasped Lizzie's fingers, as Gwendolyn's tale wrapped around her mind. "Was it dangerous, this practice?"

"At times. The sixteenth century was a wretched time for Wales," Gwendolyn continued. "King Henry banned our language and hunted the healers, directing money to priests, you see. My ancestor, Gwen Ferch Ellis, compounded salves and plasters to heal people and their farm animals, trading healing favors for food and vegetables.

"It was charms she used for healing, most often. Little prayers they were, though some folks called them spells. Gwen was skilled at her labor, so the wealthy sought her aid as well as the poor. She made the mistake of helping a powerful woman, Jane Conwy, who crossed a nobleman, Thomas Mostyn. Furious to learn a simple village healer would meddle in his affairs, Mostyn accused Gwen of witchcraft."

Mattie leaned foward, watching the flickering flames writhe across Gwendolyn's face as she repeated the tale. "Gwen's friends told her to flee for her life. But she said, 'I've done nothin' wrong. Diverse that had comen to me did beleeve I could help theim, and so I beleeved likewise.'

"The Bishop of St. Asaph asked Gwen's patients to testify against her in Llansanffraid Church. You passed the church on your way, you know. Gwen's neighbors vowed she used a fly as her familiar and killed a man she tried to heal. They hung poor Gwen from the gallows in Denbigh Town Square."

"How could they?" Mattie breathed softly, as the fire died into the night, and Gwen's story wove its spell around her. "Do you know any of her remedies?"

"That's difficult to say, but my mother told me one of her charms."

> Against adversity above wind, against adversity below
>   wind,
> Against adversity of the middle of the world,
> And against adversity in any place in the world,
> God keep you and preserve you.

"Oh, but that's poetry," said Mattie. "Or a prayer perhaps, but surely not a spell."

"Or perhaps they are one in the same." Gwendolyn rocked, her fingers still moving through the rushes.

"What are you weaving?"

"The cross of St. Ffraid."

"St. Ffraid?"

"Many names, she has. Goddess of healing, poetry, fire, and childbirth. She is said to be a source of wisdom, a protector of children."

Mattie sought the shadowed outline of her sleeping child. "May she be close tonight."

"Amen."

"In my religion, we also speak of a divine Mother," Mattie said, thinking of Eliza Snow's poem recently turned to hymn.

"She has been worshipped by many names," Gwendolyn said. "For thousands of years."

Eliza's poem—her prayer—her spell, perhaps—played through Mattie's mind and she spoke the words aloud. *"Truth is reason, truth eternal, tells me I've a Mother there."* A deep and boundless peace settled upon her heart.

Gwendolyn nodded, rocking into the night, as the fire crackled and danced against the stones of the walls. Hours stretched on until Gwendolyn's eyes at last dropped closed, her chair drew still.

Mattie felt herself alone, with only a wee hand to grasp in the darkness. Yet by turning inward in that hushed room, she found she was not alone, for if God was both Mother and Father, God knew her suffering with a mother's heart, could understand her agony with a mother's knowing, could heal through a mother's power.

Mattie leaned in the darkness to place her hands upon her daughter's head, blessing her again as strength coursed through her hands. Though darkness obscured her vision, Mattie sensed love through and from her, felt Lizzie's fever ebb, heard her breathing lengthen as she slept on, wrapped in more than simple blankets.

Of tissues are fashioned the numerous organs of motion, digestion,
circulation, respiration, sensation, etc., generally called systems.
Systems is an inadequate name for a structure so wonderful.
—MARTHA HUGHES CANNON

Chapter Forty-Four

She didn't intend to fall asleep. Sometime between midnight and dawn, as the great wheel turned forward on its axis, her head drooped forward, coming to rest against the couch. As the sky slowly lightened, she jolted back to consciousness, reaching frantic hands toward her child. Checking the rise and fall of Lizzie's chest, the flush of her skin, and gesture of her hands, Mattie read her patient, trying to determine the outcome of her story.

Sensing her mother's stirring, Lizzie's eyes fluttered open and a shard of a smile tugged at her mouth to find her mother so near. "Ta," she said softly.

Weak with relief, Mattie felt her vision blur. "Hello, mother's precious one." *Perhaps, oh perhaps the gravest danger was behind them?*

Her parents had passed through a similar night, one that ended in silence and the laborious stacking of stone. *How had she faced it, that mother of hers?* Mattie fell to her knees by Lizzie's side and, with wet eyes, said again, "Hello."

Gwendolyn stirred, laid a hand upon Mattie's shoulder, observing their patient. Lizzie gazed up in solemnity at this new person with her face wrinkled like the branches of a yew. "Ta," she repeated.

"Lovely to meet you," said Gwendolyn.

Gwendolyn insisted they stay. Lizzie passed through several crabby and cantankerous days, but Gwendolyn dosed her with a fennel decoction to help her recover. As Lizzie gradually grew stronger, she came to love the stone cottage, the gentleness of Gwendolyn's hands, and the forest creatures that made her coo with delight.

While the baby rested, Gwendolyn taught Mattie the art of the Welsh healer, advising which plants could be cultivated and compounded fresh, which needed to be dried. Together they chopped and diced, stirred and stewed, working over an ebony cauldron hung near the fire. They formed plasters and salves from comfrey and meadowsweet, brewed tinctures of rhubarb and feverfew, drew infusions of white horehound to bottle as a cough syrup. Gwendolyn crushed hedgerow plants into a poultice that improved Mattie's uterus complaint, and they drank daily from the nearby well. After a few weeks of Gwendolyn's herbs and garden diet, Mattie had never felt stronger.

"You are an encyclopedia of remedies, my friend," Mattie said, awed by her knowledge.

"As they say, the gray old woman in the corner from her mother heard a story, which from her mother she had heard, and after her, I have remembered it," Gwendolyn said with a smile. From her collection of dried herbs, she gathered seeds to wrap in leaves of paper for Mattie to plant in her garden at home.

Trying to capture the miraculous events in letters for Angus and her mother, Mattie wrote:

I caught her as she fell, senseless, gasping for breath, and went through all the horror and agony of feeling she was stiffening and dying in my arms.

Yet she knew she hadn't conveyed the half of it.

By passing through that ordeal I learned God was my friend when others were thousands of miles distant. My thankfulness to the true and living God will be a support to me as long as life and reason lasts.

Those words too, captured the smallest part of all she felt.

More at home at Gwendolyn's cottage than anywhere else in her exile, Mattie found herself enjoying letters from home like a delicious dessert, rather than the manna they'd been to her before. Gwendolyn held one aloft one day, and Mattie dragged her eyes from Lizzie who had just taken her first toddling steps the day before.

Dear Martha,

Your father and I are relieved to know you are safe and Lizzie is recovering. May this letter find you in good health and spirits, dear daughter.

I cannot tell you how difficult it is to have you and Lizzie so far away, where I cannot see for myself how you are faring, cannot help you with the burdens you carry.

How warm her mother had become in her old age, so different from the stern woman who once chastised her for her studies.

My only solace is you have friends, if not family, there to help you, and our God, to whom I pray daily to bless and keep you until you are able to return to this valley once more.

Family. Gwendolyn was far more family to them than her Birmingham cousins had been.

Your father is poorly at the moment.

Mattie's breath quickened. What if her father . . . ? While she was overseas . . . ? She clutched the paper, frantic to use her medical training on her father's behalf.

> *The doctor believes it is pneumonia, but James insists he suffers from nothing more than old age. Please remember him in your prayers. He sends his love and news that he has not yet recovered your old trunk but will keep trying.*
> *Your loving Mother*

Your father is poorly. The words spun through Mattie's head, mocking their way through her mind in a distorted refrain. *What if her father . . .* The thought forced its way in, and Mattie struggled with a fierce longing to flee home. She would not sacrifice being with Papa during his last days on earth, not even for Angus. If Lizzie could not remember her grandfather—Mattie's breath caught against the rough sides of her throat. Her daughter played on, oblivious.

Gwendolyn drew close, reading her distress. "My father is poorly," Mattie explained, noting proof the outside world could encroach upon this charmed dwelling, after all.

"Will you go to him, then?" Gwendolyn asked, still ignorant of the true reasons that kept them abroad.

"I think I must," Mattie said, counting the number of weeks before her arrest warrant would expire. If she left now, it would still be well more than a month before she could get there. Scurrying to find a bottle of ink, she penned Angus:

> *Dear Munn,*
> *I plan to secure a berth in a steamer sailing from Liverpool on the 19th. If all goes well, I will soon be in America. I may stop in Ann Arbor on my way home to have Lizzie looked at by one of my medical school professors, to be sure she is fully recovered. Then I will hurry home to Papa. If you hear news*

that indicates I must stay away longer, please write at once, sending it on to New York.

Lizzie grows stronger day by day, and I am beyond grateful our treasure has been spared. I believe positively I should have gone mad had she been taken. Still we know not how much we can bear. Many others—my own mother included—have had their darlings snatched away.

I have heard my father is ill and I'm frantic with worry. Please let me know how he is faring. I cannot bear to think of missing his final days.

Accept many kisses and love from us both. I am hoping the situation has improved after so many months. When the time is up? What then, dearest? How does the prospect look? Be frank with me.

Your own, Alace

H_2O has a great tendency to resolve itself into a gaseous vapor.
—MARTHA HUGHES CANNON

Chapter Forty-Five

Mattie wrapped Gwendolyn in a bone-deep hug, knowing that if she ever found a way to return, she would probably find her sleeping beside Mair. No common blood ran through their veins, true, but Mattie still felt that in parting from this gentle crone, her heart would be wrenched between two sides of an ocean. Lizzie clung to Gwendolyn too, grasping her fingers as though she refused to let them go.

Gwendolyn pulled Mattie's face down to the level of her own. *"Rhowch gylch i hi, arglwydd,"* she said, tucking a Ffraid's cross into her bag.

"How can I ever thank you?" Mattie asked, her eyes blurring at the edges. "I will never forget you, nor this dear place."

"It is a hard place to let you go," Gwendolyn admitted. "But you have brilliant things ahead of you, love. I am more than certain of that."

As Mattie walked away from Tythyn Bodrhyll, she glanced over her shoulder. "Ta-ra!" she called, longing for the power to leave part of herself behind, and part to travel onward.

Iron ore mined from the bowels of the earth and smelted into steel in the forges of Birmingham framed the hull of the steamship that carried Mattie and Lizzie to Liverpool. Upon the docks, crowds surged forward, eager to start life over in a new world across the sea. Carried on immigrant hopes and dreams, the ship incinerated coal to power mighty boilers. Swelling over a vast ocean of uncertainty, the steamer finally shook them down at last with a cloud of black smoke in New York harbor.

After four precarious weeks, Mattie struggled up from her narrow berth and carried Lizzie on deck to catch the first glimpse of America. A fine mist veiled the harbor, wrapping the flat expanse of water in a bolt of shifting silver. The fog obscured ships and fishing vessels alike, revealing here a disembodied mast and there a bow, like shipwrecked fragments adrift upon the water.

Searching for Lady Liberty's torch, Mattie found instead the outlines of the Washington Building and the Commodities Exchange, the industrial giants towering over New York harbor in an upward creeping mélange of steel and glass. Then the wind shifted, sweeping the veil aside, and the statue's great arm rose triumphant, casting light through the vapors.

Mother Liberty sheltered a book in the crook of her arm, copper folds of fabric falling about her bare feet planted firm on her pedestal. Holding herself with a posture of vulnerability, she appeared nearly fragile despite her bulk of strength. "Send these, the homeless, tempest-tossed to me," Mattie recited for a pensive Lizzie. "I lift my lamp beside the golden door." After so many months abroad, how sick Mattie had grown of hiding, of running, pretending, and lying. Oh, for a home of her own, a place for Lizzie to wake each morning knowing she would remain there still as night fell. And for a father who returned home each evening.

Baby and reticule in tow, Mattie struggled down the gangplank clutching the hand rope so her boots would not to slip on salt-brined wood. Humanity surged around her, pushing their way forward to Castle Garden for processing in one long queue after another. Mattie passed through examinations, paper processing, and luggage sorting, all while hefting a fussy baby in dire need of a nappy change.

Castle Garden had been built as a fort for the War of 1812, only to be roofed over later as a concert hall before converting once more into a processing center for the ever-increasing flood of immigrants. Among British, Welsh, Gaelic, Scandinavian, Romanian, and French accents, at last Mattie also picked out American English, a language with no ancient and poetic origins, but one she spoke fluently, relishing each and every word.

Attempting to track the movement of their luggage as she pushed her way through the crowds, Mattie became aware of a man moving toward her. Instinctively, she reached to protect her bags and the baby, then processed his broadcloth suit, piercing blue eyes, and a mannerism of pushing back his hat she would recognize anywhere.

Angus's arms wrapped around her, as Mattie could only exclaim, "But how?"

Tears sprung to her eyes at the wonder of finding, among thousands of people, one who knew her real name, and against whose shoulder she could, at last, set down her burdens.

She laughed, pulling him close only to draw back, devouring him with her eyes. Lizzie fussed and clutched to her mother, bewildered to find this strange man before her, and her dear mama gone mad.

"However did you manage it?" Mattie blurted.

"Can I not find a week or two to welcome my wife and daughter home?" Angus lifted a valise in one arm and a stunned Lizzie in the other, as Mattie found herself, for the first time in ever so long, with nothing at all to carry. She trailed after her husband and daughter in a daze, her arms oddly and gloriously empty.

"You are really here," Mattie said, still struggling to believe it.

"And . . . you're alone?" She looked about as if he might be hiding an entourage.

"Yes, my brave and beautiful wife, who traipsed a wide circle around this round globe to return to my arms, I really am."

"And Papa?" She grasped his arm frantically.

"Alive and recovering, my love."

"Oh, thank the heavens above."

Angus directed the porter to lift Mattie's trunk onto his hired coach. "Now, my dear, I'd like you to consider what we shall do and see in New York this precious week. You need only worry about choosing which meals you wish to taste, which sights you care to see. Let me take care of the rest. New York lies before you in all her splendor, though less elegant than the cities you've left behind. Tell me, love. How shall we spend our time together?"

Angus opened the door of the carriage and handed her up, conveying adoration with his simplest gesture. *What did she want at the end of this journey?* She hardly knew. A week with Angus in New York City—no sharing, no hiding. Only the two of them, well three . . . together.

Art galleries, concert halls, theaters, and restaurants—a wave of weariness swept over her as great and mighty as the Atlantic she had just traversed. "For now, I'm afraid divine heaven itself sounds like a comfortable bed and a good long sleep," Mattie said, slumping against Angus's shoulder, as the burdens slipped from her shoulders and exhaustion settled at the center of her bones.

"Then that is what we shall do first," Angus said. Leaning against him, Mattie could have cried with joy at the sight of Lizzie reaching for her papa's scratchy beard and giggling when she caught it, coming to know the man who was her father at long last.

The week was as heavenly as it sounded. They ate Italian oysters and pasta in Mulberry Bend, thrilled at Verdi's *Otello* at the Metropolitan Opera House, and viewed a newly acquired limestone sarcophagus in the Museum of Art, carved by hands in the fifth century before Christ. And she spent all of this, every moment, with Angus.

The smallest moments tasted sweetest: walking down Madison Avenue with Angus—wearing a hat she'd brought from England, nodding to passersby who assumed at first glance that they—Angus, Mattie, and Lizzie—were a family. "They think this is all of us," Mattie said, smiling at their lovely charade.

"For today, it is," Angus replied. Mattie strolled beside him, trying to pretend this was how she'd always lived, rather than in a crowded adobe house scratched from desert soil. In spite of her joy, she could not unsee the contrasts of the city. After all, the Vanderbilt mansion on 57th Street was not far from nearby dockyards where families stumbled off ships and into crowded tenements, nor from filthy alleyways where children pulled threads in sweatshops all day in exchange for meager sustenance. The whole world had descended upon New York City, and Mattie could not untangle the labyrinth of languages spoken on the streets, nor repress her longing to scoop up every street urchin and feed him a good meal.

They turned their steps toward Central Park, where strangers smiled at the picture of domestic bliss they created ambling over hills and along the river. "These grassy knolls and stony bridges are so like Wales," Mattie told him. "And how is Emmeline? Have you reconciled with her?"

"Well enough," Angus said, disinclined to talk about the funeral. Mattie didn't press him further, not wanting to spoil their few precious days together. Lying near him each night, she awakened to the gentle rise and fall of his chest beside her, and fell back asleep to the sound of his breathing, lulling her like a lullaby.

Though Mattie tried to hold onto their hours together, they slipped through her fingers like mist fading over New York harbor. On the night before they were to leave—he to return to Salt Lake, she to continue to Ann Arbor—they lingered over a final dinner together. Filled with his love, Mattie turned a glowing face toward him, hoping their future would hold many more days like the ones they had just passed.

But he glanced away. "I'm afraid there's something I must tell you," he confessed, and a cold fear stole round her heart at his words.

"What is it?"

"In your last letter, you asked me to be frank with you." She nodded. "Have you seen the papers since you left England?"

"You know I haven't—" She paused, realizing it was odd he had not read a paper this whole week. "What's happened, Angus?"

He carefully cut his meat. "I didn't want to alarm you. I wanted you to hear it from me, in person." He chewed and swallowed, while Mattie fought the urge to wring the words out of him. "I know how much you hoped your time abroad would change things." He fiddled with his napkin. "But I'm afraid, thanks to Congress, they could become much worse."

"*Worse?*" Mattie asked, as Lizzie made a grab for her mother's spoon. "How could they possibly become worse?"

"In spite of our work to stop it, the Edmunds-Tucker Act passed," Angus explained. "They've abolished women's suffrage in the territory."

Mattie gasped. "For *all* women?" Women had been able to vote in Utah since she'd been a teen finishing grammar school. "But how *can* they?"

"I don't know, but they have. Any man unwilling to take an oath disavowing polygamy has also lost his vote. Saints are fleeing to Canada, Mexico, and the barren edges of the territory."

"But how can such a ruling be constitutional?"

"I don't believe it is," Angus said. "But there's more, I'm afraid. The government has begun seizing Church property. They're confiscating temples, meetinghouses, and our granaries, and charging us rent for the use of them."

Mattie set down her fork. "The property *we* built? They've declared war on us, then?"

"It seems so."

Considering the thriving brothels in this city, she burned at the hypocrisy of the government's outrage over plural marriage. From Angus's expression, she knew this wasn't all. "What aren't you telling me?"

He couldn't look at her. "Many say the act will also prevent illegitimate children from inheriting from their fathers."

"Illegitimate children?"

Indignation swept over Mattie as she looked down at her daughter. The government that had done nothing to protect them from mobs in Missouri and Illinois, had stood by as they were driven from state to state, was now confiscating their buildings because of untraditional marital practices? Why couldn't they leave people alone to love as they chose? Who was the practice possibly hurting? "It's blatant religious discrimination," Mattie said in anguish. "What can we do?"

"Emmeline Wells and Zina Young are lobbying Congress, Mattie, and George Reynolds has agreed to be a test case before the Supreme Court."

"Angus, when you proposed to me, you said you believed that things would go our way," Mattie said with anguish. "*You said* the Lord would deliver us."

"And I am as sure as ever that He will, my love." Angus studied his empty plate. "But perhaps not in the way I anticipated."

The interlude in New York was not a prelude of things to come, then, but a brief taste of things she most desired that would soon be snatched away again. She did not envy the Vanderbilts their mansion, but how she longed for her parents' home, a simple structure where she could brush sorghum syrup over homemade bread for her daughter and join hands in grace with Angus each evening.

Mattie raised haunted eyes to her husband. *This. After spending months abroad to protect him. All those weeks of hiding and tossing about from pillar to post. For what? The witch hunt continued, written into law.* "And if the Supreme Court rules against us?" Mattie asked. "Whatever shall we do?"

"I don't know, my love," Angus admitted. "I'm afraid I just don't know." It was this admission, more than anything else, that turned her blood cold.

Life consists of reaction of organized matter upon incident forces.
—MARTHA HUGHES CANNON

Chapter Forty-Six

1887
Ann Arbor, Michigan

Beneath the turrets of her alma mater, Mattie frowned at students who looked far too young to be at university, as they lazed beneath trees and greeted classmates on their way to lecture.

Mattie pushed Lizzie's perambulator across the square, feeling like an irrelevant middle-aged mother. "Just wait," she wanted to tell their hopeful college faces. "You too will be here soon enough."

Her dark thoughts spiraled through the quad, as students crisscrossed and intersected, choosing paths carelessly. Mattie stopped to settle Lizzie, thinking that given the melancholic circles her mind had moved in since parting from Angus in New York, it might have been better to banish her ornery self from public until she pulled herself together.

The elms had grown. Had it truly been ten years since she dissected cadavers and spent her free time crafting taxidermy squirrels? An image of Leolin smoking his cigar and confessing his adoration entered her mind. For one moment she let her mind ramble down a length of alternate roadway where she practiced medicine with Leolin as his only wife. The boredom she had imagined years ago in her refusal now seemed as naïve as the students streaming past her.

Mattie leaned forward to tease a complaining Lizzie, and wondered at the sensations, odd and yet familiar, she'd not felt for two years past. That week in New York, as blissful as it had been, might leave her situation even more complicated.

Across the diagonal walk hurried a figure dressed in a dark skirt and white shirtwaist, child in arms. Though years had passed since Mattie had last seen Barb, her friend moved with the same vigor, though she'd filled out with the softness of motherhood.

"Mattie!" Pushing through bewildered students, Barb threw herself into Mattie's arms. After months of being so guarded, Mattie drew back, protectively wrapping her arms about herself.

Creases had formed at the corners of Barb's gray eyes, but her gaze held steady. "How I have longed to see you! Letters haven't been nearly enough."

Students moved around them, casting sidelong glances at the women. Barb hugged her again, then held her own daughter over the perambulator for introductions.

"She has her mother's intelligent forehead," Barb pronounced about Lizzie. "Another thinker."

"She is most certainly a prattler," Mattie acknowledged.

"Your gift for public speaking too, perhaps? Hello, little one," Barb said. "What a lovely little friend you must be to your mother. And this is my Ruby."

"Hello, Ruby," Mattie said to the redheaded cherub in Barb's arms.

Barb used her free hand to form a salute in front of her forehead. "Mother's friend says hello."

Ruby returned the gesture. "She also says hello," Barb said, smiling. Extending two fingers in the shape of an L, she said, "This is Lizzie." Her fingers twisted quickly, spelling out each letter of Lizzie's name, as Mattie glimpsed a road she'd not realized her friend had traveled.

Lizzie began to wiggle, trying to escape her little prison. "As long as we keep moving, she will be happy," Mattie promised, pushing the pram down the walkway.

"Like her mother in so many ways!" Barb said. "I can hardly keep track of you, my friend! England and Wales—all by yourself, with a baby in tow! What an adventurer you are. Shall we walk toward the river?"

Mattie nodded, amused by Barb's view of her time abroad, moving toward the wooded paths beyond the regimented lines of campus. "I'm afraid it was a bit of a forced adventure. Seeing Europe under different circumstances would have been delightful, but on my own with a little one, it was not much of a pleasure tour." Dappled with tree shadows, the river flowed downward near the spot where they rowed years before. The trees had grown taller, sheltering a habitat less mesmerizing than the one Mattie remembered. "Barb, however did we get so old?"

Barb laughed, a hard edge between the sounds of glee. "I don't know. One year at a time I suppose. Remember how we planned to trod the path of fame together?"

"Nothing has turned out as I imagined," Mattie confessed, daring a swift glance at Barb's sharp and honest eyes.

Mattie lifted Lizzie from her pram and set a blanket upon the grass. The little girl tried to push herself to standing, and toppled over instead. Barb set Ruby beside Lizzie and linked her pointer fingers together. "Can she be a new friend?" Ruby nodded and echoed her mother's gesture.

"When we were students, I wanted to take on the world, and I was naïve enough to believe I could do it, that life would be fair." Mattie paused. "But I've learned nothing is fair. Not for me or for anyone else." Her pitying eyes rested on Ruby, this lovely child restricted to a world without sound.

Barb recognized the glance. "I admit my goals have changed since those days. I practice medicine as I can. My husband supports my work. But at the moment, I'm more passionate about supporting other advances rather than pursuing fame for its own sake."

"What advances?" Mattie asked, intrigued.

"Ruby lost her hearing when she was a little older than Lizzie."

Mattie nodded, imagining she understood her friend's futility at finding everything is broken and can never be put right.

"Watching her world fade to silence broke our hearts, of course," Barb continued gently, "but watching the world respond to Ruby was even worse. She's a bright and curious girl, and very much the same person she was before her loss."

Ruby picked a wildflower and rushed to her mother, moving it from one side of her nose to the other. "Yes, flower," Barb said, signing back.

But Ruby wasn't finished. She gestured to her mouth, pricked her cheek with a finger and made a swatting motion.

Barb laughed. "You're right, the flower makes good food for bees." Ruby offered the blossom to Lizzie, and Mattie watched to make sure her daughter didn't pop it in her mouth for closer examination.

"Since she cannot hear," Barb continued, "many people assume her brain is impaired too. We are fighting to have her educated, but the struggle is exhausting, and if we had fewer resources, it would be impossible." Her tone grew hard, and Mattie heard echoes of the woman who had once spoken of witch burnings beneath these very boughs. "The deaf and blind should not have to live their lives at the margins of society. It is this struggle that has taken over my world, lending new direction to my work."

Mattie dropped her gaze, impressed and chastened by her first assumptions. "Ruby is lucky to have you for a mother. If anyone can bring changes about, it is you."

"I'm lucky to have Ruby for my daughter," Barb replied, as if waiting for Mattie to say more.

Watching Ruby scamper across the grass, brave and fearless, Mattie longed to lay her heart bare, to set all down before Barb's feet. She knew what the Eastern newspapers said about Mormon polygamists. Eloquent leaders denounced the practice as "organized filth" and called Utah "the brothel of the nation." *What had her friend heard? What would she believe?* Barb's friendship felt more precious than ever and she had no desire to risk it. And always, there was potential danger from whom she might tell.

"I am also engaged in a conflict I have not told you of," Mattie said haltingly. "And I am afraid I've not been entirely honest with you either."

"I imagine after so much time apart, we've both traveled some roads too difficult to share via letters, Mattie."

"Forgive me. It had been so long, and I'd very nearly forgotten how much I trust your heart."

"I understand." Barb's gaze invited her to continue.

"In truth, I was forced overseas, as there was a warrant out for my arrest."

"I must admit that was about the last thing I expected to hear from you," Barb said, laughing.

Mattie joined in the laughter, which eased the sharpness of her pain, feeling they were schoolgirls once more. "I have become a criminal for my religion, for I have married a man who has four other wives." Mattie struggled to continue. "I know what you might think of me, I've read the papers, the way they portray polygamous women, degraded and enslaved. But it's not—" She broke off.

Barb clutched her arm. "Mattie, those are the newspapers. They love a scandal. I admit the arrangement doesn't sound pleasant to me, but I *know you*. If you tell me you are happy, it is *you* I will believe."

Tears spilled freely down Mattie's cheeks as Ruby settled into her mother's lap, wrapping her arms about her neck. "I am speaking truth when I say I adore my husband above all men living. While it has not been easy to share his affection, it is far more difficult to be hunted and maligned as we have been. He spent six months in prison when Lizzie was born."

Concern filled Barb's eyes. "Oh, my friend, I'm so sorry."

"Federal agents placed a warrant for my arrest, and hunted me at work and in my home. I had to adopt a fake name and go into hiding before fleeing overseas."

"I can't begin to imagine," Barb said. "Thank you for trusting me. I promise to keep your secret safe."

"Thank you," Mattie said. "I hoped going overseas would resolve the situation, but I'm afraid things have only grown worse. They've passed laws disenfranchising Utah women and confiscating Church property."

"I thought of you when I heard about that, never imagining how much it would affect you," Barb said. "I don't see how it could be constitutional."

"It's not, yet the courts are upholding it."

"And what will you do to fight it, my fearsome, brilliant friend?"

"Fight the courts?" Mattie raised her eyes. "What could *I* possibly do? I'm only one person."

Barb smiled and bounced Ruby on her lap. "Are you, Mattie? Are you really? Because I see a woman who is also a doctor. Who is also an orator. Who is also one of the bravest, most brilliant women I know. I see a woman who faced down prejudice to graduate from two medical schools, then enrolled in oratory school so she'd be better prepared to change the world for the better." She smoothed back her daughter's fiery curls.

"That hardly even feels like me anymore," Mattie confessed, thinking how much her world had shrunk to the size of her small daughter. "I've given up all of that. I've had to." Her shoulders sagged. "I cannot fight the U.S. government. These past few years have changed and broken me."

"You do not look so broken," Barb said. "Not from where I sit."

"But the laws . . ."

"Make them write new laws, Mattie. I am no defender of plural marriage, but it's religious freedom you're speaking of, freedom to live a lifestyle of your choosing, freedom to vote. If anyone could fight for such a thing, it would be you."

Write new laws . . . Mattie's mind spun. The witch hunt acts of 1550. The banning of the Welsh language. The Edmunds-Tucker Act of 1887. The mayor of Birmingham advocating for public health. "Women have been able to vote in Utah territory since I was thirteen years old," she said, thoughtfully.

"Then you've been raised with a reality few women in this country have ever known. That's a good place to start, my friend." Barb's eyes burned with conviction. "*Go change things,* for you, for me, and for our daughters."

Chills passed over Mattie, remembering how she had not let detractors deter her from medical school. For the first time in so many months—*or was it years?*—the desire to fight stirred within her, accompanied by the beginnings of hope. As she memorized the hard, eager lines of Barb's face, past dreams morphed into the dreams of the present, and she wished she could bottle her friend's resolve in a glass vial to carry westward. "I can try," she promised.

Part Five

There are yet many realms of silence to be made vocal,
many scientific truths to be discovered, many arts to be
perfected, which require the hearts and minds of women.
—MARTHA HUGHES CANNON

Chapter Forty-Seven

SEPTEMBER 24, 1890
Utah Territory

In the dusty valley of Salt Lake, railways and rough timbered farms had begun to give way to ornate residencies transplanted from the East by hopeful hands. The granite temple that had been wrestled from the mountains and chiseled into place, now stood five stories high, bookended by six towers, its roof still scaffolded as it neared completion. Electric trolleys plied the streets alongside horses and carriages—the wheels of the future turning alongside the trappings of the past.

A nervous tension filled the streets, and the brisk autumnal air hovered, expectant and waiting. Men in bowler hats walked at a clipped pace between office buildings. Women hushed children and turned anxious eyes up the streets. Clock hands seemed to move more slowly, as a sense of anticipation settled as fine and unmistakable as dust settled at the edges of an unused room.

Outside her home of stacked red brick and gray stone, Mattie wrestled Welsh ivy back onto its trellis, wiping sweat from her brow with her sleeve, pausing from her work to look up the wide breathless street. The front door opened and a five-year-old girl, still in a plain white nightgown, shuffled onto the porch, her little brother toddling behind her. "Mother!" Lizzie called. "James wants his brefust and me does too."

Mattie put down her pruning shears and laughed, a flood of joy at the sight of her two dear ones standing on her own porch. "Is that so?" she said to the girl, as she put down her shears and removed the cloth holding back her hair.

"Yes," said Lizzie, sticking out her bottom lip.

"How do you ask for help?"

"I say 'please,'" Lizzie said, hopefully.

"Peez, peez, peez," James repeated.

"Very polite of you, loves," Mattie said, wiping her hands on her apron. "Will you take your brother inside, Lizzie, while Mother washes up?" She cast one more glance down the quiet street. "Grandmama will be here soon to play with you while Mama goes to work."

Lizzie shepherded the baby back inside. "Grandmama is coming, Jamesy," she said, and the little boy grinned and clapped.

Mattie washed garden grime from her hands and lifted James into his carved walnut high chair, making the sound of a train as she propelled him. Lizzie scaled a stool beside the chopping block in the center of the kitchen, as Mattie spooned fresh applesauce into a bowl, sliced thick bread, and spread it with sorghum.

"Good morning!" called Elizabeth, as she opened the front door and rounded the corner. Gray hair threaded generously through Elizabeth's hair, but she still managed genuine excitement for grandchildren. Not for the first time, Mattie silently acknowledged that in many ways Elizabeth's devotion to her many children and grandchildren had made her own career possible.

"Grandmama!" James called.

"My turn for the first kiss!" said Lizzie. Elizabeth laughed, bending to kiss Lizzie and then James, a folded newspaper held lightly in her hand.

Mattie rose at the sight of the paper, leaving James with applesauce on his chin. He smacked the tray of his high chair, but his mother did not notice. "Is that—?"

"Yes," Elizabeth said, handing her the paper. "I'll feed them."

Mattie snatched up the *Deseret News* and scanned down the front page.

OFFICIAL DECLARATION

I, therefore, as President of The Church of Jesus Christ of Latter-day Saints, do hereby, in the most solemn manner . . . Inasmuch as laws have been enacted by Congress forbidding plural marriages, which laws have been pronounced constitutional by the court of last resort, I hereby declare my intention to submit to those laws. . . . And I now publicly declare that my advice to the Latter-day Saints is to refrain from contracting any marriage forbidden by the law of the land. Wilford Woodruff

Mattie sank down onto a chair at the nearby table and buried her head in her arms. So the rumors were true, and this was the end of it? The end of decades of fighting and insisting that the United States would capitulate before the laws of God or receive the wrath of the Almighty? The end of talks that claimed the millennium was imminent and the principle of plural marriage was one they could never abandon? All those sacrifices, all those arrests, Angus's months in the territorial penitentiary, her time abroad—their lives tossed about like flotsam on the sea—all to arrive at this moment: "My advice is to refrain from contracting any marriage forbidden by the law of the land."

And what is your advice for those who already have? she wanted to demand of the paper.

"Mama?" asked Lizzie, her watchful eyes upon her mother.

Mattie forced her head upright. "Yes, my love?" Those perfect trusting blue eyes—Angus's eyes—the eyes of a little girl whose birth had just been declared illegitimate, her parents' marriage bonds erased with ink spread casually across newsprint by youth in a printing office.

Mattie looked into those steady, wide eyes, so quick to see humor, to connect truth in the world about her, and thought of the dark night Lizzie had swallowed enough poison to kill a grown man. She would need that strength, bless her, for the years ahead.

Elizabeth reached to take her daughter's hands, offering no words, but the simple presence of another upon whom she could rely.

She must begin as other noble women and nearly
all great men have begun, and give herself soul and
body to the acquisition of wisdom and skill, and her
very opposition and difficulties will be gain.

—MARTHA HUGHES CANNON

Chapter Forty-Eight

His heart and body worn down with long labor, James Paul lay dying. Cumulative years of work and laughter had slackened his skin, until it hung about his face in loose folds. His lips, unable to hold their form, spread wide and drooling, while his legs and ankles had swollen to many times their original size as if he were slipping earthward, cell by blessed cell. Seemingly there was no miracle this man could not manage, save the evasion of death itself.

His family had gathered, crowding into the small bedroom where he had lain each night on a bed he had fashioned, beside Elizabeth, who had slept three decades by his side. Her hands had knotted the cords and stuffed the mattress upon which he now dozed and woke, fitfully, his fingers twisting against the quilt her hands had spun, sewn, and pieced. Together they had reared the walls of this house to keep their children safe, children now grown and raising children of their own—each child a planet in the center of an orbit around which their little ones circled, spinning outward in wide and tilting arcs. The adolescents watched their grandfather, unnerved by the indignity of old age, certain they would never arrive there.

"An awful lot of you are here to see an old man," James mumbled quietly.

"All of us," Logan said, then corrected himself. "Rather—all of us except Angus."

"He wanted to be here," Mattie explained, holding his absence as a dull ache within her chest.

Little James and Lizzie held their mother's hands, touched by the grim adults paying respect to a man who seemed too good for this earth.

James drew labored breaths as if each rise of his chest was an accomplishment, one step more up the steep incline of a trail. Elizabeth curled toward him on the bed, her tears falling upon their intertwined fingers. Mary supported her mother's shoulders, Parley behind her, while Mattie pressed herself against the wall, trying not to feel the empty wall at her back. James's eyes flickered open briefly, resting upon each of his children in turn, landing upon his doctor daughter, pride in the depths of his weary eyes.

Looking back upon the thirty-four years of her life, Mattie felt she must lay her every accomplishment, her every achievement, down at the foot of this sickbed. For how would she have fostered ambition without James's encouragement and love? How different would life have been had her mother never remarried? She tearfully reflected at the small and delicately oiled hinges upon which an uncertain future invariably turned.

"I love you, James," Elizabeth whispered in his ear.

Their children echoed her words: "We love you."

"Love you."

"Love you!" little James announced, crawling into Mattie's arms, not yet understanding the weight of the name he bore.

As if released from a lifelong responsibility, James's face relaxed, his chest lifted, fell, and rose no more. A sob escaped Elizabeth as she cradled his hand to her chest.

With her intimate knowledge of death, Mattie observed from a strange and floating distance that the man her mother loved no longer inhabited the room. It was then that she felt his utter abandonment, for he had surely fled, and yet she could not imagine this wide and aching world without him. Bending herself around her son, Mattie let her tears fall thick into his hair, wishing she could hold onto him—could hold onto anything—forever.

Mattie woke with a start, heart pounding, reaching out for something to hold onto. Nothing. Only darkness and a piercing fear that had haunted her nights since Papa had died. She wanted Angus, needed his still and steady breathing beside her to stop the nightmares. But he was gone. Gone on business, gone with another family, sworn publicly to be husband to her no more. Gone, leaving only her children as a stirring proof he had ever been here at all. She fumbled in the dark for medicine to take away this dull ache, to tumble her back into the blessed forgetfulness of sleep.

Quietness descended upon the adobe home and black crepe wreathed the door. The family moved in hushed tones as they dressed James's body in his best suit, laying him out for friends and neighbors to pay their respects. James had not lived an outwardly remarkable life, so most mourners were family, though those touched by his quiet kindness and generosity felt his loss keenly; his most remarkable trait had always been his ability to deeply love.

In a nearby chapel, Angus conducted the meeting retracing the life of James Paul from Scotland to the valley. Logan spoke, Mary's oldest children sang a song, and Adam eulogized his father. A simple service soon over, the coffin closed and carried to the cemetery for interment.

Crowded into the family home, James's mourners shared a modest meal, and the day drew to a close. Angus hurried off to tend to pressing business. Mary rounded up her brood, hugged her mother, and departed. Logan and Adam and Joseph and Lotta gathered their families.

As Mattie collected Lizzie and James, she felt a definitive stillness descend upon the house. "Do you want me to stay with you tonight?" she asked her mother.

"If it isn't a bother," Elizabeth confessed. "It's awfully strange to have this house to myself. I'm sure I will get used to it eventually."

"Of course it's not a bother." Mattie tucked Lizzie and James into her old bed upstairs, the one she'd once shared with Joseph and Lotta. As they drifted into slumber, she returned to her parents' bedroom and knocked on the door.

"Come in." Seated in front of her dressing table in a worn nightgown, Elizabeth brushed out her long gray hair. The room smelled of dusting powder and old age. Papa's things lay on the dresser, untouched as if he had stepped out for a moment and would soon return.

Mattie began unfastening her own dress, changing into an extra nightgown of Elizabeth's. Watching their reflections in the mirror, Mattie realized they looked like two widows growing older, both essentially left alone.

"It was nice to see Angus at the funeral," Elizabeth said.

"We see precious little of him these days," Mattie confessed.

"This wasn't the marriage you signed up for." Elizabeth plaited the strands of her hair with knotted fingers.

"No," Mattie admitted. "It wasn't. In reality, all I ever really wanted was what you and Papa had, though I lost sight of that ideal when I fell in love with Angus. Now I fear Lizzie and James will never know their papa the way that I knew mine." Sorrow mounted near the back of her throat.

"They probably won't," Elizabeth said, placing a nightcap on her head and settling onto the mattress she'd shared with her husband. "But you forget, Mattie, you also wanted more than our life. You forget you have given them something I couldn't give you, my dear."

Mattie lay beside her mother, settling in the warmth of her presence and leaning over to snuff the candle into darkness. Ironic how she'd been so estranged from Elizabeth in her youth, and now it seemed their differences united them more than drove them apart. "In truth, we need my income. Angus's mining investments have not done well. I can only hope to give Lizzie and James a small part of the things you have given me, Mother."

"Rely upon God as you ever have and move forward with all the gifts you have to offer this world. You were right to want to give them—you always knew it. James knew it, too. It's what he would want for you."

Mattie turned toward her mother in the darkness, reaching for her arm. Though she'd stayed to comfort her mother, now she was the one being comforted. Elizabeth was right, she needed to move forward, to resume her practice, resume her nursing school, let go of expectations of how things might have been, and live in the reality of what they had, in fact, become.

*Woman is not only a helpmeet by the fireside, but she
can, when allowed to do so, become a most powerful and
a most potent factor in the affairs of the government.*

—MARTHA HUGHES CANNON

Chapter Forty-Nine

After a long day of patients and nursing school duties, Mattie sat down beside Mary in the upper gallery of the Salt Lake Theater, for a program of music ending with Adelina Patti singing "Traviata."

"I get to see you at last," Mary said, "without any of our children."

"It's a miracle," Mattie agreed, tucking back the black dotted veil of her mourning hat, as theatergoers sought their seats. "It is a bit early to appear in public, but Papa wouldn't have wanted us to stay at home for months on end."

"I wish Mama would have come," Mary agreed. "The outing would have done her good." Many prominent Salt Lake families were there. Mattie spotted Emmeline B. Wells, who had been decidedly chilly since Mattie had returned from overseas, and Mattie felt a twinge of remorse remembering the mentor Emmeline had once been to her.

The orchestra began tuning their instruments, the violas screeching out dusty notes as they cast about for the correct one.

Across the circle of carved pillars holding up the balconies, a familiar movement caught her attention. Angus, a hand tucked possessively through the crook of his arm, leaned into Amelia and patted her hand with affection. His first wife. The only one publicly acknowledged now. Mary followed Mattie's gaze. "Isn't that . . ." She let the sentence trail off.

A wad settled at the base of Mattie's stomach as the house lights dimmed and the performance began with an aria by Bellini. Though Mattie tried her best to concentrate on the lovely music emanating from the stage, she could scarcely focus as across from her another far more compelling drama played out. Lights and shadows passed over Angus's and Amelia's faces as they leaned together to whisper, and she nestled close to him.

Open acceptance and belonging rested between them. As if through a twisted fog, Mattie recalled a theater in New York, where she had basked in that belonging, knowing now it would never come again. The pain of loss was sharp enough without watching another enjoy it in her stead.

Mattie rose for the intermission, ill and shaken, dropping her eyes when Emmeline swept by without a glance. Mary leaned over after she had passed on. "Is she still distant?"

Mattie nodded, feeling the rebuff. "But she lost her daughter."

"Years ago," said Mary, as they rose to take a turn around the theater.

A night passed through Mattie's mind of woven rushes and a vigil. Emmeline's daughter Louie had lost a similar fight, and Angus had behaved deplorably. As his wife, even an uncertain one, Mattie would not publicly admit it, yet it was true. "Some losses never heal," she said.

Turning the corner, they came face to face with Angus and Amelia, who looked just as surprised by the chance confrontation. "Good evening," Angus said with understanding and apology; Amelia's eyes held only pity.

"Good evening," Mattie said, dropping a shallow curtsey and

hurrying on. And on. Right out of the theater, past carriages waiting to take theatergoers home, and into the night where she could compose her face, straighten her dress, and hide her embarrassment and rage and jealousy under the blessed soft cover of darkness.

Mary trailed after her, reaching for her sister's arm. "I'm afraid I feel ill," Mattie said, speaking truth. "I'm sorry, but I think it's best to miss the rest of the program."

"Do you want me to come too?" Mary asked.

"Of course not," Mattie said, trying to brush away Amelia's pity like a dirty bandage. "I will be fine. Finish the program. Parley will be expecting you."

"You are quite certain?" Mary asked, worried.

"I'm quite certain, Mary dear. So sorry to cut our evening short." She made her escape, slipping away, tucking herself safely beneath the veil of oblivion.

The knock came swiftly to her bedroom door the next afternoon. "Mattie?" called Lotta's voice, as Mattie groaned and fought the urge to pull the covers over her head.

"I'm sick!" she called. "Go away unless you want to be sick too."

"That's why I'm here," Lotta called back.

Mattie sighed. "Come in then."

Lotta opened the door to Mattie's bedroom where the curtains had been drawn against the garish light of day. "I imagine Mary sent you, but I assure you I will get out of bed eventually."

"She didn't send me," Lotta corrected. "Just told me you were ill."

"Hmm."

"And Lizzie and James?"

"With Sarah, of course."

"You don't look ill to me," Lotta said, opening the curtains to the daylight.

"Ugh," Mattie sighed, and put a pillow over her head.

"I've come to enlist your help with something."

"What is it?"

"You know I've been attending territorial suffrage meetings?"

"Yes." Mattie groaned.

"Legislators are threatening to remove suffrage from the constitution as a way to guarantee the bid for statehood."

Mattie sat up. "Remove suffrage?"

"B. H. Roberts is attempting to convince delegates that the issues need to be separated for our statehood bid to be approved."

"But separating them would be a fiasco."

"So says Susan B. Anthony. And Emmeline Wells. And everyone who knows anything about suffrage. But we need someone who can convince the delegates. And we also need to form a coalition to represent Utah at the women's conference for the Columbian Exposition in Chicago."

"And you think I should be such a person?"

"Well, I have tried to think of someone who is passionate about women's advancements and who also happens to be a skilled public speaker not currently involved. I only came up with one."

"Ugh," Mattie repeated. "When is your meeting?"

"Tonight."

The contaminating influence of the ballot . . .
was born of fright, produced by shadows.
—MARTHA HUGHES CANNON

Chapter Fifty

In a classroom on the top floor of Deseret Hospital, fifteen girls and women settled themselves into desks arranged in rows. Starched aprons wrapped round their waists, ending in a bow; white caps perched on their heads like jaunty handkerchiefs.

A hand-painted sign propped in the window of the school read: Highland Nursing and Midwifery School, Martha Hughes Cannon, MD. Though most of the teaching was done by nurses, as head physician, Mattie came in for occasional lectures on anatomy, germ theory, and medical procedure. Upon each desk lay copies of the book Mattie had collected in Birmingham, England, tokens of her time abroad.

"As you know," Mattie explained from a platform at the center of the room, "smallpox is a most acute and dreaded disease. With the passage of the transcontinental railroad through our territory, we are particularly susceptible to outbreaks, which have a mortality rate of thirty percent, and will leave another thirty percent of survivors blind. That number rises to fifty percent in children ages zero to five." She glanced down at her notes, wishing she could more effectively convey the suffering she'd witnessed in patients. "Are there any questions?"

Elvira Young, a granddaughter of Brigham Young with sharp brown eyes and hair knotted precisely, raised her hand. "Are those mortality rates the same in Utah?"

"So far as they've been documented, yes," Mattie said, wondering why Elvira would ask. "As you can see on page sixty-two of your text, the initial pre-eruptive stage is characterized by backache, headache, vomiting, and a localized rash, followed by the development of a prognostic rash with its focal lesions. Any time smallpox is suspected, a physician should be notified immediately, and the patient should be quarantined until the diagnosis is confirmed."

Adopting a more informal tone, Mattie explained, "As I'm sure you realize, there is no treatment for smallpox. Good care focuses primarily on nutrition and hygiene, and sympathetic nursing plays an important part. Because it can be distressing, a patient should not be allowed to see a mirror."

Kaya, a native girl who had been adopted by the Kimball family, raised her hand. "What are the rates of disfigurement?"

"Good question," Mattie said. "Among survivors, upward of sixty percent are permanently disfigured. Since the tenth century in China, smallpox has been successfully controlled by inoculation with the live virus, reducing the death rate from thirty percent to ten percent during outbreaks, though a small percentage of those inoculated contracted the disease. Far more recently, an English physician, William Jenner, noticed milkmaids were immune to smallpox and hypothesized that this was due to their exposure to a much milder related disease, cowpox. From cowpox lesions on the udder of a cow, Jenner developed an exudate, which he termed *vaccination* based on the Latin word for cow. Two-thirds of vaccinated patients will develop a localized rash, but the majority will thereafter have immunity."

Elvira Young on the front row raised her hand again. "Excuse me, Dr. Cannon, but I am surprised to hear you take up a position in opposition to statements I've heard from Church leaders. I know gentile doctors support risky procedures, but I would not think this school would support such a stance."

Mattie drew a steadying breath, as other students gaped at Elvira, who dared openly contradict the head physician. While most Church leaders were reasonable on the issue of vaccinations, Charles Penrose, editor of the *Deseret News* and husband of Dr. Romania Pratt, considered himself knowledgeable enough to write scathing editorials insinuating that members of the Church who had faith enough to be healed would not let doctors poison the blood of their children.

Elvira clearly felt it her religious duty to continue, and Mattie realized now why she had asked about mortality rates in Utah. "I've heard elders have at times laid hands upon persons with smallpox and seen their patients recover."

Realizing her students were likely to confront the same resistant attitudes, Mattie decided to dive into the controversy. "You raise an important issue, Miss Young. In my practice, I've seen incredible miracles worked by the power of faith. I consider blessings an essential part of medicine, and I seek to always involve the Lord in my work. On rare occasions, patients do recover from situations deemed impossible by science, but I believe vaccination teaches our physical bodies to recognize and mount an immune response against a pathogen. Do you not find it remarkable God designed our bodies this way? Dr. Edward Jenner, faced with such opposition, wrote, 'I wonder that they are not grateful to God for the good which He has made me the instrument of conveying to my fellow creatures.'"

Kaya Kimball raised her hand. "So you are saying, Dr. Jenner did not actually invent vaccinations, but rather discovered the body's natural ability to mount this response?"

"That would be a logical way to think of it," Mattie replied. "It may also be helpful to remember that the *Deseret News* does not speak for the whole of the Church, though the editor may sometimes forget it. Because of vaccinations, smallpox mortality rates have dropped from thirty to two percent, with an immunity that typically lasts thirty years. Does that resolve your concern, Miss Young?"

Elvira glanced up from her notebook. "Mostly, Dr. Cannon, but in all honesty, it is difficult to know who to believe. I've been told vaccinations sometimes *cause* smallpox. Or have necessitated the amputation of a limb."

"Fear is a powerful foe, Miss Young. Did you know that Utah's health officer, Dr. Theodore Beatty, offered a $1,000 reward for proof of such a case, which no one has ever claimed? A small percentage of people will have bad reactions or fail to become immune, but I guarantee that once you have seen your first case of smallpox at close range, you will be unlikely to want to try home remedies of dried onions and sheep droppings as your only defense against it."

Students tittered in response, but Mattie's voice turned serious. "Sincere prayer plus the latest advances of science remain our most effective defenses." Heads around the room nodded in agreement, and Elvira's face softened.

"Now, unless there are further questions, I will demonstrate the scratch method of delivering the vaccine to a patient, a procedure you will learn to administer yourself in a clinical setting. Are we ready?"

The classroom nodded in unison.

Mattie opened the door and welcomed her patient inside, relieved to leave the controversial discussion and wishing she could tell Romania to keep her husband in line. The fact that Charles Penrose served in the territorial legislature and his wife was a doctor made his position far too persuasive. *How bad of an outbreak would it take before these ridiculous rumors would disappear?*

Chapter Fifty-One

1893
Chicago, Illinois

From the shores of Lake Michigan arose a great commotion. Workers cleared land, assembled materials, and began erecting grandiose beams and pillars, crawling over scaffolding as they hewed a city from the morass of sand and scrubby trees in Jackson Park. Steel arrived by rail from Pittsburgh, glass from Hartford, timber cut from the vast forests of Michigan and planed in the mills of Chicago. More than two hundred buildings sprang up, neoclassical in design, with formidable porticoes and columns. Elegant statues were formed of a plaster mixture called staff, which could be shaped, hardened, and painted to gleam like marble. Driving water inland from the lake, workers formed wide canals and channels in a grand lagoon surrounded by structures reminiscent of ancient Greece and Rome. The single largest building ever enclosed rose foot by blessed foot, as men paid twenty-five cents per day conjured white castles from the shore of the lakeside.

When the buildings were finished, people came to fill them.

They filled the mining building with sculptures fashioned from pure silver and a display of Tiffany diamonds. They filled the agricultural building with a Statue of Liberty carved from salt and a Liberty Bell fabricated from wheat, oats, and rye. Thousands of engines thrummed with the new machines of industry, turning water into steam, propelling the fair with a sound so deafening, few could stand to be inside the machinery building for long. Countries vied to outdo each other, as Germany built clock towers and brought their crown jewels for display, Italy created a glass-blowing studio run by Venetian artisans. Spain, meanwhile, built precise replicas of Columbus's three lauded ships and sailed them to America. There were snake charmers from Tunisia, a golden pyramid from Brazil, and camel rides down the transported streets of Cairo. A tall and awkward man with slick black hair and a faded suit moved deliberately among the exhibits, wiring over a hundred thousand electrical lights, testing and correcting, then testing again. A wizard, he was said to be—a wizard who would light up the white city rising on the shores of Lake Michigan like a night is lit up with stars.

Artisans crafted a colossal sculpture to reign over the scene from the center of the lagoon. The Statue of the Republic, finished in gold leaf, declared her United States could no more be called a backwater nation—but one rising to become the envy of the earth. Learning from all civilizations that had come before, this country garnered nations, cultures, and people to help solve the problems facing a new century about to dawn.

After months of labor performed by thousands of hands, at the push of a button, Nikola Tesla's electric lights illuminated the shining city. Across six hundred acres, fairy lights danced through the night, as fountains sprang to life, blazing streams into the air in a display unlike anything the world had ever known.

And the world came to see it. Millions—from Syria, from Egypt, from Brazil, and from Japan. They came with their children toddling beside them, with their elderly who wanted to see the great World's Fair before they died, to have a glimpse into a future they would not live to see. They came to marvel at the world's first Ferris wheel. They came to ride camels and float into the sky in a captive balloon. They came to sip tea in a Japanese temple sheltered by a wooded island. They came to gaze surreptitiously upon belly dancers on the Midway Plaisance. They came from California to wonder at a tower made from 14,000 oranges; they came by rail from Alabama, Nevada, and Massachusetts. By horse and buggy and by foot, they came from the tenements and stockyards of Chicago, wiping the grime of the city from their feet. Scraping together the fifty cents entrance fee if they could, or looking on longingly from the Midway Plaisance if they could not.

Some months later, Mattie stumbled into all this glory and chaos, gazing about her at the city grown like a crystal garden from charcoal, sprung up overnight, formed in gracious curved lines. How she wished Lizzie and James could look upon these wonders, but they were home with their grandmother as their mother stepped into the next decade.

Stepping from the moving walkway, Mattie caught her first glimpse of the Court of Honor's monumental buildings arranged around a massive central lagoon, and could only gaze on, mesmerized.

"The fountain is simply incredible," said Emily Richards beside her, president of the Territorial Suffrage Association. She gestured to the sculpted barge in the center of the lagoon, propelled by eight female figures splashing through foam.

"Just dazzling," Mattie breathed in agreement.

"I believe the World's Congress Auxiliary is this way," said Emmeline Wells, leading the way forward. She had warmed to Mattie's apologetic gestures of friendship on their journey, and Mattie hurried after her, though she longed to explore the White City. Opposite the fountains of the Grand Basin, the women arrived at a broad, columned building. In this building of Congresses, various week-long symposia had been scheduled throughout the six months of the fair on topics ranging from religion, science, labor, to social reform—lecture invitations having been tendered to the greatest scholars and experts around the globe.

Beyond the main doors, a banner met them: Welcome to the World's Congress on the Position and Advancement of Women.

"Welcome, delegates from Utah," Bertha Palmer's harried assistant greeted. "Here is the schedule of speakers."

"Unbelievable," said Mattie, scanning the list. "It would be impossible to see them all."

"All five hundred speakers at all eighty-one sessions?" asked the assistant. "Yes, it certainly would. I recommend passing from room to room, pausing when a speaker or a topic strikes your fancy."

Amazed by the diversity of languages being spoken around them, Mattie told her companions, "I had no idea the whole world had assembled in Chicago."

"Shall we go see it?" Emily countered.

The Congress building housed a number of lecture halls where one could slip in and take a seat near the back or leave without interrupting. Isabel King from the Argentine Republic wore a fashionable hat and an elegant gown ornamented with rows of black silk buttons. "The great part of the South American population," she was explaining when they entered, "is composed of the descendants of the Spanish conquerors and colonists and the native Indian peoples; the first striving to live out a civilization commenced thousands of years ago, and having a rise in scenes and surroundings of Old World culture and luxury; the other adhering to the customs indigenous to the land of the pampas and the lasso."

"Shall we stay?" Emily mouthed.

Mattie nodded and they found a seat.

"At present," Isabel continued, "communication is so difficult between North and South America, and so convenient between North America and Europe, that many very intelligent and widely traveled persons in the United States have but vague ideas of the kinds of civilizations to be encountered among their sister republics."

This seemed fair enough, Mattie had to acknowledge. Though she knew plenty of people who had gone to Europe, only a handful had traveled southward, and if they had, it was usually to cross Panama over land, then return to the other side of North America.

"If the culture of a country is to be measured by the place a woman holds in it," Isabel continued, "then the more advanced of these southern countries must be looked upon as possessing both the highest and lowest extremes." She went on to explain the great gulf between rich and poor, while Mattie recalled the slums of New York and wondered if South America could be even more extreme in its divisions of wealth.

When the speaker concluded, Mattie and Emily stayed to hear the next person who would approach the podium. The woman couldn't be more than twenty years of age, Mattie thought, wearing layers of Middle Eastern fabrics, her dark, unbound hair beneath a decorative cap. "My name is Hanna Korany of Syria," she said in introduction. "In reporting on the status of women in my country, I start by recalling that woman in ancient Syria, Egypt, and Arabia held a prominent position in art, poetry, music, and literature. Our Arabic language is rich with feminine poetry and prose."

"I had no idea," Mattie whispered to Emily, who nodded.

"Fifty years ago," Hanna continued, "women who could read and write their native tongue were very scarce, and the fathers and mothers of that period shrank with horror from the idea of educating their daughters. But now education is awakening them from their long slumber, is opening their eyes to the sorrowful condition of the country, is stirring them up to shake off these old habits. . . . Americans, who enjoy the advantages of independence, freedom and equality, cannot readily comprehend the many obstacles that stand in the way of the Oriental woman's progress. The tide of modern progress is sweeping away in its mighty flow many of the prejudiced, fanatical ideas concerning woman's sphere and in Syria the women have come to see the necessity of education." Mattie watched the passionate young woman with dramatic brows and a regal nose continue on, speaking urgently about the need for education, realizing that her own struggles to stay in school were far from unique, and that relative to challenges this woman had faced, probably also very minor.

Hanna yielded the podium to Lady Linchee Suriya of Siam, who wore an ornate golden head ornament. She picked up a similar topic, explaining that her greatest concern for the women of Siam was that, "a girl's education is very often neglected entirely, unlike that of her brothers. At an early age a girl remains at home to take care of her little brothers and sisters, or she may go with her parents to watch the cattle graze."

Again, Mattie thought of her own struggle to stay in school as a child, feeling humbled by what she had imagined at the time to be a challenge. Her mother's opposition. Pressure to get married, to stay at home. Yet none of it had been dictated, none of it physically enforced.

Beside her, Emily looked as affected as she. "How are you feeling?" Emily asked when Lady Linchee concluded.

"A bit embarrassed by my opportunities," Mattie confessed.

"As am I," Emily agreed, "Though you must know how unique your education is. Even among American women. Or men for that matter."

"I will try to put it to good use," Mattie replied.

She and Emily stepped from the Congress building, planning to view the Viking ship from Norway and a replica of the Yucatan ruins. But they stopped first in the Woman's Building, a building designed by a woman, managed by women, and devoted to women's work in every field. Walking through the hallways, they marveled at women's scientific work, patented inventions, musical compositions, paintings, and sculptures—at baskets and embroidery created by Native American women, at walls decorated with Mary Cassatt's paintings, and at a library housing over a thousand books by women, including the handwritten manuscript of Charlotte Brontë's *Jane Eyre*.

Dazzled by all that her sisters had accomplished round the world, Mattie thought she had better increase her own efforts if she wanted to keep up.

"Where shall we go next?" Emily asked.

"We haven't seen the British Isles building yet," Mattie said, thinking of Wales.

"That's because snooty old England won't let anyone in their building without an invitation."

Mattie laughed. "Let's go to Canada then."

*If women are granted the privilege to vote, it is not going by
any means to sweep away all existing wrong in the world,
but it will be one more step toward equality before the law.*
—MARTHA HUGHES CANNON

Chapter Fifty-Two

Mattie fell into bed exhausted and arose the next morning, eager to return for more. She and Emily retraced their steps to the Congress building.

"The theme today is social reform," Mattie said, looking over the schedule. "Shall we start with Viscountess Harberton, founder of the Rational Dress Society?"

"*That* should be entertaining," Emily replied.

"I think I was an early member of her society," Mattie confessed, remembering her struggle to buy sturdy boots. The viscountess wore a cycling dress with a practical wool jacket, and tailored skirts that tucked beneath her knees. "The old idea must be eradicated that two legs are proper for a man but improper for a woman," the viscountess proclaimed. "The perpetual hampering of themselves with clothing so constructed as to make the natural functions of breathing and walking artificially laborious, and the latter in many cases almost impossible, is nearly on a par with self-mutilation."

There were a few gasps among her audience at the adoption of this daring position. "It is quite certain that a generation of women who had once become accustomed to the comfort and freedom of clothing made approximately in the shape of the human form would never consent to return to the cumbrous primitive petticoat." She argued that women need not submit to the tyranny of corset and bustle, nor hairstyles either. In cutting her curls years before, Mattie had not realized she'd already been a feminist.

Next to the podium came a woman whose simple clothing identified her as a working woman. A refreshing change to some of the glittering royalty who had stood upon the stage before her, Mattie thought. "I am Mary E. Kenney," she said, "the daughter of Irish immigrants, and I represent the American Federation of Labor. I have been asked to speak on the state of working women in America."

Miss Kenney spoke of the challenges of convincing women in factories to organize and demand better conditions. Too often, she said, they will not "because they feel their time in industry to be temporary. Also they are afraid of their bosses and losing employment, upon which they depend. Such is the existing condition of the working women in our free America, where slavery is supposed to be a thing of the past, but where it exists today in a most tyrannical form."

Clearly a woman of sincerity, Miss Kenney continued, "I work in a bookbinding factory in Albany, New York, where I am paid seven cents an hour, ten hours a day, with only Sundays off. I make $4.20 per week and I have my aging mother to support. A man doing my same job is paid $10 to $12.50 per week."

Mattie tried to imagine the struggles of the life Miss Kenney described and recalled that her mother had done similar work in a dressmaking factory in New York after her arrival in the United States. The only difference between Elizabeth's former job and her own was, once again, education.

"Is it any wonder," Miss Kenney asked, "with these fearful facts confronting them, that the masses are beginning to feel the great injustice and oppression forced upon them? We demand to be educated and to abolish a wage system that compels my sex to accept wholesale prostitution, crime, and degradation."

When she finished, the audience spontaneously rose to their feet, offering a standing ovation, and Mattie clapped as loudly as the rest, feeling that there was much great work to do upon this earth, and one would need several lifetimes to lend support to every worthy cause.

She would not have wished to follow such a speaker, but a poised black woman in a lovely lace collar and eardrops did not seem intimidated. "My name is Fannie Barrier Williams," she said, "and I was lucky enough to be raised in Brockport, New York, where my father owned a profitable business. We were accepted by our surrounding white community without question. After going to school, I took a job teaching in Hannibal, Missouri, where I found myself shattered by a racial prejudice I had never before experienced." Mattie remembered the Mormon experience in Missouri and could not feel surprised, though Utah was probably not as accepting as Brockport, New York, either.

"Today I've been asked to speak on the intellectual progress of colored women since emancipation," Fannie continued. "I believe less is known of our women than perhaps of any other class of Americans. Few can appreciate what it means to be suddenly changed from irresponsible bondage to the responsibility of freedom and citizenship! The distress of it all can never be told, and the pain of it all can never be felt except by the victims."

Mattie could not remember a time when slavery had been legal, but she recalled Elizabeth speaking of journeying westward in trains crowded with Union soldiers.

"Today we feel strong enough to ask for but one thing," Mrs. Williams continued, "and that is the same opportunity for the acquisition of all kinds of knowledge that may be accorded to other women."

Education, Mattie thought. *Again and again, the problems of the world circled around this.*

Mrs. Williams cleared her throat. "This granted, in the next generation progressive women will be found successfully occupying every field where the highest intelligence alone is admissible. American literature needs for its greater variety and its deeper soundings that which will be written into it and out of the hearts of these self-emancipating women." Thinking of gospel choirs and the patterns unique to black English, Mattie thrilled at the thought.

"If this hope seems too extravagant to those of you who know these women only in their humbler capacities," Mrs. Williams cautioned, "I would remind you that all we hope for is more than prophesied by what has already been done. Except teaching in colored schools and menial work, colored women can find no employment in this 'free' America. We plead for opportunities untrammeled by prejudice. And we plead for a breaking down of the social quarantine that is guarded and enforced more rigidly than against cholera. We ask for liberty to be all that we can be, without artificial hindrances. If the love of humanity more than the love of races and sex shall pulsate to the world from this parliament of women, the colored women, as well as all women, will realize that the inalienable right to life, liberty, and the pursuit of happiness is a maxim that can become the gospel of everyday life and the unerring guide in the relations of all men, women, and children."

Again, the audience rose, stirred to deliver a standing ovation, and as Mattie clapped, she wondered what she might do to answer such a call. Still on stage, Mrs. Williams looked down at the front row, and found the famous orator Frederick Douglass before her. "I hope you do not mind indulging me," she said, "but a hero of mine is here among us, and a champion of women, Frederick Douglass. If you don't mind, I'd like to invite him to say a word, as I'm sure I would not be the only one who would regret missing an opportunity to hear him." The audience responded in kind, and Frederick Douglass took the stage—grizzled hair brushed back, a stern, impassioned brow, and a cravat Angus would have been proud of.

Clearly moved, he wiped tears from his eyes. "I have heard tonight refined, educated colored ladies addressing one of the most intelligent white audiences that I have ever looked upon. It is a new thing under the sun, and my heart is too full to speak; my mind is too much illuminated with hope." He paused again to use his handkerchief. "Fifty years ago I was lone in the wilderness, telling my story of the wrongs of slavery, but I feel a sense of gratitude to the Almighty God that I have lived to see what I now see. A new heaven is dawning upon us, and a new earth is ours, in which all discriminations are passing away, and will pass away."

The audience rose for a third time, and Mattie struggled to her feet. In a daze, she made her excuses to Emily and hurried through the White City and the streets of Chicago to her hotel. There she spent that night scratching out words she had planned to say, writing her speech anew, crossing things out, moving words around. Awed by those who had taken the stage before her and intimidated by the thought of ascending the same podium, she hoped that what she planned to say might somehow be of value to souls engaged in such causes. Night fell, and still her pen scratched on.

*The divinity which doth hedge woman about like
"subtle perfume" has not been displaced.*
–MARTHA HUGHES CANNON

Chapter Fifty-Three

At ten the next morning, Mattie took a seat on the podium between Emily and Emmeline, while the renowned Susan B. Anthony introduced the delegates from Utah, here to report on the status of women in that territory. "The Relief Association of Utah," she said, "which is perhaps a quarter of a century old, reports thirty thousand members, several of whom are here with us today."

In true Utah form, the meeting opened with the singing of "God Is Love," with Kate Romney playing the organ. President Zina Young, wearing a homemade silk dress, spoke first and explained the silk industry the women of Utah had created. Next Emily Richards spoke of founding the Territorial Suffrage Association, addressing the legal and political status of women, including the seventeen years when women enjoyed the franchise before it had been stripped away in the controversy over polygamy. Alice Merrill Horne described the early days of Utah's settlement and the overland migration that brought them to the valley. Then Emmeline Wells reported on Utah's female authors and journalists and her storage program for saving grain. Finally, Susan B. Anthony rose to introduce Dr. Martha Hughes Cannon, rattling off a long list of accomplishments.

Approaching the podium, Mattie built upon the speeches ahead of hers, sketching out the diversity of Utah's women who continued the work of pioneers to the Rocky Mountains. "In following the migrating instinct of their forefathers," Mattie said, "these early-day women of Utah did not forget the principles for which so much had been sacrificed to establish religious toleration on the free soil of America."

Thinking of Elizabeth, she continued, "You have heard some of the experiences of our mothers in the early days; what a happy change now surrounds them in their advancing years. With all that wealth and civilization can give for the advancement of science, literature, and art, what may we not expect of the native-born daughters of this glorious land? Utah women have known the power of the ballot! We shall enjoy the feel of that strong lever in our hands again. Go home, my friends, and fight for the vote whose long silence should be broken with the sound of your own voices." The audience applauded her speech, and, though they did not rise to their feet, Mattie felt satisfied. She knew she had not quite fully captured all she had wanted to say, but Susan B. Anthony approached her, wearing a high-collared gown and spectacles, hand extended. "Thank you for your words, Dr. Cannon. You are an eloquent speaker and an asset to our suffrage cause."

"It was an honor," Mattie said to the mighty woman, now in her seventies, still fighting tirelessly, "to be here with you, and to meet you at last. Participating in this Congress has been a most inspiring experience."

Miss Anthony nodded. "I believe this gathering will advance the woman's cause one hundred years because it will impart learning in every department of life in which man has always reigned, but to which woman is and always has been eligible."

"Our final day," said Mattie the next morning, seating herself at breakfast and reviewing the schedule. "Focused on women and their relation to politics."

Alice yawned. "I'm sorry, but after speaking yesterday, I am exhausted. I don't think I can sit through any more lectures. I am going to explore the fair. Perhaps I'll manage enough energy to sip cider at the German building and eat oranges in the California exhibit."

Mattie laughed. "I won't think any less of you. Anyone else?"

"I'll go with you," Emily Richards said. "Politics interests me. And we can meet Alice at the German cider exhibit afterwards."

In the Congress building, Isabel Hamilton-Gordon, countess of Aberdeen commanded the stage, a stout woman dressed in lace and roses who seemed unaware of her own opulence. "I am the daughter of a baron," she said by way of introduction. "I received a good education at home, but my father believed a university was no place for a woman. Ironically, my parents introduced me to a number of politicians in their home, which prepared me for a life of activism helping servants obtain educational opportunities."

She looked down at her notes, and Emily whispered to Mattie, "I've heard rumors she takes meals with her servants."

"Quite scandalous, I suppose, among countesses," Mattie replied softly. Emily smiled.

"In my experience, the ideal women in poetry and fiction are generally represented in their own homes, spreading a bright and holy influence as sister, daughter, wife, and mother. Far be it from me to disparage such an ideal. I only venture to say that it is an ideal which does not include the whole of a woman's life, and that true ideals are always expanding and enlarging.

"Those for whom I speak have become politicians because we have the strong conviction that woman has a political duty, which she owes her country. And we believe man and woman working side by side, each in his or her own way, will best be able to accomplish the allotted task of leaving the world better than they found it."

"Man and woman working side by side," Mattie repeated, clapping at the countess's conclusion.

The woman who rose next needed no introduction. Those closely bound white curls topped with her iconic black lace veil immediately identified Elizabeth Cady Stanton, now in her late seventies, who seemed to have no intention of retiring from the fight that had occupied the whole of her life. From her first sentence, the audience knew they were listening to an experienced speaker, one whose voice had been raised in the halls of Congress in defense of women's suffrage. In spite of her plump, matronly figure, her voice held no softness or hesitancy, and Mattie marveled at her poise, trying to memorize each detail.

"When men say women do not desire the right of suffrage, but prefer masculine domination to self-government," Mrs. Stanton began, "they falsify every page of history, every facet of human nature. The chronic condition of rebellion, even of children against the control of nurses, elder brothers, sisters, parents, and teachers, is a protest in favor of the right of self-government."

What a brilliant point, Mattie thought.

"Woman suffrage means a complete revolution in our government, religion, and social life. In religion it means a church in which the feminine element in Christianity will be recognized, in which the mother of the race shall be more sacred than symbols, sacraments, and altars. Our civilization today is simply masculine and will be until the feminine element is fully recognized and has equal power in the regulation of human affairs. Then we shall substitute cooperation for competition, persuasion for coercion." Mattie tingled at truth, so eloquently spoken.

"This is the most momentous reform that has yet been launched upon the world," Mrs. Stanton resumed, "the first organized protest against the injustice which has brooded over the character and destiny of one-half the human race. Enough for us to see the day dawning, the coming glory on every side, enough for us to know that our daughters to the third and fourth generation will enjoy the fruits of our labors, reap the harvests we have sown, and sing the glad songs of victory in every latitude and longitude, when we have passed on to other spheres of action."

"'The highest earthly desire of a ripened mind,' says Thomas Arnold, 'is the desire to take an active share in the great work of government.'" Mrs. Stanton paused to let her audience digest this lofty claim. "Only those who are capable of appreciating this dignity can measure the extent to which women are defrauded as citizens of this great republic; neither can others measure the loss to the councils of the nation of the wisdom of representative women." Mattie felt the palpable loss in the speaker's voice, more poignant when one considered the last several days and the work these women could accomplish if given a chance.

Someday, Mattie promised herself. *Someday.*

That night, Mattie stood beside Emily as they watched a display of fireworks bloom over the Grand Basin, lighting their faces with colored fire. Overcome by the offerings of the Fair before them, Mattie was even more surprised to realize the greatest creation housed within the walls of the Exposition was the thoughts, minds, and hearts of those in attendance.

After days of such stirring speeches, Mattie felt like she had sipped a strong, intoxicating elixir and could not find her way back down from the heights. This panorama of the earth, like a globe spun round in quick succession, compressed the world into six hundred acres, but rather than evoking a sense of the vastness she'd expected, it was smallness she noticed now, the universality of human challenges and joys. Each of the speakers had played a role in this grand pantomime, and Mattie knew she too must play a part. Though she might be one lightbulb among a hundred thousand, she could scarcely let the lights go out on her watch with so much glory on every hand. Gazing across the lit expanse of darkness, she saw at last that smallness or imperfection could never be used as an excuse not to shine.

The results which have been attained speak with
such unerring logic and vindicate so completely the
argument that woman should take part in the affairs
of government, which so vitally affect her.

—MARTHA HUGHES CANNON

Chapter Fifty-Four

MARCH 18, 1895
Salt Lake City, Utah Territory

The women of the Territorial Suffrage Association remained unconvinced. B. H. Roberts, a member of the Quorum of the Seventy, stood before them in the City and County Building, hat in hand, deference and respect in his light, wide-set eyes. For the past fifteen minutes, he had addressed the association and their honored guests, hoping to persuade them to drop woman's suffrage from the proposed state constitution. Comingling the two issues was dangerous, he argued, and would postpone Utah's hope for statehood, a request that had already failed a number of times. Beyond this, Mr. Roberts contended, suffrage would hurt women themselves in ways they could not fully comprehend. Speaking from beneath a very full and unruly mustache, he counseled the women in his audience, "You are the queens of the domestic kingdom and if you become embroiled in political agitation, the reverence that is paid you will disappear."

The women did not look markedly concerned by this threat.

However, their guests, who included most of the delegates of the constitutional committee, were perhaps more likely to be persuaded.

Mattie glanced down at her notes, inspired by the women she had heard in Chicago. She wished the seated audience could have heard those incredible speeches for themselves, could have felt the electricity that charged the air, thrumming with hope. But they only had her.

B. H. Roberts concluded his remarks and sat down beside Charles Penrose, and Mattie took the podium. Graciously she thanked him for his thoughts, though she never said what she actually thought of them. Her speech would clarify that point, she imagined.

Mattie began, "One of the principal reasons women should vote is that all men and women are created free and equal. No privileged class either of sex, wealth, or descent should be allowed to arise or exist. All persons should have the legal right to be the equal of every other." She allowed these thoughts to sink in for her audience, for she knew that for many of them, they would be as alien as the thought of inhabiting the moon.

Taking a breath she retraced the history of the conflict for her audience. "Once to be born a female was to become a plaything or a slave; today in the best, most cultivated, and most powerful circles, woman is the peer of the noblest man. If women are granted the privilege to vote, it is not going, by any means, to sweep away all existing wrong in the world, but it will be one more step toward equality before the law. There will still be some drunken, brutal husbands; there will be poverty, aching heads and hearts; there will be fraud and wrong, but the skirts of the law will be clean on this one point and not compelled to bear the blame."

She could feel her audience rising with her, inspired and waiting upon each word as it fell from her lips. "And may the day be hastened when women will know all their rights, and knowing, dare maintain."

Many people congratulated her afterward, saying it was one of the best speeches she'd ever given. "I thank you, Dr. Cannon," Orson Whitney said. "Your words were most persuasive and have given me a great deal to consider."

Though she sought for him after the meeting adjourned, B. H. Roberts refused to look her in the eye.

The final contest for women's suffrage came down to a vote of the territorial delegates. Mattie and other women were allowed to watch from the upper balcony, as below, men in stiff suits decided the future of the territory. B. H. Roberts repeated his claims of fear-mongering, outlining the potential downfall that awaited them all, should suffrage pass.

"To hear him tell it," Mattie whispered to Lotta in the balcony, "women's suffrage will be the death knell of our civilized society."

Lotta wrinkled her nose. "I only wish he were less eloquent and persuasive."

Mattie nodded.

Orson Whitney arose then, and Mattie held her breath as she waited to hear which position he would take. "Woman is a wife, a mother, a cook, and a housekeeper," Mr. Whitney began, and she wondered if he had been persuaded by Roberts after all. "But while important," he continued, "these are not the sum of her capabilities. After further investigation, I've come to believe that the woman's movement is one of the great levers by which the Almighty is lifting up this fallen world, lifting it nearer to the throne of its Creator."

A smile radiated from Mattie's face, and Lotta joyfully clutched her sister's arm. "You persuaded him, Mattie. I knew you would."

"I'm sure it wasn't only me," Mattie said back, but she couldn't stop her spreading smile.

After long hours of debate, the delegates cast their final votes. Mattie and Lotta held their breath in the balcony as the ballots were counted.

"Ayes: 75, Noes: 14, Absent: 12," the speaker announced. The proposed constitution of the territory of Utah would include a clause guaranteeing the right of women in the territory to vote.

"We did it!" Lotta hissed in her sister's ear. "Mattie, we did it."

"I want to be first in line to register," Mattie replied.

No privileged class either of sex wealth or descent
should be allowed to arise or exist. All persons should
have the legal right to be the equal of every other.
—MARTHA HUGHES CANNON

Chapter Fifty-Five

The supply wagon rumbled to a stop outside the ramshackle community of West Salt Lake, and a team of nursing students descended, aprons flapping. Mattie called her students for final instructions. "Remember," she said, "you've been asked to introduce yourselves as nursing students here to help with the outbreak. Ask if anyone in the home is ill. If you have reason to suspect typhoid or any other contagious disease, give instruction for safe food and water handling, provide nutritional advice, and place a quarantine sign on the door. Be sensitive. Some patients may try to hide their illness, particularly if they have concerns over their immigration status. Disinfect your hands after patient contact. Are there any questions?"

Kaya Kimball raised her hand. "What medicinal supplies do we have to dispense, Dr. Cannon?"

"We have packets of Peruvian bark tea for reducing inflammation, especially for patients experiencing pulmonary congestion. Come and find me at once if there is any situation you cannot handle."

The students nodded, setting off in pairs. Mattie watched them go, proud of their growth and advancement. They had learned much during the past few months, and a typhoid outbreak that had afflicted close to a hundred patients, however calamitous, was a perfect opportunity for them to put their book learning to work.

Kaya Kimball and Elvira Young, arms laden with potatoes and bottles of milk, wound their way down one street, and Mattie hoped their respectful postures would inspire trust and not alarm. Fern Allred and Inez Russo gathered fresh vegetables and packets of bark tea, and set off in the opposite direction to a row of houses, where Mattie noticed fly-infested privies sat at no great distance from drinking wells.

Mattie approached a tenement directly in front of her, crowded with Italian and Greek immigrants. She spoke with a mother who had a mild case of typhoid, explaining she should boil water drawn from the wells before using it for cooking, and left her with tea to ease her labored breathing.

As Mattie left a second house, Fern Allred came running down the street, apron tails flying behind her. "Dr. Cannon, please come. We've found a child severely suffering from typhoid. Inez is with her."

"I'll fetch my medical bag," Mattie said, rushing to the wagon, and then following Fern's red braids down the opposite street. On a twisting side street, a distraught mother threw open the door.

"Mrs. Mousalimas," Fern said. "This is Dr. Cannon."

"I'm so sorry your family is struggling with illness," Mattie said. "May I come inside?"

"Come in, come in," she said, gesturing. "My children, they all had it. And now my daughter." The mother's voice broke, and she covered her face with her hands.

Three children lay together in the corner of the room on the only bed. One coughed as Mattie entered, and she noted the others breathed with difficulty. The smell of diarrhea was unmistakable.

"Fern, can you fetch mercuric chloride from the wagon for disinfecting?" Mattie asked. The student set off at once.

A little girl, around three years old, lay on a cot on the floor in front of the fire, mumbling incoherently. "What is her name?" Mattie asked.

"Althea," the mother sobbed.

"Althea," Mattie said soothingly, "I'm sorry you are hurting. I'm going to try to help." The child writhed in delirium, and Mattie held an ear trumpet to her chest. It was a miracle the child could breathe at all, her lungs were so filled with fluid. Opening the child's shirt near the top, Mattie noted the presence of rose spots across her chest. There was no question that this was typhoid at its most potent, and the child was in its final stages.

"Mrs. Mousalimas, I am so sorry, but I do not think your daughter is going to live through this. I'd like to give her a medicine called morphine to help her feel less pain, is that okay with you?" The distraught woman nodded and fell down on the bed beside her other children.

"Inez, can you assist me?" The student nodded, kneeling on the floor beside Mattie, cradling the confused and nearly unconscious child in her arms, as Mattie prepared the injection and delivered it to Althea's thigh. Within moments, the child's body relaxed, and her head dropped back as if she were sleeping. Mattie lifted the frail creature, struggling for every breath, and placed her into her mother's arms. "It's best you say goodbye to her, I think."

The mother hugged her child to her chest, reciting prayers and making a cross over her daughter's weakened form. Mattie knew this mother would give anything to heal her child.

Within an hour, Althea had passed. Mattie, Inez, and Fern sanitized the house, cleaned and dressed the body, boiled clean water for drinking, and left tea and food for the other children. "We will notify the undertaker," Mattie promised as they prepared to leave.

"Thank you," Mrs. Mousalimas said again and again.

"You're welcome," Mattie said, knowing they had not done enough. What this family needed was clean drinking water. What they needed was a house connected to a sewage system. The government of the valley had failed to provide this mother with any of that.

On the front porch, Mattie and her students sanitized their hands and removed their aprons. Inez and Fern both began weeping, confronted with their first sight of death. Now they would begin to understand what it really meant to do this work, what the hope of a future vaccine against typhoid could someday mean to the people of this neighborhood and to the world.

Back by their supply wagon, a reporter from the *Salt Lake Herald* waited to talk with the team of volunteers from the nursing school who had come to help with the outbreak. Still overcome by emotion, Mattie let Inez and Fern answer his questions. When he turned to her, she had only one thing to say: "*All* the people of our valley deserve adequate infrastructure, clean water, sewer systems, and vaccinations. These things should not be reserved for the wealthy alone."

The forty-fifth state entered the Union making
no discrimination on account of race, sex, or religion.

—MARTHA HUGHES CANNON

Chapter Fifty-Six

JANUARY 4, 1896

As if in competition with the newly dedicated granite temple, the chiseled Kyune sandstone towers and turrets of the new City and County Building soared up from a swept and sandy lot on 500 South. Topped with gargoyles, sea monsters, beehives, and the goddess Justice, the clock tower reminded everyone that time rushed onward and they best try to keep up.

Mattie drew her dressing gown around her and moved closer to the fire smoldering in its grate, scanning down patient chart notes. Snow drifted past the window, wrapping the house in the stillness of a wintery Saturday morning, and she moved on slippered feet with the practiced stealth of a mother seeking a few more precious minutes of silence before the day began.

Beyond the snow-etched windows, the shrill shriek of a steam whistle pierced the hushed morning like a bullet. Mattie clutched her chart notes, as the whistle sounded again, followed by the bellow of a cannon and a crackle of fireworks.

"Dash it all!" Mattie exclaimed, tossing her notes aside and heading to the window, seeking explanation, as James began to cry from the next room and a nightgowned Lizzie rushed to her mother, sure the world had come to a screeching halt.

In the streets below, the cacophony continued. An elderly man rushed into the road, aimed his rifle at the sky and fired, while a group of teenagers came behind him, whooping and hollering.

"Mama?" Lizzie asked, her eight-year-old eyes wide and fearful. "Is it war?"

Mattie pulled her onto her lap, motioning for six-year-old James who appeared at her doorway. "Oh no, sweetie, it isn't war." Tears streaked James's face, and sleep had tousled his curls. Emotion surged within Mattie, and she couldn't stop the exultant smile spreading across her face. "They're celebrating, not fighting, though it might be hard to tell the difference."

"Sorry they woke you, Jamesy," Mattie said, scooping him up as well, savoring the strange, bittersweet moment.

"What are they celebrating?" Lizzie asked, as more people poured into the streets, banging pans and shouting, and the sharp crackle of firecrackers sizzled through the window.

"I believe," Mattie said, pulling them closer and rocking back and forth, "that Utah just became a state."

Lizzie's face fell in disappointment. "Oh," she said flatly. "Is that all?" A man, just out of bed himself by the looks of it, paraded a U.S. flag through the mayhem, as the sounds of a military 21-gun salute discharged over the no-longer-sleeping city.

Mattie laughed at her daughter's question, thinking over the failed attempts at statehood for Utah that had spanned the past fifty years. And the sacrifice to relinquish polygamy to make statehood possible.

She wondered where B. H. Roberts might be this fine morning, and the thought forced her smile even wider. "No," she told her children. "That isn't all, or even the most important part. They are also celebrating that women can vote. After seventeen years, Mother can vote again, and when you are older, you both will as well." She paused for dramatic effect like the trained elocutionist she was: "And today to celebrate, we shall cancel all of our plans and have a party instead."

"With cake?" Lizzie asked, a little suspicious, given the wild and strange behavior unfolding in the streets.

"Yes, with cake." Mattie fetched her overcoat which she hastily threw over her dressing gown. "And also right now with noise."

At this unexpected turn of events, Lizzie began jumping up and down. "Hurrah!" she cried, hugging her brother.

"Hurrah!" said James, a little unclear about why he was happy.

In the kitchen, Mattie pulled pots and pans from the cupboards and handed them each a wooden spoon. The three sat down on the front porch in nightgown and pajamas, and joined their neighbors in pounding out the sweet sound of suffrage. Firecrackers and firearms mingled with the joyful boom of cannons, pennywhistles, and noisemakers. "Listen," Mattie told her children, hoping they'd always remember this day. "That is the sound of *franchise.*"

"Franchise," Lizzie repeated, tasting the large and luscious word upon her tongue.

The week-long Salt Lake City celebration of statehood was as grand as Lizzie could have wished. For the official celebration, a hundred-and-fifty-foot American flag, boasting forty-five stars, was draped from the ceiling of the Tabernacle. The Mormon Tabernacle Choir sang "Utah, We Love Thee," before the newly elected state governor, Heber Manning Wells, delivered an inaugural address. A parade and carriage procession wound its way through downtown Salt Lake, and a chorus of a thousand children waved miniature flags as they sang the national anthem. Bunting in red, white, and blue billowed from nearly every roof and window in the city.

The Mormons had dissolved their People's Party to alleviate criticisms of the Church influencing politics, and now Church leaders urged members to spread themselves among both parties evenly. The Republicans and Democrats scrambled to assemble their lists of five candidates each for the upcoming November election.

The story of the struggle for woman's suffrage . . . is the story of all efforts for the advancement and betterment of humanity, which has been told over and over ever since the advent of civilization.

—MARTHA HUGHES CANNON

Chapter Fifty-Seven

The decisive rap sent Mattie's housekeeper scurrying to open the door.

"Ma'am, sorry to disturb you," Sarah told her. "Judge O. W. Powers is calling."

"Thank you, Sarah," Mattie said, setting down a report from her nursing school and leaving Lizzie to play with James. She wondered what Judge Powers might possibly want; she hoped he wasn't seeking medical care outside of posted office hours.

Judge Powers stood tall and gaunt in her front parlor, dressed in a fastidious suit, with his thinning hair combed optimistically over his forehead. "May I help you?" Mattie asked.

"Please forgive my unexpected visit this morning."

"Not at all. Please have a seat." She indicated a blue velvet divan.

The judge seated himself across from her. "Dr. Cannon, I know you have taken an active interest in the women's suffrage movement, and I have enjoyed your speeches on that topic."

"Thank you," she said, flattered, for the judge was not known for throwing compliments lightly.

"You are probably aware that the two political parties are

nominating senators for the state legislature to stand for election in November."

"Yes, I am," said Mattie, wondering where he was going with this.

"And it seems fitting that we would invite a newly enfranchised woman to serve with us."

"A wonderful idea," Mattie said. "I can think of several women who would be wonderful candidates, if you came to seek my input. Sarah Kimball, Emily Richards, maybe even—"

"Thank you, Doctor, but I have come as Chairman of the Democratic Committee of Utah to ask if you would be willing to accept our nomination and run on the Democratic ticket."

Mattie's face flushed. "Heavens."

"I know it is a significant commitment," the judge replied.

"Truthfully, I've wanted to become involved in politics," Mattie said, "but I thought to try for such a thing when my children are older. And after I've gained more experience."

The judge smiled, a bit patronizingly, his mustache flaring with the effort. "When you've gained more experience? Forgive me, ma'am, but it seems to me that between your medical school credentials, your work at the hospital, your involvement in the Columbian Exposition, and your fight to include women's suffrage in the state constitution, few on the ballot could hope to match you for experience."

Had she really done all of those things? Odd how they sounded so much more important than any of them had felt at the time. Mattie drew a deep breath.

"I understand it is an important decision," Judge Powers continued. "I imagine you will need time to talk it over with family and decide if you can accept. Do you think you can let us know by Wednesday?"

Mattie nodded, struggling to clear her throat. "Certainly, that is more than fair. I thank you for the honor, Judge."

"You are most welcome," he said. "Many of us in the party feel you would be a tremendous asset to our state. We will await your decision."

When he had gone, Mattie sank back against the divan. If she won, it would mean closing her practice, or at least drastically reducing it. It would mean turning the management of her nursing school over to someone else for several years at least.

But it would also mean designing and guiding the course of this city—crafting public health projects, writing laws and working to create a more humane future. And it would mean continuing the public speaking she'd been doing as of late.

The prospect felt as daunting as it was thrilling, and she could hardly contain her anticipation when she returned to her children. Their small cries welcomed her, and she set her patient notes aside to focus on the block structure her children had laid out across the floor.

"We need a moat!" Lizzie said.

"I want a bridge there," James said, pointing.

Mattie helped them build it, one solid length of wood at a time.

Three days after sending in her formal acceptance for the nomination, Mattie stared in dismay at a note scrawled in Angus's hand. She hadn't seen him for some weeks, and now he had written to excuse his absence.

> *As you may have heard, I was honored to accept the Republican Party's nomination for the upcoming senate election. I am joined in the endeavor with several other strong candidates, including Emmeline B. Wells. We hope to bring righteous and measured experience to the city, which needs people of integrity*

at its helm to guide it aright. Very much appreciate the trust and respect the nomination indicates. I will try and do my best to live up to their estimation, and hope I may even be able to convince some Democrats such as yourself to vote for me.

Mattie laughed aloud, a rueful, twisting laugh. So she was to go up for election against Angus *and* Emmeline? If she could have chosen her opponents, *they* would be among the last she would have chosen. Both of them had twenty years of experience and far more name recognition than she did. The letter left her feeling unprepared, and a bit silly for having listened to Judge Powers's flattering words. Angus was not only president of the largest stake in the Church, the city planner of Call's Landing, a former mayor of St. George, but also brother of George Q. Cannon. Everyone in Utah knew Emmeline both as the editor of *Woman's Exponent* and the face of the fight for women's suffrage.

And what would Angus think about the two of them running for the same office—not exactly against each other—for in this race, *any* five candidates from either party could win. They could both win. Or neither of them could. *But still.*

A few days later, he rushed through the door as disheveled as she'd ever seen him, hair awry, cravat askew.

"Hello, Angus," she greeted, setting down the vegetables she was chopping for dinner.

"Papa!" Lizzie shouted, running for a hug with James close behind her. Angus hugged the children hastily, but it was clear enough they were not why he had come. His mouth worked as he tried to decide where to begin.

"Lizzie and James, I need you to fetch roots from the cellar for supper," Mattie instructed them, shooing them out the door.

"You?" he fumed, color mounting in his face. "You are running for the legislature? *When you knew I was running?*"

Mattie wiped her hands. "When the Democrats asked me to

accept their nomination, I *didn't* know you were running." She couldn't help adding, "I hadn't seen you in quite a while."

Poor man. He looked as though his world were tumbling down as he ran a hand through his disheveled hair. She'd never seen him leave his house looking anything other than fastidious. "Don't worry, Angus. You and Emmeline are far more well known than I am. I am sure you'll win."

"But you are going to stay in the race? Against your own husband?" His mouth moved as if chewing a substance he'd never tasted before. "You won't reconsider?"

"Reconsider?" she asked, feeling the sting of his question. "You mean won't I resign because you were also nominated?" She picked up the knife and continued chopping carrots. "Don't be silly. It's an election of ten candidates. The top five vote winners from either party will make up the newly formed legislature. Both of us could win, or neither of us could. It isn't anything to fuss over." She tossed the chopped carrots into a pot of boiling water. "I hope as you're here now, you'll stay for dinner?"

"Thank you," he nodded, relaxing only slightly. "I must tell you, Mattie, the Republican Party has a plan to lead this city forward, and I believe we have the backing of Church leaders, my brother among them."

"I am sure you do," Mattie said, "but the Democrats also have a plan, with plenty of leaders among us as well, including B. H. Roberts, whom you've long respected and who fought against us, just a brief time ago. I can't in good conscience join a party that fought against polygamy and women's suffrage. Besides, you know better than I do, Church leaders counselled members to spread ourselves between both parties to avoid any impressions of favoritism. So. We are a model family, are we not?"

"But, Mattie, you must see that free silver is an unsustainable concept," he began, as the children returned from the root cellar, their hands laden with sweet potatoes and onions.

Mattie smiled sweetly. "Now, Angus, let's avoid any unpleasant talk of politics over dinner with our children, shall we?"

The newspapers did not take Mattie's rational view of the matter. After releasing the full list of candidates, a new taunt appeared daily in the city papers, as editors worked to outdo each other. *The Salt Lake Tribune* went so far as to rally for a "public verbal set-to," between Martha and Angus, merrily speculating about the popularity of a public debate between spouses.

When the powerful *Tribune* backed Angus as their candidate, Mattie assumed he would prevail, and she would soon be returning to her medical practice, but the *Salt Lake Herald* advised their readers:

> Angus M. Cannon is a worthy man, against him we haven't a word to say. Only we would say that Mrs. Mattie Hughes Cannon, his wife, is the better man of the two. Send Mrs. Cannon to the state senate as a Democrat and let Mr. Cannon as a Republican remain at home to manage home industry.

Mattie laughed aloud at the jab, though she doubted Angus would find it as humorous.

The next day the *Tribune* returned to the fray:

> We do not see anything for Angus M. to do but to go home and break a bouquet over Mrs. Cannon's head, to show his superiority.

Mattie thought that comment took the whole thing a touch too far, but she shrugged it off as she'd shrugged off the others.

Though there were no public debates, there were plenty of

opportunities for speeches, and Mattie made sure to review her speaking schedule with Angus so they would not have to appear in public together, speaking in support of opposite parties.

Though she hadn't sought the appointment, after listening to Angus and Emmeline outline their plans should they win, Mattie realized that if elected, neither would attempt to address what she considered to be the most compelling issues facing the state. Emmeline's true passion was for suffrage, and with that debate behind Utah, she mostly sought the office to continue fighting the national suffrage cause. Angus, meanwhile, cared little about typhoid outbreaks, education, and public drinking water, and Mattie recognized the swiftest way to remedy these problems involved enacting legislation at the highest levels.

Doubling down on her efforts, Mattie pulled out her old textbooks from oratory school and reviewed the breathing exercises, recommended postures, and the principles of speech development, until she felt ready at last to put her elocution training to work. Emmeline and Angus both had strong public followings due to their years of community service, but Mattie determined no one would outwork her. She walked neighborhoods, Lizzie and James by her side, speaking to anyone who would listen about her public health concerns.

Mattie gave speeches at fairs, markets, and more formal gatherings. "We need a public board of health," she told listeners. "We need to work on increasing vaccinations to prevent another smallpox outbreak. And we need to do all we can to eradicate the spread of public germs in the city."

Angus, too, gave speeches of his own, and his arguments against free silver persuaded many. Emmeline stuck to the fight for women's suffrage and recounted her long experience as editor of the *Woman's Exponent*. Oddly, just before the election, Emmeline traveled to Idaho to see her daughter, which seemed strange given her desire to win, but Mattie reasoned that perhaps she felt she had such a significant lead, a brief departure wouldn't matter.

During Emmeline's absence, Mattie continued attending events explaining her belief that Utah needed public education on epidemics and drug use, and that the state urgently required a board of health.

Many times during speeches she recounted the Women's Congress in Chicago, the inspiration behind her dedication to help Utah live up to the ideals of the nation. She concluded by reciting the feminist poems of Charlotte Perkins Gilman to her audience's delight:

> *We all may have our homes in joy and peace*
> *When woman's life, in its rich power of love*
> *Is joined with man's to care for all the world.*

*With scarcely a dissenting voice, they will say to you that
woman suffrage is no longer an experiment, but is a
practical reality, tending to the well-being of the State.*
—MARTHA HUGHES CANNON

Chapter Fifty-Eight

NOVEMBER 1896

The night of the election, the Salt Lake County election office stayed open late, as ballot counters worked behind closed doors to open envelopes, complete tallies, and compute long sums of figures. In the front hall, the Ladies' Social Club threw a reception for the candidates and constituents awaiting early results.

Mattie tucked James and Lizzie into bed with a kiss, promising to give them news in the morning. "You and Papa could *both* become senators, Mama?" Lizzie asked.

"Yes, my sweet."

"If I were old enough to vote, I'd vote for you," Lizzie announced. "And Papa too."

"Me too," James agreed.

"Those are two votes I'd be mighty proud to have," Mattie said, pulling a cloak over her best silk dress and fastening her mother's cameo against the ruffles at her throat.

Angus was already at the party, cutting a grand figure in his

Prince Albert suit, Amelia's hand tucked possessively in the corner of his arm. "Hello, Angus. Amelia," Mattie said, bowing.

"Good evening," they responded.

"Is it too early to say congratulations?" George Cannon said to Angus, striding up. "I noticed the *Tribune* doesn't think so."

"Yes, congratulations," Mattie said. A *Salt Lake Tribune* article earlier that morning had claimed that Angus could not lose.

"Thank you," Angus said graciously, inclining his head. Then in acknowledgment of Mattie added, "I look forward to seeing who else will serve with me in the legislature."

Mattie smiled her thanks and moved on, greeting voters and circling through the glittering gala of Salt Lake's elite. Emmeline was there, looking just as formidable and birdlike as ever, in her elegant ruched black silk gown. "Best of luck to you, Martha," she said.

"And to you, Emmeline."

The night glittered in a world of pomp that Angus naturally belonged to, one that Emmeline moved graciously through with a rustle of her skirt—a world of gracious nods and immovable smiles, a sip from a crystal cup, a dab at the lips, and a charming murmur of assent. Here, among so many supporters, it seemed inevitable that Angus and Emmeline would make their way onto the stage of Utah's statehood, as representatives of her roots. And yet, Mattie wondered if Angus and Emmeline weren't running to preserve more of what had been than to welcome what could be.

B. H. Roberts, who had put aside the conflict over women's suffrage, and Judge Powers warmly welcomed Mattie, introducing her as the noted doctress and suffrage proponent to wealthy people in exquisite clothing whose names she would never remember in the morning.

Lotta glided across the floor, smothering her excitement with finesse. Sliding up beside Mattie she whispered urgently, "I am so proud of you!"

Mattie laughed, relieved at the chance to have a real conversation in the midst of so much posturing. "I'm afraid I haven't done anything as of yet," she retorted.

"The results hardly matter. I'm proud of you for bringing attention to such important issues and for running at all! Against your husband, no less!"

"I'm not so sure my husband is as thrilled about that as you are."

"Oh, he's plenty proud too, I think," said Lottie. "He just hides it better under all his pageantry."

"And his mustache," Mattie added, allowing herself a smile.

Judge Powers paused before them. "Excuse me for interrupting, ladies, but I simply must introduce the Kimballs to Dr. Martha Hughes Cannon." Mattie allowed the judge to bustle her away. "It is my honor to introduce you to one of the leading proponents of the national suffrage cause who hopes to work on issues of public health." Mattie still felt like an imposter when they introduced her thus, yet after so much campaigning, another part insisted: *Oh yes, that's right, I did do those things.*

Near the end of the evening, the head of the election committee clapped for attention. "I am pleased to announce, thanks to ballot counters working tirelessly, we are ready to report some early returns." He paused for applause. "It is, you understand, far too early to be definitive, but for now, the evening appears to be going to the Democrats." Cheers broke out around Mattie.

"The early front-runners appear to be George A. Whitaker, John T. Caine, and Benjamin A. Harbour!" More cheers, more applause, and the three men clambered onto the dais to give a quick repetition of their stump speeches in worn and familiar words.

Well. She'd not considered the idea that *none* of them might win—this whole silly drama for naught. Mattie clapped and congratulated the men as they expected her to. *At least, thank heavens, they were Democrats, a fact which Angus looked none too pleased about.*

Stifling a yawn, Mattie pulled her cloak around her shoulders and headed home to her sleeping children, whose heads of late had been filled with stuffy political terms like suffrage, ballot, election, and prediction. Mattie sighed into sleep, thinking of her nursing school and how to resume her previous plans, scarcely noticing anymore the emptiness of space stretching beside her.

Rapping on the front door awoke her. A sharp, insistent rapping. Mattie's eyes flew open, surprised the children had let her sleep so late, for morning sunshine streamed through her gauze curtains. The rapping came again as she drew a dressing gown around her, embarrassed she'd allowed the celebrations last night to exhaust her so. Sarah was not on hand, so she headed for the door herself, passing her fingers through her tousled curls and hoping it was no one she knew.

It wasn't. "Telegram for you, ma'am," the messenger said.

"Thank you." She took the missive with surprise.

Mattie closed the door as James and Lizzie tumbled downstairs, also clad in their sleep clothes. "What happened last night, Mama?" Lizzie asked. "Who won? You or Papa?"

"I don't know for certain," Mattie said, "But I believe neither of us did." She tore open the telegram and folded back the paper.

"Oh," said Lizzie, crestfallen. "No cake," she informed James, who yawned sulkily.

Mattie stared at the words before her:

The newly appointed Governor, Heber Manning Wells, wishes to congratulate Dr. Martha Hughes Cannon on her election to the Office of Senator in the State of Utah, November 1896. I look forward to working with you for the betterment of our society.
Sincerely, Governor Wells

It took Mattie a moment to process his words, a thrill running through her from head to foot. Tingling slightly, she looked down into the eyes of her trusting daughter and said, "There's been a change, Lizzie. This is Governor Wells writing to tell me I have won the election after all." She laughed, pure pleasure and shock at the announcement, the future shifting again with yet another swift turn of a kaleidoscope.

Senator. She was to serve as state senator. In a country where the vast majority of women could not vote. *At least, not yet.*

"Hurrah, Mama!" Lizzie shouted, turning a pirouette and hugging her mother fiercely around the knees. "Good job! You're so grown up now!"

Mattie laughed, hearing the words she often said to her daughter reversed. "Yes, I suppose I am."

Lizzie hugged James too. "Another party, Jamesy! Cake?"

"Oh yes," Mattie assured her. "We shall have ever so much cake."

When the results were finally tallied and announced, Mattie had won a seat along with four other Democrats. Neither Angus nor Emmeline had earned a seat, a fact she hoped they would forgive her for one day.

There were parties and cakes, even enough for Lizzie. Some weeks later, dressed in her finest silk, Mattie attended the swearing-in ceremony, seated beside a scrubbed Lizzie and polished James, and a beaming Elizabeth.

One by one, the new state senators were called forward in the legislative chambers of the City and County Building, past carved, wood-paneled walls and a portrait of Brigham Young. One by one, they placed their hand upon the Bible and swore to honor the oath of office. Four men. And Martha.

As she stepped across the platform, Mattie held her head high, taking each step with deliberation. Though she was a full head shorter than any of the other inductees, she knew her height was enough. As her experience was also enough. With each step across the dais, she silently repeated a name: *Trotula. Agnodice. Jacoba Felice.* She smiled to the assembled audience, in her mind, she added another, *Gwendolyn.* Solemnly, she raised her right hand before family and community and swore the oath of office, binding herself to do her best for God and country. *Barbara*, she thought. And last of all, *Lizzie.*

Mattie knew not what the future might hold, but she knew her voice would be raised in the halls of the legislature. She knew her pen would set down, in ink, her view of how the future might unfold: more just, more sane, more generous and—heaven help her—a world of greater healing. With the great handiwork of man about her—evident in the stone spires stretching skyward—it was time, at last, to build upon those efforts and begin to see what women's hands and brains could fashion, in a world that began to welcome her labor at last.

Trotula. Agnodice. Jacoba Felice. Gwendolyn. Mattie.

What could this world become in the hands of such mighty healers? She intended to find out.

Author's Note

Twenty-four years before the Nineteenth Amendment would guarantee all American white women the right to vote, newspapers around the country applauded the audacity of Utah for electing the first female senator, Dr. Martha Hughes Cannon.

During her two legislative sessions, Cannon helped with the establishment of the State Board of Health (forerunner to the Utah Department of Health), fought for mandated vaccinations, and worked for public education on drug use and narcotic addiction. Mattie introduced laws that protected conditions for working-class employees and was committed to issues that affected women and children. She called for education on behalf of the blind and deaf populations, and helped create, then served on the board of the Utah State School for the Deaf and Dumb. Mattie worked with her colleague and close friend, Alice Merrill Horne, to create the Art Institute of Utah, one of the first in the country. Dr. Cannon passed laws relating to public health, sanitation and clean drinking water, infrastructure, sewage systems, and disease control and prevention. In her third year in office, she served as chairman of the Public Health Committee.

Senator Cannon was deeply respected by her colleagues for a senate voting record independent of her husband's political views and uninfluenced by LDS Church leaders. In 1897, Angus criticized Mattie for switching her vote to a former Mormon apostle Moses Thatcher, in spite of strong opposition from himself and other Church leaders. Mattie gave a speech so persuasive in the legislature to explain her reasoning for switching, it was cheered aloud on the Senate floor, despite rules to the contrary. In 1899, when her nephew Frank Cannon asked for her vote, she insisted she couldn't oblige because she'd been elected on the Democratic ticket. When her brother-in-law George Q. Cannon ran for office, Mattie didn't vote for him either. Throughout her career, Mattie remained an active voice advocating for the national suffrage movement, and spoke on its behalf in Chicago, Washington D.C., and New York.

In January 1899, her fellow state senator, Judge Powers, nominated Mattie for the office of U.S. senator saying, "I consider her eminently qualified for the position. She is a gifted speaker, a logical and sharp reasoner." Shortly after this nomination, however, Mattie became pregnant with her third and final child, a decision deemed scandalous, coming, as it did, nine years after the Manifesto. This final pregnancy effectively ended her political career, but Mattie never regretted having her third child, a daughter she named Gwendolyn.

After retiring from public office, Mattie moved with her three children to California, where she continued her medical research and consultation for the Graves Clinic (associated with U.C.L.A.'s medical school), focusing her final years on the effects of narcotic addiction.

Her children and grandchildren remained the focal point of her personal life, and they remained near her always. Mattie's daughter Gwendolyn became an actress and artist; Lizzie became a rancher and a writer who recorded several versions of her mother's life story; and James became an inventor who established the Cannon

Electrical Company, which continues under the name ITT in California to this day.

At Mattie's funeral in 1932, B. H. Roberts, her former opponent turned ardent supporter, spoke, as did her fellow legislator, Alice Merrill Horne. Mattie asked to be buried beside Angus in Salt Lake City, finally achieving a close proximity to him in death she never enjoyed in life.

In 2019, the Utah state legislature voted to send a statue of Cannon to Washington DC to represent the state in Statuary Hall in time for the 100th anniversary celebration of U.S. women's suffrage. In the fall of 2020, Cannon's hometown of Llandudno, Wales, will also unveil a monument commemorating her accomplishments.

Martha's life exemplified the words she once wrote in a letter to her dear friend, Barbara Replogle: "Let us not waste our talents in the cauldron of modern nothingness—but strive to become women of intellect and endeavor to do some little good while we live in this protracted gleam called life."

Acknowledgments

When I began working on this novel based on the life of Martha Hughes Cannon, I had no idea we shared a common ancestor; and though I knew I had distant Welsh family, I could not guess that the search for Martha's roots would lead me to my own. My own family, like Martha's, were Welsh farmers and craftsmen for centuries. During the 1800s, rural Wales experienced a great religious revival which left people open to new sects. They sought for alternatives to the Church of England, which they associated with a ruling elite that had outlawed their language and sought to eliminate their culture. The 1840s were rife with economic challenges, and "the hungry forties" left working-class families, like mine and Martha's, desperate for alternatives, including emigration.

When missionaries from The Church of Jesus Christ of Latter-day Saints arrived in Wales during these years, they found a willing audience, though not without persecution from local clergymen. In spite of opposition, more than eight thousand Welsh men and women joined the Mormon Church during that decade, and approximately six thousand chose to emigrate. These converts left a dramatic and permanent impact on LDS culture to this day, including the formation of the Mormon Tabernacle Choir by an early Welsh convert.

My ancestors were among the earliest converts in Wales, and they chose to leave behind centuries of family connections, knowing they were unlikely to ever see their beloved homeland again. One of the best sources for understanding Llandudno during these years is an account kept by a Welsh miner, Thomas Rowlands, who recorded detailed observations about his town and its inhabitants. Rowlands records the meetings of the Mormons and recalls that when they departed Llandudno on boats bound for Liverpool (and from there, America), friends, relatives, and neighbors gathered along the edge of the Irish Sea, bidding tearful farewells to those whom they knew they would never see again.

When Mattie's parents, Peter and Elizabeth Hughes, converted to the nascent religion, their scandalized parents attempted to prevent their grandchildren's departure, so the couple, with their three young daughters, stole away without bidding them goodbye. At the age of three, Martha crossed an ocean, spent some months in New York, then, in the early days of the Civil War, set out across the plains in a wagon bound for Utah territory.

In retracing Martha's roots, I have tried to identify the ways her Welsh identity impacted her development. Certainly her love of oratory, poetry, and literature aligns with Welsh culture. Little remains to record her impressions of her native land during her exile, beyond brief mentions in letters to Angus. We know that she sought out family graves in the village of Llanddoged, and after her visit, she returned to using her father's Welsh surname, Hughes (rather than her stepfather's, Paul). We also know she named her final daughter a traditional Welsh name, Gwendolyn. These are among the only remaining clues that indicate what this journey may have meant to her.

According to census records, Martha's grandfather worked as a gardener, so it seems possible that his wife, Mary (Mair in this novel) might have been a cunning folk, as a Welsh garden is the poor apothecary's medicine cabinet. If her mother-in-law was, in fact, a healer, then Elizabeth's documented opposition to her daughter's choice of profession might have stemmed from bitterness against the woman who tried to prevent the couple's departure. This is entirely built upon my own speculation based on scanty remaining evidence.

As my family history mirrors Mattie's in its Welshness, so it does also regarding the practice of polygamy. It's important to acknowledge that, for Mormon women, the experience of practicing plural marriage encompassed a range of experiences, on a broad continuum of positive to negative. Mattie publicly defended the practice her whole life, though it is clear from her private correspondence that aspects of it caused her deep pain; it is her experience that I've tried to faithfully capture in this novel. Along with all those who have researched Mattie's life, I mourn the loss of her personal journals burned at her request upon her death, knowing she chose to take her most private struggles to her grave.

Writing a historical novel requires a voluminous amount of support and assistance, and I am indebted to the scholars who have spent years working out the details of Martha's life, including Constance Lieber, whose prolific and insightful emails have given me much to reflect on. Shari Crall's generosity and the remarkable research for her thesis (accessed at BYU's Special Collections) several decades ago proved invaluable. Martha's descendants, Arline and Blaine Brady, shared information only family members would have. Ron Fox was more than generous with connecting me with family members, including Brent and Mattie's great-granddaughter, providing rare and unpublished images, and giving me a broader understanding of the era. Historian Carol Cornwall Madsen was extremely helpful with the aspects of Martha that connect to Emmeline B. Wells. The Better Days 2020 campaign has brought long overdue attention to Martha's story and the role Utah played in the national suffrage movement. Fara Snedon's research on LDS female healing contributed enormously to this manuscript, and my sister, Abigayle M. Ellison, was an incredible resource on scientific practice, the medical profession, and Celtic ritual.

The National Library in Wales was a marvelous resource for Welsh Mormonism, cunning women, Celtic lore, and the witch trials of Gwen Ferch Ellis in Llansanffraid. One of the highlights of this project was handling Gwen's original trial documents from 1594 in their archives. Many thanks to Lucinda Smith at the archives in Llandudno, as well as to Dr. Wil Aaron, who graciously shared his resources, translated Welsh documents, and invited me over for tea to discuss Martha's story from a Welsh historian's perspective. A Clatsop Community College faculty development grant made the research trip to Wales possible.

I am incredibly lucky to have the Klickitat Writers (Afton Nelson, Keira Dominguez, and Christine Sandgren) in my corner. Their wit and wisdom never cease to thrill me, and they are gentle in their criticism, generous with their praise. Research assistants Luis Arondo and Alanna Nelson dug up all sorts of helpful details and assembled a staggering amount of information into useful formats. My Shadow Mountain editors, Leslie Stitt and Heidi Gordon are, as always, simply the best.

Last but certainly not least, I thank my children for their inspiration and support; and my husband, Andrew, who not only encouraged the research trip to Wales and commented on early drafts, but also kept me well fed so I could write. How thankful I am for his respect, loyalty, and love for myself and for the work I do.

Chapter Notes

EPIGRAPHS

All epigraphs in Parts One through Four are from Martha Hughes Cannon's medical school notebook. It is unpublished and undated and resides in the Church History Library in Salt Lake City, Utah. The epigraphs in Part Five are drawn from her political speeches and public statements.

CHAPTER ONE

The Peter and Elizabeth Hughes family departed from Wales, then sailed from Liverpool to New York on a schooner called *The Underwriter* on March 30, 1860. A fellow passenger, one-year-old Frederick Williams, died on the ship and was buried at sea. In New York, Elizabeth worked in a garment factory as they saved money to go West. Erastus Snow helped the Hughes family travel to Florence, Nebraska, where they were outfitted with oxen and wagon and joined the Joseph Horne Company crossing the mountains to Utah in 1861 during the chaos of the early days of the Civil War. In the final weeks of the journey, many in camp became sick with "mountain fever," a disease now believed to be Colorado tick fever. Ten days before the company entered the Salt Lake Valley, Annie Hughes died. There was no wood or time to spare to make coffins. The Welsh tradition, mentioned in this chapter, of lighting candles along the path to the burial site is shadowed by the superstition that if a candle glows red, the death of a man is impending. Peter Hughes died three days after their arrival; Mattie's only memory of her father was him laid out in his coffin. Though in this novel, Elizabeth Hughes is Welsh, in reality she was English; Mattie's father and his extended family were Welsh. The couple met in Llandudno, Wales, where they married and had three children. Because Peter leaves my story so quickly and I wanted to explore Mattie's Welsh heritage, which remained important to her throughout her life, I chose to portray Elizabeth as Welsh in this novel.

CHAPTER TWO

In typesetting, capital letters were found in the upper drawer, or upper case, while the lowercase letters were located in the lower drawer, or case, giving rise to the terms uppercase and lowercase letters. Brigham Young offered Mattie and other young women the opportunity to apprentice to Hyrum Parry in an attempt to remove men from doing "women's work" (see *Improvement Era,* March 1939, 114–15). Mattie became so proficient at the work she could typeset for Scandinavian papers, even though she didn't know the languages.

CHAPTER FOUR

The first year in the valley Elizabeth was given a "widow's allotment" of land on the east bench of Salt Lake. Elizabeth used a cave as a kitchen, and she and her two surviving daughters slept in the wagon bed. Eighteen months later, she married James Patten Paul, a carpenter born July 17, 1817, in East Ayrshire, Scotland. He joined the LDS Church and emigrated to the United States with his wife, Robina Gribben, and their four children in 1861. Robina died in Ohio. After Elizabeth and James married, they built a small adobe home on Elizabeth's land, and the couple subsequently had five additional children. Elizabeth sold the last of her clothing brought from Europe to buy supplies to finish the home. I am indebted to Elizabeth Cannon McCrimmon's accounts for many of the details of Mattie's childhood home.

CHAPTER FIVE

Mattie saved for months to have boots made to her specifications so she could walk the six miles every day between home, her job at the

Exponent, and her night classes at the University of Deseret. Eschewing styles of the day, she cropped her hair short because she felt it was better for her health, though she adored stylish clothing otherwise. The trunk made for Mattie by her stepfather, James Paul, can still be seen today in the Daughters of the Utah Pioneer Museum in Salt Lake City.

In writing about Mattie's life, her daughter Elizabeth recorded that Mattie's older stepbrothers, Logan and Adam, were "boisterous and loud, funny." As an actor and detective respectively, they encouraged Mattie's career aspirations. The textbook Logan reads in this scene is a fabricated mash-up of titles. The quote itself comes from Watts's *Dictionary of Chemistry,* 1888. The sharpshooter scandal Adam Paul recounts is based on an actual case he solved as reported in the *Salt Lake Daily Tribune*, August 25, 1894. A "witch's light" is a pioneer era name for an inexpensive candle substitute consisting of a rag tied around a button then set alight inside a pan of cooking grease.

CHAPTER SIX

Though in the LDS Church today women do not typically administer blessings, women routinely blessed the sick beginning with the earliest days of Relief Society through the first quarter of the twentieth century. When some men criticized them for doing so, Joseph Smith defended the practice saying, women had been ordained to heal the sick and it was their privilege to "administer in that authority which is confer'd on them, and if the sisters should have faith to heal, let all hold their tongues" (The Joseph Smith Papers, Relief Society Minutes of Nauvoo, April 28, 1842).

In 1906 the LDS First Presidency reconfirmed, "It is the privilege of any good faithful woman to anoint the sick with oil and pray for their recovery." Women were formally set apart to work as healers in the LDS temples and administered healing rituals within their families and religious communities during sickness, before childbirth, and before death. Healing was seen as a spiritual gift which complemented a woman's innate compassion, and these practices provided LDS women with a deep sense of spiritual purpose and community. In LDS settlements and along the trail westward, faith healing was used alongside herbal medical practices (the Thomsonian method became particularly popular in Utah territory). For more on the history and evolution of women healers in the LDS Church see *Mormon Sisters: Women in Early Utah* by Claudia Bushman (Logan, UT: Utah State University Press, 1997) and *Ministering: Latter-day Saint Women and Their History of Blessing and Administration* by Fara Sneddon (Champaign, Illinois: University of Illinois Press, forthcoming).

CHAPTER SEVEN

The recipe for skin salve included in this chapter comes from the recipes and notes of renowned LDS midwife Patty Bartlett Sessions who trained as a midwife under her mother-in-law, and who went on to deliver more than 3,900 babies in her career, keeping copious journals of her practice. Sessions's ancestors came from Essex, Massachusetts, mere miles from the site of the infamous Salem witch trials, and before that, England. The experience of Patty's ancestors practicing medicine in secret on an English isle is based on the view of witchcraft as an attempt on the part of peasant women to reclaim a degree of power and autonomy over their own physical health, while the dominant view of the Catholic church in the Middle Ages (and in the subsequent Church of England) viewed illness as a punishment of God, only properly controlled by male church clergy.

At many times in England over the centuries, fines and imprisonment restrained women who attempted to "use the practyse of Fisyk." During witch trials, medical experts, exclusively male physicians, were asked to determine whether women were witches and if illnesses, death, and mishaps had been caused by witchcraft. Lacking knowledge of germ theory and other scientific explanations, many mishaps were thus used as an excuse to torture and put tens of thousands of women to death. Though men were also accused of witchcraft, more than 75 percent of all witch hunt victims were female.

The *Malleus Maleficarum, or Hammer of Witches* published in 1484 by inquisition authorities taught Catholic clergy how to conduct a witch hunt and linked witchcraft with female sexuality: "All witchcraft comes from carnal lust, which in women is insatiable. . . . Wherefore for the sake of fulfilling their lusts they consort with devils . . . it is sufficiently clear that it is no matter for wonder that there are more women than men found infected with the heresy of witchcraft . . . and blessed be the Highest who has so far preserved the male sex from so great a crime."

CHAPTER NINE

Recording conference talks was a laborious process and we do not have the actual lecture given by Brigham Young, so his talk as presented here is a compilation of many talks given over the course of several years in the Salt Lake Tabernacle and from one in Idaho. Several people in attendance reported that at the October 1873 conference Brigham Young asked for female doctors to come forth and attend medical school, but this talk does not appear in the *Journal of Discourses*. Delivered when Mattie was sixteen, his talk inspired her to enroll for night classes so she could continue working as a typesetter during the day. She spent four and a half years studying chemistry at the University of Deseret (later renamed the University of Utah). I have rearranged the order of these factual events to serve the purposes of my novel.

CHAPTER TEN

The Woman's Exponent, which Emmeline Wells edited for thirty-nine years, became a popular women's bimonthly newspaper managed, written, and edited by women dedicated to strengthening LDS women across scattered settlements and educating women outside the faith about Mormonism. It reported on events related to women's rights and suffrage from Utah, the United States, and around the world. The newspaper included poems, stories, social and political commentary, humor, reports from national suffrage conventions, and current news, and set out to "discuss every subject interesting and valuable to women." The subtitle of the paper was *The Rights of the Women of Zion and the Rights of the Women of All Nations*.

The paper was distributed at the Chicago World's Fair and was used to defend polygamy on the world stage. Emmeline Wells wrote, "The world says polygamy makes women inferior to men—we think differently. Polygamy gives women more time for thought, for mental culture, more freedom of action, a broader field of labor, and leads women more directly to God, the fountain of all truth." Though Wells remained a staunch public supporter of the practice, privately, as the wife of Salt Lake mayor Daniel H. Wells, Emmeline struggled with loneliness and isolation from a husband who divided his time between six other wives. The quotes in this chapter are from *Woman's Exponent* (April 1, 1873 and Oct. 1, 1878).

Mattie became engaged to James H. Anderson, but broke off the engagement before she left for medical school. I altered his name to Jim as there is already an abundance of people named James in this novel.

As portrayed in this chapter, Mattie was blessed and set apart before she left for medical school in the Church Historian's Office. Romania Pratt went on to perform the first successful cataract surgery in the Midwest. Ellis Shipp delivered more than five thousand babies and trained more than five hundred women to be midwives.

Though we do not have the actual words used in the blessing to set Mattie apart, the words in my scene are adapted from a blessing given to Ellis Shipp by John Taylor on June 29, 1887. Some of the language in this blessing is also adapted from Susan Elvira Martineau's patriarchal blessing given February 20, 1890, by Benjamin Johnson.

CHAPTER ELEVEN

The first female student graduated from the University of Michigan in 1871, seven years before Mattie's arrival. Several faculty voted against the admission of women and offered the statement: "The medical co-education of the sexes is at best an experiment of doubtful utility, and one not calculated to increase the dignity of man, nor the modesty of women. . . . Women are qualified mentally and emotionally to tend the sick, but they are semi-invalids a large fraction of the month. There is the danger they would practice abortion to avoid having pregnancy, and childbearing would interfere with their medical careers."

Records from Mattie's time in medical school are rare, so my portrayal of the attitudes of professors toward their female students is largely based upon documented accounts of other female students. Adella Brindle, a medical student at the University of Michigan (1873–74) recalled "the coarse, ribald stories of Dr. Douglas, antiquated Prof. of Chemistry who looked upon us women as monstrosities. . . . I remember with contempt the loud and boisterous behavior of the 500 men 'medics' when we women (35 in number) entered the lecture room. . . . Dr. Palmer . . . did not approve of us, yet . . . often said we were good students, always adding, he doubted if we would ever become successful practitioners." Rhoda

Hendrick (1898) recorded the use of the phrase "hen medics." Julia Qua (1900) recalled the presence of a red line separating the seats of male students from females. Anatomy classes at the University of Michigan remained gender segregated until 1908. For more accounts, see *Women's Voices: Early Years at the University of Michigan*, excerpts available online.

CHAPTER TWELVE

In ancient Greece, Hippocrates first advanced the theory of a migratory uterus and identified poisonous stagnant humors which could only be expelled by regular coitus. He also asserted that a woman's body is physiologically cold and wet and hence "prone to putrefaction of the humors" (as opposed to the dry and warm male body). He saw this as the reason the uterus was susceptible to illness, especially when deprived of the benefits arising from sex and procreation. Hippocrates theorized that in virgins, widows, single, or sterile women, an unsatisfied uterus would produce toxic fumes that resulted in anxiety, a fear of suffocation, tremors, and even convulsions and paralysis. The use of smelling salts to return a wandering womb to its ideal place well into the early twentieth century indicates that Hippocrates's theories were still being used as a point of reference.

Dr. Douglas's lecture is adapted from the medical textbook *Insanity and Its Prevention*, by Daniel Hack Tuke (London: MacMillan, 1878) and accurately reflects the thinking of the day on female hysteria and mental illness. The metallotherapy section of the lecture is adapted from the book *Metalloscopy and Metallotherapy* by H. Gradle, *Journal of Nervous Mental Disease* (Jan–Oct 1878).

CHAPTER FOURTEEN

Though the United States produced the first female doctor of the modern age, Elizabeth Blackwell, this was only after receiving numerous denials. To one of her unsuccessful applications, a professor responded, "You cannot expect us to furnish you with a stick to break our heads with." See *Elizabeth Blackwell, Pioneer Work for Women* (New York: Dutton, 1895).

Barbara Replogle was truly one of Mattie's closest friends; however, in reality the two met at Oratory School in Philadelphia, rather than in medical school in Ann Arbor. I have tried to stay true to the impact and quality of their friendship, though I've changed many details to better suit the purpose of this book. In reality, Barbara became a noted temperance speaker. The two friends continued a written correspondence for over twenty years.

It was quite common during the Victorian era to call microscopes "magic glasses" and to keep them on hand for entertainment, and such descriptions inspired mine in this chapter. For more on this, see *Nature's Invisibilia: The Victorian Microscope and the Miniature Fairy* by Laura Forsberg, *Victorian Studies* (summer 2015).

CHAPTER FIFTEEN

The announcement of Mattie's graduation quoted in this chapter comes from *The Woman's Exponent*, July 1, 1880. To defray the expenses of her education, Mattie cleaned at the student boardinghouse; in her second year, she worked as a secretary to a wealthier fellow student from Oregon, Bethenia Owens-Adair, who subsequently became a notable female physician.

CHAPTER SIXTEEN

The character Leolin is a composite of two people: Leolin Bennet, a Cherokee medical student from Indian territory who wanted to marry Mattie in Michigan, but left school after his attempt proved unsuccessful; and John Hillary, a medical student from Maryland, who converted to Mormonism and followed Mattie to Utah after graduation, hoping to win her hand.

CHAPTER SEVENTEEN

This scene is based off of one of Mattie's first patients, Prussian immigrant, Bertha Stomlar, "the insane wife of a river boat captain." Though in reality, the incident occurred in the summer between Mattie's two years of medical school in Algonac, Michigan, the details of the case are otherwise as I've presented them. Mattie's daughter Elizabeth records that she "doctored the underlying cause and effected a cure." On August 1, 1881, *Woman's Exponent* reported the successful surgery, as well as the detail that Dr. Slocum refused to assist Mattie because he would not play second fiddle to a woman. Mattie visited the Stomlars at their home in Algonac, Michigan, on her way home from her exile in England.

Mattie was the only female admitted to the University of Pennsylvania's Auxiliary Medical Program, though the school would not allow her to do as much as her male peers. After attending lectures and writing a thesis on Mountain Fever, they awarded her a Bachelor's of Science degree, while the men in her program all received PhDs.

CHAPTER EIGHTEEN

The quote Mattie recites to herself is taken from Shakespeare's *Hamlet*. Mattie loved classic literature and theater, and attended the National School of Elocution and Oratory in order to better prepare herself to work in public health. She considered going on a cross-country lecture tour after medical school, but eventually decided against it. While her fellow classmate, Barbara Replogle, was known for her comedic presentations, Mattie was known as a tragedienne particularly memorable in her role as Mary Queen of Scots. The textbook quotes in these chapters are drawn from *Extempore Speech, How to Acquire and Practice It* by William Pittenger (Philadelphia: National School of Elocution and Oratory, 1883). While Mattie studied in Philadelphia, several anti-polygamy lectures were held, including one at Wesley Hall where Methodist Episcopal preachers presented a report on polygamy calling for Congress to "remove this great scandal from this free land."

CHAPTER NINETEEN

Angelina Fanny Eilshemius "Lina" Hesse (1850–1934) drew upon her experience canning jellies and preparing puddings in her cooking practice to make her recommendation to Robert Koch. Lina's husband worked as a physician in Koch's lab. Though Lina worked preparing cultures, maintaining equipment, and producing scientific drawings for publication, she was unpaid. For more on her unsung contribution to microbiology see *The Introduction of Agar-Agar into Bacteriology* by Arthur Parker Hitchens and Morris C. Leikind (Baltimore: Johns Hopkins University, 1938). Because Hesse was never mentioned in Koch's publications, few knew of the role she played.

Ignaz Semmelweis died in a public insane asylum at the age of forty-seven. Mortality rates in his maternity hospital multiplied six times under his successor. Semmelweis's work was not revisited until decades after his death, when in the 1880s, Pasteur, Koch, and Lister produced evidence of germ theory and provided theoretical backing for Semmelweis's work. Semmelweis preferred chlorinated lime for eliminating the "putrid smell and poisonous humors" of the autopsy room.

Robert Koch's student, Julius Petri, would invent the petri dish in 1887. Until then, glass plates topped with bell jars were frequently used for lab samples.

Physicians resisted germ theory for several reasons. Many argued that washing hands before treating each patient would be too much work, and in the long run, solving this problem required rebuilding hospitals so wash water was always within reach. Many physicians also found Semmelweis's insinuation that doctors were the cause of death to be insulting, and countered that, as gentlemen, their hands could not be anything other than clean. See also "Ignaz Semmelweis and the Birth of Infection Control" (*Quality & Safety in Health Care,* June 2004).

CHAPTER TWENTY-TWO

Emmeline B. Wells spearheaded and oversaw her grain storage project beginning in 1876. Relief Society women gleaned wheat fields and then used that money to buy their own fields, which they cultivated. All over the territory of Utah, women grew their own wheat, and shared tips for combatting pests and maximizing market profits at Relief Society meetings. Wheat profits were used to aid San Francisco earthquake survivors in 1906, famine victims in China, and maternity hospitals in the territory. Eventually the Relief Society amassed such a concentration that Wells sold two hundred thousand bushels of grain to the U.S. government in 1918 during the crisis of WWI. President Woodrow Wilson personally visited Wells to thank her for the society's contribution to wartime efforts. The remaining wheat, worth 1.6 million dollars, was incorporated into the LDS Church's welfare program. The Relief Society logo still retains wheat stalks in commemoration of Emmeline Wells's momentous effort.

CHAPTER TWENTY-THREE

Details of establishing a practice as a frontier medical woman, including a description of an appendectomy at the time, can be found in

Medicine Women: The Story of Early-American Women Doctors by Cathy Luchetti (New York: Random House, 1998).

CHAPTER TWENTY-FIVE

Eliza R. Snow's response to Mattie was given in an address on February 18, 1869. The rest of the conversation between them is my own creation. The Young Ladies' Retrenchment Association was established by Brigham Young and his daughters, and was the forerunner to the LDS Church's Young Women organization.

The documented conflict between Mattie and Romania Burnell Pratt Penrose may have been exacerbated by Penrose's husband's position on vaccinations as well as the "terrible flare up between the doctor [Romania] and the hospital matron [Jennie Whipple] in which the police were summoned," an event that occurred while Mattie was overseas. In a March 1887 letter to Angus, Mattie explained, "I tell you notwithstanding we both are considered tolerably good saints, there is an internal antipathy existing between we two women, which only slumbers while I am in seclusion but will 'erupt' when I begin to jostle in the medical field again." In telling this story from Mattie's perspective, I likely portray Romania as more at fault for their conflict than she actually was. The patient complaints dealt with in this chapter are taken from the actual registry kept by the Deseret Hospital 1886–1893.

CHAPTER TWENTY-SIX

The healing of Adeline Savage by Lucy B. Young at Deseret Hospital occurred in 1888, although there is no record indicating that Mattie was present. Some of the dialogue in this scene is taken directly from Adeline Savage's account of the event. See *My Mother Adeline* by Ruth Naomi Savage Hilton (Church History Library).

The *Young Women's Journal* of 1893 said of Lucy B. Young: "How many times the sick and suffering have come upon beds to that temple, [St. George] and at once Sister Young would be called to take the afflicted one under her immediate charge, as all knew the mighty power she had gained through long years of fasting and prayers in the exercise of her special gift. When her hands are upon the head of another in blessing, the words of inspiration and personal prophecy that flow from her lips are like a stream of living fire. . . . Volumes would not contain the myriad instances of cases of illness and disease healed by the power of God under Sister Young's hands."

CHAPTER TWENTY-EIGHT

Angus Munn Cannon's parents were converted to the LDS Church in Liverpool, England, in 1840. They decided to join the other members of the Church in Nauvoo, but Angus's mother died at sea during the crossing, and his father died in Nauvoo shortly before the family's departure for Winter Quarters. After losing both his parents, Angus was cared for by older siblings.

CHAPTER TWENTY-NINE

Though George Q. Cannon, Angus's older brother, was in the First Presidency of the Church at the time, it is my conjecture that he married Angus and Mattie.

CHAPTER THIRTY

There is no evidence that Angus's other wives knew he intended to marry Mattie. Though the official Church policy at the time dictated asking permission from the first wife, it appears that was sporadically followed, and does not seem to have been done in this instance. In fact, Angus's nephew recorded the scene Angus's wife Amanda made when she learned of the marriage: "As we reached the corner west of his house we found Aunt Amanda, whom Lewis and Mary [two of her children] were trying to get home, but who in her ungovernable rage said she was going to the U.S. Marshal's to have Uncle Angus arrested for marrying Dr. Mattie Hughes Paul. She made such an uproar in her anger that many neighbors came out to learn what was the matter." Abraham Hoagland Cannon Journal, 25 December 1884, LDS Church Archives.

CHAPTER THIRTY-ONE

Mattie did indeed pen these words to Barbara, denying her practice of polygamy. She could not have written the truth for fear of interception, but I believe she may have needed to speak of it anyway, if only as a denial of the truth. Angus was arrested in January 1885; he was sent to jail in

May and was released in December. Elizabeth Rachel Cannon was born September 13, 1885, at the home of Rachel Wooley in Grantsville, Utah. I altered timing slightly for the sake of compression.

CHAPTER THIRTY-TWO

Author Fara Sneddon explains the origins of the confinement ritual, which was at the height of its practice during these years: "Grown out of healing blessings, blessings of prophecy, and the temple ordinance of washing and anointing in preparation for the endowment, confinement blessings became more and more common as the Mormon community in Utah grew. . . . The leading women of the Church taught sisters throughout the Mormon colonies how to perform washing, blessing, and anointing in preparation for childbirth." The lines for the confinement ritual in my scene are taken from documentation done by Linda King Newell, "Gifts of the Spirit: Women's Share," *Sisters in Spirit* (Urbana: University of Illinois Press, 1992) and *Ministering Sisters: A History of Women's Administrations in the Church of Jesus Christ of Latter-day Saints* by Fara Sneddon.

CHAPTER THIRTY-THREE

Mattie was still recovering from a difficult childbirth when the arrival of federal agents forced her to flee to Centerville hidden in a bed of straw on a sheep wagon. Lizzie was blue with cold when they arrived, and Mattie feared she might be dead as she frantically resuscitated her.

Angus married Maria Bennion in 1886 just as Mattie went into exile to protect him. Angus did not inform Mattie of his intention to marry Maria, and she learned of it after the fact. The letter she wrote to him expressing her anger over the decision no longer exists, but it is clear from their subsequent correspondence that she was upset. During Mattie's exile in 1887, Angus married his sixth and final wife, Joanna Danielson, again without telling Mattie. I chose not to include Joanna Danielson in this novel for simplicity's sake.

CHAPTER THIRTY-FOUR

Emma Lazarus wrote her famous poem in 1883 to raise money for the construction of a pedestal for the Statue of Liberty. The poem was not mounted inside the pedestal's lower level until 1903, though it was in circulation well before. The statue was in the process of being installed in April 1886, as Mattie's ship sailed from the harbor, and was finished by the time she returned.

CHAPTER THIRTY-SEVEN

Perhaps Mattie assumed this alias in honor to Dr. Alice Bennett, a female physician who worked in the slums of Philadelphia around the time Mattie was in school there. Dr. Bennett was the first woman to earn a PhD from the University of Pennsylvania in 1880, and would have been known to Mattie, at least by reputation.

CHAPTER THIRTY-EIGHT

The unfortunate story of Louie Wells and her love affair with her brother-in-law, John Q. Cannon, are essentially as I've presented them. For more details on the death of Louie Wells and the tragedy of Angus Cannon's remarks at her funeral, see *Emmeline B. Wells: An Intimate History* by Carol Cornwall Madsen. See also "The Tragic Matter of Louie Wells and John Q. Cannon" by Kenneth L. Cannon, *Journal of Mormon History* (Nov. 2, 2009).

CHAPTER THIRTY-NINE

Mattie destroyed most of Angus's early letters lest they be used as evidence against them, so it is upon the first extent letter and subsequent ones that my version of their correspondence is heavily based. I have compressed the time of Mattie's exile for purposes of my narrative. In reality she stayed overseas for two years, the length of time needed for her arrest warrant to expire. Her mother's family, Fanny and Thomas Evans in Birmingham, were welcoming until they read some of her letters. Mattie reported her uncle became furious, "saying I was 'not an honored wife,' but connected with one of *those things* out there!" In addition to Warwick Castle, Stratford-upon-Avon, and Manchester (which she left after a short time for fear her presence would be reported in Salt Lake), she also visited Wales, Paris, Switzerland, and London. For the correspondence I've relied upon *Letters from Exile* edited by Constance Lieber.

CHAPTER NOTES

CHAPTER FORTY-ONE

Wild Kashmiri goats still graze on the Great Orme near Llandudno today; they were a gift to Wales from Queen Victoria in 1837.

CHAPTER FORTY-TWO

Mary Lloyd Hughes, Mattie's paternal grandmother, was born in 1779 in Llangernyw, Vale of Elwy, Wales. To avoid confusion with Mattie's sister Mary, I have used the Welsh version of her name, Mair, in this novel. The oldest yew tree in Wales is in Llangernyw and is believed to be four thousand years old. Llanddoged is a nearby village close also to Llanwrst, which overlooks the Conwy River. Much of Mattie's family is buried in Llanddoged and she visited their graves during her English exile. I have combined the two towns of Llanddoged and Llangernyw in this novel. The ivy-clad cottage that inspired my description of Gwendolyn's home has been made into a tea room in Llanwrst.

CHAPTER FORTY-THREE

Descended from the Brythonic Celtic language, Welsh was the dominant language spoken by the Welsh populace for thousands of years. In order to establish political dominance over the region, Henry VIII passed an Act of the Union in 1536, banning the language in schools and public discourse, and removing it from official status. A British Parliamentary report stated: "The Welsh language is a vast drawback to Wales, and a manifold barrier to the moral progress and commercial prosperity of the people. It is not easy to over-estimate its evil effects." Use of the language declined until the twentieth century when, in acts of defiance, road signs were reprinted in Welsh and a concerted effort to revitalize the language resulted in a popular resurgence.

CHAPTER FORTY-FOUR

Gwendolyn's poem is a variation of an old Welsh saying quoted by historian Richard Suggett in *History of Magic and Witchcraft in Wales*. Most of Mattie's letter to Angus in this chapter is adapted from her correspondence.

CHAPTER FORTY-FIVE

New York's skyline was changing rapidly in December 1887 when Mattie returned. With the early commercial use of steel, skyscrapers began rising above the churches, whose steeples had previously been the highest points of the skyline. The Produce Exchange Building was finished in 1884 on Bowling Green; the Washington Building was finished in 1884. The item described at the Metropolitan Museum of Art had recently been acquired in the Cyprus Antiquities Collection.

Utah women had to gain suffrage twice: once as a territory in 1870, and then again as a constitution was written for the new state in 1896. During the first twelve years they enjoyed the franchise, Utah women had the largest number of female voters in the United States.

The Supreme Court ruled against the Mormon Church in *Reynolds v. United States, 1879*, a decision that many scholars today say violated the First Amendment separation of church and state. Chief Justice Melville Fuller wrote the dissenting opinion for the court, accusing his fellow judges of improperly vesting Congress with "absolute power." Contemporary constitutional lawyers find the belief oath that was required of Utah's male voters a particularly egregious offense coupled with the intrusion of federal officials in private homes and the confiscation of Church property. The Religious Freedom Restoration Act of 1992 now requires government officials to show a "compelling governmental interest" before interfering in religious practice.

CHAPTER FORTY-SIX

In reality, Mattie did not see Barb when she returned to Michigan after her English exile. They planned to meet in Michigan, but ultimately did not; Mattie may have been too embarrassed about issues related to polygamy during this period to see her friend in person. They did meet again in Utah years later, however.

Mattie would have been familiar with popular anti-polygamist lecturers of the day, including Reverend T. DeWitt Talmage who stated in a sermon in 1880: "Mormonism is one great surge of licentiousness. . . . It is the brothel of the nation, it is hell enthroned. . . . Unless we destroy Mormonism, Mormonism will destroy us." *The Salt Lake Tribune* referred to polygamous wives as "Zion's roosters" and "celestial concubines." Papers in the East were even less flattering. For more on this, see *Ritualization of Mormon History* by Davis Bitton (Urbana, Illinois: University of Illinois Press, 1994).

CHAPTER FORTY-SEVEN

Not shown in this novel due to space constraints is Mattie's second exile, shortly after the birth of her son James in 1890. Though the persecution of polygamists slowed by 1889, officials still sought Mattie and Angus because of their prominent positions. James's delivery was very difficult and Mattie had a challenging recovery. When it became clear federal officials were seeking her, she took her children to San Francisco where they stayed in a boardinghouse for just under two years.

The Manifesto text is as I have presented it in this chapter, though Mattie was in fact in exile in California when it was released. In 1892, she returned with her children to her Salt Lake home and office, and Mattie reopened her medical practice. Though the Manifesto officially ended the practice of plural marriage in the LDS Church, it offered no advice to the many men and women who had shown obedience to the Church by entering into the institution during the four decades when it was openly practiced. Many women were left uncertain as to their status as wives, their ability to inherit or receive financial support, and their children's legitimacy. After the Manifesto, Angus refused to abandon his wives and continued supporting them as best he could, but with age, his financial resources declined and his relationship with Mattie grew more and more strained as time went on; their daughter Elizabeth grew to resent her father's long absences.

CHAPTER FIFTY

Charles Penrose (second husband of Romania Pratt) was the editor of the *Deseret News* and he used the paper to push his opposition to vaccination. Between this and comments by Apostle Brigham Young Jr., many people in the state were convinced the Church leadership opposed vaccination. In reality, a minority of Church leaders held this view. Due to the opposition of Charles Penrose via the *Deseret News,* Utah continued to have low vaccination rates for decades.

Brigham Young Jr. stated in 1901, "Gentile doctors are trying to force Babylon into the people and some of them are willing to disease the blood of our children if they can do so, and they think they are doing God's service." Church circulars criticized vaccination in favor of botanical and faith healing and dietary health. Dried onions and tea of sheep droppings were one of the recommended alternatives. See *The Salt Lake Tribune*, Dec. 13, 1900, Nov. 13, 1900, and Jan. 15, 1900.

In the 1890s, the issue resulted in a smallpox epidemic that could not be ignored when four thousand people contracted the dreaded disease. In 1901, the Utah Supreme Court stated "vaccination was the only safe preventive recognized and approved by medical science and by governments throughout the world." In June 1904, Apostle Abraham Owen Woodruff and his first wife, Helen, died of smallpox after declining the counsel of LDS president Joseph F. Smith to be vaccinated before the couple traveled to Mexico City on Church business. Shortly thereafter, the LDS Church agreed to take a stand in favor of compulsory vaccination.

CHAPTER FIFTY-ONE

The World's Congress of Representative Women held at the Chicago World's Fair in May 1893 constituted one of the most remarkable gatherings of women of all time. At 81 meetings, nearly 500 women from 27 countries addressed 150,000 people. The weeklong Congress was planned by President Bertha Honoré Palmer, and the speeches presented in these chapters are accurate descriptions and quotes drawn from the accounts and records of the women who delivered them. No records remain indicating which speeches Mattie attended over the course of the week she spent there. For the full text of the speeches see *The World's Congress of Representative Women*, Vol 1, 1893. For more on Mattie's speech see *Utah Historical Quarterly* 48, No. 1–71980.

CHAPTER FIFTY-FOUR

In the debate over whether or not to include women's suffrage in the Utah state constitution, B. H. Roberts was a vocal opponent, concerned that Utah's bid for statehood would be denied again should they attempt to compound the two issues. Meanwhile, Susan B. Anthony and other experienced suffragists advised that if suffrage was not included in the initial constitution, it would take years to rectify. Mattie and many other women on the Territorial Suffrage Association worked hard to petition both Democrats and Republicans on the issue, eventually convincing the delegates to vote in favor of including the suffrage clause. After the issue passed, B. H. Roberts and Mattie reconciled and, unified as Democrats, grew to be close friends and respected colleagues. For more on the fight for women's suffrage in Utah, see *Battle for the Ballot: Essays on Woman Suffrage in Utah, 1870-1896*, edited by Carol Cornwall Madsen (Logan, UT: Utah State University Press, 1997).

CHAPTER FIFTY-EIGHT

Sources disagree as to how much conflict the elections caused Mattie and Angus, and without Mattie's journals it's impossible to know for sure. Publicly Angus was always supportive and said, "I am proud of my Welsh wife." His private feelings were quite a different matter, and he was likely quite embarrassed over the defeat. The quotes from the *Salt Lake Herald* and the *Salt Lake Tribune* are drawn directly from the respective newspaper coverage. Newspapers around the country reported the election of the first female state senator including the *Detroit Free Press* that wrote on November 17, 1896: "Mrs. Cannon believes in polygamy, and is a victim of it, if victim she can be called when she can whip her lord and master at the polls."

Throughout her life, Mattie struggled with anxiety and depression that resulted in bouts of anguish and self-doubt, which I've tried to portray in part, though her mental health challenges increased in later years. To manage these and other ailments, she self-prescribed medications that are today viewed as ineffective and dangerous. Over time, she became dependent on concoctions containing atropine and small doses of strychnine. Samuel M. Brown, M.D., who read through her surviving health records also diagnosed her illness in later years as congestive heart failure. In his review of her health history, Dr. Brown commented that depression and anxiety led Martha to doubt her abilities in spite of her tremendous accomplishments, but notes that it is perhaps not uncommon that "people who are driven are not just driven, but a little haunted." See Constance L. Lieber, *The Biography of Martha Hughes Cannon: A Personal Journey*, forthcoming.

Recommended Reading

Achterberg, Jeanne. *Woman As Healer: A Panoramic Survey of the Healing Activities of Women from Prehistoric Times to the Present.* Boulder, Colorado: Shambhala, 1991.

Bushman, Claudia L. *Mormon Sisters: Women in Early Utah.* Logan, Utah: Utah State University Press, 1976.

Letters from Exile: The Correspondence of Martha Hughes Cannon and Angus M. Cannon, 1886–1888. Edited by Constance L. Lieber and John Sillito. Salt Lake City: Signature Books, 1989.

Luchetti, Cathy. *Medicine Women: The Story of Early-American Women Doctors.* New York: Crown Publishers, 1998.

Neilson, Reid L. *Exhibiting Mormonism: The Latter-day Saints and the 1893 Chicago World's Fair.* New York: Oxford University Press, 2011.

Park, Lindsay Hansen. *Year of Polygamy* podcast.

Sneddon, Fara. *Ministering Sisters: A History of Women's Administrations in The Church of Jesus Christ of Latter-day Saints.* Illinois: University of Illinois Press, forthcoming.

Suggest, Richard. *A History of Magic and Witchcraft in Wales: Cunningmen, Cursing Wells, Witches and Warlocks in Wales.* Tempus, 2008.

Ulrich, Laurel Thatcher. *A House Full of Females: Plural Marriage and Women's Rights in Early Mormonism, 1835–1870.* New York: Knopf, 2017.